THE GREEN HORNET

CASEFILES

EDITED BY
JOE GENTILE
AND
WIN SCOTT ECKERT

ACKNOWLEDGEMENTS

You hold this book in your hands through the support, patience, and assistance of:

David Grace of Loeb & Loeb, LLP representing The Green Hornet, Inc.

Michael Wm. Kaluta
(www.kaluta.com)

Matthew Baugh

Kathy Gentile

Lisa Eckert

Jeanne Schanberger

... and dedicated Green Hornet fans everywhere.

Joe Gentile and Win Scott Eckert
Co-Editors

Rubén Procopio, *Art Direction*
www.maskedavenger.com

Rich Harvey, *Publication Design*
www.boldventurepress.com

"Green Hornet" logo
rebuilt by Tracy Mark Lee

Green Hornet Casefiles Hardcover
(cover by Rubén Procopio)
ISBN: 1-933076-93-3

Green Hornet Casefiles Softcover
(Cover by Michael Wm. Kaluta)
ISBN: 1-933076-94-1

Published by
Moonstone Entertainment, Inc.
582 Torrence Ave.,
Calumet City, IL 60409
www.moonstonebooks.com

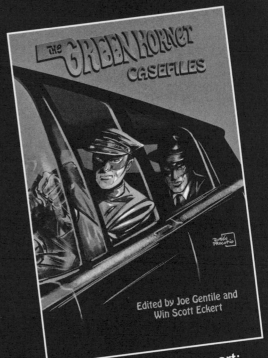

Hardcover edition cover art:
RUBÉN PROCOPIO

Softcover edition cover art:
MICHAEL Wm. KALUTA

CONTENTS

The Outlaw Hero Introduction by Ron Fortier 5

Sting of the Yellowjacket Howard Hopkins 13

Lair of the Living Dead Joe McKinney 29

Through a Green Haze Dan Wickline 47

The Black Widow John Everson 63

A Thing of Beauty Bobby Nash 79

The Insincerest Form of Flattery Paul D. Storrie 97

Bad Medicine Vito Delsante and Win Scott Eckert 113

The Gray Line Between F.J. DeSanto, Michael Uslan and Joe Gentile 123

Up in Smoke Deborah Chester 137

The Worst Angels of Our Nature Paul Kupperberg.............. 155

Now That Would Be Telling Bradley H. Sinor 173

Summer of Death Barry Reese 189

The Wet and the Wicked David Boop 207

The Carlossi Caper Art Lyon 223

Soldanus, the Sultan of Crime Gary Phillips....................... 235

The Dangerous Game Eric Fein 253

Beauty Is As Beauty Dies James Mullaney 273

Auld Acquaintance Matthew Baugh 291

Memories of My Grandfather, Raymond J. Meurer
Afterword by Lisa Meurer Long 314

Raymond J. Meurer: Man with Many Hats
Afterword by Tim Lasiuta 315

Daily Sentinel Morgue Author Biographies 317

THE OUTLAW HERO

Introduction by Ron Fortier

In 1935 George W. Trendle, the owner/manager of a small Detroit radio station, WXYZ, charged writer Fran Striker and director James Jewell with creating a new series hero comparable to their successful Lone Ranger show. After some back-and-forth between the three men, the modern day version of The Ranger evolved as The Green Hornet.

Like his western predecessor, The Green Hornet would wear a mask, be accompanied by a loyal sidekick and get around in a unique fashion. Asian valet Kato replaced Tonto and the super-modified supercar, the Black Beauty, replaced the white stallion, Silver. Upon its official debut on January 31, 1936, accompanied by a pervasive buzzing musical introduction, *The Green Hornet* was brought to full melodramatic life and his adventures broadcast through various affiliates across the country.

Listeners were introduced to crusading newspaper publisher, Britt Reid of the *Daily Sentinel*, an enterprise begun by his father Dan. Tired of the city's political corruption that remained cleverly beyond the reach of the law, Britt realized he could better combat criminals employing their own tactics against them. He assumed the role of a masked outlaw, The Green Hornet, and accompanied by Kato, also wearing a mask, set out to fight fire with fire.

Although that plot outline for the series may sound formulaic to the era, it actually contained a unique twist that clearly set it apart from the other radio and pulp crimebusters of the day. From the time The Shadow first appeared on the airwaves through to the emergence of dozens of pistol-packing pulp avengers, all of them had one thing in common, no matter how varied their backgrounds or personas; they were all considered vigilantes out to battle villainy whether the police supported them or not.

In other words, no self-respecting gang boss ever doubted The Shadow,

The Spider, The Avenger, or any dozen other such agents were anything but his nemesis. Even the public was aware of them as mystery men fighting the good fight on their behalf.

Not so The Green Hornet.

The real lynchpin to Reid's scheme was to pose as a criminal, to convince the other bad guys that The Green Hornet was actually one of them. If the very people he was targeting accepted him as one of their own, the opportunities to mine them for additional evidence would be invaluable in aiding the authorities in their daily war against crime. The psychology was simple enough: if a villain considered The Green Hornet just another competitor after the same illegal market, they would oftentimes choose to parlay rather than come out guns blasting, as they would against the traditional vigilantes. These dramatic, non-lethal confrontations provided Reid with vital information which he in turn passed along, in surreptitious ways, to the authorities.

Unlike the majority of his masked colleagues, The Green Hornet played three different roles: the crusading publisher, the green-clad criminal mastermind, and the secret warrior on the side of the law. It was a credit to Britt Reid's devotion to justice that he performed all three roles perfectly, a juggling act that would have given anyone else nightmares. His life was forever in jeopardy, either from the vicious crooks he dealt with or the police who considered him a murderer with orders to shoot on site. In fact it was Reid, the publisher, who put a reward bounty on his alter-ego to the tune of $25,000.

This singularity set him apart from his peers and contributed greatly to the show's overwhelming success, all of which led to his incarnation on film via two excellent Universal cliffhanger serials. *The Green Hornet* (thirteen chapters, 1940) starred Gordon Jones as Reid/Green Hornet and Keye Luke as Kato. This serial was so popular, the studio rushed a sequel into production and in 1941 released *The Green Hornet Strikes Again!* with Warren Hull, a veteran serial star, as Reid/Kato and Luke reprising his role as the loyal valet. It was another screen winner but would be the last time the characters would appear outside the radio broadcast booth for another twenty-five years.

The radio series lasted until December 1952, before closing up shop; a total of sixteen years and one thousand, forty-five episodes made it one of the longest running hero series ever to air.

Fourteen years later, ABC producer Bill Dozier brought the characters back in a half-hour action-packed television show which debuted on September 9, 1966. Handsome, charismatic actor Van Williams had the role of Reid/Green Hornet, now updated to a media mogul with his own television station. The legendary martial artist Bruce Lee galvanized an entire generation as The Hornet's martial arts valet/chauffeur, Kato. Wisely opting not to camp the show as was being done with the then humorous Batman starring Adam West and Burt Ward, Dozier, a childhood fan of the radio Hornet, played it straight and for one solitary season, twenty-six episodes total. American viewers were thrilled each week by the daring exploits of this colorful, crime-battling duo. Again, to his credit, Dozier kept the original formula with The Hornet walking his precarious tightrope between the police and the criminal underworld who believed he was one of their own.

Which is where I came into the picture. During that lone season between 1966 and 1967, I was a private in the United States Army and remember watching the show in our barracks dayroom whenever the opportunity arose. The show's quick pacing and Lee's amazing physical feats impressed me greatly and I became an instant fan, still having no idea of the characters' origins. Being an avid comic collector, I purchased the three Gold Key comics based on the television show that were released at the time. Each featured a photo cover of Williams and Lee in their roles and the interior art was provided by the veteran graphic artist Dan Spiegle. I sure wish I still had them now. They were very well done.

I also recall being very disappointed when ABC refused to renew the series and it disappeared without warning, leaving a legion of fans wondering what had gone wrong. In truth, nothing. Towards the end of that initial season, the bigwigs at the network came to Dozier and directed him to change the show's adult approach to mimic the camp-silliness of Batman. He refused, choosing to see it end as a quality product rather than dilute it into an object of buffoonery.

Another twenty years would lapse with The Green Hornet being relegated to a copyright-imposed limbo of sorts. During that hiatus, several comic companies approached the licensor with proposals for newer, modern versions of the green-clad avenger, but none were successful in obtaining the rights. Meanwhile I'd moved through those same years experiencing life's adventures both good and bad. By the late 1980s I'd somehow managed to stumble into a comic book writing career and landed an agent. He urged me to make the trip to the San Diego Comic-Con where dozens of editors and publishers attended, and help move my career to the next level.

Normally, ambitious writers come to this event weighted down with all kinds of proposals they hope to foist on unsuspecting editors. I only had one: a forty page proposal for a new Green Hornet comic. Allow me to back up a bit and tell you how that happened.

The year prior to this California trip, I'd met artist Steve Erwin, who was doing a cross-country junket with several Texas-based young creators hoping to build an audience for their independent comic company. That trip took them to a shop in southern New Hampshire where I was regular customer. The owner, a friend who was aware of my own burgeoning career, introduced us and for the next few hours, Steve and I got to know each other by talking comics. At one point the topic turned to those great heroes no one was using any more, a la The Lone Ranger, Tarzan, Flash Gordon . . . and The Green Hornet. Instantly we both became excited as each of shared our love of that classic '60s TV show with Williams and Lee. By the time we parted that day, we had agreed to work on a new Green Hornet proposal and try our luck at selling it.

For the next six months I worked feverishly trying to put together an extensive, exciting package that would entice a publisher to want to pursue the license on our behalf. By that time, I'd read several articles about The Green Hornet's history written by pulp historian Will Murray, another acquaintance. I wrote Will asking for anything he might have on The Green Hornet and within days a huge, fat manila envelope arrived at my doorstep filled with dozens of Xerox copies of articles on the character, covering all his various appearances from radio to comics, serials and television. This information delighted me, but it also scared me. Learning all this stuff was terrific, but the more I read, the more I realized there was no way I could simply whip up a "new" version. I had too much respect for the character's history and the people who had shaped it to simply ignore it and start anew. That would have been wrong.

But what if I could somehow incorporate those various incarnations into one long, cohesive narrative, and write a story that would pay homage to all those previous versions? This is how my family approach was born. The radio and television Hornets wouldn't be the same person, but each a different Hornet who had passed on the mask from generation to generation.

As stated above, it would take me six long months to develop a working timetable that would begin in the last few months of World War Two and end in the present. I created lots of members of both the Reid and Kato clans and dedicated myself to making them all integral pieces of a larger whole. The project had stopped being a mere comic book proposal. Instead it had taken on a life of its own, becoming the launching pad for a spectacular crime-fighting family saga unlike anything else that had ever been attempted, except for Lee Falk's classic Phantom.

The question remained: could I pull it off?

Thus I ventured into the valley of comic wonder that is the zany, madcap, over-the-top San Diego Comic-Con and proceeded to meet a hundreds new faces, many of them coming and going before my eyes like a spinning carousel of comic folks. Amidst all that meet and greet, I encountered a young artist who was then the art director for the gaming company, TSR. His name was Jeff Butler and on our very first meeting he handed me his portfolio to examine. Among the beautiful art contained between its covers I found a sexy pin-up picture of a "lady" Green Hornet and told Jeff of my interest in the hero. Sure enough, he was another fan and he commented on how sad it was that Gold Key had only done three Green Hornet comics with Dan Spiegle. Little did I realize at that meeting what was about to transpire within the next few weeks, and the journey we were going to be sharing together.

Over the next two days my agent continue to shuffle me back and forth across the convention halls until eventually I found myself talking with Tony Caputo, the publisher of the new NOW Comics out of Chicago. By the time that conversation was over, Caputo had asked me to send him plots for future issues of their Terminator series based on the highly successful sci-fi movie by James Cameron. He apparently was not satisfied with the present writer and was hoping I could inject faster paced action to the book. Now that I was close to landing a real paying gig with a mid-level outfit, my agent cut me loose, his mission completed. Left on my own, I spent the next day simply being a fan. On the morning I was to fly home, I made it a point to stop by the NOW booth to say goodbye to Caputo.

As we were chatting, the topic turned to unused, popular licensed characters. Pretty much an echo of that same conversation I'd had with Steve Erwin nearly a year earlier back in New Hampshire. And just like that, Caputo mentioned The Green Hornet and how he would love to bring that character back into the public consciousness. The words were no sooner out of his mouth, than I unzipped my attaché case, reached in, pulled out my humongous proposal, and handed it to him. I went on to explain some of what I'd done, the idea of the family approach culminating in a modern Hornet with a female Kato. He was thrilled, especially when I mentioned the last page contained the name, addresses, and telephone numbers of Leisure Concepts, the New York based firm which then handled the property for George Trendle's heirs. Caputo said he would read it carefully upon his return to Chicago and then get back to me. We shook hands and I headed home.

The following week, I submitted several Terminator plots to their managing editor, was informed they were acceptable, and soon a contract was in my hands courtesy of FedEx. Just like that.

The next few weeks I spent writing as many Terminator scripts as I could pump out. It being my first paying job as a professional, there was no way I was going to ever miss a deadline. The days flew by. Then one night the phone rang and it was Caputo calling me from New York City. He informed me he would be meeting with The Green Hornet people the next day and would be pitching them my proposal. I almost fell off the couch. I think I mumbled something about good luck, he promised to call soon as he had a decision, and we hung up.

That night was one of the longest I've ever endured. My wife, Valerie, continued to offer words of encouragement, at the same time warning me not to set my hopes too high. She is such a wise lady. Eventually the phone call came at mid-afternoon and I knew the second Caputo started talking we had it. He was wound for sound, going on and on about how the Leisure Concepts staff had found my proposal both fun and original, beyond anything Marvel or DC had ever offered them, and that they stipulated NOW Comics could have the license predicated on them producing the story I had laid out in my mega family saga.

Caputo told me to call Erwin and then start writing the actual scripts. He wanted them on his desk as soon as possible. We hung up and I immediately dialed Steve's number to tell him the awesome good news. Only it really wasn't good tidings to him. During the time between our meeting, discussing the concept, etc., he had been hired by DC Comics and was soon to start working on new monthly series for them. It would be impossible for him to do two full books a month. Both of us were crestfallen. He wished me all the luck in the world and I offered him the same, then we hung up and I sat there trying to grasp what had just happened in a matter of minutes.

NOW Comics was about to publish my Green Hornet comic series and just like that I had no artist. Which is when I remembered the affable, super-talented Mr. Jeff Butler, and his own affection for The Hornet. Scrambling, I dug up his business card and made yet another call, this one with much happier results. Jeff couldn't believe I was offering him the job of drawing one of his favorite heroes. I cautioned him the job probably wouldn't pay as much as his position at TSR. Jeff said he understood and he would deal with that. I later learned he did so by going to work the next day and giving them his two weeks notice of termination. Jeff Butler was going to be a comic book artist.

The rest, as they say, is history, or in this case, comic book history. Soon I was taking all the ideas and plots from my proposal, turning them into scripts, and Jeff was penciling them into artistic reality. He was joined on that task by the amazing inker, David Mowry, who rounded out our creative trio. NOW Comics did up a huge promotional campaign and within six short months, the first issue of the all new Green Hornet comic series was hitting the comic shops, adorned by a stunning Jim Steranko cover. The book sold through the roof and for the next year-and-a-half held its place as NOW Comics' biggest seller. In that time Jeff, Dave, and I went on an incredible literary adventure, complete with all manner of highs and lows.

I won't bore you with the lows, but will mention a few of the highs, such as all of us being guests at the first ever Green Hornet convention in Baltimore the following year, where we spent the weekend with none other than Van Williams, the actor who had so wonderfully played our hero in the '60s television series. It is a weekend none of us will ever forget.

Then there was Jeff's idea for us to do a special four issue mini-series in the vein of the old cliffhanger serials, starring the '40s radio Hornet. We pitched the idea to NOW and they gave us the go ahead to produce *The Sting of The Green Hornet*. In it Nazis spies try to kidnap President Roosevelt and take him to Germany as a hostage, to prevent the U.S. from entering the war. In the adventure, The Green Hornet and Kato cross paths with The Shadow, a soldier named Steve Rogers, and two metropolitan reporters called Lois and Clark. It was the most fun Jeff and I ever had together and that story remains a fan favorite to this day.

Ups and downs galore. In the end, I would spend three years of my life writing The Green Hornet's adventures, totaling approximately thirty-five issues between volumes one and two. It was the most successful comic series I've ever been involved with, and my name became forever associated with the character. Over thirty years later, fans, now adults themselves, still come up to me at conventions to tell me how much they enjoyed those comics and what they meant to them. Those testimonies truly warm my heart.

Of course you can't ever keep a great hero down and it was only a matter of time before The Green Hornet would return.

The Green Hornet is publisher Britt Reid, a brave, noble man fighting a selfless battle in defense of the innocent. He is a courageous soul who has sacrificed his own personal happiness in the cause of universal justice, and together with his faithful Kato, continues to wage his silent campaign against villainy behind his dark green mask.

Editors Joe Gentile and Win Scott Eckert, and the writers assembled in this book, know who The Green Hornet is. Their respect and admiration for him and what he stands for is unquestionable and their new stories continue his fantastic legacy, adding a new chapter to his thrilling exploits.

As for me, I will forever be grateful to have crossed his path those many years ago, to have become a small part of his crusade, to have helped invent new tales and in my imagination ride with him and Kato in the Black Beauty towards whatever danger awaited them. It was one hell of a ride and I wouldn't have missed for the world. Thanks for coming along.

Bzzzzzzz!
Ron Fortier
April 24, 2011
Fort Collins, CO

STING OF THE YELLOWJACKET

by Howard Hopkins

Someone was in the house.

From within his room, Kato had not heard a sound, but the intruder had set off a green-blinking light on a panel concealed in his nightstand. It was one of the many new precautions he and Britt had installed since criminals—one in particular—gained access to the home and certain secrets hidden within.

Whoever it was moved with the stealth of a ghost and had to be good to bypass the original alarm system.

Kato, still dressed in a white jacket and black bowtie, awaiting Britt Reid's return from the awards banquet, slipped off the bed, setting aside a book on advanced Gung Fu techniques he had been studying. He switched off the bedside light, plunging the room into darkness.

After waiting a moment to let his eyes adjust to the blackness, he eased towards the door. Opening it without a sound, he peered out into the hall. Yellow-amber moonlight arcing through an end window fell across the dark-green carpet in a serrated pattern, giving the impression of a giant stinger from some prehistorically large bee. The impression sent a foreboding ripple of unease through him. This was no ordinary break-in— it could not be, since older alarms had been bypassed. This was someone with skill and little or no fear. Someone who knew more than any run-of-the-mill burglar should.

The thought gave him pause. Perhaps he should signal Britt at the banquet, alert him to the threat. But that would mean returning to the room, and possibly some small sound as he activated the transmitter that would set off a warning buzz in Britt's wrist watch. He would not risk it. Every moment's delay meant whoever was below gained more access to devices that had as much potential for destruction as they did for good.

13

Kato moved like a wraith along the hall to the top of the stairs. Perhaps he could not see or hear who was below, but his years of experience in martial arts stealth made him practically invisible, as well.

He glided down the first few steps, eyes scanning, every sense alert.

Nothing. Not a whisper of cloth or the scuff of a shoe on carpet. Almost as if someone were wait—

Something hit him square in the temple just as he reached the halfway point on the stairs. It made a thin popping sound and he breathed in reflexively before realizing what the object was.

A gas dart! One of their own.

He held his breath, but it was too late. He'd inhaled some of the gas and the effects were instantaneous. The entire stairway seemed to shift sideways as psychedelic stars exploded before his vision. He was barely conscious of plunging downward; only his years of experience-honed survival instinct saving him from breaking his neck. He hit bottom hard, lying still at the base of the stairs, but hardly felt the impact.

Time stopped. Thunder filled his skull and he was uncertain whether any bones were broken. No pain, merely a distant muffled numbness.

Something stepped before his vision. Something dark, and with it the barest scent of some fruity perfume drifted to his nostrils.

He grew conscious of a figure bending over him. Studying him.

A voice came, distorted, as if the speaker were using a filtering device, making it impossible to tell whether it belonged to a man or a woman.

"Tell . . . The *Hornet*, I can get to him anytime." The figure held a dark oblong device before Kato's face. A device that even through his stupor he recognized: one of the remote boxes for the Black Beauty.

"I could kill you, you know . . . but if your boss comes around you might be useful. You do make all these wonderful toys . . ."

"I . . ." Words eluded him a moment as his mind slipped into blackness, then came back to consciousness again. "I . . . know who you are . . ."

A disguised laugh whispered out, an annoying chuckle of a thing. "Do you, now? I'm planning on making very little secret of it. There'd be no fun in that. As a matter of fact, I bet not too long from now Britt Reid will figure it out for himself . . . but it will be too late to stop what's going to happen." The figure held up the remote, uttered another chuckle. "Quite a car you two have there, Kato. A pity if it fell into the hands of the police . . . "

"W-why?" Kato struggled to lift his head, clutch at the remote. But his limbs felt as heavy as lead, refused to move.

"Uh-uh-uh," the voice said. "I never lose, Kato. The sooner Britt Reid realizes that, the sooner he'll get his life back . . . and so much more."

The figure leaned in, close to Kato's ear. "Remember, Hell hath no fury . . ."

Something dropped before his eyes. Small, round—the device the figure had been using to disguise its voice. He knew the device well, for he and Britt had designed it.

An instant later, the sound of retreating footsteps penetrated his dazed mind. The figure was gone, but still he could not move, could not follow.

Could not prevent all Hell from breaking loose . . .

The 1966 Chrysler Crown Imperial shot from the alley leading to Britt Reid's secret garage entrance, tires squealing as it rounded the corner and whipped out into the night-shrouded Detroit streets. Infra-green headlights cast an eerie sheen over the surroundings, viewable only to those wearing special polarized vision filters like the ones built into The Green Hornet's mask. A continual low buzz came from the engine. The black juggernaut gained speed, careened down a street lined with parked cars. Its front end veered into them and a horrendous crunching of metal filled the night. Parked cars flipped end over end, coming to rest like helpless turtles unable to right themselves on the sidewalk, their sides crushed, and headlights exploding into spiraling, raining shards along the street. Only scratches shown in the paint of the Black Beauty. The Chrysler was constructed like a tank. Nothing short of a missile would destroy it.

One AMC Rambler, caught by a bumper, windmilled across the street and slammed into a lamppost.

The Black Beauty swerved onto a sidewalk, aiming for a gaggle of diners just leaving the *Cordon Bleu*. Screams filled the air as the patrons scattered, narrowly avoiding being mowed down.

From the Chrysler's grill, a nozzle emerged. A thick stream of gas billowed out. Patrons collapsed an instant later, to lay unconscious on the sidewalk.

The car swerved back onto the street and an ominous buzzing of its horn rose in the night.

A Black and White whipped around a corner, in pursuit, siren blaring, blue lights flashing an eerie blue glow across buildings and pavement.

A film of spreading shiny black poured from the rear of the Beauty, laying a slick coating across the road.

The Black and White couldn't stop in time. Its tires hit the oil, instantly sending the patrol vehicle into a treacherous spin. The Black and White crashed into the rear of a parked Ford, its momentum carrying it onward, upward, and sideways. Its right side lifted and the car was airborne. It came down on its roof twenty feet on, sparks spraying like July fireworks as it slid to a halt. A dazed officer crawled from its shattered window.

The Chrysler plowed onward, an armored leviathan of black. From beneath the headlights, sixteen rocket tubes protracted. An instant later, missiles shot from their barrels. Explosions rocked the street as the missiles impacted parked vehicles and buildings. A rain of brick and mortar pelted the car and street. Flames ignited gas tanks with thunderous woofs! and great streaming phoenixes of fire clawed at the dark sky. Ribbons of flame, burning gasoline, snaked along the pavement, and billowing clouds of smoke and brick dust shrouded the street.

The Black Beauty shot through the conflagration, a great dark beast of unstoppable power and destruction, while sirens screamed in the distance and terror painted the night.

"Really, Britt Reid," Lenore Case said in a bored tone as she gave the publisher of the *Daily Sentinel* a playful smirk. "I finally get you to take me somewhere and this is the best you can do?"

Britt Reid, dressed in a dark dinner jacket and bowtie, smiled, his eyes showing a glint of amusement. With a green cloth napkin, he dabbed at the corners of his mouth, then took a sip of his wine.

"The Golden Press Awards only come once a year, Casey . . . and I couldn't think of anyone I'd rather share them with."

Lenore Case glanced about the function room at the Dozier Hotel, then at the stage where Mike Axford, the *Sentinel*'s winning reporter, stood clutching either side of the podium.

"If I wanted to listen to Mike ramble on for half an hour straight I could have just stayed at work."

"Oh, come now, Casey." The twinkle in Britt's eyes strengthened. "It's Mike night. He's been bucking for this award for a year. And he *is* our ace reporter."

"He's an ace pain in the—"

"Uh-uh," Reid said. "Look alive, he's almost finished."

Casey's eyes became even more catlike, only adding to her beauty, Britt thought. Dressed in a sparkling emerald gown with a plunging neckline, she was, indeed, a lovely sight.

"And you said the same thing fifteen minutes ago." She shook her head and took a sip or her champagne.

Britt had to admit, this wasn't exactly what Casey expected when he'd asked her to accompany him to an "event." He supposed maybe he was being a bit cruel, getting her hopes up, but he had been serious when he said there was no one else he'd rather have had come with him. Of course, he was bored to tears, but the company was as pleasant as he could have asked.

Yet, it was more than boredom causing him some discomfort. He hadn't been to a function of any sort since . . . well, since Laura. And this reminded him of that time, of her. The memory was a tapestry of conflicting emotions, good and bad.

Laura Cavendish. The woman who would be queen. The woman who knew . . . secrets.

"You're thinking about it again, aren't you?" Casey said, breaking his reverie.

"It?"

"Okay, *her*." Casey frowned.

"Do I detect a note of jealousy, Miss Case?"

"I'll Miss Case you! And you know full well what I mean and why."

Britt nodded, his face becoming a dark reflection of his thoughts. "I suppose I do. She's out there, Casey. And as long as she is, your life, Kato's, and the lives of those who live in this city are at risk."

"I wish I could say you were exaggerating, but there was always something about her . . . she was cold-blooded, like a reptile in women's skin."

"But lovely skin it is." Britt paused, eyes growing distant.

"She won't give up, Britt. I'm sure of it. She knows your secret and sooner or later she's going to use that knowledge."

He gave her a thin smile. "Women's intuition?"

She pursed her lips, eyes widening. "Remember what I said about only yellowjacket females stinging."

Britt chuckled, no humor in the expression. "Perhaps she's long gone, miles from here. Licking her wounds."

Casey cast him a dubious flick of her eyebrow. "You really believe that?"

Britt hesitated, shook his head. "No, I suppose I don't."

"Pardon me, Mr. Reid," a voice came from behind them and Britt turned his head to see a waiter holding a bottle and an envelope of mustard-yellow paper.

Britt's stomach sank as his gaze focused on the bottle.

"The young lady asked me to present this to you," the waiter said, setting the bottle on the table before Britt Reid.

"Which young lady?" Britt asked, gaze lifting beyond the waiter.

"The one right over there at the—" The waiter stopped, his gaze fixed on an empty chair at the bar. "I don't understand. She was there a moment ago."

"I'm afraid I do," Britt said, glancing at Casey, who, from the pinched expression on her features, also understood.

"Pink Champagne," Casey said, ducking her chin at the bottle.

"Laura Cavendish's favorite." Britt accepted the letter from the waiter, who bowed and walked off. A tremor of apprehension went through his nerves as he stared at the envelope.

"Licking her wounds, you said?" Casey frowned, worry showing in her eyes.

Britt sighed and opened the envelope, pulled out the slip of mustard-yellow paper. His face tightened as he read the one line of elegant penmanship.

"What does it say?" Casey asked.

"It says, 'Thanks for the loan of your car,'" Britt answered.

"What does that mean?"

Britt slowly shook his head. "I have no idea, but I'm betting nothing good." Britt stood, dread sweeping through him. Laura Cavendish was back and with some plan of revenge she was already putting into motion. But what was it?

"We leaving?" Casey asked, standing, clutching her handbag.

"We are." A note of grimness laced Britt's tone.

They hurried from the function room, his alarm increasing with every step. Something was wrong. Laura had sent that note to let him know she had opened the gambit.

Behind them a loud voice boomed from the podium: "Hey, Britt! Hold up a minute!"

"Axford beckons," Casey said, hurrying by Britt's side.

"He probably wants to brag about his award." Britt's gaze swept backward and he gave Mike a parting smile and wave, but kept on.

A moment later, they reached the street and Britt's arm shot out, halting Casey on the sidewalk.

"What is it?" she asked, voice startled.

"Look!" Britt's arm came up, index finger jabbing towards a car parked at the curb across the street.

"That's—"

"The Black Beauty . . ." Britt whispered. He bolted across the street, Casey at his heels. Stopping beside the car, he tried the handle but the car was locked tight. His gaze swept over it, noting the scraps and scratches, small dings.

"How did it get here?" Casey asked, shock on her face. "And where's Kato?"

"I don't know, but if the car's here and he's not, he's in trouble. Look at the scratches and dents—it's taken a beating and Kato's not the type to go joyriding."

Casey touched his arm. "We have to get it out of here. If Axford—"

"Hey, Britt, Britt Reid!" came a shout from across the street. "Holy crow! That's The Harnet's car!"

The sudden wail of sirens came on the heels of Axford's declaration, accompanying a squad of police cars that screeched around the corner at the end of the street.

Britt looked at Casey. "Looks like we're not taking it anywhere."

"Are you all right, Kato?" Britt asked, helping his friend to a chair. They'd arrived home a moment ago to find Kato still on the floor, groggy, but Britt was just thankful his partner was alive.

"I'll live," Kato said, shaking his head.

"What happened?" Britt asked. Casey glanced at Kato, then went to the bar flanking the right wall of Britt's living room and located a wash cloth. She ran it under cold water, then returned to them and handed it to Kato, who pressed it to his forehead.

"Someone was in the house," Kato said. "Hit me with one of our own gas darts. I think it was—"

"Laura Cavendish," Britt answered, and tossed the dart he had found at the bottom of the stairs near Kato onto the coffee table. It was, indeed, one of their own. "She apparently took the Black Beauty for a spin, too."

Kato frowned, nodded. "She had one of the remotes."

"Did a lot of damage, but at least nobody seems to have been killed."

"Where's the car now?" Kato asked.

"Impound, most likely." Britt reached into his dinner jacket and pulled out a set of car keys. "Casey, take my car. Go see if you can find out anything from Scanlon and feel out Mike for anything, too. We're going to need to get that car back . . ."

Casey shut the front door behind her and hurried down the walkway towards Britt's car, which he'd left at the curb. Britt hadn't wanted to risk taking it into the secret alley entrance with the commotion caused by the Black Beauty's rampage. Black and Whites were crawling the streets everywhere, searching for The Hornet.

A figure stepped from the shadows of a large oak, stopping her with a motion from a small mustard-yellow gun.

"Laura Cavendish . . ." Casey said, words barely audible.

"I do believe you're competition, Miss Case," the other woman said, moonlight glazing her looped blonde bun in amber. She squeezed the trigger and gas swirled into Casey's face. She collapsed, the world suddenly going black.

"And you haven't heard from her?" Britt said, standing against the bar in his living room, phone pressed to his ear. "I see . . ." A moment later he cradled the phone. Worry spread over his handsome features.

"Miss Case?" Kato said, brow knitting.

"She never reached Scanlon. Mike, either. My car is still at the curb, too. We can assume Laura has her."

"And the Black Beauty?" Kato asked.

"At Lee's Impound. Police haven't been able to get into it yet, but sooner or later they'll find a way. We have to get to it before that happens."

"Lee's?" Kato shook his head. "Why there? It is not the normal police impound. They have not used it in years."

Britt gave a distant nod. "Good question. Why there, indeed? But that's all Scanlon had. Things are being kept quiet."

"A trap?"

"Another challenge for The Green Hornet . . ."

A half hour later, Britt Reid, now in the midnight-green garb of The Green Hornet, kept to the shadows after he tucked his car in an alley five blocks back and eased towards Lee's Impound. Kato moved silently behind him.

Lee's Impound was near the Detroit waterfront, a decrepit place surrounded by a high wooden fence topped with barbed wire. The lot was seldom used by law enforcement and was long suspected of being a front for waterfront smuggling. It seemed more than a little odd the Beauty would be housed there. Which meant the police suspected he would try to steal it back and wanted a location where they could fire at will and without danger to civilians. The car's rampage had branded The Hornet a worse criminal than ever before and they were determined to trap him this time. Mike Axford was, no doubt, perched by the phone and ready with a blazing headline proclaiming The Hornet had been captured or killed.

He wondered if Laura Cavendish had planned for that in whatever scheme of revenge she had in mind.

"It looks deserted," Kato whispered, as they approached the right side of the fenced enclosure. To either side of the lot was a narrow street flanked by dark brick warehouses. On the lake a buoy clanged and the scent of diesel hung heavy in the air.

"I'm sure that's the way they want it to look," The Hornet said. His gloved hand went beneath his trench coat, came back out with his small collapsible grapple and line. He whipped the grapple in a short circle, then flung it upward. Kato followed suit.

They climbed, careful to make as little noise as possible. He felt positive police were waiting for them, but he no desire to make it easier on the law. Reaching the top, clinging with one hand to the line, he paused, scanning the dark grounds.

"There," The Hornet said, ducking his chin at the darkened shape of a vehicle towards the center of the lot.

"Right out in the open," Kato said.

The Hornet nodded. "Convenient."

"There should be dogs," Kato said. "Drug lords down here use Dobermans."

"Maybe they didn't want them getting in the way." The Hornet, using his free hand, the other gripping the line, slipped his Sting from beneath his coat. The foot-long device telescoped and emitted a high-frequency sonic beam. Sparks shimmered into nothingness as he cut a swath through the barbed wire.

"That attracted no attention," Kato said, as The Hornet returned the Sting beneath his coat.

"I had little doubt it would be ignored. They're waiting."

Kato slipped a small oblong object from his pocket, clinging to his own line with on hand. He aimed the object at the Black Beauty, pressed a button. The car remained stationary.

"Spare remote doesn't work," he said.

"Laura thought of everything," The Hornet said. "She disabled the remote drive."

Kato nodded, pressed another button. A front and back door whisked open.

"But not the opener." Kato tucked the remote back into his pocket. "What are our chances of getting to it without being ambushed?"

"Zero to none, I'd say. But we have no choice. I'm not willing to let the police find a way into it and discover some potential clue back to us."

The Hornet glanced at Kato, who nodded. "Check."

They went over the top of the fence, slid down their lines. At the bottom, they flipped the grapples loose and secured them to their belts.

With another glance at each other, they bolted for the car.

Flood lights blazed blinding white light across the yard before they made it twenty feet.

"Stop where you are, Hornet!" a voice boomed from a blow horn. You're under arrest!"

The Hornet and Kato halted, their backs to one another. Kato's hands came up in a defensive position; The Hornet's rose in a boxing posture.

They were surrounded by uniformed men, guns drawn. The men began to close the circle, one liberating a pair of handcuffs from his belt.

"It is worse than we thought," Kato said, eyes roving behind his mask. He kept his head tucked.

"Let them close in. They won't be able to shoot without risking hitting their own men."

The policemen advanced in increments, plainly wary or the two supposed criminals.

Ten feet . . .

"Head to the Beauty," The Hornet said. "Don't stop to look back."

Kato nodded, feet shifting a fraction.

The Hornet felt his heart skip. He had planned for a trap, but this was a bit more complete than he'd anticipated. These weren't criminals, either; they were hard-working cops doing their duty, and for all intents The Green Hornet was a criminal.

Five feet . . . four . . . three . . .

"Now . . ." The Hornet whispered.

"Ki-yiii!" Kato yelled and swung a leg up and back in a spinning kick that met one cop's gun hand, knocking the weapon from his grip.

The Hornet surged forward, fists pumping. He had calculated correctly—they didn't dare fire at this close range for fear of killing one of their own. He had anticipated close combat, though he'd had a moment where he worried they'd simply start shooting.

The Hornet's hand darted beneath his coat, came out with a small green gun. Gas spurted and a cop fell.

Behind him, Kato's feet whipped out and his hands lashed.

"Pile on them, boys!" one of the cops yelled. "There's too many of us—they can't take us all down!"

The cop was right and The Hornet knew it. He was certain Kato knew it, too. Despite the melee and sudden confusion, the city's finest would get their act together in another moment and crush them under the weight of sheer numbers.

With a yell, Kato came off the ground, both legs snapping out sideways, each connecting with a cop's chest. He came down in a half-crouch, an opening in the circle of bluecoats now before him. In nearly the same move he sprinted towards the Black Beauty.

It was a ten-yard dash, but he was now in the open, a sure mark under the glare of a dozen arc lights.

"Dive!" The Hornet yelled. His foot swept out, connected with the back of an aiming cop's knee, and took the man off his feet—but not before the bluecoat pulled the trigger.

Kato, at The Hornet's shout, dove into a forward roll. The bullet tore through empty air where he had been an instant before.

Kato came to his feet, momentum thrusting him towards the car, and plunged into the Black Beauty. The front door swung shut on his heels and seconds later the engine buzzed to life.

Two men, those not stunned by the sudden turn of events, grabbed for The Hornet's arms. The Hornet's fists whipped upward, one still gripping the small gun, and connected with each cop's face. The men staggered and The Hornet plunged forward.

Guns raised.

"Shoot to kill, men!" the lead cop ordered. "Don't let him escape!"

Outlined in the stark glare of the lights, The Hornet was perfect target. He made it ten feet, fifteen—

The Black Beauty's tires spun, spewing gravel as Kato rolled the wheel and sent the vehicle fish-tailing between The Hornet and the circle of cops.

The Hornet dove into the back seat, door sweeping shut behind him.

Guns roared and lead spanged from the car's armored plates. Windows of bullet-proof glass spiderwebbed, but held.

"Let's roll, Kato," The Hornet said, shoving his little gun beneath his coat.

The Black Beauty shot forward, Kato's gloved hand tight on the wheel. With a flick of a switch on the dash, the rocket muzzles extended beneath the headlights.

Before them, the wooden fence exploded as rockets hit, splinters lacerating the air while bullets from police guns pounded the back of the car.

The Black Beauty arrowed through the opening and out into the night.

"The recorder light is blinking," Kato said, gazing into the rearview.

The Hornet frowned. "No doubt a lovely parting gift from Laura Cavendish. She always did have to have the last word. Play it."

"She certainly made herself intimate with our equipment." Kato jabbed a dashboard button.

Laura Cavendish's annoying little chuckle came from the speaker and Britt Reid, beneath the mask and fedora, cringed. Her tone, one he'd once thought like windchimes on a summer morning, now sounded like nails dragging across a blackboard.

"My-my-my, you always do manage to pull off the most amazing escapes. And I assume if you are listening to this message you have, indeed, escaped and have your precious car back. You know where I am. We spent many happy nights here. They were happy for you, weren't they? I'd be crushed if they weren't. Come to me. And leave the trained chimp behind. If you don't, Miss Case will simply be beside herself . . ."

The message ended and Kato jabbed a button. "You know where she is?"

The Hornet nodded. "Trendle Apartments. I've kept a check on her place; it's been empty since she disappeared. Someone's been paying the rent on it but I haven't been able to trace it back to the source. Let's roll!"

Kato swung the car in a U-turn, tore up a side street, silent running.

"Why would she tell you where she and Miss Case were?" Kato asked. "It's another trap?"

"It's an offer . . ."

"An offer to kill you this time. I am going in with you."

"No, Kato, if she wanted us dead she would have killed you earlier tonight. I don't know what she meant by Casey being beside herself, but there was something threatening in her voice. If she sees you with me . . . Casey's dead. Better you stay behind . . . Cheetah . . ."

Kato flashed The Hornet a humorless smirk in the rearview, but remained silent.

Twenty minutes later, The Hornet's sting telescoped and the lock on the door leading to Laura Cavendish's apartment exploded in a shower of sparks. He placed a gloved palm on the door and shoved it inward. The last time he'd been in the apartment, he'd thought Laura Cavendish had fallen over the balcony to her death. He wondered if that wouldn't have been for the best.

The Hornet froze, a wave of dread washing through him. The room was dark, except for a dim light cast from a mustard-yellow, low-watt bulb on a couch-side lamp. In the center of the room, Lenore Case, still in her emerald gown, lay on a slanted wooden board attached to a pivoting base. Her wrists and ankles were held to the board by straps and a gag was laced between her teeth.

But that wasn't what stopped The Hornet short. For to the left, anchored to a track in the ceiling and secured with a hinged clamp to the wall, was a half-moon-shaped blade of steel, a pendulum.

The Hornet took a step forward, only to be halted by a voice that came through a hidden speaker.

"No-no, Britt," Laura Cavendish said. "You wouldn't want to be the cause of another split personality, would you?"

The Hornet looked about, searching for some sign of the woman who spoke. He gripped the Hornet Sting still in his hand tighter. It would not stop the blade, but if he could spot some type of activation switch . . .

"What do you want, Laura?" The Hornet said, eyes roving behind his mask. Dammit, where was that switch?

"I want you, Britt. To rule this city beside me."

"You know that won't happen. And you know I'm not a real criminal."

"Oh, but it's such a short step over the line, Britt. You have a choice, you see. Join me or Miss Case gets a tragic case of split ends . . ."

"You're insane . . ." The Hornet said.

"I'm ambitious . . . time's up, Britt. The Lady or the Tigress?"

Laura Cavendish always had shown a flare for the melodramatic, but something in her had snapped. He could hear it in her voice. She hated losing and that had become a mania.

"No way!" The Hornet's fingers tightened on the sting, whipped it towards the pivoting base of the board upon which Lenore Case was secured. A screech came from the loudspeaker and suddenly the clamp holding the pendulum sprang open.

The pivot exploded in sparks as the sonic beam hit and The Hornet flung himself forward in nearly the same instant—straight for Lenore Case.

He hit hard atop her. The pendulum swept downward, cleaving the back of his coat in two, but missing his flesh, as the pivot buckled and the board, along with him and Lenore Case, wrenched free and slammed into the floor.

The Hornet was up in a heartbeat, careful to avoid the swinging blade. He unbuckled Lenore's straps, pulled the gag from her mouth.

"That room!" Lenore said, voice quivering, and pointing to a door. "She's been going in and out of there."

The Hornet nodded, helping her up. "Kato's waiting in the alley. Go to him."

Before he finished speaking, The Hornet was leaping for the door. He tried the handle, finding it locked. The Hornet Sting obliterated the lock. Returning the Sting beneath his coat, he kicked the door inward.

It took him only a cautious moment to discern the room was empty. He discovered a microphone and transmitting apparatus on a desk near the bed, so she must have been in the room only a moment before he burst in.

After checking the room's only closet, he made his way to an open window across from the bed. Peering out, he spotted nothing to indicate she had gone down or up, no ladder, ropes. The roof lay two stories above and he wondered . . . it would have been possible for someone to climb up a line and retract it.

He withdrew his own grapple and line from his belt, dangled it out the window. Whirling it in a short circle, he let it fly upward with a flick of his arm. It hooked the lip of the low ledge running along the roof. He tested the line to make sure it was secured solidly, then slipped out the window and began to climb. The ascent was perilous, despite his skill, and if Laura was waiting for him with a gun . . .

She was waiting, but unarmed, as far as he could tell. She stood on the opposite ledge, her mustard-yellow great coat rippling in the breeze that wafted across the roof. A fedora of the same color perched atop her blonde locks and her emerald eyes peered from behind a mask that was a mustard-yellow duplicate of his own.

"You like it?" she asked, a cold smile on her lips. "I modeled it after your outfit, after all."

The Hornet took a step, paused. "I'm not much for the color . . ."

Laura Cavendish laughed her haughty little chuckle.

"I got lucky last time, Britt. When I went over the balcony. I used to be a gymnast, you know. I caught the line you'd left hanging. Quite by accident, in fact. I should have died."

"You've lost your mind, Laura. I'm turning you over to Scanlon."

She uttered another laugh. "Oh, but you can't do that, can you, Britt? Because I'd tell . . . I'd tell everyone Britt Reid, publisher at large, is the notorious Green Hornet."

"I'll take that chance to save Casey and the innocent people of this city."

She peered at him at long moment. "You would, wouldn't you? So damn righteous . . ." She turned, looked down, then back to The Hornet. "I won't lose, Britt. You know I can't. You'll come to me . . . You'll beg me . . . I *will* have you . . . or I'll make your life a living hell."

Laura Cavendish stepped out into space, vanishing downward in an instant.

The Hornet ran to the side of the roof, peered down. There was no sign of her.

"I wish she'd stop doing that . . . " he muttered.

An hour later, Britt Reid, Kato, and Lenore Case walked into Britt's study to find District Attorney Scanlon seated behind the desk.

"Frank!" Britt said, a smile on his lips. "To what do we owe the pleasure?"

The D.A.'s eyes narrowed behind his horn-rimmed glasses, his features grim. "I'm afraid it's not much of a pleasure with Laura Cavendish still on the loose."

"Why's that?" Britt asked, a slight smile on his lips.

"She'll be back at some point, you know that," Scanlon said. "The Yellowjacket's not about to just let you be."

"That's what *I've* been telling him!" Casey said, shaking her head.

"I think you both worry too much," Britt said with a chuckle. "I'm sure wherever she is she's—"

"If you say licking her wounds, *I'm* going to dress in a bad color and sting you!" Casey said, smirking.

LAIR OF THE LIVING DEAD

by Joe McKinney

East Michigan, near the channel islands, just south of Milleville Beach. January, 1967.

A narrow country road dead ends at the water's edge, where a sixty-foot trawler waits in the dark, rolling easily on the icy waters of Lake Erie.

Above the road is a meadow, weed-strewn and brittle beneath a blanket of ice. The land curves upwards like the sides of a bowl toward a black line of skeletal trees. The sky is a lowering mass of gray clouds, laced through with lightning.

A mournful, almost plaintive moaning splits the chill night air.

Eleven shambling forms, moving with the jerks and fits and the drunken stagger of dead men climbing up from their graves, form an uneven skirmish line and move down the meadow to the road where a pair of lumbering cargo trucks are closing on the trawler, and a meeting with the living dead.

In the cab of the second truck, The Green Hornet and Kato rode beside Earl Brunig, head of the Red Hand Gang. Brunig was a corpulent man with shoulders as wide as the grill of a Buick. He held the steering wheel like it was The Green Hornet's neck and he was dead set on doing some strangling. He'd said little on the hour-and-a-half drive up from Detroit, and not just because the icy roads and the strong Canadian winds of the impending storm had made the driving difficult. He was too busy trying to hold on to what was left of his pride.

The Green Hornet expected as much.

For almost a week now, he and Kato had been closing in on Brunig and

29

his gang. A recent police raid on a warehouse owned by one of Brunig's associates had turned up a cache of Russian-made military assault rifles smuggled in through the Canadian border. Unable to link Brunig directly to the guns, and unable to determine what Brunig's gang intended to do with the weapons, District Attorney Frank Scanlon had asked The Green Hornet to investigate.

And The Green Hornet, in his own inimitable style, had gone straight for the jugular. He told Brunig he was muscling in on the action, and that he'd be taking half the profits on the guns. After getting one of Kato's lightning fast roundhouse kicks to the chin, Brunig had reluctantly agreed to the deal.

But cowing Brunig didn't put The Green Hornet any closer to learning who was behind the weapons smuggling operation, which was what really mattered. Brunig was just a marionette. The Green Hornet had realized that from the start. Someone else was pulling the strings. And if he didn't figure out who that was, Brunig would simply get replaced by another marionette.

The big man downshifted and the truck's engine groaned in response. The trawler was waiting just ahead, and The Green Hornet could see a few dim shapes moving around the beached prow.

"How long do you think this will take us, Brunig?"

"Don't know," Brunig growled. "Twenty minutes, maybe. We get loaded up and back to town while we've still got the cover of darkness."

"That's it? We don't set up another shipment?"

"No," Brunig said sharply, "we don't. We get the guns. We store them. We don't ask questions."

The trucks skated to a stop on the icy road and the men climbed out.

The Hornet, an imposing figure in his midnight green trench coat and face mask, rounded the front of truck and faced Brunig and his gang, some of whom were still limping from their fight at the warehouse the night before. Behind The Green Hornet, Kato blended into the darkness and waited to strike down anyone daring to make a move in anger against The Hornet.

The effort was hardly necessary, though. The Red Hand to a man had hate in their eyes, but none dared issue a challenge.

The Green Hornet and Brunig walked up to the boat, gravel crunching beneath their shoes, and stopped in front of the trawler's skipper. His name was Torrence. He was a tall, slender man in denim overalls and a heavy black turtleneck sweater. His eyes were buried in a nest of wrinkles and his mouth was almost completely hidden behind an immensely bushy salt and pepper beard.

"What's this then?" the skipper demanded. "You the new partner?"

The Hornet caught the elongated vowel in the middle of the word "partner" and thought, Boston? New England coastline, maybe?

"That's right," The Hornet said.

Torrence stood with his shoulders squared to The Hornet. The wind was knifing in off the water, making the air feel like a hard twenty below, but the New Englander didn't seem to notice.

"I don't like it," said the skipper. "No, sir, I don't like it."

"What don't you like?" The Hornet said.

"I don't trust a man who wears a mask."

He turned to his crew of three and ordered them to shove off.

"That would be a stupid thing to do," The Hornet said.

Torrence wheeled around, his eyes suddenly glinting with anger. For such a slender man he carried himself with absolute confidence. "What did you call me?"

The Hornet had already noticed the bulge of a pistol under the man's sweater at his right hip. And now he was noticing the balled fists at the man's side, the flat-footed stance, the chin thrust upwards in defiance.

Definitely raised in a New England fishing community, The Hornet thought. A man with no fear of a fight.

Kato appeared at The Hornet's side.

"No," The Hornet said, "there's no need."

He turned to Torrence.

"I didn't come here to fight with you," he said. There was a gleam in The Hornet's eyes that made Torrence blink. "And I don't care if you trust me or not. I'm here to make money, plain and simple. You want to make money, you'll work with me."

Torrence remained where he was, staring at The Hornet. The crew had appeared on deck with assault rifles, and the Red Hand Gang was also looking antsy. The only sound was the creaking of the trawler as it rolled upon the waves.

But then, just as the tension between them seemed to be at its thickest, Torrence's face wrinkled up in disgust.

"Oh God," he said. "What's that smell?"

The Hornet had smelled it too. Something dead, like a corpse two weeks old.

"There!" one of Torrence's crew shouted. He pointed toward the far side of the road, and as The Hornet turned to look, shots rang out.

The Hornet stepped back just as another of Torrence's crew jumped down and opened fire with a fully automatic Russian-made rifle. The night air, so quiet a moment before, was filled now with the sounds of gut-wrenching moans and the staccato bark of gunfire.

The Hornet saw a group of men staggering across the road, their gait stiff and uncertain. He focused on the man out in front. There was something wrong with his face. His mouth looked slack. He was covered in open, oozing sores and dried blood. His eyes were the milky white of a dead man's.

More moaning filled the space around them, sending a shiver down The Hornet's spine.

"Shoot him!" Torrence shouted.

The lead man's body convulsed as the men fired their weapons into his chest.

But he didn't fall.

He moaned once more, and then his hands came up and he was clutching at the air between them as if in supplication.

"What the. . ." said the man next to The Hornet.

Dead men, The Hornet thought as he watched the figures stagger across the road, advancing right into the hail of bullets. My God, they're the living dead.

The Hornet was a veteran crimefighter, and yet his blood ran cold at the sight of the zombies attacking the Red Hand Gang. Bullets didn't stop them, and their smell was enough to raise the bile into The Hornet's throat. Their moaning had already caused one of Torrence's crew to flee back to the boat, screaming.

And then Torrence himself was in front of The Hornet. He pulled his pistol from his hip and emptied all six shots into a zombie's chest.

It did absolutely no good. The zombie seemed to shiver, but that was all.

A moment later, he was staggering forward again, hands outstretched.

"You did this!" Torrence shouted at The Hornet.

"No," The Hornet said.

Torrence waved at his crew. "Fall back to the boat! We're leaving!"

But the men were cut off. Several of the zombies had got behind them and were blocking the path to the boat. And now most of the men were out of ammunition. One of the zombies fell on a member of the Red Hand Gang and dragged the man down to the icy road, screaming and flailing his arms like a drowning man.

"To the trucks," Brunig shouted. "Hurry!"

The men scrambled away, sprinting past The Hornet as they abandoned their useless weapons and Torrence's trawler for the safety of the trucks.

It all happened so fast The Hornet barely had time to register that he and Kato were being left alone with the zombies. He turned to see Kato knock one of the living dead to the ground with a leg sweep, and when he looked back, Brunig was staring at him from the passenger window of the rearmost truck as they trundled off down the road.

A sickening moan snapped The Hornet's attention back to the fight.

One of the zombies was looming over him, hands outstretched, the face beyond the hands slack with an utter lack of emotion.

An accomplished boxer, The Hornet hit the zombie with two hard left jabs and then a crushing right-handed haymaker.

But the blows did nothing.

The zombie staggered backwards, then raised his hands and came at The Hornet again. Backing up, The Hornet lost his footing on the ice and fell flat on his back. He found himself looking straight up into the sightless white eyes in the dead man's skull.

The zombie reached for him, but before the hands could close on The Hornet's throat, there was a dull sounding thwack as a six inch long hornet-shaped steel dart lanced into the zombie's wrist. A moment later a puff of green gas billowed upwards from the dart and into the zombie's face.

The zombie glanced to his left, where Kato was running towards the fallen Hornet, but otherwise showed no ill effects from the dart or the gas.

The Hornet crab-crawled backwards, away from the zombie. The stench of death was overpowering, and though he had never fled from a fight before, that smell, and the sight of a dead man walking, shook him to his core.

But a moment later Kato was there and jabbing a sidekick into the zombie's throat. The kick lifted the zombie off his feet and sent him sprawling on his back across the road.

From where The Hornet sat the only part of the fallen zombie that was still visible was the soles of his shoes, but that was enough. For even in the dark he could see a faint pattern of green ink on the shoe leather. He leaned forward and could just barely make out the design of a five dollar bill. As the zombie sat up and stared at them, completely unfazed by Kato's mule-like kick, The Hornet could only blink in confusion.

"What the. . ."

The other zombies were closing in around them now. The moaning was deafening, the stench enough to bring tears to The Hornet's eyes.

Kato bladed his hands out in front of him in a classic wing chun fighting stance, ready to take on the horde, but The Hornet scrambled to his feet and pulled Kato back.

"The Black Beauty," he said, and took what appeared to be an eight-inch-long remote control from his trench coat pocket.

Kato nodded that he understood.

The Hornet made three quick keystrokes on the remote, and suddenly the scene was lit by a faint green light from the headlights of a customized 1966 Chrysler Crown Imperial, the Black Beauty.

The car skidded to a stop on the road and The Hornet and Kato ran for it.

Kato jumped in the driver's seat and The Green Hornet slid into the back as the zombies lumbered after them.

"Get us out of here," The Hornet said.

Kato, unflappable, merely nodded. He put the car in reverse and accelerated away from the cluster of zombies, who were suddenly engulfed in a haze of ice and powdered airborne snow.

"Behind us!"

Kato glanced in the rearview mirror.

Two of the zombies were blocking the roadway, tall snow banks on either side of them.

He didn't flinch.

He gave the wheel a hard one-half turn and simultaneously dropped the gear shifter into drive. The car spun 180 degrees, rotating around the zombies in a flawless J turn that left the Black Beauty pointed down the road.

Using the vehicle's momentum he drifted sideways through a tight curve and regained control as they came out the other side.

Then he glanced in the rearview mirror again and caught The Hornet's eye.

The Green Hornet let out the breath he had been holding, then nodded at his old friend.

"Nice driving," he said. "Thanks, Kato."

The storm had rolled in during the early morning hours and settled over downtown Detroit like a blanket, obscuring the upper stories of the soot-stained brick buildings in a swirling gray screen of falling snow. Derelict men in shabby clothes hunted for shelter in the doorways and alcoves while skeins of airborne ice snaked around them. Weak orange lights glowed faintly from snow-blasted windows, the lure of the warmth within cruelly remote. And down these mean streets a long black Chrysler struggled with the loose powder and ice that the municipal snowplows had yet to clear.

When at last the car stopped at the curb, a man in a tailored black overcoat stepped out, gave a furtive glance up and down the street, and then disappeared into a dark, graffiti-soiled alleyway between two large buildings, his shoulders hunched forward against the windy cold.

The man paused at a boarded over doorway. District Attorney Frank Scanlon gave another furtive glance toward the street, then slipped quickly through a hole in the boards.

Britt Reid paced his study like a caged leopard. In his hand was a five dollar bill he had spent the last twenty minutes pondering.

A faint chirping stopped him in his tracks and his eyes snapped to his desk.

The chirping came once more, and he moved quickly to the bookshelf behind his desk. There he tilted down three of the hardbound books and turned to the fireplace on the opposite wall.

As he and Kato watched, the entire wall rose into the ceiling, revealing a metallic, open-faced elevator shaft within.

Scanlon was standing there, his overcoat tossed carelessly over his shoulder.

A short metal ladder dropped from the elevator platform and Scanlon stepped down gingerly. The man was built like a railroad spike, tapering to a point somewhere below his feet. He handed his coat to Kato and shook hands with Britt Reid.

"I'm glad you called me," he said. "I was getting worried."

"It was a busy night," Britt said.

"So I gather."

Kato appeared at Scanlon's side with a hot cup of coffee on a silver tray. Scanlon took it gratefully and held the cup between his palms for a long moment before drinking. He closed his eyes and savored the flood of heat entering his body.

"Ah," he said, setting the cup back down on Kato's tray. "That warms the soul. Thank you, Kato."

Kato nodded smartly.

"This has to be the worst winter I can remember," Scanlon said. "Which reminds me, I asked the State Police to check out the landing area you told me about. No signs of a struggle. No bodies. No boat. Nothing."

Britt nodded thoughtfully. "That fits."

"Well, I wish you'd explain it to me. Last night you were talking about zombies. What gives?"

"They weren't zombies. I watched one of them take a full magazine from a Russian-made assault rifle. Kato gassed another of them with one of his Hornet darts. Nothing stopped them. They moved like dead men. They even smelled like dead men. But they weren't zombies."

"What do you mean they smelled?"

"Kato," Britt said. "Show him."

Kato took a small glass vial from his white valet's jacket and pulled out the rubber stopper. He held it up and gestured for Scanlon to take a whiff.

Moving cautiously, Scanlon leaned forward and sniffed the vial.

He backed away immediately, his face scrunched up in disgust like he'd just bit into a lemon. He put his knuckles up to his nose and tried to rub the smell away.

"Oh God," he said. "What is that?"

"Cadaverene," Kato said.

"What?" Scanlon looked to Britt for clarification.

"Kato was able to manufacture it for me earlier this morning," Britt said. "It's a chemical developed to simulate the smell of rotting human flesh."

Scanlon looked as though the smell was still deep in his nostrils. "But why would anybody make that?"

"Disaster workers use it to train cadaver search dogs," Britt said. "But I think what you're really asking is why anybody would pour this stuff all over themselves and wander around like the living dead. The answer to that is I don't know."

The phone rang before Scanlon could respond.

Kato picked up the receiver and said, "Mr. Reid's residence." The faint hint of an accent was still noticeable beneath his precise English. He looked at Britt and put a white gloved palm over the mouthpiece. "It's Miss Case."

Britt took the phone from him. "Yes, Miss Case. What is it?"

"I looked into known counterfeiters in the Detroit area, like you asked me," came his secretary's voice on the other end of the line, "and I think I found a good lead. Do you remember an article we did three years ago, on a man named Carlton Miers?"

"Carlton Miers, yes of course. He was brought up on federal charges three times back in the fifties, but he's been quiet for nearly a decade."

"That's right. But he has a house up at North Pointe."

"North Pointe? That's less than five miles from the attack last night."

"Three and three-tenths of a mile, actually."

A smile played at the corner of Britt Reid's mouth. Casey, he thought, you're the best.

"That's fine, Miss Case. Thank you."

"Yes, sir."

Britt hung up the phone and said, "Looks like we're going to pay a visit to Carlton Miers this evening."

"Miers?" Scanlon said. "But I thought this was about gun running? What am I missing?"

"I'm not sure yet," Britt said. "But I think the gun running and the five dollar bill impressions I saw on that zombie's shoes are connected. And I think maybe Miers is the man behind it."

"That would fit. But can you prove it?"

"No. But you can bet The Green Hornet will."

Carlton Miers' home was a wind-blasted three story Victorian right on the edge of Lake Erie. There were very few trees out here, no well-manicured shrubs or ivy-covered stone walls. The house stood alone, a silent, dilapidated sentinel overlooking a wasteland of snow and barren emptiness.

That's the home of a man who would use troops disguised as the living dead, the Hornet thought. But to what purpose?

That was the question that still eluded him.

In his head The Green Hornet went through what he knew so far.

He had a gang of gun runners who were obviously working for someone bigger.

He had another gang of men who could take fire from assault rifles without flinching, who could get a face full of gas from Kato's darts without any noticeable ill effects, who stank like two-week-old corpses, and yet were clearly not zombies. They had, after all, stolen Torrence's boat and all its cargo. What would the living dead care for weapons?

And at least one of them had an ink stain from a counterfeiter's five dollar plate on the bottom of his shoe.

Add to that the final piece of the puzzle—Carlton Miers, veteran counterfeiter. He was the key to this. And hopefully the bluff The Green Hornet was about to play would prove that.

The Green Hornet and Kato slipped the locks on Miers' window easily and slipped inside without a sound.

They took up positions behind a heavy red curtain and listened to a man's voice on the other side, reading in a low, eerily dulcet tone.

"'No pestilence had been ever so fatal, or so hideous. Blood was its Avatar and its seal—the redness and the horror of blood. There were sharp pains, and sudden dizziness, and then profuse bleedings at the pores, with dissolution.'"

"What is that?" Kato said, mouthing the words silently.

"Edgar Allen Poe," The Green Hornet said, "from 'The Masque of the Red Death.'"

There was a shrill giggle from inside the room, and the reading resumed. "'The scarlet stains upon the body and especially upon the face of the victim, were the pest-ban which shut him out from the aid and from the sympathy of his fellow men. And the—'"

The man's voice suddenly broke off. And when it came again, all the ease had left it.

"Ah God! It's freezing in here. I thought I told you to close the window."

"I did, Boss."

"Well it doesn't feel like it."

"I'll check it, Boss."

The Hornet and Kato waited behind a heavy read curtain, and when Miers' thug threw it open, they exploded into the room.

The Green Hornet launched a ferocious haymaker into a henchman's chin and sent him sprawling. Kato stepped around The Hornet and launched a wheel kick into another man's ear, dropping him to the ground like he was a bag of bricks. A third man lunged at Kato with his hands outstretched, but stopped when he saw the blade of Kato's right foot suddenly poised in mid-air in front of his eyes.

As he stood there, frozen, Kato wagged his toe back and forth in front of the man's face, and the man seemed to get the message. *Don't even think about it.*

"Enough!" Miers said. He had a hardback book in his hands and he slammed it shut with a thunderclap that silenced the room. "Who do you think you are, Hornet, barging in here?"

He was a tall, cadaverous man with very pale and graceful fingers. Blue veins showed through the skin at his temples. His lips were pallid and his hair as delicate as cobwebs upon his brow. Only his eyes showed the heat still burning within the man.

"You know me," The Hornet said. "That's a good sign."

"Of course I know you. What are you doing in my house?"

"I have a business proposal I want to discuss."

"I think you're in the wrong house, friend."

"No, I'm in the right house, friend. Last night, I was with a man named Brunig who was trying to buy some guns off a ship's captain named Torrence."

"I have no idea what you're talking about."

"I'm talking about zombies, Miers. The zombies you used to steal the guns from Brunig and Torrence last night."

That made Miers pause, but he recovered quickly.

"Zombies, you say? Listen, Hornet, everybody knows I love a good horror story. That's no secret." He held up the book in his hand. "But that's all they are, Hornet. Stories, nothing more."

Miers waved them away with a haughty, almost feminine wave of his pale fingers, but The Hornet was not to be put off.

He stepped toward Miers. "'But then without those doors there did stand the lofty and enshrouded figure of the lady Madeline of Usher. There was blood upon her white robes, and the evidence of some bitter struggle upon every portion of her emaciated frame. For a moment she remained trembling and reeling to and fro upon the threshold—then, with a low moaning cry, fell heavily inward upon the person of her brother, and in her horrible and now final death-agonies, bore him to the floor a corpse, and a victim to the terrors he had dreaded.'"

Miers stood aghast.

One of his henchmen struggled to his feet, still trying to shake the ringing from his head, and made a move toward The Hornet.

"No!" Miers shouted at the man. "Stop." To The Hornet he said, "I'm impressed. You know your Poe. Am I to believe you've memorized 'The Fall of the House of Usher?'"

"I know lots of things, Miers."

Miers leaned against his desk and crossed his arms over his slender chest. "Such as?"

"I know the fear you can drive into a man when he thinks he sees a dead man walking. That's the key to this. There's more going on here than just gun-running. At first I thought it was just counterfeiting, but now I know it's even more than that."

"You've got me curious, Hornet. What else, exactly, do you think I'm up to?"

"You're the man behind Brunig, and probably half a dozen small timers just like him. You sent his gang out to make pickups from Torrence. You let a few get through, but when it's time for the big shipments you went in with your crew of zombies and stole the guns."

"To what end, Hornet? What would be the point?"

"You're an anarchist."

"A what?" Miers looked amused, and he traded a smirk with his bodyguards.

"You heard me. First you designed and built the ultimate terror weapon in your zombies, which are nothing more than men dressed in head to toe body armor that's been soaked in Cadaverene. They're invulnerable to weapons and they can terrorize a civilian population into blind panic. Then you use those zombies to stockpile large caches of weapons throughout the city. And then the counterfeit bills. That's your biggest stroke. You work on two fronts. You destroy the economy by disrupting the value of its currency while at the same time driving its populace mad with fear. What's left would be nothing more than a post-apocalyptic ruin—controlled by you."

The smile had slipped away from Miers' face, and with that The Green Hornet knew he'd hit the mark.

"What do you want, Hornet?"

"I want a big bite of the pie before you make it go rotten."

"How big?"

"That's negotiable. But first I want to see the size of your operation."

Miers looked like he was trying to drive nails into The Hornet's face with the force of his stare.

"When?"

"Tonight," The Hornet said. "It's ten o'clock now. Shall we make it three hours from now?"

"Fine. Do you know Dreamland Pointe?"

"The graveyard of ships?"

"That's it."

The Hornet nodded. "We'll be there."

"I can't wait," said Miers.

In the back seat of the Black Beauty, The Green Hornet did a function check on the Hornet Sting, a telescoping metal baton capable of emitting a high-frequency sonic wave that could cut stone, metal, and glass with surgical precision. It had two folding grips that allowed The Hornet to wield the Sting like a machine gun and he clicked both of these into place, checking the mechanism, making sure it was perfect.

Kato watched him in the rearview mirror.

"Do you think he'll really lead us to his operation?"

"I think so, Kato, but not by choice. If he's as smart as I think he is, he'll use the three hours we gave him to dismantle his operation. We need to get to him before that happens."

Kato nodded.

"Do you have him on the scanner?"

"Yes. They haven't moved. We should come up on them around this next bend."

"Good. Go to silent running, Kato."

Kato gave another nod. His fingers glided effortlessly toward the controls, and a moment later, the Black Beauty disappeared into the night, becoming as silent as the falling snow.

Dreamland Pointe, The Green Hornet reflected, was the perfect place for an operation like the one Miers was running.

The Hornet and Kato were kneeling behind a bank of snow, watching the shoreline, where the broken skeletons of hundreds of scuttled boats lay creaking and groaning beneath the gathering ice. Skeins of icy snow darted across the landscape and out onto the frozen surface of the water. Fresh fallen snow, gray and dirty, covered every hull, every battered, ghostly wreck. There were boats out there as large as a freighter and as small as a shallow water fishing boat, but to a vessel they were true derelicts, far, far beyond the possibility of salvage.

And that was why this place made so much sense. There wasn't a trace of development for thirty miles. In the summer the land was a swampy wetland filled with mosquitoes so large you could put a saddle on them. In the winter, with the ice entombing everything and the boats moaning as their timbers were slowly ripped apart by the elements, the place had the feel of a graveyard. The boats, especially the larger freighters, would provide a perfect shelter for Miers' counterfeiting operations, and the water would provide an easy escape across to Canada should the cops ever get close enough for a raid.

"Very clever," The Hornet muttered.

They were watching the deck of one of the larger freighters, where a man in a zombie outfit stood watch. He had pulled his armored face mask back over his head and smoked as he leaned over the railing, where row upon row of jagged icicles gave the prow of the ship the look of a mouth full of teeth.

Not far to the right of the freighter they could make out the dark outline of Joe Torrence's trawler.

"You see any others?" The Green Hornet asked.

"That one there," Kato said, pointing at the zombie guard still puffing away at his cigarette. "And two more walking aft. There."

"Okay, I see them. Let's go aft and take care of those first. Then we'll make our way forward. We saw eleven last night. We should see at least that many now."

The two crimefighters climbed aboard near the stern of the wrecked freighter and made their way silently across the deck. Leading the way, Kato came up behind three of the zombies. Their stench carried on the cold, crisp air. Each carried a Russian-made assault rifle.

Kato tapped one of the zombies on the shoulder.

He turned around and got Kato's heel planted severely in his teeth, snapping his head back with enough force to send a numbing jolt down the man's spinal column. He stood perfectly straight, arms swinging drunkenly at his side, while Kato chopped his hand down on the bundle of nerves at the base of the man's neck.

He dropped to the deck in a motionless heap.

The other two zombies were too startled to react, and their moment of indecision cost them. With his fingers extended, Kato jabbed one of the men in the Adam's apple, right at the seam where the face mask met the collar of the body suit, and he doubled over, gasping for breath.

Kato vaulted over the man's back, turning a midair cartwheel, and brought the heel of his shoe down on the third man's nose like a hatchet.

The three men were unconscious in less than five seconds.

Kato turned in time to see The Green Hornet pull a fourth man from the shadows, flip him bodily into the air, and slam face first into the deck.

The man tried to roll over, but couldn't manage it. He slumped to the deck, unconscious.

"Grab some of that rope over there," said The Green Hornet. "Let's bundle them up."

When the men were secured, The Green Hornet opened a hatch and he and Kato dumped the men, one by one, down into the darkness of the hold.

"Bring me that metal bar over there," The Hornet said.

Kato handed him a long piece of metal tubing and The Hornet slid it through the hatch handles, katy-barring the hold.

"That'll take care of their rear escape, Kato. Now let's go get that other guard."

They made their way forward on the gangway until they reached the observation deck immediately below the bridge. Icicles hung down from the windowless bridge, shielding them from the orange glow of the zombie guard's cigarette.

The Green Hornet scanned the deck and liked what he saw. There was what had evidently been a large pallet of bricks stacked above the deck on a small construction platform. The bricks were little more than dark nuggets at the heart of blocks of ice now, but they would do.

The door to the hold was open, and a buttery yellow light seeped out from the aperture. They could hear Miers barking orders to his men from inside the hold, and from the sound of things, they were in the process of bringing the equipment topside. No doubt to relocate to a small boat so they could make their escape.

They weren't too late.

"I'll take this one," said The Green Hornet.

And with those words he eased himself over the edge of the railing and down onto the deck.

He wasted no time with stealth. Not now. Not while the prey was so close.

The zombie guard turned when he heard boots clicking on the icy deck behind him and brought his gun up to fire.

But The Hornet was faster.

He leveled the Hornet Sting and a high-frequency sonic beam shattered the mechanism of the rifle, flinging it from the man's hands and sending it skittering harmlessly across the deck.

The zombie body armor made the man's movements clumsy, and when he tried to catch The Hornet with a wide right hook, The Hornet was able to slip under the man's arm, twist it down hard, and toss the man forward in an awkward somersault.

He landed with his heels hanging over the lip of the ship's hold, and before he could recover, The Hornet gave him a kick that sent him tumbling down into it.

Then The Hornet and Kato stood at the edge of the hold, looking down at Miers and two of his henchmen.

"You tried to cheat me, Miers. Nobody gets away with that."

Miers said nothing. Instead he motioned to his henchmen to head to the rear of the ship.

"It won't work, Miers. You'll find the only other way out blocked."

Miers looked alarmed.

"What's your game, Hornet?"

"I told you. I wanted in."

"You want in, you can have in."

The Green Hornet shook his head. "I think it's too late for that now, Miers. I don't believe in giving people second chances."

"Second. . ." Miers shook his head. "What are you talking about, Hornet? What are you going to do?"

"I'm talking about 'the thousand injuries of Fortunato,' Miers. You remember what happened to him in 'The Cask of Amontillado,' don't you?"

Miers nodded. His face was looking almost as green as The Hornet's mask now. Even in the low light The Hornet could see the man's Adam's apple pumping like a piston in his throat. "The narrator sealed him into an alcove behind a wall of bricks."

"Exactly." The Green Hornet held up The Hornet Sting for Miers to see. "And like the narrator from 'The Cask of Amontillado,' I too am a mason. Here is my trowel."

The Hornet stood and nodded to Kato.

The next moment, a huge hatch fell shut over the hold with a booming metallic echo that rolled over the icy stillness of the graveyard of ships.

From inside the hold, Miers' voice was pure panic. "For God's sake, Hornet, don't! For God's sake, Hornet. Hornet! *Hornet!*"

As The Green Hornet leveled his weapon at the struts holding the platform erect, he could still hear Miers' maniacal screams from below. He was screeching, begging, cajoling, cursing, even giggling.

The sound sent shivers down The Green Hornet's spine.

"Stand back," he said to Kato.

He fired the Hornet Sting, and the immense mountain of bricks and ice on top of the platform came tumbling down over the hatch, burying Miers with his zombies and his madness just as soundly as Poe's narrator had sealed up Fortunato and his jingling bells.

As the dust and ice settled, The Hornet turned to Kato. "Check them."

Kato knelt next to the rubble, prying away their body armor and checking their pulses.

"Are they all alive?" The Hornet asked.

Kato nodded.

"Good. I'll call Scanlon and have them picked up."

Britt Reid sat at his desk at the *Daily Sentinel*, Miss Case by his side. All that morning he had been especially sensitive to smells. His coffee carried warm notes of clove and cinnamon and cream. And Miss Case, in her sleek black skirt and white blouse, smelled very nice. He could pick up the subtle floral notes of her shampoo, the clean smell of baby powder on her skin.

It was almost intoxicating.

Scanlon's voice in his ear shook him from his reverie. "None of his men are talking. From what it looks like the guns have just disappeared into thin air."

"And you have no idea how many rifles Miers managed to cache around town?"

"None. It could be in the thousands."

"Okay," Britt said. "Thanks, Frank."

"No, thank you."

Reid smiled and hung up. Once again the clean, wonderful girl smell of Lenore Case filled his nostrils.

"What does that mean that they couldn't find all those weapons?" she asked.

He looked at her and smiled tiredly. "I don't know, Casey. But if those weapons find their way onto the streets of Detroit I think we might have some pretty rough weather ahead."

"That gives me chills just thinking about it."

He put his hand over hers and their eyes met. "Me too," he said. "Me too."

In the early morning hours of July 23, 1967, the city of Detroit erupted in a riot that went on for five days and eventually became one of the most violent and destructive events in American history. In the wake of that riot, National Guardsmen, supported by the U.S. Army, recovered vast stores of weapons and ammunition from Detroit's numerous abandoned buildings. But no public statement was ever made as to how those weapons got there in the first place, or what might have happened had they made it onto the street.

THROUGH A GREEN HAZE

by Dan Wickline

The old Ditchburn Cruiser slammed across the waters of Lake St. Clair like a ricocheting bullet, the crescent moon more than enough light to guide Eugene "Pops" Roberts on his journey from the shores of Canada back to Detroit. Twelve thirty-inch by thirty-inch boxes were probably more weight than the old boat was meant to carry, but the more cargo, the more Pops got paid. And Pops was all about getting paid.

This was more than a normal smuggling run for him. This was going to be his last. Between the stress of ducking the cops and the cold night air, smuggling was a young man's game, and Pops was no longer young. His once jet-black hair was now dominated by gray, and his forehead seemed to expand each morning he looked in the mirror. His slender build had stayed the same, but he found that he lost his balance more easily, and the mornings after his excursions were getting harder on the old bones. His age now matched his moniker and it was time to call it a day.

Pops had worried how his boss would take the news. It's not like his line of work came with retirement benefits and a gold pocket watch. Most of the time you got out by way of a bullet or a prison cell, but Jimmy was a boss that understood loyalty worked both ways and was okay with it. More than okay, really. He knew Pops had been smart. He never looked in the boxes he carried. He never asked any questions and never knew anything more that his own role in the business. Change docking spots and times and there was nothing Pops could give the cops even if sweated. Jimmy just asked him to do a few more runs until they got a replacement set up. Jimmy had called him that morning to tell him it was all set. This would be Pops' last trip.

Pops breathed a sigh of relief as it appeared on the horizon, the marker he always used to guide himself home. An easy thing to see from hundreds of yards out, the thirty-foot tall cow painted on the side of the Henderson Meat Packing Plant. The company had gone out of business many years before, but no one touched the place. Maybe the owner wanted too much money, or maybe the idea of painting over the cow turned off potential buyers. Either way, the empty building was the easiest thing to pick out in the distance and guide Pops home.

He laid on the throttle a little more, racing as much toward his future as he was his drop point. Monday morning he was going to be working a newsstand on Fifth and Avery selling copies of the *Daily Sentinel* to all who passed by, making new friends, talking to people, passing the day. It sounded a thousand times better than freezing his butt off as he bounced over the water every couple of nights.

He was now close enough to the docks to see the giant cow's dopey, grinning face. He always thought if the cow knew what was going on inside the plant, it wouldn't be smiling. It wasn't the mural that got Pops' attention, but the light on in the window beside it. There were never any lights on there, especially at this time of night. Curiosity kept him staring at the window, which was fortunate or he would have missed seeing something (or someone) crashing through the window and out toward the lake.

Then, the building exploded, setting the night sky ablaze with light. The thirty-foot cow no longer had a head and fire raced through the meat packing plant. Pops pulled the throttle back and turned the boat hard to port. His drop point was about to be flooded with firemen and cops. He had to go to plan "B." There was a place he could hide his boat for a day or two if needed, and he would call Jimmy in the morning to set up a new drop point. He wasn't out of it just yet, though.

Pops opened the engine up just a little. A speeding boat would get attention where a slow moving boat would appear to be just another curious on-looker. He would casually drift off into the darkness. Then he saw it, floating in the water just ahead of him, the thing that crashed through the window just before the explosion. It wasn't a thing, though. It was a man and he was in need of help. Pops paused for a moment, looked back at the twelve boxes on his boat, and thought to himself that it would be better to just keep going. He may have committed many crimes over the years, but had never taken a life. Not stopping to help this man would be just as bad.

He pulled the boat in alongside the floating body, using a pole hook to catch onto the guy's coat and pull him into range where he could reach down and grab him. It took every ounce of strength Pops had left in his old muscles, but he finally got the guy over the side and onto the deck of the boat. Luckily the guy had been floating on his back, so he was still breathing. Pops stood to get a better look. A long trench coat, decent suit, but the thing that made him almost stop breathing was a recognizable mask on the man's face.

Pops had just rescued The Green Hornet. His newsstand now seemed very far away.

The shortest distance between two points is a straight line, unless you're Lenore "Casey" Case and you're trying to get to your desk in the morning.

She could take the straight line approach through the main newsroom doors right by the elevator, or she could take the hallway to the left, go through the break room, past the typesetting department and enter through the side door near the service elevator. She picked the long way every morning, as it got her to her desk outside Mr. Reid's office faster. Yes, the shortest distance is a straight line, but Michael Axford sits along that line and she'd be stuck hearing stories for a good ten minutes or more.

Casey unlocked the outer door to the office, put her stuff down on the desk, and turned to start the coffee brewing when she heard the outer door open again. She turned, expecting to find that Axford had followed her in to tell her about some crazy story he was on. Instead, she found a very different, but equally familiar face looking back at her. A face that seemed very worried.

"Kato, what are you doing here? What's wrong?"

The small Asian man turned and closed the door behind him before speaking. He wanted to make sure no one else could hear.

"It's Mr. Reid. We were out last night following a tip on the bomber case. We were told to look into the old Henderson Meat Packing Plant. I checked downstairs while Mr. Reid went to the upstairs office. After few minutes, I heard a window shatter, then a second later, the office blew up."

"Blew up? No. Tell me he got out!" Casey's heart sank as Kato told his story; she was not ready to lose Britt Reid yet.

"I think he might have. The fire spread too quickly for me to get to the office, so I went outside and saw a small boat pulling someone out of the water before leaving. I had no way to give chase and I can't say for sure if it was Mr. Reid, but he hasn't come home. I was hoping he was here."

"I haven't seen him yet, this morning. Let me check something." Casey went around her desk and grabbed the phone. She dialed up the desk of the City Editor. "Gunnigan, it's Casey. Any big stories come in overnight? Nothing? Okay. Thanks."

She hung the phone up and sat down in her chair. As an assistant and secretary to Britt Reid, she had also become one for The Green Hornet. Her boss' duel identity meant that any night she could get a call saying he was wounded or dead. She could even be arrested as an accomplice if the truth ever came out. Those were all scenarios she had thought about long and hard, but the idea of him missing, not knowing if he was alive or dead, had never entered her thoughts.

"If The Green Hornet had been turned over to the cops or dropped off at a hospital, someone would have called in, even if it was just a body. The person pulled out of the water couldn't have been him." Casey tried to find solace in her own words.

Kato thought for a moment, then responded: "Unless the person in the boat can't go to the cops. It was a very small boat and it was very late at night. Most likely he was a smuggler coming back from Ontario. I should go back down to the docks and see if I can find who he is and where he hides his boat."

Casey felt just a tinge of hope at Kato's suggestion. Only a tinge, though, since to the world The Green Hornet was a criminal, and if the smuggler decided to turn him over to one of The Green Hornet's many enemies. . . The very thought was too much for her. She had to do something herself.

"I'll get a hold of Scanlon, let him know what is going on, and ask him to let us know if he hears anything."

"Good. I'll check back with you in a few hours."

Kato turned and left, closing the door behind him. Casey picked up the telephone once more and began dialing the District Attorney's phone number. Her mind now focused on finding her boss.

The sun filtered through the dirt-stained window of the rundown bait shack. The glare hit across his closed eyelids like a search light, guiding him to consciousness. Every inch of his body hurt like the devil, and the paper-thin mattress he laid on did nothing to help. He sat up on the edge of the small bed and looked around the room. Wood. Everything was made of wood: the walls, floors, ceiling, furniture. And it all had that worn, damp look that characterized buildings down by the water. But why was he there?

His head pounded like a mariachi band that had been paid to play all night. He reached up to rub his eyes and felt an odd material on his face. He stood slowly, his legs wobbling a bit in protest before finding their strength. He paused for a moment before taking a step. When that was successful, he took another and another until he was across the room standing in front of a piece of mirror that had been nailed to the wall with a thin piece of wire. He looked at his own reflection but a stranger looked back. A stranger in a green mask. He thought if he took the mask off, it might help, so he reached up to remove it.

"No! Don't do that!" Pops raced into the room, grabbing the man's arms with both hands. "I don't want to die!"

"Die? What are you talking about? I was just going to take off this mask to see if—"

"If you take off that mask and I see who you really are, then you'll have to kill me. The Green Hornet would never let someone know who he is behind the mask."

"The Green Hornet? Is that who I am?"

"You mean you don't remember? You were down at the docks when an explosion sent you into the lake. I fished you out and brought you here."

Pops calmed down and moved toward the wooden table and chairs in the corner of the shack. He tossed a copy of the paper on the table then took a seat. He gestured for The Hornet to sit as well.

"What was I doing at the docks? And who or what is The Green Hornet?"

The Hornet sat down opposite of Pops. His memories were foggy at best. He couldn't remember his name, where he was, or why he was wearing a mask, but he could remember simple things like what a newspaper was or how to tie his shoes. He hoped the old man across from him could fill in the blanks.

Pops did his best, telling The Hornet everything he knew, the problem being that Pops only knew The Hornet by rumors and reputation. He knew him as a criminal, a scourge of the dark streets of Detroit, someone that cops chased and the criminals avoided. The Hornet didn't see the city divided up equally like Pops' boss did. The Hornet demanded a cut of any action he came across or he would put you out of business.

Even without his memories, what the old man was telling him didn't feel right. Then he saw the look in Pops' eyes, the fear of being the guy to feed the hungry bear. Whatever he felt, he knew Pops believed every word he said, and every word made The Green Hornet out to be a horrible and evil man.

"I need to check in with my boss and reschedule the drop. I'll see if he knows of a way to contact your people. I know you have a least one guy who drives you. If we can reach him, we can get you home." Pops headed over to the door. "I'll grab us some breakfast on the way back. Just sit tight."

With the slam of the old wooden door, The Green Hornet found himself alone again in the old shack with nothing but a copy of the *Daily Sentinel* to pass the time. He questioned if he could be the man that Pops described, or if it was all some horrible mistake. Just because he wore the mask, that didn't make him the man, did it? And who was the man behind the mask? Too many questions and no answers to be found.

He flipped open the paper and found an article on the bottom of the front page with the headline:

Green Hornet Strikes Again

Maybe Michael Axford would have a different opinion of the man he was supposed to be.

Jimmy "Six-Gun" Scalera flipped over two pairs, jacks and fives with a nine kicker. Of the other five men at the table, only two still held cards and one of them tossed his face down into the pot with a "beats my aces." That just left the Brick. Billy Wayne wasn't the sharpest tool in the shed, but he was built like Frankenstein's Monster with a set of meat hooks the size of boulders, and he hit with the strength of a battering ram, hence the name Brick. He held three queens, a winning hand, and the pot was enough to pay his rent for the next two months at the fleabag apartment off 3rd. He showed just a hint of a smile, which was rare as he was missing his front tooth and didn't like people to see the gap, but the smile caught the attention of someone else at the table, Billy Tonks.

Billy was Scalera's right hand man and handled all the dirty work. Billy subtly made eye contact with Brick and shook his head. The big lug stopped, the smile disappeared, and he tossed his cards facedown into the pile as well.

Jimmy swept the pot pack with a quick chuckle. "I so love playing with you boys. I make more here than I do on the rackets."

In the corner of the room the phone rang. Billy stood and made his way toward the phone, passing by Brick and slipping a twenty into his top pocket. Everyone knew Jimmy was the boss, but Billy would take care of the boys fairly. He picked the receiver and answered.

"Yeah. What? Oh hey, Pops. No idea what happened down there, but you did the right thing. You remember the drop point we used back in

October? That should be clear now, I'll send someone to meet you just after—" Billy stopped in midsentence and just listened. Then he replied with, "Okay, hang on just a minute." He turned toward Jimmy with a surprised look on his face. "Hey Boss, you're gonna want to hear this yourself."

Jimmy got up and headed for the phone. He hated to deal with minutia, but Billy wouldn't call him over if it wasn't important. Billy handed him the phone and stepped aside.

"Yeah, Pops, what's shaking?" Jimmy's face made that same expression he had when he won the pot a moment before. "Really? You don't say? Yeah, I think I know how to contact his driver. Bring him here and we'll get him home safely. Noon is fine. See you, then."

Jimmy hung up the phone and turned to face Billy. The boys at the table turned to see what was going on. Jimmy spun the ring on his left ring finger. It had belonged to his father; he'd worn it since his father was killed. He died in a three-way gunfight with the cops and The Green Hornet. The cops may have shot him, but it was The Hornet who got him there in the first place, and Jimmy had wanted a chance to even the score ever since.

"Seems Pops pulled The Green Hornet out of the lake last night. The poor fellow has no memory and Pops hoped we could help him get home." Jimmy continued to spin the ring. "Billy, I want you to go out and find another half dozen guys, big guys, guys that can cause serious damage. Get them here before noon."

"You don't think Brick and the others will be enough to handle one man? Even if he is The Green Hornet?"

"Oh, I'm sure they could, but I don't just want him handled. I want The Hornet broken, bloodied, and begging for me to kill him. Then I'll take his mask off, find out who he is, and bring every one he loves down to watch him die."

Kato returned to the site of the explosion dressed in a pair of denim jeans and a black pullover in an attempt to blend in with the other dockworkers. As he moved down the docks away from the meat packing plant, he found the men became more open to chatter. They speculated at the cause of the explosion. Some figured it was the bomber that had already hit a train station and took out a television broadcast tower, but none of them could explain why hitting an empty building would fit in with the other two.

Someone else was certain that it was the owner of the building doing it for the insurance money, thinking it would get blamed on the bomber. The most farfetched theory involved a pocket of methane gas having been caught in the building and finding a stray spark. There was no mention of a survivor or any reference at all to The Green Hornet.

Kato continued on for another hour before he finally caught sight of something interesting. Billy Tonks, right hand man for Jimmy "Six-Gun" Scalera, was making his way toward another familiar face, Ray Stone. Sweet Ray, as he was called in the ring, was a golden gloves champion for six months before rumors of his fights being fixed got him kicked from the sport. It was never proven, but the rumors were enough to destroy his reputation. Now he spent his days unloading boats and nights as hired muscle for local loan sharks.

Kato grabbed a crate from a pallet to help blend in and headed out on a path that would take him directly into earshot of Tonks and Stone.

"Hey, Ray, why don't you come by Jimmy's for lunch today, just before noon. He's got a little something for you to help with." Tonks spoke in his friendliest voice.

"The wife made me a nice pastrami on rye that I've been looking forward to. I think I'll stay here and eat it. Jimmy's jobs tend to get me dirtier than I like." Stone tried to dismiss the man.

"It's up to you, but he was going to take good care of you. If you don't want to take a few swings on The Green Hornet, though, that's fine by me."

The smile that earned him the name "Sweet" came across Ray's face. "The Hornet you say? I can always eat that sandwich on the way to Jimmy's."

Tonks turned to walk away and bumped directly into Kato. He staggered a step or two before regaining his balance. Kato didn't miss a beat, kept moving forward with the crate like nothing happened.

"Watch where you're going, idiot!" Billy called after him.

"So sorry. Me watch next time." Kato called back but never stopping. If he moved quickly he would have just enough time to change into his fighting togs and get over to Jimmy Six-Guns' place.

Pops' old pickup bounced along Jefferson Avenue. Ten to twelve meant they should get there with a minute or two to spare. The Hornet sat back in the truck, his head low to hide the mask from passerbys. He wondered to himself how someone could get anything done while wearing a mask. Sure, it hid one's identity, but it also called a lot of attention. He tossed that on the list of questions for which he had no answers, deciding instead to turn his attention to his newfound friend.

"I really do appreciate you pulling me out of the drink last night. Not many guys would have done that."

"I may bend the law of man by moving some boxes from one side of a lake to another, but I never hurt anyone and I couldn't just sit by and watch someone die. It's just not my nature."

"I appreciate it just the same. You tell me I'm a criminal, so I should have a stash of cash somewhere. Once I get my memory back, I'll send you some, to fix up that shack of yours at least."

"Don't worry about that place. Once I drop you off and retrieve my shipment from last night, I'll never look at that place again."

"Oh? Is it compromised now that I know where it is?"

"I guess it is, but that's not the reason. Last night was my last run. Come Monday you can find me on Fifth and Avery shilling copies of the *Daily Sentinel* to all who pass by."

"Good for you."

The truck swung into the parking lot of an unmarked warehouse on McDougall and the two got out of the cab. The Hornet reached back for his hat but there was none. That was important. Not the fact the hat was missing, but the fact he knew it was missing. It was the first positive sign about his memory since he woke up that morning, and he was going to say something to Pops, but the old man had already reached the door to the warehouse and was holding it open for him.

The Hornet walked inside slowly. His gut told him he could trust Pops, but the hairs standing on the back of his neck told him to not extend that trust to anyone else. They walked into the back office where two men stood in the room. Pops introduced them as Jimmy Six-Gun and Billy Tonks.

The Hornet's eyes searched around the room. The table in the corner had what looked to be an active card game going with at least six players. The cushions on the couch against the west wall were still depressed from someone sitting on them, and a fresh set of condensation rings were collected on the window sill looking out toward the parking lot. He guessed that there would be a half finished beer can in the trash by the door . . . a door that was left slightly ajar.

"Ah, The Green Hornet. So nice to meet you after all this time. I contacted your driver. I'd expect him to be here at any minute." Jimmy spoke with his arms out wide and a used car salesman's smile. "Have a seat. Can I get you something to drink?"

"I'm fine, thanks." The Hornet moved slowly across the room, putting as much distance between him and the other door as possible, positioning himself with his back to the wall. He may not have his memories, but his instincts were still sharp as ever.

Billy crossed over to Pops with an envelope in his hand. The Hornet had to wait to see how this was going to play out. He kept his eye on Jimmy, who had adjusted his shoulders for the third time since they came in. His watch said he was right handed, which meant his gun was under his left arm. Even if he was a quick draw, The Hornet knew he could cover the distance fast enough to keep him from getting a good shot off, but where was Tonks' gun and was the number of thugs in the back room ten or twelve?

"Here you go, Pops. This will cover your last run with a little extra. Consider it a retirement gift." Billy smiled at the old man as he gave him the envelope.

"That's really nice of you, Mr. Scalera."

"Now why don't you go ahead and head back to the shipment. Once you drop it off, your life of leisure can begin." Billy slapped him on the shoulder.

Pops hesitated. "I've got plenty of time to make the drop. You want me to stick around till his driver shows up?"

"We're fine here." Jimmy spoke up again. "He'll probably be pulling into the parking lot as you leave."

Pops looked over to The Hornet. The old man looked unsure, like he genuinely wanted to make sure that the man he had saved got home safely.

"I'm going to be fine, Pops. Go ahead and get out of here." The Hornet lied in hopes of getting the old man out of there before the thugs in the back got too impatient.

Pops nodded, waved his hand in a goodbye gesture, and headed back out to his old pickup. He knew the tension in the office was beyond thick. It was really none of his business and he had done the right thing by fishing the man from the water. He was now going to finish up his last job.

The truck fired up on the second turn, and a few second later Pops was back on track for his happy retirement.

"So, no memory at all, eh?" Jimmy walked over to the table and started spinning one of the chips. "You don't remember who I am? Who my father was? Nothing?"

"Your father? Was he more than the two-bit thug that you are?"

Jimmy flashed a second of anger before regaining his composure. "We're past the pretense, then?"

"Just waiting to see how much you're going to babble on before calling in your hired goons from the other room."

"Come on in, boys!" Jimmy called to the door in the back. In walked ten dangerous looking men led by the Brick and Sweet Ray Stone. They spread out behind Jimmy like it was team photo day for the Lions.

"You tricked my father into meeting you for business, but all he found was the cops and they filled him with lead."

"I'm sure it couldn't have happened to a nicer guy, but I can't remember a bit of it."

"Going to be a wiseass till the end, eh? Boys, beat him till he remembers everything. Then start over again."

A single man walked forward. He stood around six feet tall and had a body built by years of hard work and hard drinking. The bent and smashed nose on his face said he had taken a few punches, and the flat knuckles on his right hand said he had given a few as well. The crowd behind him started to egg him on.

"Get in there, Verne!"

"Hurry up, man! I want my shot!"

"A sawbuck says you don't even get a punch in on him!"

The Hornet scanned the room once again. He could make a break for the door or window, but he wouldn't get more than a few feet before one of them caught up. His only option was to fight and he hoped he knew how, because Verne was now standing two feet in front of him.

"We drew straws. I won."

Verne swung with a right-handed haymaker, just about lifting off his heels in an attempt to put everything he had into it. The Hornet blocked it with his left arm, the force sending pain straight to his elbow. The move left Verne open and a quick chop to the throat left the thug gasping for air. The Hornet followed by driving his knee into Verne's midsection, and the hired muscle crashed to the floor in a heap.

The Hornet turned just in time to see the heel of a work boot flying toward his head. He ducked under the kick and then shot forward, driving his own shoulder into his assailant's groin. Now completely off balance and in the air, the man could do nothing as The Hornet rammed him head first into the wall.

"You morons were really planning to go one at a time?" Jimmy spoke up. "His memory may be gone, but obviously he can still fight. So stop standing around like it's a game of freaking craps and jump the mook."

Five of the thugs raced toward The Hornet with Brick in the lead. The dense giant slammed straight into his opponent's chest, knocking him off his feet and driving him full force into the wall. The Hornet felt the air rush out of his lungs as another of the hired muscle cracked him across the jaw. One at a time he stood a chance, but now he was about to be buried by wave after wave of vicious attacks. He refused to give up, positioning himself to try and take as many hits as he could with his arms and legs, but after a few minutes it wouldn't matter.

Tonks shouted out over the noise of the beating. "Stay away from his head. Jimmy wants him to be conscious as long as possible."

"And don't knock his mask off!" Jimmy added. "I get to do that!"

The Hornet could feel each of Brick's giant knuckles as they hit his arms and sides. Then, the pounding was immediately replaced by another thug's fist and then another. He felt a different set of very quick fists working on his kidneys, fists that knew exactly where to strike. His body, already battered from the explosion, wouldn't be able to take much more of the pounding. He just needed an opening, a chance to fight back.

He got that chance as a flash of black crashed through the office window. The small Asian man hit the floor rolling and was back up on his feet in the blink of an eye. From his right hand he let three hornet-shaped throwing darts fly. Two of them found their marks, dropping their victims quickly. But that still left six thugs pounding on The Hornet, not to mention Jimmy and Tonks.

Kato had to give his partner a chance to get up. He ran toward one of the closest henchmen, grabbed him by the neck, and swung his feet around as quickly as he could, catching Sweet Ray in the back and knocking him across the room.

His movement was so fast the others were stunned, but The Green Hornet wasn't going to waste his opportunity. He put everything he had into an uppercut to Brick's jaw. The giant staggered backwards and The Hornet cracked the next closest thug across the nose with his elbow before quickly stepping toward Brick again with a jab to the solar plexus. He side-kicked another thug and connected a cross into the side of Brick's head.

Sweet Ray was back on his feet and could care less about Kato. He was there to take down The Green Hornet. He stepped in between Brick and the masked man, throwing a quick left at The Hornet's jaw. Ray moved in to follow with a powerful right, but The Hornet had his guard up and took the punch with his forearm. The two well-trained fighters began sparring in the middle of a warzone. Punch for punch they went, the fallen champ versus the man of mystery, a fight boxing fans would pay a king's ransom to have seen.

Normally, Kato preferred to fight his battles with his hands, but they were still vastly outnumbered, so he went once more to the hornet darts he had tucked in his belt to put their opponents to sleep. He jabbed one into the neck of the closest thug, spun around and ducked under a lunge, jamming a second dart into the new attacker's leg, and hurled a third dart across the room and into the arm of a thug about to go after The Hornet with a lead pipe. That left three fighters, Jimmy, and Tonks. Kato was suddenly grabbed from behind by a giant, his arms pinned against his body.

"This will keep you from jumping around so damn much," Brick growled into Kato's ear.

Jimmy Six-Gun watched as his plans fell apart. His ten hired goons were dropping like flies, but he was not going to let the chance to avenge his father go. He drew his gun and took aim on The Green Hornet. Billy Tonks grabbed his arm before he could fire.

"What are you doing? You could hit one of our guys!"

"Get off me!" He pushed Billy aside. "The Hornet dies now!"

Jimmy aimed and fired. With a thunderous crack, the .357 slug raced out of the barrel, crossed the twenty feet of open floor space, and ripped through the flesh and bone of Mike Kirby before embedding itself deep in his right ventricle. Kirby had worked for the crime boss since he turned sixteen, thought of Jimmy like an older brother.

Now Kirby had one of Jimmy's bullets in his chest. He was dead before he hit the floor.

Kato ignored the gun shot. He had to get free. He brought his left heel up as hard as he could into Brick's groin. The big man's grip loosened just slightly, but enough to reach a nerve under Brick's left arm. Applying pressure made the whole limb go dead. Kato slammed the back of his head into the bridge of the giant's nose. Kato dropped to the ground as Brick reeled. A roundhouse kick to Brick's jaw hurled him flying back into the poker table, flipping it on its side and sending the giant crashing to the ground. His head hit the floor hard enough to knock him out.

The gun shot pulled Sweet Ray's attention away for just a split second, but that was more than his opponent needed. The Green Hornet landed three successive quick jabs to the boxer's face, and then slammed an uppercut into his kidney, followed by a knockout punch right across the side of Ray's head. The ex-champ hit the floor like a wet sack of cement.

Billy Tonks had watched Kirby fall, then Brick, and finally Sweet Ray. Now, there was only Jimmy and himself to stand against The Green Hornet and his companion. Billy was never known for being stupid, so as Jimmy raised his gun again to fire, Billy slipped out the back door and ran for his car.

He had suddenly grown very tired of Detroit.

The Hornet saw Jimmy out of the corner of his eye. The thug was about to shoot again. The masked man dove behind the overturned table, where he found his black-clad companion. Kato handed him a foot-long metal baton. Had he stopped to think about what he was doing, he wouldn't have been able to extend The Hornet Sting to its telescopic three feet or pop out the handle. He was continuing to run on instincts.

Kato rolled to his left, drawing Jimmy's attention. The masked man jumped to his feet and fired the Sting. The buzzing sound made Jimmy turn back, but before he could fire, the Sting's sonic wave shattered the pistol's firing mechanism.

Jimmy dropped the gun like it was a hot potato. His rage was boiling over at seeing the man who had cost him his father. He raced full speed toward The Hornet, leaving his feet as he dove the last few yards. Jimmy hit hard against the masked man's chest, send them both tumbling across the floor.

The Sting flew from The Hornet's grasp. His body had taken more abuse in the last twelve hours than half a dozen men could handle, but he wasn't going to lie down and die now. He slammed his elbow into Jimmy's mid-section and the gangster drove a rabbit punch into The Hornet's side. They traded a few more body blows before The Hornet got his best opening and delivered an open palm strike to Scalera's brow. He followed it with a left to the temple, the force of the blow being enough to get Jimmy off of him. The Hornet jumped back to his feet and delivered one last punch to the gangster, putting him down for the count.

Kato grabbed his partner by the arm. "We have to go. I called Scanlon just before I came in. The cops will be here any minute."

The Green Hornet could barely stand, doing his best to keep from passing out. He still didn't know who Kato was, but the hard-fighting Asian had come to his aid and had earned his trust. Kato slipped his arm around The Hornet and guided him out to the waiting Black Beauty.

Kato steered the Black Beauty away from the warehouse while The Green Hornet, dazed and barely awake, sat in the back. He told the driver what he remembered, about Pops pulling him from the lake, waking up in the shack, and having no memory of anything prior to the explosion.

Kato answered as many questions as he could. That The Green Hornet was really Britt Reid, that he posed as a criminal so he could strike at the heart of Detroit's organized crime families, and that the two of them worked secretly with D.A. Scanlon to bring down the gangsters that the police couldn't touch.

"Is any of it coming back to you?"

"It all sounds familiar, but it feels like it's all from a movie I saw long ago." The Green Hornet closed his eyes, trying to find a way to focus through the haze in his mind.

"Then you don't remember if you found out anything about the bomber before the explosion? He threatened another bombing today at two p.m."

"I wish I did."

"I'll take you back home now to rest, and call Miss Case to let her know you're okay."

"Miss Case?"

"She's your secretary at the *Daily Sentinel*. You call her 'Casey.'"

"Casey." And after a pause, "The *Sentinel*."

The image of Casey flooded The Hornet's mind: her smile, her laugh, and then the explosion from the night before. Memories started racing through his mind: his father working at the paper, Axford railing on about The Hornet, the first time he put on the mask, the shootout with Jimmy Six-Gun's father, blue prints of a familiar building, schematics of a printing press, a bomb rigged to go off when a file cabinet drawer was opened, and finally the window of the meat packing plant as he leaped through it. All his memories jammed back together like pieces of a jigsaw.

"Kato! Take us to the *Sentinel*. Now!" The Hornet said, snapping alert.

The Hornet grabbed the phone in the back of the Black Beauty and dialed the familiar phone number.

"Casey! I'm fine, we can talk about that later. Shut down the presses and evacuate the building. The bomber's next target is the *Sentinel*."

As the car raced across town, the green haze that had filled The Green Hornet's mind cleared up completely. After twelve hours of amnesia, concussion from the explosion, and a severe beating by hired thugs, his body screamed out for rest.

Any normal man would do just that, but The Green Hornet was no ordinary man. He was a hero and there were more lives to save.

THE BLACK WIDOW

by John Everson

"Looks like we got us another one, Britt!"

Mike Axford stood in front of Britt Reid's desk, triumphantly shaking a small piece of paper from his reporter's notebook. His face was almost as red as the short crop of hair on his head. "Roger Coury, the bigshot CEO of Coury Pharmaceuticals, never came home last night. The police, they're keeping it hush-hush, but there's a search goin' on."

Britt cocked an eyebrow. "Maybe he got lucky, Mike. Some guys don't go home every night, you know."

The *Daily Sentinel*'s most curmudgeonly bulldog reporter laughed and pointed to the headline of the morning's paper sitting smack dab in the middle of the editor's desk. "Come on now, you know better than that. Four of the city's top suits disappear . . . only to turn up a few days later laid out to rest in the park? And now a fifth has gone missing?"

The banner headline of the morning's paper screamed:

The Black Widow Strikes Again!

Beneath it, next to a column of type, was a photo of a body laid out on a park bench. The face was obscured; the lens focused on the chest of the man. The outer dress shirt had been unbuttoned and pulled aside, leaving a plain white t-shirt. In the center of the shirt was a drawing in what looked to be red marker or lipstick.

The drawing was in the shape of a heart.

"I've been following this case for the past two weeks and you know what I noticed?"

Britt shook his head.

"All of the victims were seen down along the Strip just before they disappeared."

"What's your point, Mike?" Britt asked. "Lots of people walk the Strip

. . . that's why it's called the Strip!"

"Ah, you know as well as I do what kinda lowlife trading goes on down there," Axford retorted, his Irish accent thickening with excitement. "That's not the sorta place where the head of a million dollar company hangs out. Somethin' drew them there. I want to stake the place out; see if I kin come up with any leads on Coury. Maybe we can save him before he turns up on a bench like the others."

The reporter pushed a petty cash requisition form across the desk for Britt to sign. As the pen flashed across the slip, Britt looked at Mike and cautioned, "Don't spend this all at the bar. If you're going to see anything, you'll need to stay sharp."

Britt had two phones at his desk; one sat unobtrusively on top, in standard black. But the other was hidden from view inside a drawer. It was bright red beneath its rotary dial, though the dial was for looks only— the line only went to one place. It also was electrified. When it rang, the whole body glowed with light. As Britt handed Mike back the petty cash form, the phone inside his desk began to ring. A red glow was visible from the crack of the drawer. Britt opened the drawer and nodded dismissal at Axford.

"Reid here," he said, grabbing the handset. Mike disappeared down the hall to finance, and on the other end of the line the city's District Attorney, Frank Scanlon, said just four words:

"We've got a problem."

"You want to talk about it?" Reid asked.

"Half an hour?"

"See you there."

The buzzer sounded in the study of Reid's townhome just as he arrived himself. Britt walked to the bookshelf and lowered three fake hardcover volumes to activate the false fireplace front while Kato slipped silently into the room. He stood at the ready near the entrance, awaiting instruction from his boss.

Scanlon strode off the elevator and into the plush room without pause. "Kato," he nodded, and locked eyes with Reid.

"You've heard about Coury?"

Britt nodded. "Axford is off to the Strip to stake it out. He says all of the Black Widow's victims have been seen there shortly before they disappeared."

Scanlon nodded. "That's true. But there's something else. Something we haven't told the press." The District Attorney looked around the room, as if making sure there were no eavesdroppers other than Kato. Then he took off his glasses and twirled them by the long black plastic end as he looked the city's best known media magnate in the eye. "Britt, I'm worried," he said. "There are no ransoms, no demands . . . we don't know what it is she's after. But she's taking down the top businessmen of Detroit, one by one. And they all have had contact with her beforehand."

Scanlon replaced his glasses, reached in his pocket and pulled out a crumpled envelope. He handed it over to Britt, who unfolded it and looked at the red heart drawn on the back. He opened the flap and saw that it was empty inside, and then ran a finger across the design and brought his finger away smudged crimson. He held it up to his lips and nodded. "Lipstick," he said.

"Yes, lipstick," Scanlon acknowledged. "The exact same lipstick that's been found on the shirts of all the victims.

"And the envelope?"

"We've found one of these envelopes somewhere in the offices or apartments of each of the past four victims."

"What about Coury?"

"He hasn't been missing long enough for it to be official. The police don't have a search warrant to go through his things," Scanlon said.

"The Hornet doesn't need a search warrant."

Scanlon shook his head. "Be careful, Britt. She's dangerous. And we don't know what she's after. Even if you find her calling card there, it doesn't tell us anything more than we already know. Which is a lot of nothing."

The Black Beauty roared to life under the chauffeur's steady hand and pulled out of the hidden exit from Reid's townhome. Britt enjoyed being the beneficiary of the skill of Kato's driving. The man could pull a hairpin turn around a tenement so tight that you couldn't fit a penny between the side view mirror and the brick wall.

The Hornet checked off his equipment as Kato swung the car from corner to corner, only a faint engine buzz left in their wake. "Hornet Ring," he said, and held out a hand to reveal the emerald stone of a signet on his finger. The ring allowed him to always stay in direct contact with the Black Beauty.

"Hornet Sting," he said, again following his preparatory ritual of checking the weapon. He slipped the baton into his overcoat and held up a long-barreled pistol and pronounced "Hornet Gun." Satisfied, he said, "Let's roll, Kato!"

He barely heard the squeal of the Black Beauty's rubber on midnight asphalt. He was already lost in thought as he considered the game at hand. The first victim had been Travis Anthony, the shipping magnate of Detroit Docks Inc. The second had been Benjamin Soumis, the president of the board of the Empire Bank chain. Third came William Breedlove, the founder of Pipes R Us, one of Detroit's largest plumbing service chains. And finally number four had been Sardina Martel, president of Middleton Medical, a large hospital on the west side.

Seemingly they had nothing in common, though in his identity as Britt Reid, owner of the city's largest newspaper and television station, he knew them all. As leaders of industry in Detroit, they all attended the same social functions, sat on the same boards of directors, gave to the same charities.

The hum of Black Beauty suddenly powered down, and Kato exited the car, pulling the door open for The Hornet.

They stood at the back of a high-rise complex, its glass tinted steely silver, its stone façade a dull gray. Without a word they ran to the loading dock and tested the door next to the accordion dock entry. It opened without protest, and they moved through silent hallways to the back elevator.

Roger Coury's apartment was on the 27th floor—the penthouse suite.

The Hornet and Kato walked down the short hallway from the elevator to the floor's lone door and took up positions on either side of the doorframe. The Hornet rapped on the white wood three times and flattened himself to the wall. When no response came, he knocked again. Then, satisfied that nobody was inside, he pulled a gadget from his pocket, a special lock-defeating device, and inserted it into the keyhole. Holding it against the doorknob, he activated it with a thumb. The hallway buzzed for just a second as the device powered up, and then suddenly a faint click came from the lock mechanism, and The Hornet turned the knob.

The door opened easily, and then they were both inside the dark front room of one of Detroit's richest pharmaceutical magnates. Kato closed the door quietly behind them, and turned the bolt.

They split up and stalked the shadowed rooms within, quickly casing the joint and ensuring that it was, indeed, unoccupied.

"Nothing, Boss," Kato said, when they reconnoitered to the front room.

The Hornet nodded, green mask eerily luminescent in the near dark. "Same. Let's see what we can find at the desk."

The room stepped up to a raised office lit by a window covered in translucent drapes. A dark wooden desk dominated the middle of the space, surrounded by bookcases and a wide wooden filing cabinet.

The Hornet stepped quickly up the two steps to the office level and, using a small flashlight, began to investigate the papers stacked and shuffled on the desktop. After a moment, finding nothing of any obvious import, he pulled a trashcan out from beneath the desk and looked through the papers there while Kato stood guard at the front door. It didn't take long before he stood up triumphantly with a wrinkled envelope in hand. On the back of it, the shape of a heart was easily discerned, even in the shadows.

"She's got him," he said.

"Now what, Boss?" Kato asked quietly.

"We get *her*," he said simply.

Just then, a click sounded behind them; a key in the lock. Kato leapt to the center of the room in a battle stance, ready to take down whoever was about to enter the room.

"No, Kato," The Hornet hissed, and launched himself from the desk to the front room. "Hurry," he implored as he darted for cover into the nearby kitchen. Kato followed and they reached the safety of shadows just as the door opened fully and four figures stepped into the room.

The first, The Hornet recognized as Roger Coury. The man was noticeably pale, even in the dark of the shadowed room. The light from the hallway followed him in and played off the glistening bald patch at the top of his head as he walked into his apartment followed closely by a man holding a gun to his back.

Another man followed the first two, and quickly stepped up the stairs to the office area, clearly intending to stand guard over the room.

The last and final entrant was a woman. Dressed all in black, she nearly melted into the night, but for the pale frisson of her face against the shadow, and the glint of her eyes in the faint light from the draped window.

Coury and the gunman crossed the room and the pharma magnate lifted a surreal painting of red and blue geometrics from the wall directly in front of his desk. Behind the painting lay the front of a safe. His hands spun the combination, and with four quick flicks of his wrist he opened it, to withdraw a sheaf of papers.

"Thank you, my dear," the lady in black murmured, and easily lifted the paperwork from his hand. "You've been a good boy, you have," she said. "And now . . ."

The man closest to her handed the woman a thin tube with a needle and a plunger. It looked like the kind of shot you'd get at a hospital. But The Hornet didn't think Roger was going to get better if the needle touched his veins.

No, he would get much, much worse.

"Now," he whispered, and The Hornet and Kato sprang into the front room. The guard at the far end of the room pulled a gun and fired off three shots that ricocheted off the wall behind The Hornet. Kato launched himself across the room in five steps and lunged at the man, jabbing out with a one-two that connected squarely in the chin with the room's watchman. With punch one, the man's gun flew one way, and with punch two, the guard dropped, hard. He didn't get back up.

Meanwhile, The Hornet pulled his gun on the other henchman and suggested, "I think you have some things that I came here to find."

The man threw himself to the left and rolled, coming up with the intent of jumping The Hornet, but instead, he met the ready fist of The Hornet. He took a cut on the jaw, and tried to rally and punch back. Instead, The Hornet delivered three fast jabs to the man's gut. The unexpected blows left the man stunned and off-balance, and he staggered back across the room, looking for an out. But he wasn't getting off that easy. The Hornet Gun flashed to life. A spit of green gas jetted across the room, catching the man in the face. He went down without another sound.

But as The Hornet and Kato took care of the guards, the Widow was spinning her own deadly web. When The Hornet finally was free to help Coury, he saw that he was too late. The Black Widow held a black blade to the man's neck as she stepped steadily backwards, towards the door.

"One wrong move," she promised, "And I'll take him out now. I mean it!"

Stalemate.

The sound of distant sirens cut the silence in the wake of her threat. And then she moved fast and was gone out the door, with Coury in close tow.

"Quick Kato," The Hornet said, "pull them together."

They dragged the two thugs to the center of the room. The Hornet ripped a cord off the back of a lamp, and secured their feet together. Kato followed suit with their hands as The Hornet slapped his trademark Green Hornet seal on the shirt of one of them, along with a quickly scribbled note: "Breaking and entering is a crime."

The sirens were louder now, and The Hornet stood and looked once, quickly, around the room. Satisfied that there was nothing more to be gained from the scene . . . and nothing left behind, he nodded once at Kato and as one, they ran for the door.

The dust from Black Beauty's tires still hung in the air when the first police cruiser pulled up in front of the building.

"I knew that green devil'd be involved in this somehow!" Axford complained. His face was once again as red as his hair. "Here I am, staking out the strip, and Lowery gets the scoop!"

He threw down the morning's paper on Britt's desk and pointed to the headline:

Coury Pharmaceuticals CEO Missing
Green Hornet Leaves Note at Scene

"What did the note say?" Britt asked mildly. "Was it a ransom?"

Axford snorted. "No, some nonsense about breaking and entering being a crime. And he left behind two guys tied up. The police are still trying to get something out of them."

"Did you find any leads yourself?"

The ex-cop shook his head angrily. "Somethin' will turn up today, I kin feel it."

"I hope so," Britt said calmly, encouragingly. But inside, he was echoing Axford's urgency. Coury didn't have much time. Hell, maybe his time was already up. Britt had to do something.

"Mike," he said. "I want you to go to the offices of all five of the people who have disappeared. Interview the people they worked with. Find out if they had noticed anything different about their employers . . ."

"But Britt, the police have done all that already, we have their statements," Axford protested.

"The police have," Britt said. "But you haven't. And remember your credo. If your mother says she loves you . . . check it out."

Britt watched Axford gather some things and stomp out of the newsroom, clearly unhappy to be shunted away from where he thought the action was going to be. And *shunt* was the right word. Because as soon as Axford left the newsroom, Britt Reid gathered his own things and headed down toward the waterfront. He had his own questions to ask down on the Strip.

The day was gray and the breeze off the river cold as Britt walked down the sidewalk in front of the bars and restaurants and houses of ill-repute that dotted the waterfront. He'd worn an old sweater and blue jeans and hoped that out of his normal element, he wouldn't be recognized. He intended to be seen simply as someone curious, not as someone from the *Sentinel*.

He walked into a bar that boasted the exposed thigh of a woman on its marquee amid the words "Get A Leg Up." But when he entered the dark room inside, the scene wasn't one to suspect you would ever get a leg . . . or anything else up. A haggard-looking man with shoulder length gray hair wearing three shirts sat nursing a beer in one corner, while an equally disenchanted barmaid sat behind the bar. She set a paperback novel down on the wood at Britt's entrance, but otherwise didn't move.

Britt pulled up a stool at the bar and reached into his back pocket for a crumpled envelope.

"What kin I getcha?" the woman grumbled.

"How 'bout the phone number of the woman who draws these?" he said, setting down the heart-embossed envelope on the wooden bar.

"I dunno what yer talking about, Mister. But we don't give out no phone numbers here. You get 'em if you can. We just provide the liquor to letcha."

"I'm not some piker looking for a pickup," he said, frowning his displeasure. "You saying you've never seen an envelope like this?" he asked. "We could play wordgames about this all afternoon, but I really don't want to spend that kind of time here, and I know you've got better things to do. So give it to me straight and let's cut to the chase."

The barmaid feigned boredom. "Are you drinking, or not? I've got a book to read," she groused.

"I'm drinking if you can tell me anything about these hearts," he said.

The older woman shook her head and a silvering curl slipped down to cover one darkened eye. "Then I guess you're going dry," she said.

Britt shrugged and left the bar, walking into the next one, just a door away. But his reception there, and at the next place, and the next, was much the same.

When he returned to the office, he held no more information than before he had left. He leafed through the articles about the Black Widow that his own paper had published, and set the envelope he'd rescued from Coury's place next to them. He knew all of the men who had died. But what was the connection . . . ?

"Can I get you anything, Boss?" The voice was quiet but warm.

Britt looked up from his thoughts to see Casey leaning over the side of his desk. Her dark eyes offered a shoulder to cry on, and, he thought, more.

"Thank you Miss Case, but I think I've had enough for one day."

"Drinking on the job, Mr. Reid? I wouldn't have thought . . ." There was a flash of mischief in Casey's eye, but he didn't encourage it tonight.

"Unless you're offering me the whereabouts of the Black Widow, I don't think you can get me anything right now, Miss Case."

"Suit yourself," she smiled, and disappeared from his office. Britt soon followed her, troubled by the images of Roger Coury's sweating, reddened cheeks as they disappeared out of the doorway of his own apartment, a cloud of black behind him.

"This was just delivered downstairs for you," Casey said. She dropped an envelope on the desk in front of Britt. "Feeling better today?"

He nodded. "I hate not having a lead."

"As much as you hate not having coffee?" she asked.

"More," he said. "But if you're offering . . ."

"Black and hot, coming up," she promised, and breezed out the way she'd come in.

Britt turned the mail over in his hands. It was a simple white envelope, with no return address. On the front it simply said: "Britt Reid."

With a letter opener, he slit it open.

Inside, there was a single sheet of white paper. He unfolded it, and smiled when he saw the signature. Ahead of that, it read:

"Britt Reid—

You were on my list, but apparently you won't wait. Leave it to a reporter to be impatient.

Come to the Lusty Lady on the Strip tonight at 11 p.m. Tip the girl dressed in black and say you've been looking for an angel in black. She'll take you to where you need to go.

Do not tell anyone about this note.

Do not call the police.

Follow these instructions to the letter, or by midnight Roger Coury will be waiting for you on a park bench. But he won't have much to say. He'll be dead."

Beneath the words, the letter was signed in a large, red, lipstick heart.

Just then, Mike Axford poked his head into Britt's office. "Today's gonna be the day, Britt, I can feel it. I'm *this* close to finding out how The Hornet ties into all these disappearances. I'm going to have page one for ya tomorrow!"

"Hmmm," Britt said simply, and contemplated a long day of waiting. He hoped Axford stayed out of trouble in the meantime.

When the day's stories were all finally put to bed, Britt quietly packed his things and headed back home to pick up Kato. Britt Reid was going to the Strip. But he intended for The Hornet to be close behind. It was just a little inconvenient that the bait happened to also be the hook.

The Lusty Lady was everything that the name suggested it would be. The inside was dark, seedy and smelled of mold. Or something worse. Britt took a seat at a small cocktail table, and in moments a tall blonde with a red corset and a bow in her hair to match strutted over, and bent down so that Britt couldn't help but notice her ample assets as she asked, "How 'bout a drink, sailor?"

Britt ordered a beer and contemplated the clientele around him. Scantily clad women in outfits that left little to the imagination moved between the dark shapes at the tables like bees to flowers. The men were quiet, but the voices of women filled the bar, as they coaxed every last dollar from their patrons for drinks and . . . other services.

"How are you doing tonight?" a crystalline voice asked.

Britt looked up to see a raven-haired girl in a black evening dress standing at his table. It was not his previous waitress.

She wore black sheer gloves. And black nylons and heels. Even her eyes were black. Her lips though . . . her lips were red. Fire engine *it's-a-flaming-emergency* red.

"Good," Britt said. He should have been rattled, but he wasn't. Inside he only smiled. The game was afoot, and he *lived* for the game.

Britt reached into his pocket and pulled out a five dollar bill. He offered it to the girl. "I've been looking for an angel in black," he said.

She raised one eyebrow, but otherwise did not respond. She tucked the bill into her cleavage and nodded. "Follow me," she said.

They walked past the bar and through a small corridor that led behind the bar. They passed one room with a closed door, and then another. And then they came to an open door, and the Angel in Black faded back, disappearing back the way they'd come. But a cool hand took her place on Britt's arm almost immediately.

"You've been looking for me, I believe." A woman's grip tightened on his arm and pulled him into the open room.

"Actually," he answered, "I've been looking for Roger Coury. Word on the street is he's taken up with a Black Widow. I wanted to help."

"Help the Black Widow?" she teased. Her voice was cool as an icepick.

"No, help Roger Coury find his way back home. The police say a couple of other thugs have been sleeping there lately."

"Hmmm . . ." she said, leading him steadily past a furnished room and then into another hallway where a large window broke the wall. "You sleep where you can," she said. "As you'll see, Roger's sleeping with me."

She pointed through the dark glass window in the hall and Britt saw the familiar balding pate of Roger Coury inside. His eyes were closed, but he was standing. His arms were tied at the wrists above his head. The rope ran up to a steel spike hammered into the wall. The man was essentially hung from a hook.

But it was the other person in the room that gave Britt pause. Standing next to Coury, in almost the same pose—eyes closed, arms above his head—was Mike Axford.

"Normally, I have the opportunity to talk with my suitors a bit more," the woman offered. "We meet, we talk . . . we drink . . . I show him mine, he gives me . . . his."

"What is it you're after?" Britt demanded.

"What, you want me to just broadcast it to the newspaper?" she laughed. "That would ruin my whole persona."

She slipped an arm around his throat, and Britt felt the bite of a blade against his neck.

"On the other hand, I don't suppose you'll be telling the newspaper anything, will you?" she said. "I'm surprised you haven't figured it out yourself though. I mean, being a reporter and all."

"Color me clueless," Britt said.

"Mmmm. And what color exactly would that be?" she replied. Then she pulled him around to face her. Britt saw the light in the black of her eyes. It was like an alluring tunnel to the end of time. Her gaze seemed endless. Her lips were painted a deep red, but the rest of her was all in black, just as her errand "girl" had been. "I gave my heart to the water," she said presently. "Does that help?"

When he didn't respond, she laughed again, a high-pitched giggle of obviously self-reflective pleasure.

"I would think you, as a member of the board of directors of Pier One—only the largest port and entertainment complex we have here in Detroit—might have recognized that your fellow investors all seemed to be disappearing. What's interesting is that prior to ending up, so unfortunately, on their last walks in the park, they've all very legally and completely signed away their interests in Pier One to a handful of different corporations—corporations that I happen to own."

"Why do you still have Roger here?" Britt asked.

"I like to make sure the paperwork really does go through," she grinned. "After all, it wouldn't do me much good to kill them, if their holdings didn't end up in my control legally and without question afterwards."

She pushed him backwards, pinning him to the wall next to the window, and pressed herself close. He could smell the jasmine of her perfume as her eyes loomed ever-wider in his face. Inescapable. "Let's talk about *your* holdings in Pier One," she suggested.

"I'd rather not talk business right now," Britt grinned.

The Black Widow did not answer his smile. "That wasn't a request, really," she said. "You do understand that?"

She pushed him into a small room and shut the door behind them with her foot. "By the figures I have, you are a nine percent owner in the Pier One collective. When I have Coury's and your shares fully within my control, I will have the dominant interest in Detroit's waterfront. And I have a few ideas for its development . . ."

"I'd prefer to keep with the plans we had already agreed upon for the waterfront," Britt said. In the midst of his sentence, he brought a leg up to kick the Widow in the side, and at the same time, let his body drop to avoid her response. He rolled away as she struck out with her knife and screamed in anger and pain at the same time.

"I'll let myself out," he said, and mimicked his best track runner's sprint back towards the door from which he'd come. At the same time, he was triggering the alert in his pants pocket that gave Kato fair warning.

Black Beauty would be powering up and waiting to roll.

But it wasn't that simple. Before he'd cleared the door, three men detached themselves from the shadows and sprang after him, even as the Black Widow sank to the floor in pain and surprise.

Britt rounded on the first and landed a fist in the man's jaw that echoed through the room. His knuckles felt white-hot and broken as he turned, but there was no time to worry about his hand. Instead he continued in a flurry of motion to face his next opponent. His heel connected with the second man's chest, and as the man staggered backwards, Britt pressed the attack.

A roundhouse kick and another fist to the third thug's face followed. Pain shot up to his elbow and now Britt was sure he'd broken a knuckle. But he didn't slow.

Britt dashed back down the hallway and through the Lusty Lady. As he stepped onto the street, a gun popped off three shots behind him, but he didn't slow. Instead of racing down the main drag, he turned the corner and ducked into an alley, waiting for Kato and the Black Beauty to answer the call of his transponder. He didn't want to go far from the joint . . . because he was going back in. Fast.

The green lights filtered into the alley and he was in the car almost before they had reached his hiding place. In moments, he had completed his change in the back seat and his mask was in place. The Green Hornet was ready to face the Black Widow. And he had an advantage—because he knew things she didn't know he'd know.

"Roger Coury—and Mike Axford—are both in a room behind the Lusty Lady club," he told Kato. "We don't have long, or they won't be there anymore. Not in a way worth saving, anyway."

Kato pulled Beauty up behind the Lusty Lady and the two got out and entered the club via the receiving door in back.

"This way," The Hornet said, and led Kato to the room where Roger Coury and Axford were hung from hooks. "Let's get them down now," he said, but before they could undo the knots from the prisoner's hands, the door opened to the room and the Black Widow returned.

"Ahhh . . . The Green Hornet," she said. "Again you're buzzing around my web. Still trying to get in on a cut of my action, hmmm?" she said. "Well, there is no cut available." She motioned to the remote corners of the room and suddenly there was movement. "Wrap them up," she said. Hands grabbed at The Green Hornet's arms. But . . . capturing The Hornet was about as easy as catching the wind.

Kato didn't wait for a command. He twirled in the air like a top, catching three of the Black Widow's henchmen with the cutting edges of his feet.

The Hornet didn't wait for Kato. He had counted on his partner launching into action. In seconds, The Hornet had turned from dealing with her bodyguards to taking on the woman herself, directly. His attack took her by surprise, and he quickly pinned her arms behind her back. She kicked out, using her only weapon, and The Hornet lofted her in the air, a blue-black cloud above his head as he worked to avoid the daggers of her heels.

The Hornet threw her to the floor, and the Widow cried out sharply in pain as she hit the ground. He didn't wait for to recover. Instead he dove next to her and pinned her arms to the floorboards, anticipating an attack. But none came. She remained still. From behind, he heard Kato working over the Widow's henchmen with a series of painful whoomps, smacks, and gasps.

With his free hand, The Hornet traced the subtle slant of the woman's cheek with his finger. She was coolly beautiful . . . and out cold.

At least, he thought she was. Until her knee caught him in the gut and she turned the tables, straddling him for just long enough to laugh and say, "Gotcha," before she leapt off and darted from the room.

Kato sprang to his side.

"I'm all right," The Hornet coughed, and rolled to his feet. "Let's get Coury and Axford out of here. She won't go far. This is her web."

Together they found the door to the Black Widow's "prison" room. Kato pulled Coury from his hanging position and helped the man to the ground, as The Hornet freed Axford.

"I knew you had to be behind all this," Axford mouthed off when he saw The Hornet. "So why help us now?"

"My grudge is with the Black Widow, not you," he growled. "I'd like you both to get out of the way."

Coury leaned on Axford as the feeling struggled to return to his arms, and Kato ushered them both through the club and out to the street.

"Would you come back to the paper and give us a statement?" Axford asked Coury, before leading him to his old red Plymouth, parked just two blocks away.

"Wait here," The Hornet cautioned Kato. They stood at the base of a stairwell at the back of the Lusty Lady. "This is her lair . . . she's up there somewhere. And I have just the thing to make sure she doesn't slip past us."

The Hornet disappeared for a few minutes to retrieve something from the trunk of the Black Beauty. When he returned, he held a long, narrow spray bottle in his hand.

"Walk ahead of me, Kato," he said, pointing up the dark stairs. "And remember . . . if things go bad up there, do *not* run down these stairs."

With that, The Hornet began to spray each step behind them, as they mounted the stairs. When they reached the top, they found themselves in a long, empty hallway. The Hornet sprayed the floor near the stairwell, and then motioned Kato to follow him down the dark corridor.

"A spider never abandons its lair," he whispered.

The hall appeared empty. A room on either side proved unoccupied. But The Hornet was certain. He moved down the hallway to the end. A closed door was all that existed past a certain point. The two stationed themselves on either side. The Hornet grabbed the handle, twisted and pulled.

It opened.

At a desk across the room, the Black Widow sat. In her hand was a gun. It was trained on The Green Hornet.

"Come into my parlor," she said. "And please understand, that's not a request."

"I always thought the Black Widow mates before she kills," The Hornet mused aloud. "So far, you've been most unromantic."

"Against the wall," she demanded, motioning with the gun. "And your sidekick too."

They followed her demand, and the Black Widow stood, her raven dress glimmering as it slid down to mostly hide the creamy curve of her calves. But if it covered her legs, it did little to hide the lure of her chest. She stepped towards The Hornet and Kato, a secret smile twisting the corner of her mouth.

"You wanted romance," she asked. "I had something else in mind. Something more along the lines of an exterminator. For pesky insects."

She held the gun up until the barrel pointed directly at The Hornet's nose. Her hand was steady, and her eyes narrowed.

"I'm sure you came here for a piece of this action," she said. "But this action is all mine."

She pulled back the hammer on the pistol, and Kato dropped and rolled. The distraction did exactly what he intended. The Black Widow took her eyes and the gun off The Hornet for a split second and she fired off a shot at Kato. But he was already inches away from where the bullet bit into the wood, coming up in a kick to her firing arm.

Even as Kato connected with her forearm, and the Widow's pistol ricocheted in the air, The Hornet pulled his own Hornet Gun and aimed it at the Black Widow.

"So much for romance," The Hornet said, and fired. A green plume of gas jetted out of the long pistol, catching the Black Widow in the face. Her eyes widened, and without a beat, she ran from the room. But even before she'd passed the door, she was stumbling, as if drunk. Once past the door, she fell to the ground, but lurched to a half crouch again as The Hornet and Kato followed her through the doorway.

She looked backwards, for a brief second, her eyes confused and tired. And then she was at the stairs. She stumbled down the first step, then the second, and then . . . stopped. She was trapped . . . her feet glued to the steps. She opened her mouth to say something, but the words never came.

Instead she slumped down in a waterfall of black silk and deadly cunning across the back steps of the Lusty Lady.

The Hornet leaned over her and jotted a brief note on a scrap of paper. He used the sticky back of his Hornet seal to attach it to her chest. "Caught in the web she wove," he wrote.

He and Kato leapt down the stairs, and ran from the building. Somewhere in the distance, sirens wailed.

"Here's the final," Casey said, and dropped the morning's *Sentinel* on Britt's desk. Axford was already there waiting. The reporter grinned, and read his page one headline aloud:

In the Battle of the Spider and
The Hornet, Coury Goes Free

"Thank God for turf wars," he said. "Or Roger Coury and I would probably be dead by now. The Hornet set us free just to spite her, I think."

"You don't think it was because he was simply being a good citizen, protecting the rights of the good people of our city?" Britt asked with the faintest of grins.

"C'mon, Britt, lookit who yer talkin' about. This isn't Batman for cryin' out lout, it's that devil, The Green Hornet!"

Behind him, Casey gave Britt a knowing smirk and returned to her desk, without saying a word.

A THING OF BEAUTY

by Bobby Nash

"Do we have an agreement?"

Genevieve Lilly stared daggers across her imported ivory-topped desk in the study of her luxurious penthouse apartment at the masked man dressed in deep midnight green. If her icy demeanor bothered him, he showed no sign. Even the two bodyguards she hired for the meeting did not faze him. Especially since he had brought his own black clad backup with him.

"Don't make me ask you again, Lil," The Green Hornet said.

She stood, never taking her focus off his dark, unblinking eyes. The last thing she wanted was to give in to this criminal mastermind, but with his reputation for ruthlessness, she knew he wouldn't think twice about dismantling her organization if it suited his purpose.

"Alright," she said after a tense moment of silence. "You win. We have an agreement . . ." She paused. The next word out of her mouth would be one of the hardest she had ever uttered.

"Yes?" he prodded.

"Partner."

"Partners. Okay, so break it down for me, Lil. What's the plan?"

Genevieve Lilly was a master thief, considered one of the best in the world. Her specialty was diamonds, which had garnered her the nickname Diamond Lilly. She did so love those shiny baubles. She smiled as she lowered herself seductively into her oversized desk chair. "Plan?" she asked with just a trace of amusement. "There is no plan."

"I'm in no mood to play games," The Green Hornet said as he took a step forward.

One of Lilly's guards countered the move, positioning himself to step between the boss and her new partner if need be.

Lilly noticed The Hornet's silent partner tense, a hand moving inside of one of the sleeves at the end of his tunic. From their first, more volatile meeting the day before, she knew the guard did not stand a chance against The Hornet's bodyguard and his lightning fast reflexes. She raised a hand to halt her muscle before the smaller man could make his move. The last thing Diamond Lilly needed was a fight in her exclusive penthouse apartment, even though her guards outnumbered his two to one. She had grown rather fond of the building's four star accommodations in the short time she had been there and didn't want to lose it, which is exactly what would happen if the men decided to shoot it out.

"No games, Hornet," she said with authority. "There is no plan until tomorrow. I have my sources pulling together research on the target, security, and personnel. It would be foolhardy to formulate any kind of plan without that information."

He leaned on her ornate oak desk, his knuckles popping and smiled at her. "I've got to hand it to you, Lil, you're every bit as good as I'd heard you are. You only made one mistake."

"And what pray tell was that?"

"You tried to set up shop in my town without paying the proper respect. That lack of manners has cost you fifty percent of any job you pull in my town. Something to ponder in the future, should you ever decide to return to Detroit."

Lilly's jaw twitched as anger colored her cheeks. She quickly hid her ire behind a smile as brilliant as any diamond she had ever pilfered. "Come back tomorrow night at this same time," she told him. "We can discuss the plan in detail at that time."

"That is acceptable."

"Very well. I believe you know the way out."

"Until tomorrow then, partner," The Green Hornet said as he and his masked sidekick quickly disappeared through the same balcony doors they had used to make their unannounced entrance.

Once they were gone, Diamond Lilly let out a breath. The Green Hornet was gone for the moment, but he was a problem that would not go away on its own. That's why she had called in outside help after her first run in with the masked man the night before.

"So that's the infamous Green Hornet," a deep voice said from the doorway of the adjoining room.

"Yes." Lilly's gaze fixed on the balcony doors as the new arrival stepped out onto the balcony and watched as The Green Hornet and his partner descended down the fire escape before speeding away in his modified car. "Magnificent," the man whispered before closing and securing the balcony doors once he was back inside.

"As you can see, he's become something of a problem for me since I arrived," Lilly said. "I'm a relatively small fish compared to others in my line of work, Mr. Biggs. I simply do not have the resources to deal with this situation on my own. You, however, come highly recommended. Mr. Lord informed me that you could help solve my particular little problem."

Sanford Biggs stepped next to the desk. At six foot four, he towered above the demure woman sitting behind it. He was dressed all in black: slacks, turtleneck, and sport coat, which made him look even taller. His short cropped black hair and trimmed goatee bore the only telltale signs of the man's age, as flecks of white had begun to intermingle with his jet-black hair.

"What is it you expect me to do, exactly, Miss Lilly?

"I'm relatively fond of this city. Unfortunately, the only way I can stay is if The Green Hornet goes."

"Perhaps vagaries and innuendo are fine when dealing with others, but if you wish to hire me to go toe-to-toe with one of the country's biggest criminals then you have to say the words. Just so there are no misunderstandings."

She sighed. "The Green Hornet is a problem, Mr. Biggs, one that must be eliminated. I want him dead."

The big man smiled.

"Call me the problem solver."

Lenore Case tried to cut Mike Axford off at the pass.

Unfortunately, once Mike sunk his teeth into something, he was like a bulldog with a steak. There was no way you were going to make him let it go and you just might lose an arm in the attempt. While this was an admirable trait in a reporter, and one of the reasons his stories often made the front page, it made Miss Case's job difficult at times, but despite his rough edges, of which he had plenty, Lenore loved Mike like a father.

This particular morning, Mike was hell bent for leather on talking with his boss, Britt Reid, publisher of the *Daily Sentinel*. Normally, this wasn't a problem as the publisher had an open door policy with all of his employees, but she knew that he was tired and not particularly in the best of moods this morning. As one of only a handful of people who knew of Britt's double identity as The Green Hornet, it was up to Lenore Case to help protect that secret from everyone. That included Mike Axford, who considered The Green Hornet public enemy number one. Mike was on a crusade to catch the masked criminal in the act and see him behind bars.

Obviously, she couldn't let that happen.

"Trust me, Casey," Mike said in his usual loud baritone. "He'll want to hear this. We're talking front page stuff here."

"Can't it wait a little while, Mike? Mr. Reid's a little preoccupied this morning."

"That's perfect! I've just the thing to perk him up!"

"Mike . . ."

"It's okay, Miss Case," Britt Reid said from his now open office door. "I've always got time for one of my ace reporters. What can I do for you, Mike?"

The reporter beamed with excitement. "I've got him red-handed this time," he almost shouted. "I've got The Green Hornet dead to rights!"

"Why don't you come in, Mike. You too, Miss Case. Let's not disturb the bullpen."

Britt shut the door after they were all inside and he made his way to his desk and sat down. Mike and Casey stood across from him.

"What's your mind, Mike?"

"I'm telling you, we've finally got him, Britt. There's no way that blasted green hooligan is going to get away with it this time."

"Specifics, Mike. I run this newspaper on facts, not speculation. We have an editorial page for unproven theories and speculation. What can you prove?"

"Well, how's this for starters? I followed up on that diamond thief ..."

"Alleged diamond thief."

"Okay, okay, *alleged* thief," Mike said as he tapped a finger on the boss' desk. "I did some digging. She's wanted for questioning in a string of diamond heists from New York to California and all points in between. It took some doing, but I was able to track her down right here in Detroit."

"That's great, Mike."

"On a hunch I staked out her place and sure enough, guess who showed up?"

"The Green Hornet?"

"That's right, Casey, the blasted Green Hornet!"

"Do you know what they talked about, Mike? Tell me you had a photographer with you."

Mike hung his head low. "I'm sorry, Britt.

"Mike." He dragged the word out a couple extra syllables.

"But I know what I saw!"

Britt sat back in his chair and rubbed his chin with his index finger, a habit he usually fell into when making a story decision. "Okay, Mike," he said after a moment. "Run with it. We'll start with a small piece in tomorrow's edition and you can follow it up with an expose they day after for the Sunday edition."

"Why wait?"

"Because I want you to get back out there and get some proof before we slap this on the front page. I don't like retractions, Mike. They leave a rotten taste in my mouth and we've already had a few this year. No more, you hear me? You get those facts and I'll give you the front page. Deal?"

"Deal."

"Off you go then. I want to see copy on tomorrow's piece before I go home this evening."

Dismissed, Mike Axford left the office much the same way he had entered it, in a huff. Casey closed the door after he was gone.

"Is there anything I can do to help?" she asked softly.

"No," Britt said as he rubbed the bridge of his nose. "If I stall Mike any more than I already have he'll start to get suspicious. Don't worry. If all goes as planned, Mike will have one whale of a front pager after The Green Hornet gets finished with Diamond Lilly."

"Good. You look like you could use some rest. Maybe a night out."

"Wouldn't that be nice?"

"Do you need anything else, sir?" Casey asked before opening the door. "Perhaps an aspirin?"

"That would be perfect. Thank you, Miss Case."

She smiled. "You're welcome, Mr. Reid."

The Green Hornet followed Kato into the garage.

With practiced ease, the masked driver turned a specific ratchet on the tool wall, which opened a hidden compartment. A simple push of a button and the garage was awash in green light. Another button extended steel beams from beneath the front and rear ends of Britt Reid's sporty Chrysler 300 convertible while clamps moved into position to hold the car in place.

Another button rotated the garage floor, securing Britt Reid's car in an underground bunker while bringing The Green Hornet's customized Crown Imperial, known far and wide as the Black Beauty, to the surface.

A final button released the clamps holding the car in place and deactivated the Black Beauty's security system, releasing the door locks. While Kato closed the hidden compartment, his partner climbed into the back seat.

Seconds later, Kato was behind the wheel.

"Check the scanner, Kato."

Beneath the center console was a row of unmarked buttons. Kato depressed one and the scanner rose from its nest in the Black Beauty's trunk. A confirmation beep told him that the scanner was working perfectly. He resealed it once more inside its housing. "Check," Kato said.

The Hornet pulled a weapon from its cradle in the armrest. "Hornet Gun," he said as he inspected the piece of equipment. It passed. "Check." He flipped open a small device and powered it on. It hummed. "Hornet Sting," he said. "Check."

"Let's roll, Kato."

Rising on hidden hinges, the rear wall of the garage opened, revealing a path across the patio outside Britt's study. The Black Beauty rolled easily across and through a second false wall into the abandoned warehouse next door.

Minutes later, the lovers on the old Kissin' Candy Mints billboard split as the Black Beauty roared through the hidden exit into the night.

Kato parked the Black Beauty beneath the cover of trees.

Across the street from the building where Genevieve Lilly lived, they sat there in silence and watched the building. Neither Kato nor The Green Hornet trusted Diamond Lilly, so they proceeded carefully. They expected some kind of double cross and were going to be prepared for it.

After ten minutes with no movement, they were satisfied that none of the diamond thief's henchmen were lying in wait to ambush them, the duo made their way to the emergency fire escape at the rear of the building. They climbed.

True to her word, Diamond Lilly was once again behind her desk in the study. She had maps, blueprints, and other assorted papers scattered across the top of her desk where she and four of her operatives discussed tactics.

The balcony door was locked, but it didn't take long for Kato to jimmy the lock. The masked men entered the way they had the two previous nights. To her credit, Lilly hid her irritation at the interruption this time.

"I believe we had an appointment," The Green Hornet announced.

Diamond Lilly looked up from the papers and offered a crooked smile. "Of course we did. Please, come in." With a flick of her fingers, she motioned for her men to step away from the desk so her new partner could come closer.

"I see you've been busy. I'm impressed, Lil. You do know your stuff."

"I pride myself on my thoroughness."

"Why don't you go over the plan, partner?"

Diamond Lilly pointed to the floor plan on the desk. "We'll start with the basics," she began.

Sanford Biggs loved a challenge.

During his illustrious career he had chased the most prized items, seized every opportunity that came his way, and braved dangers that would have sent a lesser man crying to his mother's side. As a result, he had amassed one of the world's most illustrious collections of rare antiquities and unique one-of-a-kind items. If not for the fact that the majority of his collection had been obtained illegally, he could have made a fortune by selling tickets.

He took great care in planning and researching the items he desired for his ever-expanding collection. In truth, getting "*it*" was most of the fun. He put a great deal of thought into each quest before going after that which he wanted.

However, sometimes the rare and unique managed to find him.

Such was the case of the customized black Crown Imperial parked just a few feet away from him. When he had seen The Green Hornet and his partner drive away in that beautiful machine the night before, he knew that he had to have it. Unlike many of his conquests, The Green Hornet was known as a man not to trifle with. If he was going to take the Black Beauty for his own, he would have to act quickly and decisively. Since the lovely Miss Lilly was paying him to eliminate The Green Hornet, he would have not only the villain's vehicle for his collection, but also his mask and whatever secrets the Black Beauty held beneath her steel frame.

Biggs' men were watching the building while he did his work. Like the rest of his collection, the men and women who worked for Sanford Biggs were each unique in some way. Each of his employees was considered the best in their field. Second best would never do. He had assembled a one-of-a-kind team and they had yet to be defeated. That was a fact for which he was immensely proud.

Based on The Green Hornet's reputation, he assumed that the car was booby-trapped. It made sense that the villain would want to keep his getaway vehicle safe since his partner had not remained behind to keep an eye on it.

If his last two visits with Diamond Lilly were any indication, Biggs knew the meeting upstairs would be as brief as possible. The timeframe available would not allow him adequate time to disable the car's security before The Hornet returned, but Biggs had planned for that.

He pulled a small silver box roughly the equivalent size of a pack of cigarettes from his pocket. On one side was a flat magnet. A small inlaid switch and an antenna were located on the side. He extended the antenna and activated the device. It emitted a tiny *beep, beep, beep* that informed him it was in working order.

Biggs knelt next to the Black Beauty. He could still feel the warmth of the engine as his hand snaked underneath the wheel well to attach the small transmitter to the Black Beauty. The transmitter's powerful magnet snapped against the metal and held fast.

Once the transmitter was in position, Biggs returned to his car at the end of the block and checked the signal strength. "Loud and clear," he told his driver, Davis Walker, who despite the irony of his last name being Walker, was also considered one of the best wheel men in the country. Biggs had paid top dollar to have the man on his team. "Are you certain you can crack whatever security he's got on that thing?"

"I've not run across anything yet I can't handle. I doubt that'll change tonight."

"You'd better be right about that," Biggs said with just a hint of menace. "The transmitter has a range of one mile. As long as you don't let him get farther away than that we've got him."

"Piece of cake, Boss," the driver said. "Nobody out-drives me."

"That is why I hired you."

"Yes, sir. What do we do now?"

"Now," Sanford Biggs said as he leaned back in his seat and crossed his arm. "Now we wait."

"There they are, Boss."

As predicted, The Green Hornet and his sidekick had not stayed inside Diamond Lilly's office very long. She and Biggs had discussed the meeting prior to her new partner's arrival. Biggs had asked her to stall and delay The Green Hornet's departure as long as possible. She said she would do her best, but he knew better than to count on anyone outside of his crew. He was surprised she had managed to keep him occupied as long as she had. He would have to compliment her on her skills once the contract was fulfilled and he collected his fee.

The masked duo wasted no time as they piled into their ride and sped away.

"Get after them, but don't let them spot you," Biggs ordered Walker.

"You got it."

They pulled out onto the nearly deserted street behind the Black Beauty, but stayed back. "Scanner's working perfectly," the driver said.

"Of course it is," Sanford Biggs said. "Second best will never do."

The two of them drove the rest of the way in relative silence, broken only when Biggs gave orders to turn, to speed up, or to slow down. Walker obeyed each directive without comment. With what Biggs was paying him, he could handle the boss' heavy-handed management style.

"Where are they going?" he asked aloud, not really expecting an answer. "Looks like a residential area coming up. We must be close. There's no way they can hide something as unique as this car around that many people."

"They're turning," Walker said.

"Stay sharp. This has to be it."

Kato parked the Black Beauty inside Britt Reid's garage and closed the door.

Normally, a quick repeat of the steps he had performed earlier that evening would have the Black Beauty once again securely entombed beneath the garage. Tonight, however, Kato had other plans. He had ordered some parts for their rolling arsenal and was anxious to get under the hood.

"The new four-barrel carburetor, headers, and pop up pistons I ordered for the Beauty came in today," Kato reminded his partner. "I want to get those installed tonight so we're in top form before the diamond job."

"No problem, Kato. Keep the car up here in the garage if you want, but make sure the outer doors are secured." As he stepped out of the car, The Green Hornet pulled a pocket watch from his midnight green coat pocket. Turning the dial to 1:50, he pressed the stud. A small antenna ratcheted up and beeped, its signal sent. "You can attend to the Black Beauty after we finish up with Scanlon."

The Green Hornet walked up the steps with Kato just a step behind.

"Frank will be here soon, Kato," Britt said as pulled off his mask, coat, and hat and handed then over to his valet.

"Of course," Kato said. "I'll be ready."

Sanford Biggs tapped his fingers against the dashboard.

He and his driver sat parked on the side of the road. Just seconds earlier the tracking signal being sent by the transmitter had ceased. It was illogical to assume The Green Hornet's driver had spotted them because they had not made any evasive maneuvers. The Black Beauty and the transmitter had simply vanished.

"Where do you think they went?" Davis Walker asked for the third time.

"Quiet," Biggs said. He did not raise his voice, but his tone was intense and full of authority. "I'm thinking."

"Sorry, Boss."

"I knew he would have a place to hide it, but where? It has to be shielded wherever it is. There's no way The Green Hornet could keep something as illustrious as that beauty of a car without having a clever place to hide it. It's much too distinctive to leave where someone might see it. That means it's hidden somewhere inside one of these buildings."

"That's a lot of room to cover."

"Indeed." He pointed toward an alley off to the right. "I'm going down the alley to get a closer look. You take the car around the block and see if there are any other promising entrances. Then park out of sight across the street until you hear from me. The signal was right around here before it stopped. Let's take a look and see what we can see."

"You got it."

Sanford Biggs walked into the alley, staring at the lovers on the tattered billboard frozen in perpetual lip lock at the end of the line. The buildings appeared deserted. Windows in the upper floors were either blacked out or broken. Off to the right there were stacks of boards leaning against chipped bricks. Slats of old lumber had been nailed over a side door. On the left were old garbage cans that had been picked over by homeless felines out looking for a meal. It smelled like someone had urinated in the alley. The farther along he walked, the worse the smell became.

Headlights spilled across the walls half a second before he heard the distinct sound of wheels making a turn into the alley. Without a thought, he pressed himself into a shadowed nook behind the garbage cans. As he suspected, a car pulled into the alley and stopped near the mouth. He let out a breath when he realized it was not The Green Hornet.

If not The Hornet, then who? Biggs wondered. *One of his flunkies, perhaps?*

He watched as the driver doused the lights and killed the engine. He walked with purpose toward a crack in the wall. With little effort, he ducked through the opening and stepped inside.

A secret door! Biggs couldn't believe it. He had noticed the same slatted boards himself, but suspected nothing until he saw the stranger step inside. It was a perfect deception. Stepping back into the alley he signaled for Walker to join him. Once the man reached him, Biggs pushed open the hidden entrance and stepped inside cautiously.

Holding back, Biggs watched as the man they had followed unlocked a heavy steel door then stepped inside something that looked like a larger version of a dumbwaiter. The door slid shut and the whir of hydraulics filled the empty space as the steel door closed.

With his ear against the door like a nosy neighbor, Biggs listened to muffled voices coming from beyond the dumbwaiter. He could hear men talking, but most of what was being said was hard to make out. Whoever it was he had followed, it was now clear he either worked for or with The Green Hornet. He tried to pry open the door, but it wouldn't budge.

"There's no handle," Walker whispered. "Looks like it is activated from wherever it is this thing goes."

Sanford Biggs cursed under his breath. If he could have taken out The Green Hornet and company, his contract would be fulfilled and he would have plenty of time to abscond with his prize.

"Come on," he said. "Let's see where this goes."

They continued on until they came to a dead end in front of another locked door.

"Can you pick it?" Biggs asked.

Walker smiled at the stupid question.

Seconds later they stood in a garage painted a shade of the lightest green.

Sanford Biggs smiled as he looked over the prize that would very shortly become the highlight of his collection.

Walker whistled softly. "Ain't she a thing of beauty?"

"Yes she is," Biggs said proudly. "Now let's get to work."

Unaware of the unwelcome guests in the garage, Britt and Kato met with District Attorney Frank Scanlon in Reid's private study he used as an office. The D.A. arrived as he usually did, riding the secret lift hidden behind the fireplace.

"I swear I'll never get used to that thing," he remarked as hydraulic levers lowered the fireplace back into position.

"Good to see you, Frank," Britt said. "I think we can wrap up Diamond Lilly tomorrow. We discussed her plans at length tonight. Here's everything she gave us."

Kato handed over a folder and Scanlon began flipping through it immediately.

"This is good stuff, gentlemen. The D.A. in LA will be happy to hear that too. He's the one that gave me the heads up on her coming here in the first place. Apparently, she was quite the problem out there. They couldn't corral her, but they'll be just as happy if she doesn't come back."

"Lucky for them you've got an inside ace, eh?"

"Yeah. Lucky them," Scanlon answered while reading. "Oh, there was one other thing?'

"What's that?"

"One of Sergeant Burke's snitches told him that there's some hitman in town and that he has a contract out on The Green Hornet."

"Does the sergeant have a name?" Kato asked. If he was concerned, he hid it well.

"No. Burke tried to squeeze him for more, but that's all he could get. I've got some people looking into it. Perhaps you two should lay low for a little while," Scanlon said. "Just as a precaution."

"I appreciate the concern, Frank" Britt said, flashing a playboy smile that melted the heart of many a woman. "But you know I can't do that. I've got a date tomorrow and I'd hate to keep Diamond Lilly waiting."

"At least promise me you'll both be careful."

"We always are, Frank. We always are."

"Okay," Scanlon said as he pushed the thick horn-rimmed glassed back up on his nose. "You win. Now, why don't you explain the plan to me so we can set the trap."

Kato took the papers and spread them out on the desk.

"Okay," Britt said. "The first thing she needs is a way inside."

Davis Walker was worth every penny.

Sanford Biggs was no slouch when it came to bypassing security systems, but even he had to marvel at the skill of the thief and driver he had hired to help him claim his latest prize.

The Green Hornet's reputation cast a lengthy shadow. Even outside of Detroit. Thanks to the articles by the *Daily Sentinel*, most by the crusading journalist Mike Axford, The Green Hornet remained prominent in the public eye. In this city he was public enemy number one.

Just spending a few minutes studying the car confirmed that the man's reputation was well deserved. He had expected some form of security. They found more than expected. First, there were electrodes built into the door handles. If someone attempted to open the door while they were active, they were in for quite a shock. Walker talked Biggs through the steps to disable the electrodes while he waited for sensation to return to his right hand.

Once that was done, they moved on to the second layer of security. They traced a lead from the door to a series of small jet nozzles underneath the car. The nozzles were connected to a canister holding some form of gaseous material. Unsure whether the gas was lethal or not, they simply disconnected the leads.

"With this level of security they must use some kind of remote control to activate and deactivate it," Walker said once he was sure the driver's side door was safe to open.

"Makes sense," Biggs agreed. "I wouldn't be surprised if we find more obstacles before we're through."

"Agreed. Let's be cautious," Walker said before adding, "You do understand that The Green Hornet probably has a way to track the car. They'll follow it wherever we take it."

Biggs smiled. "I'm counting on it."

They worked on the car for another ten minutes. Biggs kept a wary eye out in case the car's owner or driver returned. While he was not afraid of a face-to-face confrontation with The Hornet, he preferred to avoid it until after the Black Beauty was in his possession.

"We're golden," Walker said with a smile as the Black Beauty's engine came to life.

"Fantastic!"

Britt Reid was tired.

The meeting with Scanlon had been productive, but lengthy. It was almost two in the morning and he still had to get up for work at the *Sentinel* in a few hours.

"I'm turning in, Kato. I suggest you do the same."

"What about the upgrades to the Black Beauty?"

"I think those can wait until morning. Why don't you go and tuck the Beauty in and we'll pick back up in the morning."

"Okay, Britt. Good night."

"Good night, Hayashi."

Kato cut through the kitchen to the steps leading down into to the garage. He had been looking forward to working on the Beauty, but the yawn he was unable to stifle confirmed just how tired he was. Britt was right in suggesting they each get some shuteye.

When he stepped into the garage it took his weary senses a second to comprehend what he was seeing. There were two men there.

And they were doing something to his car.

"Hey!" Kato shouted.

The taller of the two intruders moved quickly. One second he was about to get into the passenger side door, the next he had a gun slung over the roof and opened fire.

Kato moved faster. He dove back through the door into the stairwell as bullets tore into the plaster wall where his head had been just half a second earlier.

He heard the sound of the Black Beauty's purring engine and the squeal of tires on concrete as the automobile tore off through the fake rear wall of the garage and across the patio. Kato ran back into the garage just in time to see the taillights disappear.

Britt entered the garage sporting The Hornet's mask, but the same clothes he had been wearing when they met with Scanlon. "You okay?" he asked his friend.

"Nothing hurt but my pride, Boss. They stole the Beauty."

"Anybody we know?"

"I didn't recognize them."

"Did they get a good look at you?"

"I don't think so. It all happened fast."

"Suit up, Kato! We're going after them!"

"You think this was one of Lilly's men?"

"We'll ask him when we catch him, Kato."

Kato was behind the wheel of Britt Reid's convertible, with the top up, The Hornet in the back. Neither of them wore their masks and had on long coats on the off chance anyone noticed them. They were only a minute behind the thieves, but that could mean miles thanks to the Black Beauty's souped-up engines.

The Green Hornet had the remote control turned on. "Activating scanner," he said as he pressed the appropriate button. "Let's hope this works."

"They'll probably hear the scanner doors open."

"We'll have to risk it. We have to know where they're taking the Beauty."

For a tense moment that felt like an eternity, they waited in silence. The Hornet released the breath he had been holding when the first trill beep emitted from the remote.

"I've got a signal. They're heading toward the docks."

"I'm on it, Boss," Kato said as he jerked the wheel. "I know a short cut."

The *Bigg Dipper* was anchored at pier three.

Sanford Biggs had spent a considerable fortune converting the massive cargo carrier into a floating museum and his permanent residence. From the outside it looked like any other grungy hauler working the open seas. There was nothing special about it.

The inside, however, told another story entirely. Sanford Biggs' personal living area was immaculate, rivaling any five star hotel. The crew quarters were also impressive. The man liked to keep his team happy and adding small luxuries to their cabins was a small price to pay for their servitude.

The pride of the vessel was the museum.

Were he to open it to the public, the museum would rival even the best of those around the world. He did, on occasion, show off his collection to clients. Some of the highlights of the private exhibit included various tribal head masks from multiple cultures such as spears from Africa, a well preserved Roman shield, and a federal marshal's badge believed to have belonged to Wyatt Earp. There was also a glowing green meteorite; the remains of a crashed experimental airplane that had been shot down over Switzerland in 1939; the mask, hat, and pistols of a famous lawman in the old west; and a bat shaped metal throwing weapon. There were other items there as well. Paintings from all over the world, sculptures, gems, and assorted trinkets lined the display cases.

Davis Walker parked the Black Beauty on the loading platform and remained in the car as it was lifted onto the ship and then lowered into the hold.

Biggs supervised the work, smiling as he watched his latest prize settle into its final home. Next to the spot reserved for the car were two bare mannequins. Once he had disposed of The Green Hornet and his partner, he would add their distinctive costumes and masks to his collection.

Who wouldn't pay to see that? he wondered.

The Green Hornet and Kato watched the Black Beauty being lowered into the hold.

"There was a report last year about the *Bigg Dipper*," The Green Hornet said, trying to mentally recall the information. "The ship's crew was wanted in connection with trafficking stolen goods. The man suspected of being behind it was named Biggs. I can't remember his first name, but that was him getting out of the Beauty."

"I spot seven men, but there might be more," Kato said as he looked through the binoculars. "What's the plan, Boss?"

"Let's go introduce ourselves and get back our car."

"Good plan."

"Let's go, Kato."

The men ran across the dock, kept hidden by crates and containers as they made their way to the *Bigg Dipper*. There were two guards at the bow and two at the stern, moving in a rotating pattern, always within line of site of the other. The two men who took the Beauty had gone below. The seventh man worked the crane from the bridge.

"Those two are yours," The Hornet said as he pointed toward the bow. A large chain held the anchor. That was Kato's entrance. "Off you go."

Kato was more agile than his partner so he could easily handle climbing up the chain faster. The Hornet took the less difficult, but more exposed route, directly up the gangplank.

The first guard swung around at the sight of the midnight green blur heading toward him, but he wasn't fast enough. The Hornet dropped the man with one well-placed punch. He turned to face the second man, but stopped short. Kato had already taken out his two guards and was in the process of taking out the third. Sometimes The Green Hornet forgot exactly how gifted his partner was.

The duo moved with stealth toward the hold. A stairwell led down from an open bulkhead door. Aside from The Hornet darts, which Kato kept, all of their weapons were inside the Black Beauty. Kato had divided the darts between them so they both had weapons.

"It looks like a museum," The Green Hornet whispered. "Look at all of this . . ." his mouth went dry when he saw the lawman's hat, mask, and pistols. "Do you know what these—"

Before he could finish, Kato nudged him aside as the enemy attacked. Five very large men came at them. A tall man with the sword came at The Hornet, slicing away at the air. The Hornet leapt backward as the sharp blade just barely missed his stomach. The front of his shirt was not as fortunate. He recognized the man as the one who had been in the passenger seat of the Black Beauty.

"Biggs!"

"So you're The Green Hornet, eh?" Sanford Biggs said.

"That's right."

"I'm not impressed." He swung again.

"Give me time," The Hornet said as he ducked under the swing.

The other four men surrounded Kato. They were not brandishing weapons, but from their moves, he knew they were each trained in various martial arts techniques. Kato fell into a fighting stance. It wasn't often he had the opportunity to truly test his skills against well-trained opponents such as these. Despite the seriousness of the situation, he smiled. He curled his fingers and invited the attack.

The sword crashed again, shattering a glass display case.

This is ridiculous, The Hornet thought as he dodged left. Then he spied the swords and shields hanging against a nearby bulkhead. He feinted, then reversed and threw himself in the direction of the weapons.

He grabbed a large shield and deflected the next strike. As his opponent drew back, The Hornet used the shield like a battering ram and lunged forward, knocking the man into the Black Beauty. He slammed the hand holding the sword against the frame until the man released his grip.

Before Biggs could recover, The Hornet caught him with an uppercut that knocked him over the hood of the car.

Kato whirled a kick into the face of his opponent, spun around, and tossed a hornet dart at another, taking both out of the fight at once. The other two advanced on him, but Kato held his ground. He leapt into the air, his left foot snaking out as he did so and catching one of them in the nose. The last man blocked the attack, lancing a blow off Kato's chin. Kato landed in a fighting stance.

The big man lunged forward and Kato feinted to block, but twisted away at the last second. The attacker was unable to stop his forward motion in time and ran through the other man, who Kato recognized as the driver who stole the Black Beauty, with his sword. A roundhouse kick doubled the man over and a chop to the back of the neck took the fight out of him. All four men were down. One would not be waking up.

Kato wiped a trickle of blood from his lip when he saw his partner chasing the tall man up the ladder to the catwalk that ran the entire length of the hold.

"There's nowhere to run, Biggs! It's over!"

"Never!" Biggs shouted as he swung the sword again. It hit the handrail and the catwalk shuddered under the vibration. The Green Hornet moved fast, pinning Biggs' sword hand to the rail. A pinch and twist maneuver Kato taught him, and the sword fell away.

Biggs took a swing at The Hornet, who dodged. The swing went wild and he lost his balance and went over the railing.

The Green Hornet snagged him in midair and held fast.

"Oh no, you don't," he said between gritted teeth. "You and I have some unfinished business. I believe you have something that belongs to me."

"Somehow I doubt the mighty Green Hornet is going to just let this go."

"Perhaps we can make a deal," The Hornet said, his muscles aching.

"Go ... to ..." Biggs started as he wiggled free of The Hornet's grasp and fell backward. He landed with a heavy thud that echoed throughout the hold.

The Green Hornet watched from the catwalk as Kato ran over to check the body. After a moment he looked up and shook his head. Sanford Biggs was dead.

"Get the Black Beauty back on the platform and we can lift it up," The Hornet said once he was back in the hold. "I just have to do one thing first."

Minutes later the Black Beauty roared away into the predawn night.

Frank Scanlon was entranced.

He had listened to Britt and Kato relate the details of the theft of the Black Beauty and the showdown aboard the *Bigg Dipper*. Once they were back in the car and safely away, The Hornet had called the D.A. at home with the details of his encounter with Sanford Biggs. The police arrived shortly thereafter and took Biggs' men into custody.

"The only thing I don't understand," he said once they were finished. "Everything in the museum was tagged, labeled, and easily accounted for. Except for one empty case. Do you know what was in the case and what happened to it?"

"I do, Frank. It was an heirloom that was stolen from my family many years ago, something that belonged to my grandfather. It's in a safe place and I intend to see it stays there."

"That's good enough for me, Britt."

"Thanks, Frank. Now, as for Diamond Lilly . . ."

THE INSINCEREST FORM OF FLATTERY

by Paul D. Storrie

Lonnie Donovan took a long pull on his cigarette and watched the mist rising up from the river. The day had been sweltering hot, but the temperature had dropped a good twenty degrees after nightfall. Lonnie was thankful for that. It meant less griping from the six-member crew he had loading the 18-foot panel truck that was parked next to the riverfront warehouse.

Officially, the place was supposed to be full of toy tea sets from Taiwan. Unofficially, there were boxes scattered all through the place packed with all sorts of stolen goods. His crew was removing a truckload of cigarettes that had been hijacked off a truck in New York about a month before and brought by boat across Lake Erie a couple weeks after. Now Lonnie was set to distribute them to vending machines all over the city and make a bundle in the process.

As he flicked his still-smoldering butt away, Lonnie noticed a soft hissing sound nearby. Turning, he was surprised that the mist seemed to have thickened into a dense fog that rolled towards him. Then a shadowy figure began to emerge from it, tall and wearing a fedora.

Donovan flinched. "Lookout boys!" he rasped. "It's The Green Horn..."

More details registered as the figure stepped free of the smoky tendrils obscuring him. He was wearing a long purple cloak over a dark pinstripe suit, with a lavender shirt and a white tie. His face was hidden by a purple hood and a pair of amber-lensed goggles like open cockpit pilots used to wear.

"You ain't The Green Hornet," Donovan said.

"No," a muffled voice replied. "I'm not. I do, however, have a proposition for you."

97

Donovan laughed. By this time, his crew had eased around the truck, eyeing the strange newcomer. Every one of them was a big, mean scrapper. Those were the kind of men Donovan always picked to work with.

"I ain't got time to waste on some cheap knockoff!" Donovan said. "Get 'im, boys."

As the goons started forward, the cloaked man raised his right hand and made a slight gesture. Before Donovan's crew could reach him, another, bigger man stepped out of the obscuring cloud. He too wore amber-tinted goggles, but his went with the old-style, leather driving helmet that covered his head. A driving scarf was tied around his lower face. His clothing was different too: a linen duster over dark pants, a white shirt, and a tweed vest, with calf-high laced boots.

Strange as his clothes were, that wasn't what grabbed the attention of Donovan and his goons. It was the drum-magazined Thompson gun he held firmly in his leather-gauntleted hands. The muzzle flashed and the Thompson's distinctive ratta-tat-tat echoed across the river.

Donovan clenched his eyes tight, waiting for the .45 caliber slugs to rip into him. It struck him as funny that the last thing going through his mind was, *"I thought it would be louder."*

The machine gun's chatter stopped. Donovan pried open his eyes, amazed to still be standing. His men were sprawled on the ground all around him. He couldn't understand why there wasn't any blood.

Then one of them moaned. Donovan's head snapped up to look at the purple-clad gangster and his gunman.

"They ain't dead!"

His reaction brought a muffled laugh.

"No, they're not. This time, my friend was using rubber bullets. You and your associates are no good to me dead. As I said, I've got a proposition for you..."

"Councilman Davis to see you, Mr. Reid."

The publisher of the *Daily Sentinel* looked up from his seemingly never-ending pile of paperwork at the sound of his secretary's voice. They'd worked together for years, but every time he saw her, he was struck by how beautiful she was, by her auburn hair and deep brown eyes. Beyond that, she was a smart, independent, exceptionally competent woman who shared his most important secret. It was unfortunate that their working relationship made their mutual attraction . . . difficult.

Pushing those thoughts aside, he said, "Show him in, Miss Case."

Reid rose from his chair and came around his desk to greet the man who entered. Councilman Nolan Davis was tall, blond, and handsome, with a winning smile and blue eyes that practically sparkled with sincerity. Like Reid, he was dressed in an expensive, stylish suit.

Lenore Case asked, "Shall I hold your calls, Mr. Reid?"

He nodded. "Thank you, Miss Case."

She left the room, closing the door behind her.

As she did so, Reid and Davis exchanged a firm handshake.

"Good to see you, Nolan. It's been too long."

"Likewise, Britt. I guess with you running the paper and me running the city, we've just been too busy."

Reid laughed. "You're not running the city yet, Nolan. Mayor Fields still has a few months before the election. In fact, last I heard he was ahead in the polls."

Clapping Reid on the shoulder with his free hand, Davis said, "An endorsement from the *Daily Sentinel* could help change that!"

Reid gestured at a chair in front of his desk, then returned to his own. As the two men sat, Reid asked, "Is that what this visit is about? I told you before, I've got to be careful. Given how long we've known each other, Fields could easily suggest I was biased."

Davis shook his head. "I know, I know. Anyway, I'm not really here about that. I'm actually more concerned about why the *Sentinel* hasn't been reporting on this Purple Gangster character that's been stirring up so much trouble the last few days."

Reid leaned back in his chair, steepling his fingers. "You and Mike Axford," he replied, referring to the *Sentinel*'s top crime reporter. "He's been trying to push a story through, but Gunnigan won't run it."

Davis looked curious. "Why's that?"

"We haven't been able to get any official confirmation he exists from the police, for starters. So far all Mike's got is rumors of a costumed crook with a big wheelman partnering up with some lowlifes to pull a few lucrative jobs. Gunnigan doesn't like running stories based on anonymous sources and I can't say that I blame him."

Davis nodded. "Would it help if I went on the record?"

Reid sat up straight. "Of course. What more can you tell us?"

"Did you know that one of those lucrative jobs this Purple Gangster pulled was robbing a city payroll truck?"

"That I hadn't heard."

"Not surprising. Fields is working hard to keep this out of the public eye to hide his own incompetence. Bad enough that The Green Hornet has been running loose under his watch. Now there's another one following in his footsteps. Something needs to be done!"

"And you figure you're the guy to do it? I'll be honest with you, Nolan, I've known you since we were kids and I never figured you for public office." Reid smiled and said, "You were a bit on the wild side, before you joined the Army."

Davis smiled. "You were always the steady one, Britt, but things changed for me while I was overseas. I learned the value of discipline and the importance of doing what needs to be done, no matter how difficult or distasteful it might be. You know as well as I do that Fields is a career politician and crooked to boot. All he cares about is staying in office and getting fat on the taxpayer's money, not what's best for the city."

"I'm not sure I can argue that," Reid replied, a slight frown flickering across his face. "If you don't mind my asking, are you going to be able to finish out the race? I'd heard that your campaign was having some money troubles."

"Off the record?" Davis replied. "We did have a bump in our funding. Looks like things have smoothed out, though. I fully expect to sitting behind the mayor's desk once all the votes are counted."

He nodded towards the door. "And you'd better be careful. Once I'm in office, I may try to steal away Casey to be my personal assistant. She's one of a kind, Britt."

"That she is," said Reid. "Believe me, I won't let her go without a fight."

Davis smiled. "Well, maybe I should go talk to Axford about this Gangster fella? I expect you've got work to do."

"You're certain you want to go on record? It might not win you any friends down at police headquarters if they're trying to keep it quiet."

"I'm sure," Davis replied. "What is it you newspaper men always say? The people have a right to know?"

"So, do you think he's right?"

"I don't know, Kato. I checked with Scanlon. So far, all the police have to go on is secondhand stories. Is it worth worrying the public over someone who may not even exist?"

It was a few minutes after nightfall as the two men entered the garage attached to Britt Reid's home. They were no longer dressed as the newspaper publisher and his faithful valet. Instead, Reid was wearing the midnight green suit, topcoat, fedora, and mask of The Green Hornet.

Kato was clad in the black chauffeur's uniform of The Hornet's silent and dangerous assistant.

"Your friend seems to think he exists," Kato said as he walked past Reid's car. On the back wall, several tools were handing from hooks and brackets mounted on pegboard. Kato reached up and twisted the center of a ratchet handle. Just to his right, a small panel slid back, revealing a set of push buttons.

"True," The Green Hornet replied, "but Nolan is fighting an uphill battle against Mayor Fields. He's desperate for anything that'll make Fields look bad."

Kato punched a button, switching the overhead lights to green. "I saw that Arlan Thompson endorsed him. Do you think that will help or hurt?"

"Hard to say, Kato. Thompson was a sports hero and he's a decorated veteran, but he's still a black man. The Civil Rights movement is changing things, but some people still can't see beyond the color of a man's skin."

"You're telling me?"

"Touché."

Kato punched another button and a set of clamps popped out of the floor, locking onto special brackets welded to the bottom of Reid's car. "How is it that they know each other?"

"They met in the Army. Thompson was the sergeant who showed a wet-behind-the-ears Lieutenant Nolan Davis the ropes when they were both stationed in South Korea."

"That's where Thompson was injured, yes?" Kato pressed a third button and a large section of the garage floor turned over, swinging the mundane vehicle underground and revealing The Green Hornet's rolling arsenal, the Black Beauty.

The Hornet nodded. "Training accident. Being drafted didn't hurt Elvis' career any, but once Arlan 'the Tank' Thompson tore up his left shoulder, he was done as professional boxer."

"Shame," Kato replied. "I saw him fight. He was good." For Kato, that was high praise. He hit another switch, releasing the clamps that held the Black Beauty in place.

The Green Hornet nodded. "Might have given Clay a run for his money in the Olympics."

"Muhammed Ali, you mean," said Kato.

The Green Hornet nodded. "Of course. But he was still going by Cassius Clay when he took the gold in Rome."

Kato pressed one final button and the Black Beauty's doors sprung open. He swung the panel shut and slid into the driver's seat as The Green

Hornet climbed into the back.

"Check the scanner, Kato."

Opening a panel beside his seat, Kato activated a test sequence that raised the flying camera from the hatch in the trunk, then lowered it back in place.

"Check."

The Green Hornet then made sure his gas gun was loaded and ready. "Hornet Gun, check." Setting the gun aside, he flipped open the end of his telescoping Hornet Sting. A low hum filled the car. He snapped the end closed again. "Hornet Sting, check."

He gave a grim smile. "Let's roll, Kato."

"So, what's the story on this place, Boss?"

The Black Beauty was parked on a tree-shadowed lane next to a riverside estate in Grosse Pointe.

"I'm wondering if this so-called Purple Gangster might have some connection to the old Purple Gang."

Kato looked surprised. "The Mob from the Twenties? Are any of them still around?"

Reid nodded. "One in particular I'd like to talk to. Maury Saul. He was pretty high up in the organization. Then he got sent up for tax evasion."

"Like Capone."

"Exactly, but he's been out for a few years. He lives here with his son."

Minutes later, The Green Hornet and Kato were making their way, swift and silent in the darkness, across the estate's carefully trimmed lawn. When they neared the house, they could see light streaming from glass doors that opened onto a flagstone patio.

Drawing closer, they looked into a large wood-paneled room with tall bookcases and a stone fireplace. Despite the late summer heat, there was a fire blazing and the shrunken old man who sat in a large leather chair beside it had a blanket over his legs.

Kato quietly slid the tip of a Hornet dart into the narrow gap between the door and the jamb. In seconds, he had snicked back the bolt. Though they made little noise as they entered, the old man became aware of them as they did.

His sunken eyes swung towards them and made a careful appraisal.

Then he gestured with bony fingers at the open doors.

"Shut those. Can't stand the draft."

Kato gave The Green Hornet a quizzical look. The Hornet shrugged. Kato closed the doors.

"So, the infamous Green Hornet, eh? To what do I owe the pleasure?"

"I'm looking for information, Saul. Seems that someone is trading on the reputation of your old gang. I'm wondering what you know about it."

The old man coughed out a laugh. "This Purple Gangster, eh? Yeah, I've heard the rumors. Can't tell you anything, though. He's got nothing to do with me." He coughed again, harder. "Kind of a kick, though. Reminds me of the old days."

"The old days are gone, Saul. I don't like the idea of this Purple Gangster muscling in on my territory."

The old man bobbed his head. "I can see how you wouldn't. In my day—"

The main doors into the room swung open. A man stood there, maybe thirty years old with curly black hair, wearing cotton slacks, a polo shirt, and deck shoes. He had a book in his left hand, a finger between the pages to hold his place.

"Dad? I thought I heard—The Green Hornet!"

Kato took a few quick, catlike steps towards the door and stood ready to act.

The Green Hornet turned to the newcomer, a cold sneer on his lips. "I was just asking your father about his past, Mr. Saul, and . . . The Purple Gangster."

The old man cackled. "Oh, his name isn't Saul. It's Sales. Being Maury Saul Jr. was bad for business, so he changed it to Martin Sales. My name wasn't good enough for him, but he was sure happy to use my money to start up his business."

The younger man flinched, but he glared at The Green Hornet. "We've got nothing to do with any Purple Gangster and we want nothing to do with you. My father's past is past and the sooner this Gangster is out of the picture, the happier I'll be. I hope the police catch him, but if the two of you wipe each other out, I won't shed any tears."

Turning his head, he shouted down the hallway, "Harris, get in here. Now!"

Kato started towards him, but a minute shake of The Green Hornet's head stopped him in his tracks.

Seconds later, a tall, broad-shouldered man in corduroys and a sleeveless T-shirt stumbled into the room.

"Where's the fire, Boss? I . . ."

He stopped cold when he spotted The Green Hornet and his silent companion.

"Some bodyguard you are," the old man sneered.

The bruiser's eyes darted to Sales. "You want I should . . . ?"

Before Sales could respond, The Green Hornet moved towards the patio doors. "We've got all the answers we need. There's no percentage in roughing up your goon just because we can."

As The Hornet reached the doors, Kato tensed as if he were about to strike. The bodyguard took half a step back, but gave a defiant glare.

Then Kato spun and followed The Green Hornet into the darkness.

In minutes, they were back in the Black Beauty.

From the back seat, The Green Hornet asked, "Well, Kato, what do you think?"

"Not a very informative conversation, except . . ."

"Except that The Purple Gangster is supposed to have a big man backing him up."

"You think that Sales could be The Gangster?"

"I don't know, Kato. His disgust for his father's past seemed genuine, but it could be an act."

"So, what next?"

"Let's keep an eye on the house. If he's The Purple Gangster, he might be headed out later tonight."

The next morning, a weary and frustrated Britt Reid received a clandestine visit from District Attorney Frank Scanlon. A lean man, with dark, widow's-peaked hair and horn-rimmed glasses, Scanlon entered Reid's home through a special entrance in the study. Reid and Kato were waiting for him, alerted by a buzzing signal that sounded throughout the house.

"Something's got to be done about this Purple Gangster, Britt."

Reid nodded. "We were up most of the night following a lead, but our suspect spent the time drinking at the Keyboard Lounge."

"Well, while you were out listening to jazz, The Gangster and his crew knocked over the diamond exchange. By the time the police were able to answer the alarm, he was already gone."

"How do you know it was him?" Kato asked.

Scanlon frowned. "He's taken another page out of The Green Hornet's book. He left a calling card at the scene with a picture of a purple Tommy gun on it."

"Not much room for doubt, then," said Reid. "You said 'by the time the police were able to answer the alarm'—what slowed them down?"

"A rash of petty crimes and false reports, that's what," Scanlon replied. "No doubt planned by The Gangster."

Reid looked thoughtful. "It wouldn't be enough, though, to simply cause some trouble. He'd have to know exactly how many policemen were on duty and how many would be dispatched to each type of crime."

Scanlon's eyes went wide. "You think he's got inside information?"

"Could be," said Reid. "It would explain how he was able to plan the city payroll heist." He snapped his fingers as a smile lit up his face. "What's more, it may give us a way to trap him!"

"Send up the scanner, Kato."

The Black Beauty was parked in an alleyway between W. Hancock and Warren, just off of Woodward in the Midtown district. The Maccabees Building, former home to WXYZ Radio, loomed just ahead.

The Green Hornet carefully adjusted the controls to the small television screen that would receive the images broadcast by the Scanner. It warmed up quickly and resolved into an aerial view of the nearby streets.

A few minutes later, Kato asked, "You think this will work?"

"Scanlon pulled some strings to leave the 13th Precinct shorthanded tonight. There are a number of prime targets in the area, so we'll see if The Purple Gangster takes the bait."

"Hope it doesn't take too long. I'm none too happy sitting this close to a police station."

The Green Hornet didn't answer. His attention was focused on an 18-foot panel truck that was pulling up to the loading dock behind the Institute of Arts. He maneuvered the Scanner for a better look. Seven big men climbed out of the truck, looking around nervously.

"Seems like a strange time for a delivery," he said quietly.

Then the door next to the loading dock opened. A masked figure gestured for the men to come inside.

"We've got him, Kato. Let's roll."

Lonnie Donovan and his crew made their way quietly through the dimly lit halls of the museum, carrying priceless paintings back towards the van. The Gangster said he and his big pal had taken care of the guards, but it never hurt to be careful.

Donovan had been surprised when The Gangster suggested hitting the art museum. "How we gonna fence any of that stuff?" he'd asked.

The Purple Gangster had just laughed. "We aren't. We're going to ransom it back to the museum. It should make quite a splash in the papers."

Donovan wasn't sure he wanted one of his jobs getting a whole lot of ink, but The Gangster hadn't steered them wrong yet. Since they'd teamed up with the masked man, Donovan's crew had raked in more cash in a week than they'd pulled in the last two months.

In the loading bay, Donovan noticed that his boys were taking a breather. He figured they deserved it. They'd already hauled a bunch of paintings there, ready to load into the truck once they'd gathered everything The Gangster wanted.

He pulled out a cigarette, meaning to relax for a minute himself. Then he heard a strange, buzzing noise that rose to a high-pitched whine. It ended in a sharp bang, followed by a long hiss.

One of his men, Vernon, eased over to the door and peered out.

The door flew open, slamming into Vernon and sending him flying. A heartbeat later, a slim, black-clad figure launched himself into the room. He was followed by a man in midnight green.

Lonnie dropped his unlit smoke and dashed back into the museum. He doubted the boys were going to hold The Green Hornet for long and The Purple Gangster needed to know the competition had arrived.

Not twenty steps down the hall, the sounds of fighting echoing behind him, Donovan slammed into a half-seen obstacle and stumbled back. It was The Gangster's wheelman.

The man reached out his left hand, grabbing Donovan to keep him from falling down. Donovan heard a grunt of pain. Letting go, the wheelman rubbed his shoulder and asked, "What's going down?" Donovan was pretty sure it was the first thing he'd ever heard the guy speak.

"It's The Green Hornet!"

The wheelman gave a noncommittal grunt as The Purple Gangster stepped out of the shadows. "Unfortunate," he said, "but not unexpected. Let's go see if we can reason with him."

The wheelman shoved Donovan back towards the receiving area. As they walked, Lonnie tried to explain there was no reasoning with The Green Hornet. "If he decides you're invading his turf, he takes you down. That's that."

The Gangster merely said, "We'll see."

The three men stepped into the receiving area just as The Green Hornet's assistant dropped the last of Donovan's muscle with a roundhouse kick.

The Gangster gave The Green Hornet's assistant an admiring nod. "Nice form," he said.

The Green Hornet gave his purple-cloaked doppelganger an appraising look. "So, you're The Purple Gangster? You've been copying my act."

The Gangster shrugged. "They say imitation is the sincerest form of flattery, right?"

The Hornet and his partner moved forward, their every step full of cautious menace.

"I'm not flattered."

"Then I don't suppose I can offer to cut you in? There's plenty to go around and no need to fight over it."

"I don't share what's mine."

"Then I guess you leave us no choice." A quick glance was all it took to signal the big man beside him. The wheelman swung his Thompson gun out from under his duster where it had been hanging by its leather strap.

Almost faster than the eye could follow, The Hornet's partner produced a hornet-shaped dart and hurled it with uncanny accuracy. Humming with speed, it wedged in the barrel of the machine gun.

At the same time, The Green Hornet sprang forward, throwing a powerful right cross. The Gangster dropped into a defensive crouch, blocking the blow with his forearm and launching a forward kick that The Hornet just barely evaded.

The wheelman popped the machine gun's strap and thrust it towards Donovan as The Green Hornet's partner leapt towards him. The big man raised his fists to protect his face, his elbows in tight to protect his ribs. Seeing this, the man in black spun low, sweeping the bigger man's legs out from under him. The wheelman landed heavily on his left shoulder, letting out a grunt of pain.

Panicked, Donovan tried to use the machine gun as a club, swinging with all his might at The Green Hornet's driver. The other man faded away from the blow like smoke on the wind. Then he glided forward, snapping a backhanded blow into Donovan's face. The machine gun clattered to the ground and the man followed after it with a quieter thud.

As The Gangster's wheelman clambered to his feet, sirens began to sound in the streets nearby. Hearing them, the purple-cloaked man called out that it was time to go.

Falling back, both men produced fist-sized canisters and tossed them to the ground. Smoke poured from them with a fierce hiss, quickly filling the room.

As the vapor billowed up, both The Green Hornet and Kato quickly produced the small gas masks they carried and put them on. Though they had no trouble breathing, the smoke was too thick for them to see anything more than the occasional flash of glowing amber-tinted goggles.

Crouching low, The Green Hornet made his way cautiously towards the door. The last thing he wanted was to put his foot through a priceless Monet or Rembrandt.

As he expected, Kato was waiting for him outside.

"We'd better make ourselves scarce. The police are almost here."

They squeezed past the truck. Its engine, which The Hornet had disabled with The Hornet's Sting, was still leaking sweet smelling steam.

They ran for the Black Beauty. As they got close, The Green Hornet used the remote control he carried to open the doors. Seconds after they slammed the doors shut again, the engine gave off its peculiar buzz and they raced away from the scene.

Kato looked in the rearview mirror, seeing the pained look on his friend's face. "You saw what I saw?"

The Green Hornet nodded. "You mean about your dance partner's reaction when he fell on his left shoulder? I'm afraid so. Tell me, what fighting style was The Gangster using?"

Kato frowned. "Looked like Hapkido to me."

"Which is Korean?" The Green Hornet grimaced behind his mask at his partner's nod. "I was afraid of that. I guess we've got all the answers we need, Kato, whether we like them or not."

"'Gangster's son offers reward for Purple Gangster!'" Mike Axford read aloud. "Now don't that beat all?"

The craggy-faced crime reporter had invited himself into Britt Reid's office to talk about the headline on the latest edition of the *Sentinel*. He never seemed to consider that his boss might have more important things to do than chew the fat with him.

Running a hand through his thinning red hair, he asked, "Now why is it that The Green Hornet's been running around for a so long now and nobody's offered a reward for him? Certainly not a hundred thousand dollars! To be paid in cash, no less! Why, this Purple Gangster's only been tearing up the town for a couple weeks. Why is everyone in such a lather about him?"

"Hard to say, Mike," Britt Reid replied. "Maybe because the election is coming up? Besides, this Sales seems very anxious to have The Purple Gangster out of the spotlight so that people will stop talking about his father's past."

Axford grimaced. "That's the problem with this town. Out of sight, out of mind. Once The Gangster's caught, this Sales will go back to spending his daddy's ill-gotten gains and no one will pay any attention." He gave a heavy sigh. "Well, maybe things will change if your friend Nolan Davis wins the election."

Reid shrugged. "It'd be nice to think so."

Standing, he gestured towards the door. "Now, if you'll excuse me, I've got someplace I need to be."

Axford eased up out of the chair and gave a knowing smile. "Hot date, eh?"

Reid returned the smile. "Can't hide anything from you, can I, Mike?"

Lights blazed in the windows of Martin Sales' riverside mansion. New outdoor spotlights shone out over the lawn. The incandescent display seemed like a desperate attempt to drive back the night's darkness as far as possible.

In the den, Maury Saul watched his son pacing.

"Sit yourself down and stop twitching, boy. You're making me tired just watching you."

His son gave him a cold stare. "Easy for you to say. You don't have a hundred thousand dollars cash lying around just waiting for someone to steal."

The old man snorted. "You may have cleaned it up, but it started out as my money. Don't you forget that."

"Sorry to interrupt your touching family moment, but we need to have a word about a price you put on my head."

Father and son turned to see the patio doors were thrown open. The Purple Gangster stood in the door frame, cloak billowing slightly in the breeze. Behind him loomed his wheelman.

"Might as well put in a revolving door," Maury Saul murmured, "for all the good that one does."

The Purple Gangster moved into the room and off to one side. His partner advanced, raising his Thompson gun to cover the old man and his son.

"Let's all just keep our heads," said The Gangster. "No one needs to get hurt. All I want is the money you're offering as a reward for my capture. That's not too much to ask, is it? I promise you, I'll put it to better use than most."

"Somehow, I doubt it."

Now it was The Gangster's turn to whirl at sound of a voice behind him. The Green Hornet was on the patio, his Hornet Gun in hand and his black-clad assistant by his side.

The wheelman spun too, bringing his machine gun to bear. The Hornet's driver was faster. A flying kick sent the Thompson gun spinning.

"Give it up, Gangster," said The Green Hornet. "Your smoke bombs aren't going to work in the open air and the other door is barred. The only way out is through us."

"Suits me," growled the wheelman. He launched a fierce right cross that Kato barely managed to evade. The smaller man immediately threw a lightning punch into the wheelman's gut, twisting at the hips, putting his whole body into the attack. The larger man just grunted at the impact.

Meanwhile The Purple Gangster moved forward, taking a stance that left no doubt he was familiar with a fighting style of the Orient. The Green Hornet merely raised his gun and shot a stream of gas into the other man's face. The Gangster laughed.

"Did you really think I wouldn't be prepared for The Green Hornet's famous gas gun?" he asked. "I studied you very carefully before I started my criminal career. You were my inspiration, after all."

The Gangster closed the ground between them in a few gliding steps. He waited until The Green Hornet threw a punch, then pivoted, catching the other man by the wrist, and sending him tumbling head over heels.

He was surprised to see The Hornet execute a picture perfect forward roll and come to his feet.

"I have learned a few things from my partner," The Hornet with a grim smile.

The wheelman circled Kato, jabbing and feinting, trying to use his reach. The smaller man relied on his speed, dodging and weaving, letting the bigger man come to him, tiring him out.

"Dance all you want, little man. I only have to hit you once."

"Maybe so," Kato agreed, "but you still have to hit me."

Ducking under the big man's next blow, he threw an elbow into the other man's ribs, then bounded to the side and threw a kick that landed in the exact same place. "And in the meantime, I'll be hitting you."

Nearby, The Green Hornet edged towards his opponent, feinting with his left. When The Gangster tried to trap his wrist again, The Hornet yanked it clear at the last second, using the momentum to put everything he had into a devastating uppercut. The Gangster slid a half step back, just enough for the punch to miss. Except that The Green Hornet hadn't been trying to punch him at all. As the other man moved back, The Hornet grabbed the loose hem of his purple hood and jerked it clear, revealing the startled face of Councilman Nolan Davis.

"Not quite the straight arrow you'd like people to believe, are you Councilman?"

Davis' eyes blazed. "Don't for a minute think I'm like you! I'm doing what has to be done to show the people what an inept, ineffectual mayor they've got."

"And all that money you stole?"

"The system is twisted," Davis spat. "Corrupt. I poured every cent I could raise into my campaign and it wasn't enough. If I had to use dirty money to make sure I could clean up this town, well . . . the irony isn't lost on me."

The Green Hornet sneered and said, "Then maybe you'll get a kick out of this too." Then he pointed towards the sky. Davis looked up to see The Hornet Scanner hovering above. Doing so gave it an absolutely clear view of his face. "I managed to break into the DSTV signal. The whole city just learned who The Purple Gangster really is."

Furious, Davis rushed forward. The Green Hornet merely raised his gun and sent a second jet of gas into the Councilman's now-unprotected face. Davis stumbled, then slumped to the ground. The Hornet dropped the purple hood beside him. The miniature gas mask inside it, probably very like his own, clattered on the patio stones.

That sound drew a quick glance from The Gangster's wheelman. That distraction was all Kato needed. He launched a front kick almost vertically into the big man's jaw. When his opponent staggered back, Kato threw another barrage of fists, pressing his advantage. The wind rushed out of the larger man's lungs. A flying spin kick finished it, sending Davis' partner toppling to the ground.

Looking up, The Green Hornet faced the camera. "I want the whole city to know, this is what happens when you tangle with The Green Hornet."

Then he pulled the remote from his pocket and shut off the transmission. Looking over towards Kato, The Hornet saw he was tying the big man's hands and feet using the long, leather laces from the man's own boots.

Sirens were sounding in the distance, growing closer.

"We'd better get out of here, Boss. I guess the cops watch TV."

Nodding, The Hornet looked into the house where Maury Saul and his son looked on. "You played your parts well," he told them. "Spin this right for the cops and the reporters and you'll look like heroes. I don't want anyone knowing you offered the reward on my say so."

Sales shook his head. "Believe me, I don't want anyone thinking I've got anything to do with you."

The old man merely sniffed and said, "I ain't afraid of you, but I'll keep my trap shut for the kid's sake."

Then The Green Hornet and Kato turned and moved swiftly into the shadows.

The next night, there was a somber gathering at Britt Reid's home. Reid and Kato were joined by Lenore Case and Frank Scanlon, assembling everyone who knew the truth about The Green Hornet in one room. Even though The Hornet had triumphed, no one felt much like celebrating.

"It's a terrible shame," Casey said. "He started out with the best intentions and it all turned out so horribly wrong."

"I still can't believe it," said Scanlon. "I really thought that Davis might be what this city needed."

Kato shrugged. "The one I feel sorry for is Thompson. He only went along with it to help out his friend."

"Kind of like you, eh, Kato?" said Reid.

"Not really," Kato replied. "You only pretend to break the law."

"We both know that's not really true, old friend. We're very careful to avoid harming the innocent, but along the way we break our share of laws. I can't help thinking that a misstep here or there, some slightly different choices, and I could have ended up just like him."

"Oh, Britt!" Casey gasped. "Don't even say that. That's not true."

Reid gave her a sad smile. "Isn't it?"

"It isn't," Scanlon said. "There's a fundamental difference between you and Davis, Britt. You believe that one man can make a difference. He believed that he was the *only* man who could. It might seem like a small distinction, but it's what keeps you pretending to be a criminal and allowed him to actually become one. It's why the city is lucky to be rid of The Purple Gangster, and luckier still to have The Green Hornet."

BAD MEDICINE

by Vito Delsante and Win Scott Eckert

Detroit, Autumn 1964

Donald Legoni, aka "Donny Legs," was always in over his head, thought he seldom knew it. The nickname "Donny Legs" was ironic, having nothing to do with his height. It had to do with the fact that Donny's reach always exceeded his grasp.

"You don't move an operation into Detroit and take on The Green Hornet head to head," the other players had told him. "You start small and stay small, unnoticed even, so you can be ignored."

That never suited Donny Legs. He thought for sure that he could beat the odds, yet here he was getting his backside, and his counterfeiting operation, handed back to him.

Donny watched as The Green Hornet brought his cousin Louie to his knees, an allegory for the current state of Donny's business. To his immediate right, Donny could see The Hornet's bodyguard take on two of his heaviest hitters.

He was the scary one, Donny thought. He had no name, was dressed in black, and he utilized at least three different Oriental martial art fighting styles at once.

Donny turned away from the carnage, trying to find the nearest escape route, but The Hornet and his bodyguard were upon him.

Donny stood up, like a man, as his father had taught him, and offered no resistance. As The Hornet's midnight green gloved fist shot forward like a bullet from a pistol at close range, Donny realized he was, once again, in over his head. He fought to stay conscious, and remembered something important, something that at first felt unconnected, but something that he knew would make a difference.

Maybe he was standing in shallow waters after all. He passed out, finally, with a smile on his lips.

Several months later, Britt Reid, publisher and owner of the *Daily Sentinel* and DSTV, stood at the window of his penthouse office, lost in thought as he contemplated the crisp light peculiar to sunset in autumn.

Donny Legoni was in custody and now going on trial, and the intervening weeks had seen more victories for The Green Hornet and his masked bodyguard.

But today, things had taken a drastic turn for the worse, both for the city of Detroit, and for The Hornet.

He checked his watch, moved to his desk, pressed a buzzer. "Miss Case, would you come in please?"

Lenore "Casey" Case promptly entered. Reid thought she was stunning, with her auburn done up in a loose bun, and attired, smart as always, in a pink pencil skirt and matching jacket. Her cat eyes usually sparkled with humor, belying her professional attitude.

But tonight they were grim.

"Yes, Mr. Reid?"

"It's time for the evening newscast. Let's check out the competition tonight, channel 8."

Casey nodded and went to the television. As she did so, Mike Axford barged in uninvited. "Britt—"

"Not now, Mike, we're about to check out the channel 8 news." Britt was irritated, but concealed it well.

"Yes, but—"

"Mike," said Casey, "hush." She pointed to the television.

"Tonight, on Eyewitness News 8," began the voiceover, "reputed mobster Donald Legoni goes on trial tomorrow on racketeering, counterfeiting, and extortion charges."

Britt had to admit that the anchorwoman, Diane Westfeldt, was striking, and her appearance on the nightly newscast was becoming a big deal. Men throughout Detroit were paying attention to Westfeldt's broadcast, and Channel 8's ratings were increasing. Reid's DSTV had some competition on its hands.

The image switched from the broadcast's logo to shots of Legoni being escorted through the City Jail in cuffs. Then Westfeld reappeared on-screen, looking directly into the camera, her face grim.

"More on the Legoni trial in a moment. But first, this just in . . ." The reporter stopped for a second to collect her thoughts.

"Governor Mathis is considering a full quarantine on Greater Wayne County, and has alerted the National Guard to activate, in case it becomes necessary to block all access to Detroit and its surrounding suburbs."

A graphic with the words, "Hornet's New Sting?" appeared on the screen to her right.

"The reason?" she continued. "According to unconfirmed reports, the gangster known as The Green Hornet has threatened to unleash what has been dubbed a 'green plague' upon the city."

The screen cut to the Governor's news conference from earlier in the afternoon.

Britt, Casey, and Axford watched as the channel 8 newscast replayed Governor Mathis' statement, and then switched to a live shot in front of City Hall.

Arnold Tasker, News 8's on-scene reporter, usually was stoic in the face of adversity. Tonight, however, as he began to read off a list of alleged plague symptoms, his voice cracked a bit.

"If you or anyone in your household exhibits any of following symptoms, it is imperative that you seek medical attention immediately."

He began the list: dizziness, shortness of breath, blurred vision, light-headedness . . . .

Tasker looked back into the camera and cleared his throat. "Reporting live from the steps of City Hall, I'm Arnold Tasker. Back to the studio."

Britt nodded and Casey turned off the set.

"This is what I'm talking about, Britt!" Axford exploded. Britt knew the look on his face; Mike wanted the plague story.

Reid and Casey listened to Mike explain why he should investigate The Hornet's connection to the illness.

"We've finally got something that we can tie to The Harnet, Britt. He's finally gotten his hands dirty!"

Britt knew better than to give Axford free reign on this one. He needed to divert Mike so that he was free to investigate himself, as The Hornet.

"What do you say, Chief?"

"No, Mike," Britt said, his gray eyes cold.

"No?" Mike couldn't believe his ears. "This is the story of the year. A plague attack in Detroit and a masked gangster is to blame. This will make headlines across the country . . . across the globe!"

"The Legoni trial, Mike. This plague is just a rumor." Britt put his hand on Axford's shoulder, and without squeezing, he gave a strong indication that it would be best not to push the matter. "I need you at the Legoni trial and that's final."

He knew the former police officer wouldn't like it, but then Mike always respected authority. That's what had made him such a good cop.

Mike headed for the office door. Then he turned and said, "Your father would have put me on the Harnet story." The door closed behind him and Britt, normally calm and cool, ran his fingers through his hair in frustration.

"He didn't mean anything by it, Britt," Casey said. She pushed a lock of auburn hair away from her heart-shaped face. "He was just trying to—"

"Press his luck and see if I'd cave," Britt finished. "I've known Mike for years, Casey, and he's right. For him, this would be a big story." Britt sat down behind his desk, his father's the desk. "I've got to keep him away from this plague case so I can investigate it myself."

Casey, ever attentive, brought Britt a glass of ice water. "Any ideas who would do something like this?" she asked. "If it's true, the scale of it sounds like something Dr. Fang—"

"She's dead," Britt said abruptly, then was instantly sorry.

He hadn't gotten used to the new dynamic between him and Casey. She had recently discovered his dual role as The Hornet, during the Dr. Fang affair, and had insisted on helping him wherever she could. He was coming to value her new role as a trusted confidant, but hadn't fully adjusted to it yet.

And he didn't know what he would do if she were ever hurt in the course of assisting him.

Britt took a sip of water and started again, contrite.

"Casey," he said, "it's all rumor and innuendo right now. Someone's trying to frame The Hornet, obviously. But right now there's no proof there even is a green plague."

"What's the next move, then?"

"The Green Hornet will put out some feelers tonight. Then . . . we wait."

When Britt Reid's office phone rang, the *Sentinel* publisher answered immediately. But before he could even utter the first syllable in the word, "Hello," Mike Axford was already talking.

"Two days in and all we've done is finish jury selection. Britt, this plague story is taking over every newspaper in town but the *Sentinel*, and I'm here watching lawyers choose between housewives and butchers!"

"Mike, the Legoni trial is important." Britt was starting to get upset. Inside, he knew that Axford was doing this on purpose. He wondered how his father had dealt with reporters who thought they knew better. "You know the conviction rate of criminals in this city, possibly better than anyone. This plague nonsense—"

"It's not nonsense, Britt!" Mike interrupted. "Two witnesses fell ill and had all the symptoms. Both are at Henry Ford and neither is expected to make it through the night. The green plague is legit!"

Britt started to consider this new information. If he could get close to either of these two witnesses himself, he'd be able to see if Mike's claims were true.

"Stay with the trial, Mike," he said as he hung up. He immediately pressed the button on the intercom. "Miss Case, could you come in please?"

Casey entered the room, and saw the look etched across her friend's face. He was no longer Britt Reid. "Please place a call to District Attorney Scanlon, and put on the scrambler."

She nodded, pulled the scrambler phone from its secreted spot in one of the drawers of Reid's desk, dialed, and handed it to Britt.

"Hello, Frank." Britt didn't have to disguise his voice, as Frank Scanlon was one of three people who knew Britt's alter ego. "There are two witnesses from the Legoni trial convalescing at Henry Ford Hospital, supposedly suffering from the so-called green plague. I would like to talk to them."

On the other end, Scanlon gave Britt their names and room numbers. After thanking the District Attorney, Britt turned to Casey. "Please have my car brought car around, Miss Case. I'll be working from home the rest of the afternoon."

It was time for The Green Hornet to get involved.

The Black Beauty was perfection on wheels, the product of Detroit engineering . . . and Britt and Kato's constant tinkering.

While it appeared to be a normal Chrysler Imperial Crown on the outside, it performed like a tank, a weapon that once pointed could eliminate anything in its way.

When the car hit the streets, it did so with a fury that could only be described as primal. But as the heroes drove around the city, they noticed something odd. It wasn't uncommon for the citizens of Detroit to run in fear from The Hornet, but normally, the criminal element would view any incursion of those polarized green lights as a trespass on their territory and would respond in kind. Once, a rival gang had opened fire without provocation on the Black Beauty, prompting swift retaliation from the two masked men.

Tonight, however, the streets were clear. Everyone, even criminal rivals, was afraid to catch The Hornet's plague.

After parking the Black Beauty in a dark alley, the two crimefighters scrambled up a shadowed fire escape and through a hospital window, unobserved, entering the quarantined room occupied by the two ailing witnesses. Kato scanned the room, careful not to make a sound as there were armed guards on the other side of the door.

The Green Hornet looked over the patients' charts, but nothing indicated a plague, a disease, or even the flu.

"Unless I miss my guess, these two were poisoned," he said, using sign language.

Kato's replied, also signing, "But if they were poisoned, then there is no airborne plague."

"That's my operative theory, Kato," The Hornet signed back. "Someone poisoned these two, but who? And why?"

As if on cue, one of the witnesses fell into cardiac arrest, and an alarm went off. The Hornet flicked something on the floor, and the two vigilantes hurdled through the window and scurried back down the fire escape.

Once inside the Black Beauty, Kato turned to The Hornet and said, "I saw you toss that Hornet seal down on purpose. Why?"

"Kato," The Hornet said, "despite the fact that we're obviously not to blame for what's going on, maybe it's best the public actually believes there is a green plague and that I'm responsible."

As Kato started the car, The Hornet added, "It may help us flush out who poisoned those two witnesses."

Kato began to drive and asked, "Where to?"

The Hornet had no chance to answer. Headlights shone directly into the Beauty. A police cruiser now blocked their egress.

Two cops got out, shielded by their car doors, revolvers trained on the Black Beauty. "Kato, we can't be caught. Evasive maneuvers."

Kato revved the Beauty's engine. He flipped a switch and a nozzle emerged from the front grill of the car. With the flip of another switch, knock-out gas spewed forth. The effects were immediate, and the patrolmen fell unconscious as another prowl car arrived.

The second two cops wasted no time firing their weapons on the Beauty, testing the bullet-resistant frame and glass. Kato hit the gas, spinning the tires, and immediately shifted into reverse.

The Beauty thrust into the street behind it, and with Kato's quick spin of the wheel, the vehicle turned ninety degrees. The car shot forward, and Kato flipped a third switch. Oil sprayed out from the Beauty's bumper and the second pair of patrolmen, in pursuit of the masked men, immediately succumbed to the slick pavement.

Kato cracked the slight smile of an adrenaline junkie. He looked into the rearview mirror and said, "That was close!" He didn't have a death wish, but he did love to test what the Black Beauty could do.

The Hornet smiled in return. "Home, Kato."

Mike Axford was in the *Sentinel* offices early, before any other staff, typing up his report of the prior day's events at the trial.

Britt Reid was used to this; Mike was a cop earlier in his life, a good cop, and some habits died hard. The reporter noticed his boss, grumbled something under his breath, and went back to typing.

Britt, an excellent reader of body language, knew that Mike still resented being assigned to the trial, and hoped he wouldn't hold a grudge.

He leaned on the corner of Mike's desk and said, "So . . . you might have a point about the plague."

Mike immediately looked up with an "I told you so" smile.

"Those two Legoni witnesses died last night, in the hospital," Britt continued. "If The Green Hornet killed them, then there obviously must be a connection, right Mike?"

Axford was about to say, "Right," but he stopped.

"No," he said, questioning it himself. "Legoni and The Hornet were rivals. Why would The Hornet kill two witnesses for Legoni?"

Britt could tell that Mike was starting to see things from a different angle. The reporter looked at his typewriter, thought for a moment, and looked back up at Reid. "You know, the day before those two dead witnesses got really sick and were hospitalized, all the witnesses reported feeling a little queasy after lunch."

"They all took lunch together?"

"Yes, Scanlon's investigator was keeping them all sequestered, even during lunchtime. Food was ordered in."

"And they all felt unwell?" Britt pressed.

"Yes, but only those two—the two who died—felt sick enough to ask for a doctor," Mike replied. "Fortunately there was one there in the courthouse, on other business, and he volunteered to treat them there so as not to delay the trial."

"Except," Britt replied, "they got even sicker and ended up in the hospital. And then they died . . . supposedly of the 'green plague,' at the hands of The Green Hornet."

Mike looked at Britt, and this time, the "I told you so" smile was replaced with a "How'd you know" look.

"I was reporting on the green plague this entire—"

"Mike," Britt interrupted, "get down to the courthouse right away. We might have had a break in this story!"

"Yeah, yeah, right away," Axford said as he grabbed his coat.

Britt handed Axford his notebook and pen and said, "You call me if anyone else falls ill. If Legoni kills off enough witnesses, Scanlon will have no case."

After Mike Axford rushed out the *Daily Sentinel* office, Britt flipped through Mike's notes. There, he found the name he was looking for, the name of the doctor who had treated the nauseous witnesses.

Things were coming to a head.

Nighttime.

Dr. Rand Falwell was sitting behind his desk; a small banker's lamp threw a yellow cone of light across the side of his face.

A face that reflected shock and alarm when The Green Hornet and Kato kicked in his office door.

The doctor instinctively tried to run, but Kato stopped his progress with a swift karate chop to the sternum that sent him backwards. As the doctor crashed down, The Hornet placed a small recording device under the doctor's desk and activated it.

Falwell stood up slowly, trying to catch his breath.

"Do you know who I am?" The Hornet asked.

"You're . . . you're The G-Green Hornet," the doctor stammered.

"There's something you need to know about me, Dr. Falwell. I don't kill my enemies." The Hornet walked around Falwell's desk, to get closer to the physician. "The reason why is . . . I don't have to."

The Hornet continued, "I find that intimidation, fear, and the promise of swift retaliation are motivation enough without having to resort to murder."

Falwell was overweight and sweating. His heart raced and his hands shook.

"I believe," The Hornet said, "that a defeated man can say so much more alive than dead." The Green Hornet looked to Kato and nodded. Kato reached out and grabbed the fat doctor, lifting him to his feet with almost supernatural strength. "But I promise you that if you do not tell me who put you up to this, my partner here, who does not have the same ethical code that I do, will kill you."

It was an empty threat, but Falwell didn't know that. He hyperventilated a bit, then caught his breath. "Legoni! Donny Legoni set this up!"

"Why? How? I want answers, Dr. Falwell."

"He . . . I can't tell you. He'll kill me!"

Kato tightened his grip on Falwell's lapel, and the doctor relented. "He wanted a failsafe, a plan so that if and when he got caught, he'd have an out."

"He ordered the hit on those witnesses?" The Hornet asked.

"Yes," the doctor said. "I was the Legoni family doctor and I owed them . . . too much."

Kato loosened his grip and Falwell walked over to his desk. He opened the top drawer, pulled out an envelope, and tossed it on the desktop. "They blackmailed me. I didn't want my wife to find out."

"But why spread the rumor that I was responsible?" The Green Hornet asked angrily. "I could come down on you and Legoni harder than the police."

"If the public believed it was you," Falwell said, "then they'd spend all their time trying to bring you in, leaving Legs—"

"—free to wreak havoc on the trial, with witnesses dying off from the 'plague.' Everyone would be looking for me, not the real culprit."

"Exact—" The doctor's words were cut short as he was shot in the side. The Hornet and Kato turned quickly to find Louis Legoni, Donny's cousin, holding a smoking gun. Behind him stood six of Legoni's men.

"And now that the doc is plugged, we'll just ice the two of you and let the fuzz clean up the corpses."

Before Louis could blink, Kato whipped two darts into his hand. Louis dropped the gun and it discharged, bullets striking the ceiling.

Quickly, the gangsters entered the room to engage the two masked vigilantes in hand-to-hand combat. The odds were seven to two—heavily in their favor, as The Hornet took two of them out himself with a one-two combination, both knockout blows.

Meanwhile, Kato silently engaged three of the thugs and made it look easy. He fought each man simultaneously, timed strikes and blocks making the quick fight look like it was moving in slow motion. Each punch was met with a block, a parry, and an even stronger strike by the Asian bodyguard.

Before long, all three men were down and just one of Legoni's men was left. Kato, with the speed of a hummingbird's wings, struck a swift Wing Chun chop to the throat and knocked him breathless.

At the same time, The Hornet raced to catch Louis Legoni, who saw the odds dwindling and rushed from the room. They crashed into a makeshift lab in the next room, thousands of clear plastic capsules spilling to the floor as The Hornet tackled Legoni. Taking a dominant stance, The Hornet pinned the bigger man down and rained fist after fist upon the criminal's face and head. One final hammer-punch put the mobster out for good, just as Kato entered the room.

"The doctor will be all right, Boss, I stopped the bleeding."

"And the evidence?"

Kato held up the small recording device.

"Let's get that to the District Attorney right away."

As the police and emergency medical personnel entered the office, they found seven gangsters, all unconscious, and Dr. Falwell, holding a bandage to his side. The Green Hornet and Kato, however, where nowhere to be found.

"Falwell's official statement was that he spread the false plague rumors to the media and administered the poison that killed the two witnesses; he made the poison up to look like real medicine in the lab in his own office. Falwell's pre-trial hearing is scheduled for next month."

Mike, sitting in Reid's office, closed the morning edition of the *Daily Sentinel* and looked at his boss. "Well, I hate to say it, Britt, but you were right. The Legoni trial was the more important story."

"Mike, I never had any doubt that you could and would get to the truth." Britt reached out across his desk to shake Axford's hand. "You're a great reporter, Mike. I'm glad we could work out our differences."

Mike nodded, awkwardly. "Well, gotta run! Gotta find the next scoop!" He grabbed his hat and coat, opened the door, then turned and said, "Still, I feel like I was so close to getting The Harnet this time."

He exited as Casey entered, closing the door behind her. She set a cup of coffee on the desk and looked at Britt archly.

With a sly smile, she said, "Closer than you think, Mike."

THE GRAY LINE BETWEEN

by F.J. DeSanto, Michael Uslan and Joe Gentile

Looking through the fresh cracks in the window, Britt Reid stood stunned, lost for a single cohesive thought. Of their own accord, his eyes systematically glanced back and forth over his beloved city of Detroit. The harsh daylight exposed it for what it was . . . broken, disassembled like a discarded jigsaw puzzle.

Small mobs of people scurried from one storefront to another, smashing windows with crowbars and fearlessly taking whatever they wanted, and with a righteous verve. Vehicles were overturned by angry throngs looking for any kind of release that presented itself.

Fires were scattered throughout Britt's view, casting an eerie post-apocalyptic pall over the jagged landscape. From the safety of this office, uncomfortably warm since power had long since vanished with the destruction of a local power station, he stood transfixed.

Trancelike, his mind barely recognized the chaos as reality, for it was twisting and turning, surreal . . . a bad movie, or a nightmare from which he couldn't wake up.

"There's no way to win," he acknowledged privately. At least he thought it was a private musing.

"Did you say something, Mr. Reid?" a voice asked from behind him. Britt turned around to find a man standing in the doorway. His face was obscured by the short-brimmed fedora so popular just before men's hats fell fully out of fashion amid the recent British invasion of "mod" styles.

"Just thinking out loud, sir," Britt said, as the man motioned for Britt to take a seat. "Thank you for seeing me, Doctor."

"Of course, Mr. Reid, I know you've been under a lot of stress. I've long followed your editorials and the policies you set for *Daily Sentinel*. I know you strive to be honest and fair to all Americans, despite your city, and our country, being torn apart by prejudice and misunderstanding. You have helped the cause. Now, how can I help you?"

Britt's took a deep breath, and seemed to deflate, as he looked down at the ground.

"You are troubled, Mr. Reid?" the Doctor asked.

Without looking up, and with a low voice that seemed to come from somewhere else, Britt said: "Doctor, there's something I need to share with you. I need to trust you, and I'm about to bet my life that I *can* trust you. Everything that's happened down there to this once proud city is . . . I just wanted to make a difference. But I may just be part of the problem."

"Part of the problem? Mr. Reid, I'm afraid I don't follow."

"I know this will sound crazy, Doctor, but I need you to understand. That's why you have to know the truth. I *am* responsible for this. I'm not just the publisher of *Sentinel*. I'm also The Green Hornet!"

Days Earlier

At the back table of Stryker's Hideaway on Treadwell Avenue in downtown Detroit, District Attorney Frank Scanlon checked his Timex. He was the type of bureaucrat who took pride that his watch kept precise time and only cost $9.95. He was also the impatient type . . . anxious, a perfectionist, all qualities that won him the D.A. job over others who were more politically connected.

Suddenly, all heads turned as the high-profile publisher of one of the two most powerful newspapers in the city entered the dimly-lit restaurant with an air of quiet confidence. His chiseled good looks and tailored Italian suit signaled to the upper crust diners that Britt Reid was a rising star in Detroit society's firmament. Ushered to Scanlon's table by a pretty young hostess, with blonde hair and a curvy figure, Reid turned his charm up a notch.

"Thank you, Candy, I would have never found the D.A. without you. And you DO know what 'D.A.' really stands for, don't you?" Smiling, Britt whispered something into her ear. Scanlon's smile turned to a scowl while the hostess' eyes opened wide as she slipped the confirmed bachelor her number in a not-so-subtle fashion.

"Sit down . . . Mr. *Hefner*, is it?" joked an exasperated Scanlon. Britt's demeanor quickly changed from light-hearted to dead serious. Britt was puzzled. "This lunch 'date' with Britt Reid is unusual, even for you, Frank. What's going on?" asked the publisher.

The D.A. grabbed a thick file from his oversized legal briefcase and slid it across the table. "I need your help," Scanlon said.

Curious, Britt opened the file. "I've spent months trying to gather this," Scanlon stated. Britt was amazed to see evidence of the existence of a speakeasy on the west side of Detroit.

"12th Street," Scanlon said. "If we start here, we can take every one of these illegal booze joints down. Plus there seems to be a connection to something even more dire, as you can see."

Britt studied the documents and leaned in for "The $64,000 Question." "You need our mutual 'friend' to get involved here? That explains the free lunch," he wise-cracked.

"No, no," Scanlon replied. "We're going to do this straight. I need the *Daily Sentinel* publisher to expose these bastards so the police can shut them down. No matter how popular they are with the locals, they're illegal under the ordinances of Detroit. And when word gets out, perhaps we can flush out the real truth behind some of this damn street lunacy, as many of these outbreaks occur very near to these places."

Britt closed the file and put it in his briefcase. "Well, my friend, while this sort of strategy didn't work very well for Eliot Ness in Chicago in the '20s, it's your shot to call. I'm here to serve my city, and you have my attention with that behind-the-curtain stuff. I'll run this on page one of *Sentinel*. And I'll even ask our buzzworthy friend to back you up . . . just in case."

Scanlon smiled and firmly shook Britt's hand. He quickly stood up, gathered the files back into his briefcase and bid his much needed ally adieu.

"Hey! Where you going?" Reid asked. "You invited me to lunch!"

"Lunch? I have work to do! Who the hell has time for lunch?"

As Scanlon made his exit, the hostess came rushing over nervously.

"Is everything all right, Mr. Reid?"

With a sincere look copied directly from Rock Hudson when he starred with Doris Day in *Lover Come Back*, Britt pulled Candy down next to him, informing her that he'd been left to dine alone, and that no three-star restaurant hostess would allow this atrocity to happen to a patron. He was very, very clear it would mean the world to him if she joined him now for lunch. When he swore he'd make it right with her boss, Candy's thin shell melted like the inside of an M&M on a hot summer day in Detroit.

The *Daily Sentinel* headline screamed:

SPEAKEASY EXPOSED!

Britt Reid's perception of right and wrong, justice and injustice, were resolute, but not as black and white as his newspaper was. That club was against the law and had to be shut down. Scanlon's evidence was compelling and irrefutable, but it was really the other part of Scanlon's investigation that intrigued him, and about which he felt a strong sense of urgency. It was all about corruption, and it was not going to stop. The police were taking the lead in the operation and The Green Hornet would wait in the wings to back-stop them in case anything went wrong. But what could possibly go wrong in such a routine police action?

Everything.

Detroit . . . and the country itself, was about to change, profoundly and permanently.

It was time to roll. The Black Beauty, a huge advancement to the concept turbocharged car Reid had first seen demonstrated at the New York World's Fair back in '64, was equipped for anything. Hopping in, The Green Hornet and Kato raced into the night, prepared to support the police in tonight's inner city action, and hoping to be of use in uncovering something much deeper.

The police, while busting the speakeasy, underestimated the dissatisfaction of the people in the neighborhood. Detroit was a city sitting on a powder keg of emotions . . . emotions of people who felt they were trapped in their lives with no chance to escape because of their color and class. With one simple bust, the police broke the people's spirit, not comprehending that they were ready to fight back. The citizens felt oppressed . . . disrespected . . . angry. Sitting in The Black Beauty, a stunned Green Hornet and Kato watched everything rage out of the control of the police. Riots now erupted on the streets of Detroit. Agitated crowds began looting. Fires flared everywhere. Hatred based on race, economy, and the feeling of being backed into a corner boiled-over from block to block. Collectively, this was a force greater than anything The Green Hornet could ever have imagined.

Shocked by the sheer intensity of the mobs, by the warlike level of fighting erupting from every street corner on this steamy summer night, The Green Hornet, for the first time in his career, questioned his supporting role in this terrifying crisis. The rules had changed and, like America, he was paralyzed.

He could see Kato's agitated frustration of inaction. "Kato, if we enter the fray, we'll only make this situation worse."

Kato turned around to face The Hornet. "At first, I was ready to stop these rioters by whatever means it took. My perception was they were tearing apart the country they were privileged to live in. But sitting here, watching this all unfold, witnessing people being brutalized by the authorities who hide from reprisals behind their badges, I feel the need defend these people."

"Kato, there is more than meets the eye happening here . . . you can't just go out there," said The Hornet.

"I'm a man of peace," Kato replied. I was raised in a culture of order over chaos. Order cannot be restored by oppression and the splitting of skulls. I, too, am a minority in this great country. If it is to remain great, I must go to these people and help them find peaceful ways to prevail in their struggle. This is no longer about crime and punishment. It is about civil rights and equality."

"How are we to help here? There's no peaceful way to do anything right now, and us adding even more violence is like pouring gasoline to a fire."

Kato got out of the Black Beauty, and looked his partner in the eye, and softly said: "I don't know the answer . . . but I can't do nothing."

Knowing he couldn't leave Kato alone out there, The Hornet reluctantly exited the car. It didn't take more than ten seconds, and they found themselves surrounded by what looked to be ordinary folks. But these people all had the look of mob-mentality in their eyes, and they both knew this was going to be a big problem, because they were considered by the public to be rich gangsters. And "the rich" were not welcome.

It was too late to get back into the Black Beauty, as both of them were swarmed over by the mass of humanity screaming for their blood. Baseball bats were in vogue and used to pummel, releasing the pent up rage that people held so dear. The Hornet and Kato faced the problem of trying to defend themselves while not hurting anyone.

The two friends stood back to back, shouting at the top of their lungs to be heard over the crowd, trying to install calm, but the yelling fell on deaf ears. They held their arms up trying to ward off the blows, but there were just too many, and flesh gave way to hard wood. The Hornet fell to the pavement, on his knees.

In between a forest of legs, he could see the sanctuary of the Black Beauty just feet away, but to get there, he would have to really hurt some people. His hat fell to the ground and got trampled into a thin mat. He spit out blood and his vision blurred, as the street came up to greet him. He did the only thing he could do. He reached into his coat pocket for the small remote control of the Black Beauty. Trying to squint to clearer sight, he pressed what he hoped was the right button.

A huge blast sent debris and dust everywhere, as rockets launched from the black car into a nearby empty building. Since most of the crowd was surprised by the blast, there was a moment of opportunity to move. The Green Hornet was up and limping quickly to get into the Black Beauty's front seat.

He waited, expecting Kato to be there as well. Kato did not show. Worry took over The Hornet, and adrenalin kicked in, which cleared up his vision. He saw his friend. Kato was about twenty yards away, lying on the ground, battered and bruised, amidst a throng of rioters who were still shell shocked from the rockets.

The Hornet slammed the Beauty into gear and stomped on the accelerator. The car leaped the curb, traveling the distance to Kato in a split second. Seeing the big black behemoth hurtling towards them, the crowd split like the Red Sea.

Drawing his Hornet gun, The Green Hornet jumped from the car as it screeched and lurched to a stop. He sprayed the throng, turning in a circle, and bodies hit the ground. Those that were far enough away from the gas to not be affected, fearfully did not move to stop him.

He knelt down by his friend, and upon seeing Kato's eyes closed, emotion got the better of him. "What is wrong with you people? How is this helping anything? We weren't here to hurt anyone."

"Right . . . The G-Green Hornet coming in peace to help us poor r-regular folk . . ." came a soft voice from nearby.

The Hornet turned with a sneer towards the voice.

"What is your problem?"

Then he saw the boy behind the voice. A young kid, couldn't be more than thirteen . . . looking wide-eyed at The Hornet, scared motionless.

He knew the boy was right. How was anyone to know that they were actually trying to help? No one knew the truth of their charade, which seemed right then to be not one of his best ideas. His eyes calmed and his own voice softened.

"I'm sorry. I won't hurt you. I know this all seems confusing, but we did come to help. Would you help me with my friend? He is badly hurt." He put his hand out palm up to the frightened boy.

The boy looked down at all of the people affected by the gas, and then looked up at The Hornet shaking.

"They're just asleep, son, I promise you. Please help me."

"Okay."

Between the two of them, they managed to get Kato into the passenger side of the Beauty.

The Hornet crouched down to talk to the boy face to face.

"Where do you live?"

"Just down the street."

"Get home now, son, and stay safe."

Before he was even done speaking the boy was running.

The Hornet looked around at the gassed crowd, and some faces registered with him. He knew some of these men. But, his brain was not processing as usual, so it wasn't all sinking in yet.

Inside the Beauty, The Hornet drove like a man possessed, as he knew he had to get Kato some medical attention as soon as possible.

Punching a button on the console, The Hornet said through gritted teeth: "Casey?"

"Britt?"

"Casey, get that doctor friend of yours to meet us at my place, and make it quick!"

"Britt, what happened?"

"Casey, there's no time, just do it now!"

Looking down at Kato, he couldn't help but think it was his fault for getting his friend involved in his madness to begin with.

"Hold on, Hayashi, we're almost there. Stay with me."

As Britt Reid, he put Kato in the hands of the good doctor and Casey, and he was told that they wouldn't know anything more about his friend's condition for a couple hours. Although he was aching all over, he felt that he had to do something; he couldn't just sit around. Refusing Casey's strong suggestion to stay put, he took off in the Black Beauty.

He drove around the city like a bat out of hell. When he saw a mob up to no good, he drove right for them, scattering them like leaves in a storm. It didn't matter if the group was citizens, police, or criminals. . . . The line between was nothing but gray. After they moved out of the way, he would lay down a blanket of gas from his Hornet gun.

"Any word?" he hoarsely asked after pressing the button on the console.

"Nothing yet, but Britt, please . . . please come home."

There was no real logic to his actions, for sometimes he would just gas a street corner of people while passing by, and sometimes he would rev the Beauty at them, or drive onto the sidewalk if he thought that would do anything. It was all on instinct now. When all of his gas supply was gone, he suddenly felt the effects of the day, and his body screamed at him.

"Britt . . . Kato—" Casey came through the radio.

The Hornet gunned the motor, and the Beauty launched homeward like a missile. He didn't hear anything else Casey said.

At Kato's bedside, the bedraggled Britt grabbed his friend's hand in both of his. Casey was by his side, looking at both men with concern. The doctor had long since left.

"Hayashi."

Kato opened his eyes and a small smile appeared on his lips. "Mister Britt, you look like I feel."

Britt smiled, and Miss Case let out a little gasp of relief.

"You should see the other guy," Britt said.

"I am sorry to have left the car."

"You just are a caring man, my friend."

"It looks like you saved my life . . . again. Thank you."

"No one's keeping count. Rest up, and then we'll talk." Kato closed his eyes again, and Casey hugged Britt, and half of him wanted to never let her go.

The next day, Britt returned to his office to find his loyal assistant, the savvy and stunning Lenore Case, watching the riots unfold on national television. Detroit was burning on prime-time in millions of homes across the country. He was concerned for Casey's safety and told her to remain in the Sentinel Building until the rioting was quelled.

"This is wrong, Britt. The rioting puts innocent people in terrible jeopardy and will economically and socially destroy Detroit for generations to come. "Anything your . . . *friend* can do?"

"I honestly don't know yet." Britt said. Casey stood in surprised silence. She had not heard him like this before. But her reverie was interrupted when dozens of FBI agents flooded the *Sentinel* offices.

"What the hell?" Reid said.

Moving like a running back shouldering through a line of defenders, Britt got to the front of the line of agents, with his eyes ablaze.

"What do you think you're doing?"

"The FBI is commandeering your offices; seems pretty cut and dried. Here is the official paperwork. You will step aside." The lead agent, in a suit and tie with a crew cut, handed a pack of paper to Britt. Britt handed the papers to Mike Axford, who was standing almost on top of him with his mouth open.

"The hell I will," Britt exclaimed, grabbing the agent's shoulder; all eyes of which of the *Daily Sentinel* staff were on him and he agent.

"Mister, if you don't remove that hand, you will be lead out of here in handcuffs, or worse."

The other agents had spread from the conference room, and had not only taken over half the newsroom, but had commandeered the majority of the *Daily Sentinel*'s phone lines. Reporters longer could access their typewriters. Reams of carbon paper were seized by the agents, who furiously ground out files and dossiers on what seemed to be half the city's citizens. Purple spirit masters churned through hand-cranked mimeograph machines, spewing wanted posters for every rioter whose photo the Bureau was able to snap amid the chaos in the streets.

"Britt, these bureaucratic yes-men will not only take over our phones and equipment, preventing us from getting the news out when the city needs it the most, but they're also clearly intent on stopping the dissemination of information altogether!" Mike Axford yelled, purposefully loud enough for every agent usurping the newsroom to hear. "This isn't a matter of us getting our work done. It's a matter of dire public safety!"

Ed Lowery and Gunnigan stood by their boss and Axford, showing solidarity.

"What is the hold up here?" asked a very calm voice that hid something quite opposite underneath.

"Mister Reid, is it?" J. Edgar Hoover flatly smiled as he entered the room, and with that, only the hard breathing of the *Daily Sentinel* staff could be heard. Hoover's presence took over the room. "I would suggest you return to a calm state, and I am sure you will see the right thing . . . the *patriotic* thing, to do."

To Britt, it seemed that the man enjoyed that power a bit too much.

"Mister Hoover, I need my office back now . . . as well as my newsroom, my conference room, my phones and my equipment. We've got an important job to do and a responsibility to our city."

"Do you now?"

"Yes, and I need your men cleared out."

"I'm sorry, Mr. Reid," responded Hoover with serpentine calm, the sort that comes just before the paralyzing strike, "but that simply will not be convenient for us."

"I'm also sorry, Mr. Hoover," Reid replied between gritted teeth, "but

I am the owner of this building and this still America; you cannot just take over. I believe that sort of thing went out some time ago, around the time freedom of the press was established."

Hoover slowly stood up and pointed his index finger at Britt. "I have always suspected you for a liberal fop."

Britt moved close to Hoover, now completely calm, and leaned down. He looked him right in the eye, inches away, and whispered. "You must have me confused with someone who cares what you think. You have chosen the wrong guy to play this on. You need better Intel. You're done here. Get out."

Hoover was speechless, but it didn't take more than a second for him to recover. "Well, Mr. Reid, have it your way, for now. And may I add you are not even a shadow of the man your father was. John Henry Reid always saw his duty to his country clearly. But, yes, this is, indeed, America. And, indeed, you have every right to order me off your premises. But I have rights, too, Mr. Reid. The right to have the IRS investigate you . . . the right to have selected policemen follow you everywhere you drive, or even walk, so that for your own safety, they can pull you over for any and all perceived problems or violations . . . the right to have public safety officials inspect these offices daily with a fine toothed comb, also for your protection, in case they see any and all perceived safety problems or violations," hissed Hoover.

Reid smiled. With arms folded, his eyes just bore through Hoover like a drill. "Your time is coming to an end."

Hoover marched out of the office and ordered his men to close up shop.

Moments later, the office erupted in joyous shrieks, pats on the back, and pride in their boss. Britt was in no mood to celebrate.

This whole mess had just gotten messier.

While in the quiet cockpit of the Black Beauty, The Hornet began to put the puzzle pieces together.

He recognized known mobsters, not rampaging rioters, shooting police. These men were inciting the police action.

He also recognized known mob henchmen disguised as policemen, beating rioters to a pulp just to agitate the enflamed people in the streets. The Detroit mob was capitalizing on this chaotic opportunity to take out their rivals and claim new territories. Or worse, to take over the city itself.

Knowing now that there was a larger plan afoot, The Hornet hopped back in The Black Beauty and, before speeding off, called the D.A.

"Frank, your fears are justified. The riots are being encouraged and choreographed. Get your most trusted to the heart of the city. We need to make sure our rescue workers are protected."

Immediately thereafter, Reid not only unleashed Mike Axford and the newspaper staff with information about the disguised mobsters, but also ordered Casey to put his television station on live twenty-four hour coverage of unfolding events in Motown.

Meanwhile, Scanlon and the mayor were coordinating fire control and the protection of all firemen and policemen combing the inner city, in service to the people and property of Detroit.

They had reached out for help from every power-broker in the city: United Auto Workers President Walter Reuther; the heads of the "Big Three" automakers; and even Motown's own Berry Gordy, Jr.

When Reid arrived at City Hall, Scanlon excused himself from the makeshift command center and they adjourned to a private chamber.

"Britt," said Scanlon, "I just received a call from J. Edgar Hoover, himself. He said if we don't send in a massive anti-riot police force and the National Guard, there'll be copycat riots everywhere from Watts to Harlem, from Newark and Asbury Park, New Jersey to Miami . . . all as seen on God-damned TV!" The D.A., like other city officials, had never been so challenged in his life.

"Frank, you can't place all your bets on Hoover and the way he perceives reality," Reid advised, fresh from his own run-in with Hoover. "His actions are colored by his old school way of thinking. I don't think he's color-blind. Our world today clearly is no longer simply good versus evil, black or white. Our world is gray. And we need to solve some horrific problems instead of breaking heads. So let's get to it. And the first big problem for you and me is the mob."

Scanlon was as equally prepared as Reid for the daunting task at hand. "Based on your . . . uh . . . The Green Hornet's observations, we now know we're dealing with dozens of fake cops who've been committing many of the atrocities, fueling the flames of hatred amid the rioting. We need to get them off the street pronto."

"That's one part of the problem, certainly," Britt replied.

Scanlon sighed and he removed his heavy black-framed glasses, rubbing the reddened indents on the bridge of his nose, then spoke again:

"Unquestionably, we have a long-term mission here, same as all of society around us. It may well take generations to change things, for society to evolve, but today all we can do is identify those impersonating officers and outside agitators who are using the riots as a cover for murder."

"Agreed, Frank. And it's also time for The Green Hornet to ride," Reid said.

"Britt," Scanlon added, "your father would be very, very proud of you."

Reid choked up with unexpected emotion. "Thanks, Frank. You have no idea how much that means to me today."

That night, from out of the darkness, came the thundering engine roar of the great car, the Black Beauty, and The Green Hornet rode again. Along with the faithful Kato, the daring and resourceful masked rider of the urban terrain again led the fight for law and order in Detroit. Nowhere in the pages of that city's history could one find a greater champion of justice.

Almost immediately, The Hornet and Kato were in the thick of the action. Armed with extra gas cartridges, the sting of The Green Hornet was able to put the guilty to sleep, cart them off, and dump them near the police's temporary mobile detention units. What The Hornet's gas gun was unable to do, Kato's fists of fury and knowledge of the body's pressure points did. The unconscious bodies of carefully identified felons piled up across the still smoldering city streets. But the tide had turned. The worst would soon be over . . . for everyone but The Green Hornet.

Some inner city dwellers heralded The Hornet as hero when they spied him taking down one bad cop after another. But when they saw him immobilizing people they didn't know were mob-controlled outside agitators, they harassed and hounded The Hornet and attempted reprisals.

Guilt-ridden for the role he may have played in inciting the riots, Britt Reid changed tactics and The Green Hornet moved his war against crime directly against the Detroit mob itself, and its godfather, Joseph Zerilli.

Calling on all the sources of the *Daily Sentinel*'s crime reporters, Britt identified the current locations of many of Detroit's ranking mobsmen and capos. One by one, they were accosted in their safest havens and threatened by a masked man in green they had always assumed to be the head of some rival gang, seeking control of the city rackets.

He was out for justice, not out for himself. He believed in the power of the human spirit, not in the power of the buck or the bullet. In the end, The

Green Hornet was red, white, and blue, and the Mafia was forced to play by a whole new set of rules—The Green Hornet's rules.

Today

"That's my story, Doctor, and the reason I asked you here today," Britt Reid confessed as he sank further into the once plush chair. "The Green Hornet was created to fight crime from within, by being disguised as a criminal. I just don't know if what I'm doing is, well, what I should be doing."

"Mr. Reid," the Doctor responded, "you are, by definition, one of the unsung heroes of this tortuous story. One man alone is not the root cause of centuries of slavery, oppression, repression, bigotry and hatred. We are at one more of the countless turning points where the actions or inactions of each individual, each unique human being created in God's image, can allow us to rise above our circumstances and not be subjugated by them. By choosing the path of non-violence, like Jesus, Moses and Mohammed, like Gandhi and Buddha, like your own great-uncle, you will be one instrument in the effectuation of change in America."

"But, Doctor," Britt countered, "I don't know how to—"

"Stop right there," the Doctor cautioned. "Not 'I' . . . but rather, 'We.' *We* will work together to take care of the issues of humanity and human rights that underlie the events of our history. If Detroit is ever to heal ... if America is ever to heal . . . every American will have to find a Green Hornet inside him or herself. You just keep fighting the good fight, for that's all that can be asked of anyone, no matter how it's disguised."

With these honest and impactful words of encouragement, the Doctor stood up to tend to the work at hand. A visibly moved and appreciative Britt clasped the Doctor's hand in both his own hands. "Thank you for the help and for the much needed inspiration. If there was one person on earth with whom I could honestly share my secret and my burden of being The Green Hornet, it clearly was you, Dr. King. God bless you, sir."

"And God bless you, Mr. Reid, and this once great city that one day will rise up and be great again."

UP IN SMOKE

by Deborah Chester

It was Britt Reid's birthday. A select gathering of friends, business acquaintances, and employees from his newspaper and television station filled his home. A quartet played soft music in the background. Waiters with trays of champagne and canapés circulated through the crowd. Reid, suave and broad-shouldered in his dark tux, stood smiling near the fireplace, accepting congratulations. Two beautiful young women stood next to him.

His valet Kato, attired in a correct white jacket, came up with a wrapped gift and handed it to Reid with a slight bow. "This was just delivered, Mister Reid."

"Oh?" Taking the box, Reid glanced past Kato's shoulder toward the door. "A guest didn't bring it?"

"No. The messenger said you were to open it immediately." Kato's dark eyes met Reid's. "I took the liberty of scanning it for anything unpleasant," he whispered.

Reid understood his meaning. This week had seen the launch of his newspaper's most recent crusade against organized crime. Bombs and other nasty surprises were always a potential form of retaliation.

Curious, he hefted the package. It was surprisingly light for its size and wrapped in gold foil. His name was written across it in ornate letters, but there was no card.

"Open it!" cried Jessica on his left.

"Hurry!" said Linda on his right.

Pulling away the paper, he smelled the full-bodied aroma of fine tobacco even before he saw the distinctive artwork on the wooden lid. The box held Cuban cigars— thick, long, expensive ones. Very illegal ones. Since President Kennedy had slammed the embargo on Castro's country in 1960, choice, hand-rolled cigars like these weren't supposed to cross the U.S. borders. Frowning, Reid shut the lid swiftly and looked up to see Frank Scanlon watching him through a pair of thick-framed glasses.

The District Attorney beckoned. Excusing himself, Reid led Scanlon into his book-lined study and shut the door on the babble of voices and music.

"Cuban cigars?" Scanlon asked, frowning at the box still in Reid's hand.

Reid put it down on a table. "Anonymous gift."

Scanlon opened the lid. "Quite a generous one. These are Partagás. Among the best."

Reid shrugged. He was no connoisseur, but his father had kept H. Upmanns on hand. There were a few still preserved in the humidor simply because they were now so rare and hard to get. An entire box of these large Partagás was very generous indeed, but Reid was leery of expensive, anonymous, and illegal gifts.

"I got a box just like them yesterday," Scanlon said. "So did the mayor. So did the chief of police."

That caught Reid's interest. "Bribes? From whom?"

"That, we don't know. Customs is keeping a tight watch on the lake for smugglers, but there've been no arrests."

Reid nodded. *Habanos* were legal in Canada, which had no trade embargo on Cuba. With Detroit located on Lake St. Claire right across from the Ontario border, smuggling was always a possibility. He thought of the elderly men quietly smoking in the cigar room at his club. There'd never been any question that there was a certain amount of small-scale black marketeering going on, but this kind of overt bribe seemed unnecessarily bold.

"It's not a bribe," Reid guessed. "It's a message."

"Meaning what?" Scanlon asked. "I can't think of anyone in the local mafia that would make a gesture like this. And to what purpose? With the *Sentinel* stepping up pressure, I think they'd be more inclined to retaliate than send gifts."

"Maybe that's it," Reid said. "Maybe someone new is moving in."

Scanlon sent him a sharp look. "Maybe. Some Canadian thug named Duluth stirred up a little trouble last month, but after the welcome we gave him, he decided to stick to the north side of the border. I haven't heard of anyone else."

"I've been keeping my eye on the Brazzi operation lately."

"The beer distributors? Come on! They've been importing Canadian beer legally for thirty years."

Reid shrugged. "Nick Brazzi died a few weeks ago."

"Killed, wasn't he?" Scanlon took off his glasses and polished them. "The investigation was inconclusive."

"Meaning whoever did it was too clever to leave incriminating evidence. His son, Tony, has taken over. He's young, and not terribly good at business. I expected him to sell out to one of his father's competitors. He didn't. Instead, he's started some rapid expansion."

"That doesn't make him a racketeer, though," Scanlon said. "And it doesn't answer the question of who's handing out these cigars."

Nodding, Reid picked up his box and started to throw it in the wastebasket.

"No! Don't do that," Scanlon said.

Reid grinned at him, extending the box. "You want them?"

Temptation flitted across Scanlon's face, but he shook his head. "I have a box, too, remember? My ethics won't let me smoke them, but I can't bear to throw out such artistry."

Shrugging, Reid put the box on his desk. "A supplier would find cigars a lot more profitable than, say, beer or other imported products. The Hornet will do some checking, see what's coming into town."

Scanlon picked up one of the Partagás and rolled it carefully between his fingers before putting it back and closing the lid firmly. "Let me know what you find out."

The following morning, Reid sat at his office desk at the *Daily Sentinel*, reading the early edition. The phone rang, and his secretary's cool efficient voice said in his ear, "There's a visitor here to see you. A Mr. Duluth. He doesn't have an appointment. Do you have time for him, or shall I ask him to come back?"

Reid frowned, his senses suddenly on alert. "Thank you, Miss Case," he said. "Show him in."

A moment later, Leonore Case ushered in a squat, barrel-chested man in a tailored camel hair jacket and highly polished shoes. He wore his black hair sleeked back from a face as craggy as a bloodhound's. "Mr. Reid!" he boomed with false jollity, sticking out his hand. He had a grip like a stevedore's, with old calluses still roughening his broad, fleshy palm. His voice was deep and gravelly, his vowels carrying that peculiar Canadian inflection. "Kind of you to see me like this. I know you're a busy man. Duluth, here. Leo Duluth."

"What can I do for you, Mr. Duluth?"

"Just coming by to make your acquaintance. I hope to do business in your city, yes sir. Hope to do business here, and whenever I get started in a new venture or a new town, I like to know the movers and shakers, so to speak."

So much for Scanlon sending this character north of the border, Reid thought. He kept a polite smile on his face, however, as Casey returned to place steaming cups of coffee on the desk for him and his visitor. The curvy secretary was wearing a vivid green mini-dress that brought out the auburn tint in her shoulder-length brown hair. Her gaze swept coolly over Duluth's frankly appreciative grin and she turned to Reid.

"Will you be needing me, sir?"

"Not at present. Thank you, Miss Case."

As she exited, closing the door behind her quietly, Duluth put his fleshy lips together and emitted a low wolf whistle.

Reid's brows snapped together. "Is there anything else?" he asked sharply.

Duluth, still grinning, moved his gaze back to Reid's face. His eyes, dark under jutting brows, were like cold little stones. "Yes sir, there sure is. I wanted to see if you enjoyed your birthday, Mr. Reid. Many happy returns of the day, and all that."

Certainty clicked in Reid's mind. He leaned back in his chair, his gaze intent and wary over his steepled fingers. "You sent the Partagás."

Duluth growled a sort of chuckle. "Glad to see that you appreciate the brand, Mr. Reid. Hope you noted the generous ring size and color of the wrapper. *Colorado maduro*, it's called. Gives the cigar a good, rich flavor."

"Cuban cigars are illegal in the States, Duluth."

"Bah!" Duluth waved that away as though swatting a gnat. "What do politics matter to men of the world, eh, Mr. Reid? You've got a lot of influence in this community. You can help smooth my path, if you will, and I'd appreciate it if you'd do just that."

"I publish a newspaper," Reid said coldly. "I'm interested in reporting truth, not in smoothing paths."

"Hey, come on! I made a friendly gesture of good will. All I'm asking for is a little good will in return."

"Exactly how?"

Duluth shrugged his heavy shoulders under the expensive tailoring. "Just good will. You know. I'm trying to start a business here, and I want people to like me. You follow?"

Reid didn't thaw. "The District Attorney seems to think your business ventures aren't good for Detroit. Maybe you should consider staying in Ontario."

Duluth's jovial grin vanished. An angry flush darkened his cheeks as he stood. "Look, I'm taking on an American partner, so there's nothing you—or that Scanlon—can do about me crossing the lake, see? And you got nothing on me. Hey, I'm just trying to be friendly. Set up some mutual good will, maybe even buy an ad in your fancy newspaper. Yeah, a big full-page ad."

When Reid said nothing, Duluth's flush grew darker. He spun about on his heel and marched out, slamming the door.

Casey came in, glancing over her shoulder as she shut the door. "What did that ape want?"

"Good will," Reid said thoughtfully.

When she shot him a puzzled look, he smiled and asked her to put the phone on scrambler for him. Then he called the District Attorney.

"Scanlon here. What's up, Britt?"

Reid filled him in, then said, "I have a hunch his choice of American partner might be Tony Brazzi. It's worth checking into anyway."

"This guy must be crazy, announcing himself this way."

Reid smiled. "Egotists aren't known for their modesty. But if he's really looking to stick his fat fingers in several pies, then maybe he'd like to do a little business with The Hornet."

Two nights later, at his home, Reid had just put on his snap-brim hat and green mask, ready to go out as The Hornet, when the phone rang. It was reporter Mike Axford.

"Mike? What's going on?"

"Sorry to bother you at home," Axford said gruffly over the line. There was static on the connection, and a lot of background noise. "I'm calling from the waterfront. I can't get Gunnigan. Brazzi's boats just docked."

"Isn't this an odd time of night for them to come in?" Reid asked.

"You bet! The custom inspector's going onboard right now, but there's a bunch of goons hanging around, none of 'em local. Can't tell if they're armed or not, but it looks like there might be trouble. I need a photographer, but Gunnigan's not answering and I don't know how to reach Binny without bringing in Lowery. Don't need *him*."

Despite himself, Reid grinned. Ed Lowery was the *Sentinel*'s star reporter, and Axford—although competent enough—was not. Naturally Axford would want to protect his scoop.

"Gunnigan's probably down checking the Linotype," Reid said now. The machine that handled the hot-lead type had been threatening to break down all day, and Gunnigan was a hands-on type of editor. "Isn't there anyone else in the newsroom?"

"Sure, but I'm not sharing this story," Axford said. A bell clanged in the background, and Reid could hear the sound of shouts. "Just get me a photographer!"

"Right away," Reid promised, thinking fast. Just then, his newspaperman's instincts were at war with his crimefighter persona. The latter won. "Make sure you hurry back to the *Sentinel* and file your story before the paper goes to bed."

"I figure even if there's no fight with customs I should tail these guys back to their warehouse."

"You've got enough story now."

Even through the static, Reid could hear Axford's growl of frustration. "I'll have a *better* story if I—"

"Mike, just do what you're told. You're too good a reporter to step over the line and get yourself arrested for trespassing."

"I'm too good a reporter to leave a hot story in the middle. Old man Brazzi never ran his boats at night. No, and he never used goons for protection either. If that's not suspicious, what is?"

"All the more reason for you to get busy writing copy," Reid said.

"Holy Crow! Your father wouldn't pull a man off a good story just as it's about to break."

Reid's mouth tightened. "Let's leave my father out of this discussion."

"We've been running a hard-hitting crusade lately, at least until now. Maybe you've decided to smoke those cigars you got the other night."

Anger swept Reid before he contained it. He'd known Mike forever and considered him a friend, but the red-headed ex-cop could really ruffle his temper at times. Trouble was, tonight as The Hornet, Reid intended to pay a visit to Duluth in the warehouse district. Although Britt Reid probably could have reached Duluth with a phone call, The Hornet had been forced to call in favors from a few underworld connections to negotiate a meeting with the man. Reid didn't need Axford snooping around there at the same time.

After a moment, he said in a voice of forced calm, "I'm going to overlook that last remark, Mike. No one at the *Sentinel* is pulling back."

"Yeah, okay. I was out of line there. But sufferin' snakes! This is breaking news."

"Just make sure you stay at the docks where the action is. No poking around the warehouse yet."

"It'd be a perfect time to snoop while Brazzi's occupied here."

Reid tried to keep his impatience from his voice. "I want you to stay put in case Duluth shows up."

"Duluth?" Axford said blankly. "Oh, the goombah that sent you the cigars? You think he's muscling Brazzi?"

"That's what I want you to find out. See if the two of them are connected," Reid said, rolling his eyes at Kato, who was standing nearby clothed in his dark chauffeur's uniform and black mask beneath his peaked cap. As Reid spoke, he buttoned his dark green top coat. "Run it down, okay?"

"Sure, okay," Axford said reluctantly. "But I still think I ought to tail these guys as soon as customs lets them go."

"No. Come straight in and file that story. I want it for the morning headlines."

"But—"

"You've got your orders," Reid said firmly and broke the connection.

Kato's dark eyes met his in concern. "Do you think he will obey you?"

Reid was worried. "For his sake, I hope he does. And ours. One of these days he's going to get too close to The Hornet and blow my cover." Pausing only to make a swift call to dispatch a photographer, he led the way to the garage. There, a push of a button set the floor rotating, revealing the rakish Black Beauty, gleaming and ready to roll.

Kato got behind the wheel as The Hornet slid into the specially equipped Chrysler's spacious back seat. Almost reflexively, he checked the gas charge on his Hornet gun and flicked on his Hornet sting to make sure the sonic weapon was ready. All the while he was thinking things over, wondering if he could persuade the arrogant Duluth to take The Hornet as a partner in his smuggling scheme. Attempts to talk to Tony Brazzi had proven unsuccessful, so he felt he had no choice but to deal with Duluth more directly. He hoped, for Tony's sake, that the young man wasn't involved. But from what Axford had said, it looked like his suspicions about Tony might be correct.

As the garage door opened, the car engine buzzed to life. The Black Beauty rolled forward into the street, its infra-green headlights shining ahead.

The Hornet drew a deep breath, feeling the stirring anticipation of being on the hunt. No matter the degree of danger, he never tired of taking on criminals. Just like his father, and his great-great-uncle before him, he believed in bringing down evil wherever he found it. It was time for The Hornet to get busy.

Duluth failed to show. A messenger was waiting at the rendezvous point, looking uneasy and nervous.

"Mr. Duluth says he's sorry. Somethin' came up. He'll get in touch."

"What kind of kiss-off is this?" The Hornet asked angrily, keeping up his tough persona. "I'm offering your boss a sweet business proposition, and he's too busy to show up? Come on!"

"Somethin' came up," the man repeated. "It ain't personal."

As the messenger's car sped away, Kato glanced in the rearview mirror. "I wonder if the trouble at the docks is what came up. Could be the link between Duluth and Brazzi that we're looking for."

"Maybe."

"Do I tail the messenger?"

The Hornet frowned, considering it. "No. Pushing Duluth too hard too fast will make him suspicious. Let's wait for things to cool down at the docks, then check out Brazzi's warehouse instead."

The hour was late. The waterfront stood quiet, with no evidence of cops or customs agents now. The Black Beauty, rigged for silent running, rolled along the dockside street with no more noise than a shadow. The Hornet saw the starlight reflected in the black waters of Lake St. Claire before Kato turned down a side street and headed deep into the warehouse district. A few minutes later he pulled up in an alley and killed the engine.

Getting out, The Hornet looked up at the building's long brick profile. About a half block ahead, men were busy unloading a truck and wheeling beer kegs through a rear door. Keeping to the shadows in the poorly lit alley, The Hornet and Kato moved as close as they dared.

By the muffled sound of things, some kind of activity was going on inside the warehouse besides stacking kegs. The Hornet heard voices, a thinly pitched one raised in argument and now and then a deep, gravelly comment. A few minutes later, Duluth emerged, his stocky barrel-chested silhouette unmistakable.

Watching from the shadows, his eyes intent behind his mask, The Hornet saw a second man join Duluth. Hatless, the other man looked thin and slight in comparison to Duluth's bulk. The dim alley light shone on his pale brown hair. Recognizing Tony Brazzi, The Hornet narrowed his eyes.

"You've got to find another system," Tony was saying in an aggrieved tone. "This isn't going to work. We nearly got caught tonight."

"But we didn't," Duluth said. He stuck a huge cigar in his mouth and flicked a wooden match with his thumb to light up. Tipping back his head, he exhaled a long stream of smoke into the night air. "Ah. Perfect."

"I'm telling you they're suspicious. They were asking all sorts of difficult questions, and that reporter—"

"Don't worry about him. And don't worry about the customs agents." Duluth clapped the younger man hard on the shoulder, making him stagger. "The key to dealing with authority is not changing your routine. We took that risk tonight, yes sir, changing your boat schedule, but it was a necessary risk. Now we keep up the new schedule, and they get used to it. They won't bother us again."

His deep laugh boomed out briefly. "The next shipment will be twice as big."

"Twice—"

"That's right. I'm expanding fast. This city's ripe for the taking. The other racketeers think they're running this town, but they'll find out otherwise. No one has my vision, follow?"

"But if—"

"The Green Hornet's promised me trucks, lots of trucks."

In the shadows, The Hornet and Kato exchanged a silent look of surprise.

"And I would have had that deal sealed tonight," Duluth went on, "if you hadn't panicked and needed me to hold your little baby hand."

"But—"

"I can spread this operation through the whole state before any competitors know what's blowing past 'em. I don't sit on my thumbs and wait for things to happen, no sir. I *make* things happen."

"Yes, but if we're caught ... if I'm caught, the whole business ... everything my father worked for ... will be gone. I don't think we should—"

Duluth twisted Brazzi's coat front enough to lift Tony onto his toes. "Listen to me, punk," he said, rough and low. "You leave the *thinking* to me, follow? I give the orders, and you do what you're told."

"But—"

"Shut up! I need you for just one thing, and that's to ship beer. You do that, you follow the shipping schedule I gave you, then we'll get along fine. Now, I don't want no more babysitting, follow? You keep this place locked up. The trucks will be coming in tomorrow, and when they do, be sure you're out of the way."

Thrusting Tony Brazzi aside, he strode off into the night, his hat pulled low and his thick shoulders thrusting forward. Brazzi stood in the alley until the workers came out and drove away. Then he locked up dejectedly.

Before he could walk away, The Hornet gestured to Kato and stepped out into view, blocking Brazzi's path.

"Having trouble, Tony?" he asked.

The young man jumped, clearly startled, and looked around swiftly as though to run. But Kato was faster, hemming Brazzi between them.

"H-hornet!" Brazzi squeaked. "What're you doing here?"

"Sure you want to be mixed up with Duluth?" The Hornet asked. Through his mask he could see beads of perspiration on Brazzi's pale brow. The young man's eyes were shifting from side to side. He looked hunched, nearly sick. Clearly he was unsuited to a life of crime. "He's bad news, Tony."

"Yeah. Yeah, I guess so." Brazzi squared his thin shoulders. "Or maybe you're just trying to cut me out. Is that it?"

The Hornet stepped closer, keeping a wary eye on Brazzi. He didn't think the young man was armed, but Brazzi was the type that could easily lose his head. "Sure, I'd love to cut you out," he said now. "Do you want to sell your fleet of boats?"

"Just keep away from me!" Brazzi took a clumsy swing at The Hornet.

Ducking the blow easily, The Hornet punched him in the jaw. With a faint noise, Brazzi crumpled to the pavement.

The Hornet knelt and rifled his pockets for his keys, which he tossed to Kato, who caught them deftly and unlocked the warehouse door. Then, as The Hornet stepped inside, Kato picked up Brazzi by his shoulders and dragged him over the threshold, shutting the door quietly.

When Kato threw the light switch, a dim row of bulbs burned along the ceiling joists high overhead. The interior of the warehouse was shadowy and smelled of sawdust and the pungent aroma of beer.

The floor was wet where numerous aluminum kegs had been emptied of their contents. Packing sawdust had been spilled and tracked everywhere. Over to one side away from the mess, a number of small crates stood stacked neatly atop wooden pallets. Prying one open, The Hornet pulled out a small stainless steel canister slightly thicker than a coffee Thermos. It was still wet and obviously had been immersed in a beer keg, just like the other canisters in the crate. Unscrewing a tightly fitted lid, The Hornet peered inside, finding it packed with cigars. Silently he handed the canister to Kato.

"Hermetically sealed, with precision machining," Kato said, looking it over. "This damp sponge keeps the cigars humid, and when these tubes are concealed inside the beer no customs inspector is likely to find them."

"Even narcotics dogs wouldn't be able to sniff this contraband," The Hornet remarked. "And with the beer coming over legally, no one's going to look too closely at the cargo. As smuggling schemes go, it's simple enough to be brilliant."

"Okay, so I did it once," a voice said rather wildly a short distance behind them. "But that doesn't mean I'm going through with it forever!"

The Hornet and Kato spun around to find Brazzi standing rather shakily upright. He was holding a board taken from one of the broken pallets lying nearby, and his eyes were round and shiny like wet marbles.

"I don't care what you and Duluth cook up between you," he said. "I can't go through with more of this. Take my boats. Take my warehouse. I–I just want *out!*"

The Hornet stretched out his hand. "Tony—"

With a shout, Brazzi swung the board at him. The Hornet ducked back just as Kato sprang between them, shattering the board to splinters with a perfectly executed blow. Lightning fast, Kato's hand jabbed forward and knocked Brazzi back, sending him sprawling. Moaning, he didn't get up.

Kato straightened from his kung fu stance, looking almost disappointed. "He is no fighter."

Just then, Brazzi rolled over and fired a pistol. The shot hummed between The Hornet and Kato, traveling wild to ping off a metal post. Twisting around, Kato hurled a Hornet dart at Brazzi, pinning his sleeve to the floor. As Brazzi struggled, crying out, The Hornet drew his Hornet gun and, holding his breath, fired green sleep gas directly into Brazzi's face.

Brazzi went limp, and The Hornet was just stepping back from him when he heard a sound at the back door. He glanced at Kato, and together they ran to the front of the warehouse. Someone shouted, and The Hornet quickened his stride.

Pulling out his Hornet sting, he flicked it open to its full three-foot length and aimed it at the front door. The sonic blast blew out the lock, and The Hornet kicked the door aside so that it swung crazily from its top hinge. Kato jumped through first, dropping into a crouch as he checked for danger from all directions.

There came another shout, but The Hornet had already gained the street. He and Kato ran for the shadows, whisking themselves out of sight just as Mike Axford came shouldering his way past the smoking door. The Hornet glanced back with a scowl.

Once again, Axford had done exactly what he'd been told not to do.

The man was like an old bloodhound that couldn't be pulled off the trail.

"One of these days, Mike," The Hornet whispered in annoyance as he and Kato hurried away. "One of these days."

The next morning the *Daily Sentinel*'s headlines screamed: "Cops Close Smuggling Ring!" It went on to describe the midnight search of Brazzi's boats, police confiscation of the beer kegs and steel canisters found in the warehouse, and Brazzi's tearful confession that after his father was killed he'd been coerced into cooperating with the smugglers. Brazzi was currently being questioned further by the District Attorney's office. It was a hard-hitting news story, full of the kind of excitement, fact, and speculation that sold copies. The only trouble with it, as far as Britt Reid could see, was that Duluth wasn't firmly implicated. Still, as long as Brazzi feared the Canadian mobster enough to cover for him, there wasn't much that could be done . . . unless Reid's masked persona found a way to lure Duluth into the open. If the Canadian was as greedy as Reid suspected he was, he would be eager to find a new partner on the American side of the border, someone to continue smuggling while the heat remained on Brazzi. That's where The Hornet needed to step in.

Now, Reid and his editor Gunnigan stood in the newsroom at Mike Axford's empty desk.

"Haven't seen him today," Gunnigan groused, rubbing the back of his head. "Lowery's walking around, looking like he bit something sour. It's not every day that old Mike scoops him."

Reid frowned. "Well, when he does turn up, tell him I want to talk to him."

"Sure thing, Boss. But not until I skin a piece of his hide! If he thinks writing a front-page story gives him a free pass to ditch work, he can think again."

But Axford didn't come in or call. The story was still breaking, especially from the D.A.'s office. Police were combing the warehouse district in search of more contraband and watching the Detroit River like hawks. A fuming Gunnigan had assigned Ed Lowery to cover the activity. Meanwhile, the editor was pacing the office, still muttering what he was going to do to the missing Axford.

By evening, they were all worried. The police had orders to keep an eye out for the brash reporter. Some of them were friends with Axford from his old days on the force, and still considered him one of their own.

Reid stopped at Lowery's desk, where his star reporter was busy typing, a pencil rammed behind his ear and his hat perched on the back of his head. Picking up the page next to Lowery's typewriter, Reid read it swiftly. As usual, he was struck by the clean, crisp quality of Lowery's prose.

"Good reporting," he said.

"Thanks." Lowery finished typing his sentence, then stopped and gazed up at his boss. "I'm thinking they got to Axford."

Reid nodded. His stomach was in knots about it. He wanted to go after Duluth in the worst way, but he knew he had to be patient. "I'm afraid I agree with you."

"They killed old Nick Brazzi. They won't hesitate to kill again, if they need to." Lowery's gaze was steady on Reid's face. "I know this Duluth character came in, flaunted his plans in your face. You think he'll try to blackmail the *Sentinel* now with Mike?"

Reid's jaw tightened. "It's possible."

"Mike knows the score. He wouldn't want you to cave in."

Reid said nothing. His veins were humming; his muscles were steel cords.

Lowery sighed. "I got all my feelers out, looking for this guy. Soon as I pick up a lead, I'll—"

"Thanks." Reid rested his hand briefly on Lowery's shoulder, and walked on. It was time, he thought grimly, for The Hornet to take Duluth down.

Darkness held the city hostage. Clouds hid the stars in the sky. The lake lay black and bottomless beyond the piers. And in the night, a shadow raced through the streets . . . the Black Beauty en route to meet Leo Duluth. Via a small-time hood named Jimmy Fingers, who would snitch on anyone for a sawbuck, The Hornet had put out word that he was still willing to talk to Duluth, and finally the Canadian had sent Jimmy Fingers back with a succinct message: "Brazzi's out. Let's deal."

Now The Hornet rode in the back seat of the Black Beauty, his mask in place, his hat pulled low over his eyes. His weapons were ready.

"We've got a good advantage, Kato," he said. "Duluth doesn't know that Axford works for me. He's expecting The Hornet to side with him, not take vengeance."

Kato glanced in the rearview mirror. "His mistake."

Minutes later, Kato wheeled the big Chrysler around a corner, then braked at the sight of a patrol car ahead. Swiftly he turned down an alley, running parallel to the street of dark warehouses. "So how do we go in?" he asked. "Fighting? Or talking? Duluth may have decided to dispense with you and keep all the action for himself."

The Black Beauty was slowing to a halt. The Hornet checked his weapons again.

"We'll go in talking," he said and got out of the car. "At least, I'll go in. You stay back at first, and then let his men bring you. They'll be less on their guard if they think they have us cornered."

Nodding, Kato melted into the shadows. Drawing a deep breath and steeling himself, The Hornet entered Brazzi's warehouse through the back door. Although the police had sealed it with crime scene tape, someone had obviously broken the seal and unlocked the door, which now stood slightly ajar. Cautiously, every nerve tight and alert, The Hornet stepped inside.

"That you, Hornet?" Duluth's gravelly voice called out.

The Hornet slipped his hand into his pocket, closing his fingers around his pistol of sleeping gas. "Yes," he replied.

Footsteps scraped across the cement floor. The Hornet turned, and there ahead of him stood squat, top-heavy Leo Duluth, looking bulkier than ever in a double-breasted camel hair topcoat. Four goons armed with guns stood behind him, their eyes alert and stony in the dim light.

Kegs and steel canisters had been cleared away. The Hornet supposed the police had been thorough. Over to one side, Mike Axford—gagged and bound—was sitting on a haphazard stack of pallets. His eyes widened at the sight of The Green Hornet, but the gag kept him quiet.

"Where's your wheelman?" Duluth asked. His voice was grim and rough, no jollity in it tonight.

"We've got him," someone answered.

The Hornet glanced over his shoulder and saw an expressionless Kato walking up with his gloved hands held high. A man prodded him from behind with a pistol. The Hornet slowly eased his hand from his pocket. Sleeping gas wasn't going to work against bullets.

"So, Hornet," Duluth said, "you don't trust me."

"Should I?" The Hornet asked, keeping his voice cold and clipped. "After the mess you and Brazzi made of things."

Anger contorted Duluth's craggy face. "Look, we were betrayed by that chicken-livered little piece of—"

"You picked Brazzi. You brought him in."

Duluth pointed at him. "You don't judge me, Hornet. No matter what that stupid paper says, nobody runs this operation but me, follow?"

"What operation?" The Hornet asked coldly, edging a few steps away from Kato. "Looks to me like it's in pieces. You wouldn't be blaming Brazzi just to hide your own incompetence, would you?"

"Now see here!"

"You promised me a supply of Cuban cigars, and instead they've been impounded by the police. My trucks are sitting empty, and I've got nothing from you. I'm not impressed, Duluth. Not impressed at all."

"Then I've got something that *will* impress you," Duluth said. "I'm going to take care of this newspaperman, yes sir. Sneaking into warehouses, snooping where he don't belong, tipping off customs. Reporters, they're supposed to sit on their bums and write, not go sticking their noses in what don't concern them."

The Hornet almost smiled. "What's the matter, Duluth? Is your ego bruised because your name wasn't in his story? I heard you went around to the big-wigs in town, boasting and handing out bribes. Is that how you run a smuggling operation, by stirring up the authorities first? Pretty stupid, if you ask me."

Duluth glared at The Hornet. "Who're you calling stupid? I don't like that. No sir, I don't like that one bit."

"Who cares what you like?" The Hornet asked, his mind going in several directions as he tried to think of a way to get Axford out of here. "If you kill him, it will bring all the cops down on us, and Britt Reid will be screaming for our heads. He can put your face on television and stir up a manhunt—"

"Yeah," Duluth said, grinning. "I'll be on television. Not bad."

"You won't be so happy when you're holed up, hoping the cops don't rake you out. Why didn't you leave the reporter alone? Now we've got a witness. His ears are wide open."

"So?" Duluth gestured. "I told you I'll take care of him while I teach that fancy newspaper publisher a thing or two. And I'm going to pay Brazzi back but good for squealing. Yes sir, I'll make all of Detroit sit up and notice. You follow?"

The Hornet flicked another wary glance around the warehouse. The armed men were between him and both exits. Kato could take care of several of them, but how to free Axford remained the problem. Meanwhile, The Hornet kept Duluth talking.

"Big talk, Leo. So far, talk's all I've seen from you."

Duluth shrugged and pulled out a long cigar. "You ever smoke a fine Partagá, Hornet? It's like a work of art. You don't roll it between your fingers. You don't chew on it. You treat it with respect." As he spoke, he snipped off one end of the cigar with a pair of small brass cutters, then flicked a wooden match with his thumb and held the small flame near the tip of the cigar. "You never touch the match to the foot of the cigar, see? You toast it, yes sir. Toast it until the tobacco starts to burn."

"So what?"

Duluth put the cigar in his mouth, rotating it gently as he drew on it. He seemed lost in a dream. "See how I'm turning the head of the cigar to get an even burn started? You never want an uneven burn." He held the cigar in his thick fingers and blew very slightly on the side of the cigar. "Now I'm intensifying the heat right here in this spot, letting the cigar stabilize and correct the burn. It should be done proper, Hornet. This ain't some cheap stogie, follow?"

"Thanks for the lesson," The Hornet said warily, tensing as he saw one of Duluth's men place dynamite beneath Axford's pallet.

The reporter's eyes bulged above his gag. He struggled harder against his bonds.

"But," The Hornet went on, trying to keep his voice even and unconcerned, "I can't practice on fancy cigars since the police have them."

"I can get more," Duluth said. "Plenty more. But first, I'm going to settle a few scores."

His henchman uncoiled a long fuse from the dynamite across the floor to Duluth, who took a big puff of his cigar, then used it to light the fuse.

At that moment, The Hornet exploded into action, spinning around and slugging the nearest man within reach. As his opponent went sprawling, The Hornet followed him down, punching him again. A shot zinged over The Hornet's head, and he rolled to one side, just as Kato leaped over him and kicked a gun from someone's hand. A third man raised his pistol, but Hornet darts flew faster than thought, nicking the man's fingers so that he yelled and dropped his weapon.

Gaining his feet, The Hornet tackled another gunman before he could shoot Kato from behind, and hit him hard, knocking him out. Meanwhile, the fuse was burning fast, blazing across the floor. Stamping it out while Kato fought and felled the last henchman, The Hornet saw Duluth scuttling into the shadows behind a row of shelves. When he followed, Duluth tossed his precious cigar into a pile of packing sawdust, and it caught fire immediately, blazing up so that The Hornet took an involuntary step back. As much as he wanted to catch the smuggler, it was more important to get Axford away from the dynamite. Only he couldn't save the reporter's life without blowing his cover.

Hesitating only a moment, he made his decision and started for Axford when Kato's savage yell brought him up short. Another Hornet dart whizzed through the air, striking the rope that bound Axford's wrists.

Yelping in pain and surprise, the reporter brought his wrists forward and scrambled away from the dynamite. The fire, fed by the spilled sawdust, was heading in that direction. It was only a matter of time before the whole place went up.

But instead of running for his life, Axford rushed toward The Hornet. "I'm finally going to collar you!" he yelled.

The Hornet scowled. The ungrateful . . .

"Duluth's heading out the front!" Kato shouted and intercepted Axford with a swift cross kick.

The reporter went down with a muffled grunt. Leaving Kato to deal with him, The Hornet spun away, sprinting through the flames and smoke after the smuggler. Hampered by his bulk and lack of condition, Duluth had no chance of outrunning someone as fit as The Hornet, who grabbed him at the door. Duluth flung a wild haymaker at him, but The Hornet ducked expertly, feinting with two swift jabs before his right hook connected with Duluth's chin. Then, clutching a fistful of heavy camel hair overcoat, he manhandled the sagging, half-stunned crook out into the street.

A police siren wailed in the distance. Glancing that way, The Hornet turned his attention back to Duluth, who was trying to swing again. The Hornet's uppercut left the mobster sprawling unconscious on the pavement. Flexing his hand, The Hornet turned back for the others just as Mike Axford came running out the door. The warehouse blew, sending great gouts of flame and black smoke out the broken windows. The door went sailing by, but The Hornet hardly noticed as he was knocked off his feet.

Tumbling across the pavement, he lay stunned a moment, his ears deafened, his vision seared by the blast. Fire blazed up through the old timbers of the warehouse, and with a groan the roof fell in, sending sparks and cinders shooting high. Some of them landed on the adjoining roof, which began to blaze.

Dazed, knowing he had to get out of here, The Hornet thrust himself upright. He wanted to scream Kato's name, but gritted his teeth against the impulse. The very idea of Kato trapped inside that burning building made him wild, but as he started back inside, orange-white flames filled the gaping opening that was once a doorway, blazing too tall and hot for even The Hornet to jump through. Even so, he ventured a few steps closer before being driven back by the intense heat.

The sirens were wailing even louder. When police and fire vehicles came into sight, he turned, staggering, to run.

"No, you don't," Axford said grimly, catching hold of The Hornet's sleeve. One of the red-haired reporter's eyebrows was singed off, and his rumpled suit was covered with soot and tiny burn holes from flying cinders. His eyes held the fury of triumph. "This time I've finally got you!"

The Hornet's fist drove deep into Axford's solar plexus, doubling him up. Twisting free, The Hornet ran for the shadows, stumbling back to the alley and the Black Beauty. Heartsick, he hardly cared about getting away. This time, the price of bringing down another racketeer had been too high.

Without Kato . . .

"Hurry, Boss," Kato said, emerging from the shadows behind the car to push The Hornet into the back seat. "You took your time."

"Kato!" The Hornet said gladly, hardly able to believe his eyes as Kato slid behind the wheel and sent the Black Beauty speeding away just in time. "How did you get out of there?"

"Back door," Kato said. His chauffeur's cap had a burn hole that was still smoking, and his uniform was covered in ashes and sawdust. As he wheeled around a corner, he glanced in the rear view mirror and met The Hornet's eyes. He smiled. "Plus, I ran very fast. Otherwise, I would have gone up in smoke."

THE WORST ANGELS OF OUR NATURE

by Paul Kupperberg

Warren T. Reynolds III rapped his gold Cross pen sharply against the sweating crystal of the water pitcher with a vigor the seventy-three-year-old vice-chairman of the board of Reid Communications usually reserved for cheering on his beloved Tigers. The clear, fragile beat pierced the excited rumble of voices filling the room like noxious smoke and, finally, after what seemed like an eternity of outrage and admonition, silenced the indignation.

Reynolds waited until he had everyone's attention, until all eyes were on him and the proverbial pin might have been heard dropping against the mahogany conference table, and then he waited several moments more. To make certain they understood that age and laconic manner aside, Warren Reynolds was in fact running the show this morning.

"And that brings us to the final item on our rather burdensome agenda. Do you have anything to say for yourself, Britt?" he said to the tall, dark haired young man in the exquisitely tailored English suit badly in need of a pressing, slumped in a chair at the opposite end of the long table. Britt Reid could have used a run through the dry cleaner himself, or at the very least the services of a razor and pocket comb. The usually fastidious Reid looked as though he had gone sleepless for days, his insomnia fueled by alcohol and guilt, and his usually handsome features smeared across a face that appeared to have taken at least one recent beating.

Between Britt and Reynolds, on either side of the table, sat the corporate gauntlet, the eleven members of the board of directors. Instead of clubs and pikes, they clutched reports and legal documents with which to beat him.

"Warren," the younger man said, "I know it looks bad, but there's an explanation for. . ."

Reynolds was equipped with a bludgeon of reports and accountings of his own. Unlike the others, he appeared to regret having to wield it.

"The evidence," he said with a final shake of his grayed head and a father's disappointment in his voice. "I'm sorry, son, but unless you can refute the evidence, it doesn't matter how much I once may have believed in you."

Britt flinched. A newspaperman even in disgrace, he caught Reynolds' use of the past tense. Coming from one of his father's oldest friend, Reynolds knew it would hurt, but figured it small payback one such as himself might exact on a recalcitrant child for the damage he had done to the Reid name and the memory of a brave man who died in prison for other men's crimes.

Britt Reid swallowed and stood, pushing back his chair.

"I ... I'm ... sorry, Warren ... gentlemen," he said, and then fled the room.

Warren T. Reynolds III allowed the silence to last just until the door hissed closed behind Reid. Then he said, sadly, "I move that, effective immediately, Britt Reid be removed as chairman of the board of directors of Reid Communications and, further, he be suspended from all fiduciary responsibilities and positions within the company until the conclusion of a proper investigation. All in favor, say 'aye.'"

Eleven voices responded without hesitation. "Aye."

In the elevator, Britt Reid said, "I didn't think it was going to be this painful."

"These men knew your father, have known *you* since you were a child," Hayashi Kato, behind him, said. "You had to expect they were going to be disappointed."

"I was ready for that. What gets me was how *quick* they are to believe I embezzled that money from my own company."

"If you were shown the same evidence they were, what would you think?"

"I'd like to think in that situation I'd give a guy the benefit of the doubt."

"You know that's impossible, right? You knew what you were getting into when you started this, Britt."

The elevator chimed and opened its doors onto the lobby of the *Daily Sentinel* Building.

"I know. But why are they in such a rush to believe in the worst angels of my nature?"

"Because," said Hayashi, "they all believe in their own."

For a man of action, Mike Axford was surprisingly adept at doing nothing. It was a skill he had picked up by necessity, as a cop often forced to sit for hours on end on stakeouts. These days, the pursuit of his duties as a crime reporter for the *Sentinel* still required time spent rooted in one spot waiting for something to happen, or somebody to make an appearance. He figured if he had a nickel for every hour he'd spent crammed into a car or loitering outside some office building, nightclub, or private residence, he'd have himself a whole hell of a lot of nickels by now.

Axford was a big, burly man with a thinning patch of red hair he kept covered by a battered fedora, and a hound dog face dominated by a nose to make any Irishman proud. Between being a copper and becoming a reporter, he had performed another job on the payroll for old man Reid: young Britt's bodyguard. He knew his connections inside police HQ and the city's criminal underworld, combined with his dogged determination to track down a suspect, or a story, regardless of obstacles, made him a natural reporter, even if his grasp of grammar and spelling argued against it. He half-suspected that Britt made him a reporter after the senior Reid died just to stop the big man standing over him like a protective mother hen. "Don't worry about the grammar," Britt told him. "That's what the rewrite desk is for."

Problem was, Axford *was* a protective mother hen. His loyalty to the boy and his concern for his well-being hadn't ended when he put away his piece and picked up a pencil. Britt was in trouble and Mike Axford's instinct was to jump in with both fists swinging.

Except there was nothing to hit and nothing to do except wear a trench in the sidewalk opposite Britt's townhouse and wait. He knew the answer to the question he had, but he had to hear it from Britt's own lips. That ass Gunnigan on the assignment desk had labeled Britt a crime story and tried to send Mike out to cover the witch hunt. Mike, normally content to merely give the editor a hard time, had told him to shove it and left Gunnigan fuming at his desk. The story, if there was a story, belonged in the financial section. Or let fashion take it, for all he cared. The story was going to be written, there was nothing he could do about that. It just wasn't going to be written by him.

Mike Axford had started his search late last night. A buddy in the D.A.'s office let it slip that some of Reid Communications shareholders with clout and concerns about Britt's honesty had lodged complaints against his boss. An arrest was imminent. But the kid never showed up. Frequent calls to Casey back at the office throughout the night brought him the reasons why, beginning with a shouting match and forced expulsion from "Butch"

Weiner's gambling den when the loan shark refused to extend Britt credit. That was followed by a drunken scuffle at Frizzy Lenore's joint when the inebriated young publisher got too familiar with "Gat" Dooley's escort *du jour*. The evening ended early that morning with a swim in the fountain outside the Hilton Hotel that concluded in a ticketing for public nuisance instead of arrest only because the old harness bull who fished Britt from the water had known his pop and couldn't bring himself to bust the kid.

It was no use chasing after him. By the time they got the call, Britt had already moved on to his next round of mayhem in another part of town.

Mike checked the time. It was exactly two and three-quarters minutes later than it had been the last time he looked. But this time, when he looked back up, he was rewarded with the sight of a *Sentinel*-owned company sedan gliding down the street.

"What'd you know," Mike said out loud. "Watched pots do boil. Eventually."

He pushed himself away from the wall he had been holding up for most of the last few hours, and cut across the busy street to arrive at the opposite curb at the same time as the limo.

Hayashi had already come around the car and was reaching for the handle to open the passenger door for his boss. He had on that tough guy puss he used whenever he was protecting Reid. It hurt Mike's feelings that Britt's chauffeur thought he had to use it on him.. He always thought he and Kato got along alright. He had to know Mike would do anything for Britt. If they would let him.

"Hey, Kato," Mike said.

He was answered with a curt nod and a suspicious look. Hayashi's hand was on the door handle but he made no move to open it.

"I'm here on my own. Gunnigan wanted me on the story, but I told him to go screw," Mike said. "Besides, you don't think you can stop me from talking to him if I really wanted to, do you?"

Hayashi allowed a faint twitch of his lips to pass briefly for a smile. "You could try."

"But I ain't gonna have to, am I?"

Hayashi's glare softened and he flicked his wrist to open the door. "Of course not. Sorry, Mr. Axford. I guess I'm just on edge."

"Yeah, who isn't?"

Britt, the flesh around his left eye the color of eggplant, stepped from the sedan's passenger seat. He grinned at Axford but the old cop couldn't see any happiness in the younger man's bloodshot eyes, just exhaustion and maybe, for the first time he could remember, a little bit of fear.

"Hey, Mike. What's going on?"

"Funny. That's just what I was gonna ask you, kid."

Britt shrugged. "Nothing much. I've just been out celebrating."

"What've you got to celebrate?"

"My retirement," Britt Reid said. "The board voted me out of my own company. To tell you the truth, I sort of saw it coming, so I decided to treat myself to a little *pre*-retirement ... Kato, what's the word I'm looking for?"

"Debauchery?" the chauffeur suggested.

"Exactly. Yes, it was quite an unforgettable night. Well . . . so I've been told. I personally don't recall anything that happened much after about 10 p.m.."

Mike laid a beefy hand on Britt's sleeve. "We don't have time for this, Britt. Is there something going on I should know about? I wanna help, you know that."

Behind him, Mike heard the squeal of automobile tires, several vehicles all taking the turn too quickly. Without looking, he knew that sound. He'd heard it often enough in his career, on the street and from behind the wheel of one of the police cars arriving in a hurry to arrest some perpetrator for his crimes. Usually there were sirens involved, but in deference to the high tone of the neighborhood, they settled for flashing their gumballs as they came to screeching stops around the parked limo. Cops began piling out of wildly flung open doors, weapons in hand.

Britt smiled sadly and clapped a hand on Axford's broad shoulder.

"Thanks anyway, Mike," he said. "But I think it's up to the lawyers now."

Britt Reid raised his hands in the air and nodded solemnly at the approaching cops and said, "Gentlemen."

"You took a real gamble there, Boss," Kato said from behind the wheel of the Black Beauty.

"Not really," said Britt from the back seat. "I'm a rich guy being booked for a white collar crime. It was a pretty safe bet the court would take away my passport and grant me a huge bail. Which they did. Thanks for the change of clothes, by the way."

"You've been wearing those for two days, the last one spent in central booking and the courthouse holding cell. Besides, you need to be properly dressed for tonight's activities."

"Fortunately, I ran into Judge Pszenica, an old friend of my father's, and he lent me a razor and let me use the shower in his chambers this afternoon. He told me I stank."

"You did. So, where to?"

Britt dropped his filthy slacks to the floor and pulled on the fresh pair in midnight green that he found folded neatly on the seat behind him. A crisp white shirt, midnight green tie, and jacket were added, along with the mask and fedora of the same hue.

"The corporate world's not the only front that's been under attack, and we've been out of touch with the other side of business for a couple of days. Let's stop in at Geronimo's and see what's been going on in our absence," said The Green Hornet.

Warren Reynolds and David Hitchcock sat side by side on the wooden bench in the steam room at the Club. Hitchcock was ten years Reynolds' junior and sixty pounds his inferior, a rail thin man with a ridiculous handlebar mustache who, while incapable of recognizing the absurd when he saw it in the mirror, was nonetheless a shrewd businessman with holdings in steel, shipping, oil and communications, including a seat on the Reid board.

"I assume you heard what happened to Bill Mason this morning?" Hitchcock said.

Reynolds shook his head. "No. With this thing with Britt, I haven't been paying attention to much else."

"He lost the proxy fight against Peninsula Partners. They pulled the majority share out from under his feet and left him out high and dry."

"Any idea who the principles behind Peninsula are? They've been picking up companies all over the city. And not always in the most polite way. They've been sniffing around Reid Communications lately, I hear."

Reynolds' expression gave away nothing. "You know I can't comment on that, David, especially in light of Britt's situation."

"Damned shame about the kid," Hitchcock said. "I never thought he was the type."

"Everyone's the type, I suppose," Reynolds said, his eyes closed, breathing in the steam.

"Even you, Warren?" Hitchcock said with a chuckle. Warren Reynolds was well known as a businessman with morals, a straight-shooter with a lucky streak as wide as his native Michigan.

"Depends," the older man said, wiping a bead of perspiration from his shaggy brow. "What would I be doing it for?"

Hitchcock blinked. "Sorry?"

"I wouldn't do it for money. I have more than enough of that to last me and my heirs for a few generations to come. What, then, would be the burdensome agenda turning me to crime?"

The steam room door opened, and another Reid board member, Steve Gilbert, the six-times married CEO of Tuff-Parts, the auto parts manufacturer, entered tucking a towel tightly around his trim, gym-toned waist.

"You're a thief now too, Warren?" Gilbert said, settling on the bench opposite the two men.

"Hypothetically. Dave wanted to know if I could be corrupted."

"Like your young Mr. Reid?"

"That remains to be proven," Reynolds said.

"I don't know. The indictment was pretty convincing," Hitchcock said, smoothing his steam-wilted mustache.

"Nonetheless. Britt's alleged fraud and embezzlement . . . why did he do it? Since when has he ever given a good goddamn about money, other than as a tool to do some good or chase after some woman," Warren Reynolds said. "And, much as myself, his resources are more than ample to see to his wants and needs, no matter how expensive. So, I ask again: What was his motive?"

"Power," said Gilbert. "The amount of money Britt *allegedly* stole could buy a lot of influence under a lot of tables."

"But the idea that Britt would use stolen money in the pursuit of his philanthropic goals is. . ." Reynolds started to say "absurd" before Gilbert interrupted: "That's assuming Britt Reid is the man you've always believed him to be."

"Who among us is who other people think we are?" Hitchcock said.

"Certainly not I," said Reynolds with a shake of his head.

Mike Axford could hardly bring himself to read the entire indictment against the boss. He found it hard to believe the flurry of charges for embezzlement, money laundering and securities fraud were being leveled against the same Britt Reid he knew. The one who was honest to a fault, the kind who re-filed his income taxes when a mistake in his favor had been discovered by his accountant, and who returned the extra change mistakenly handed him by cashiers. He made sure the *Sentinel* was scrupulous in its fact-checking and, when caught in an error, would print a retraction with the same prominence as the original story.

The boy wasn't a thief, no matter what evidence the D.A., S.E.C., F.C.C., I.R.S. or any other damned jumble of initials claimed to have.

But Britt wouldn't deny it. His only comment in court or to the press had been the "not guilty" plea he entered at his arraignment. A man under these circumstances feels he's been unfairly accused, he says something. Hell, he screams it for all the world to hear.

But Britt Reid had no comment.

And Mike still couldn't bring himself to believe the worst. Something was up. It was a good thing he was a reporter whose job it happened to be to find out what that thing might be.

"C'mon, Leo," he growled, "you're the head numbers man around here. Could Britt have done what they're saying he did, and if so, how'd he do it without you noticing anything for so long?"

Leopold Grant was not a sentimental man. An accountant by training and temperament, he viewed the world in terms of black and red, profit and loss. Human foibles were not quantifiable on the ledger page and therefore not of great interest to him. He did not seem particularly upset or offended that the reporter was practically accusing him of incompetence.

"A ledger book can be made to say anything you want it to say," Grant said. He wore a light gray suit and white shirt that matched his ashen complexion and thinning slicked back white hair. "Numbers are fungible."

"Fungi*who*?" Mike said. "What's this got to do with mushrooms?"

"Fung*ible*," Grant said. "Interchangeable with something of equal value. One can make a monetary exchange do anything one wishes, all depending on what you call it and where you place it in the ledger book to determine its value to a corporation. Some such manipulations are perfectly legal, some barely so, and many blatantly illegal. As long as all the numbers add up in the end, regardless of where they are in the book, Mr. Reid could have been doing almost anything he wished with vast sums of money and I would have had no way of knowing until it came out in a full audit."

"So . . . you're saying the boss *could* have done this?"

"Mr. Reid?" The left side of the accountant's mouth quirked upward for a fraction of a second before settling back into its normal bottom line. "No way in hell."

The shooting was already underway when the Black Beauty turned the corner.

On the southwest side of the city, block after block of businesses and homes stood empty, abandoned and neglected, or gutted by fire and vandalism. From the decay, like the few remaining teeth in a broken, old man's mouth, establishments such as Geronimo's stood, never to flourish, but at least surviving.

The bar's plate glass front, "Geronimo's" spelled out in a graceful arc of peeling gold gilt against a face made opaque by decades of grime and grease, flashed madly like a light show in accompaniment to the syncopated crack and pop of small arms fire inside.

"Trouble, Boss," Kato said. He wore a high collared black chauffeur's jacket and cap, his eyes hidden behind a black mask.

The Green Hornet took the Hornet Gun from its clip in the Black Beauty's door and carefully checked its charge before slipping it in the right hand pocket of his overcoat. Next, he filled his hand with the comforting weight of the Hornet's Sting, making certain as he always did, that it too was fully charged.

"Can't say I'm surprised. We've been expecting this," he said.

"How do you want to go in?"

The Green Hornet leaned back in his seat and reached for the safety strap.

"Hard," he said.

Kato hit the gas and the Black Beauty's silent, powerful engine buzzed to life as he swung the wheel hard to the left, framing Geronimo's façade in his headlights.

The great car surged forward and pounced from the curb, leaping through the grimy plate glass and into the hail of gunfire.

Slugs ricocheted and pinged off the side of the customized Chrysler Crown Imperial's armored body as it sailed through the shower of shattered glass, then hit the sawdust covered floor and skidded a full one hundred and eighty degrees before her brakes grabbed hold and she screeched to a stop.

Surprised momentarily quieted the guns on both sides. As one, The Green Hornet and Kato flung open their doors and threw themselves to the floor.

"Hornet!"

It was one of The Green Hornet's men, a piece of red-haired muscle with one eye they called McSquintin. The Hornet had taken down this small neighborhood gangs' boss a month earlier but had spared a number of street-level thugs and mobsters to serve as the nucleus of a mob of his own. It was an experiment, a way to more deeply penetrate the underworld from within, using his gangsters to counter the actions of other gangs. McSquintin was scrunched up behind an overturned deuce, trying to shield his immense frame with the tiny table made for two. A .38 all but disappeared in his meaty paw.

Shooting resumed. On the far side of the bulletproof Black Beauty, along with the sounds of scuffling feet, came the muffled thud of Kato's fists against the shooters' flesh and their grunts as they hit the ground as dead weight.

"Who are they?" The Green Hornet said.

"Dunno," McSquintin snarled. "Four bastards came in, pulled down masks before we could get a look at 'em. Didn't say nothin', just started shootin'. They got Nunzie behind the bar and Wino Willie took one in the arm. Wasn't nobody else here yet, the stupid galoots."

A last shot cut the air just before the sound of a breaking bone and a yelp of pain put an end to the commotion.

The Green Hornet got to his feet. McSquintin, less certain of Kato's abilities, hesitated before following suit. No one shot at him. The driver was coming around the car, dragging one of the masked gunmen behind him.

"This one's still awake, Boss," he said. "Mostly."

Kato dumped the man against the Beauty's bumper. The Hornet knelt in front of the man and yanked the ski mask from his head. The face was dark and cruel, scarred and twisted like a man who had spent too many rounds in the boxing ring at the mercy of superior fighters. A face that broken did not belong to a man who went down easily.

"Know him?"

McSquintin squinted his good eye and nodded slowly. "Yeah, I think so. Pug, used to take dives under the name Kid Reingold. Last I heard he was breakin' arms for the Wallace gang."

"Wallace is dead," The Green Hornet said.

"So is 'King' Johnson on the east side, O'Brien and Graydon on the north, and the Fargo Twins in the suburbs," Kato said. "Want to bet Reingold and his pals are working for the same 'Mr. X' who's been killing the bosses all over town?"

"No bet. We figured he would be turning his attention to us sooner or later. He was just saving the best for last," said The Hornet. He lightly tapped gloved fingers against Kid Reingold's cheek. "Ding, ding, champ! There's the bell. Wake up. It's time to answer some questions."

Kato was ready with a capsule of ammonium carbonate which he broke under Reingold's oft-broken nose. The biting smelling salts cut through the daze and Reingold gasped and gagged, sitting up straight and shaking his head.

"Heh? Who'dahell?" he rasped.

"Got it in you for another round, Kid?" The Green Hornet said.

The boxer growled and lunged to attack. Kato's polished black boot on his chest kept him in place.

"I ain't tellin' you nothin', big-man," he growled.

The Green Hornet smiled and held up the Hornet's Sting. With a snap of his wrist, it sprang open to its full three-foot length.

"You gonna beat on me, that it?" Reingold said with a ragged laugh. "I been beat so much I don't remember what it feels like not t'be gettin' hit."

"I don't just hit," The Hornet said and he pointed the Sting at a chair. He activated the high-frequency sonic cutting device, a brief burst, but enough that with a high-pitched whine, one wood leg shattered as though exploded from inside and the chair toppled to the floor.

Reingold's eyes went wide.

"Imagine what it can do to flesh and bone, Kid."

In truth, The Hornet would never use the Sting on another human at such a lethal setting. At low power, the Sting was harmless, capable of little more than a startling shock.

Not that Kid Reingold had any way of knowing that.

If there were anything more boring than corporate financial reports and federal regulatory filing forms, Mike Axford hoped to heaven above he never had to read it. He could barely make heads or tails out of the dense paragraphs of tiny print with all their multiple-claused "heretofore" and "whereas" filled sentences, but, having spread the word to all his contacts and snitches in the department and on the streets, there wasn't much else he could do until somebody got back to him with something. Anything.

Mike's mole inside the D.A.'s office told him the investigation had been triggered several months back by the receipt, from an anonymous source, of incriminating documents from inside the Reid organization. The lead proved solid and led to a series of irregularities that were traced, not without difficulty, back to Britt Reid. A pal at City Hall confirmed a lack of possible political motivation for Britt's problems; the current administration enjoyed the support of the *Sentinel* and was not at all pleased to have yet another of the city's business leaders proved to be corrupt. "Off the record, it's a damned epidemic," the third deputy mayor in charge of public outreach whispered into the phone. "What's he, like the fifth or sixth corporate big shot indicted since last year? The city's got enough public relations problems without this crap."

The phone on his desk rang, making him jump in the late evening silence of the newsroom.

"Axford here."

From the other end came the sound of shallow breathing, followed by a high-pitched, hurried voice saying, "Dat you, Mike? It's Ratso, man."

Gus "Ratso" Jablonski was a low level hired hand for the Slavic mob on the east side. One look at Jablonski's rodent-like face was enough to secure his nickname; that he picked up extra cash by ratting out colleagues to reporters and cops allowed the little gangster to enjoy a secret laugh at those who stuck him with the name in the first place.

"What've you got for me?" Mike said, reaching for a pencil.

"My resignation, dat's what," Ratso squeaked into the phone. "Dey just popped Boss Siroky and his boys . . . I'm gettin' outta town before dey come lookin' for da rest'a da crew."

"Jeez, Ratso," Mike said, scribbling furiously across the face of a copy of Britt's indictment. "You sure? Nothing's come in over the police radio..."

"Just happened, Mike, I seen it," the snitch whined. "Took 'em out in da alley behind Lumpy's joint . . . you know how da boss loved his pierogies. Look, I need some dough to get outta town, Mike."

"Who made the hit, Ratso?"

"I was too busy kissin' pavement to see nothin'."

"Not the trigger men. Someone's been taking out bosses all over town. That's the name I want."

"Don't nobody know a name, 'cept he calls himself da Silver Mist. C'mon, Mike, about dat dough . . . ?"

"Yeah, sure, Ratso. I'll leave it in the usual spot."

. . . Someone's been taking out bosses all over town . . .

"T'anks, Mike, t'anks a lot. You was always a gent, even when you was a cop."

. . . The fifth or sixth corporate big shot indicted since last year . . .

"Good luck, Ratso."

Mike Axford would never deny he was a dud when it came to higher mathematics, but he did have a knack for simple arithmetic. It was a trait shared by most policemen and reporters, the ability to quickly add up two and two to find the answer that is so obvious as to be overlooked or disregarded as coincidence.

Heads of the city's major companies being dislodged from their seats through a recent flurry of corporate buyouts and takeovers or criminal indictments.

Heads of the city's criminal mobs being dislodged from their seats through the underworld version of the corporate takeover, the hit.

Coincidence?

Two plus two still equaled four, didn't it?

Mike was still shrugging into his jacket as he ran for the elevators.

The Green Hornet's jab mashed Dino Pavia's nose flat against his face. The gangster's arms windmilled wildly and the .45 flew from his hand before his backwards stagger was checked by the wall.

"I said *no* guns," The Hornet hissed.

Pavia growled and, ignoring the blood streaming from his broken nose, launched himself off the wall and charged the man in midnight green.

The Hornet glanced over at Kato, who lounged casually in the doorway, and shrugged. When Pavia was nearly on top of him, he popped off another jab at the man's ruined nose. This time, Pavia yowled in pain and stopped dead in his tracks to clutch at his bloodied face.

"Ow, ow," he said, hopping up and down. "Jesus, Hornet! That hurt!"

"It got your attention," the masked man said. "What's the idea of pulling your piece on me, Dino?"

Blood spilled from between Pavia's fingers. He pulled the wad of red silk from his breast pocket and stuffed it against his face.

"New boss, new orders," the gangster said with an embarrassed shrug. "Sorry, I got carried away."

"So you're working for the man who killed 'Kid' Johnson?"

Pavia spit blood and growled a curse. "Yeah. Why not? A paycheck's a paycheck."

"Who's signing the check these days, Dino?"

The other man managed to grin around his pain. "Paycheck's a, what'd you call it? A metaphor. This's a cash business and mostly it doesn't matter who's handing me the cash, *capice*? The boss says it's like when one company buys out another one, only sometimes, it's gotta be a hostile takeover. It's just business, no hard feelings."

"This philosopher have a name?"

Pavia shrugged again. "Likes to call himself the Silver Mist. He don't show his face. He's just a voice over the radio or telephone, but he's pulling all the strings."

"The mobs all have agreements to keep to their own territories. . ."

"Like I says, new chairman, new rules. Talks like that all the time, 'consolidation,' 'growth phase,' 'contract renegotiation' . . . sounds like the business section in the newspaper."

"I don't suppose you know where I can find the chairman of the board," The Green Hornet said.

"Hey, you know I'd help if I could," Dino Pavia said. He pulled the silk handkerchief away from his nose and inspected it briefly. "But I got no clue. Like I said, he don't never show his face."

The masked man's eyes bore into Pavia's.

"But I'm next on his hit list?"

"He calls you the 'final item on a burdensome agenda.' He's offering a *big* bonus to the man who takes you down."

The Hornet's eyes flicked to Pavia's fallen .45 and then back to the gangster's face. "You're not thinking of claiming the bonus, are you, Dino?"

Dino laughed. "Yeah, 'cause I'm that stupid. Like I say, I don't care who makes my payday, 'Kid' Johnson, Silver Mist, Green Hornet, or Barry freakin' Goldwater. This's between you and him . . . and, uhm, sorry again about drawing on you. Guess you kind of startled me."

"You always were the nervous type, Dino," The Green Hornet said.

In the Black Beauty, Kato said, "'Contract renegotiation?'"

"Sounds more boardroom than back alley, doesn't it?"

"Someone trying to corporatize the mob?"

"Or someone corporate applying his expertise to a hostile takeover of the mobs from the outside."

"Either way . . . I'm beginning to think *your* boardroom and back alley problems may be related."

"If they are, there should be something or someone connecting them."

The Green Hornet opened the compartment holding the car's radio telephone and lifted the receiver to his ear. He gave the operator a telephone number in Washington, D.C. and waited.

"Mr. Tolson, please," he said when the other party answered. "Britt Reid. Yes, he'll know."

Kato eyed his boss in the rearview mirror. "You went straight to the top, didn't you?"

The Hornet crossed his legs and said, "I thought it best not to risk any slip-ups, all things ... ah, yes, hello. Good evening, Clyde, so sorry to bother you at this hour ... thank you, that's very kind. I think I'm getting close ...

yes, I agree, especially with that indictment hanging over my head.

"No, we're not ready for your boys to move in quite yet. Well, I need you to run checks on a few names . . . no, not through the criminal database. The S.E.C. and F.T.C. . . . mm-hm, that's right. You can? Thank you, Clyde. Yes, I'll hold for your secretary . . . with luck, this should all be over by tomorrow. Have a good night, Clyde. Please give my regards to Edgar."

The Green Hornet covered the mouthpiece and smiled. "Our F.B.I. at work!" he declared, then spoke back into the telephone. "Yes, I'm here. Okay, ready for those names?"

In the driver's seat, even Kato was surprised by the list of names that followed.

"You want we should do *what*, Boss?" McSquintin said, his one eye going wide.

"Run away," said The Green Hornet. "Leave town. Get lost. Go hide under a rock, whatever you want, just *don't* be here."

"But this Silver Mist palooka . . . you just gonna let him waltz in and take over our territory?"

"He's not taking over anything. I just need a few hours to take care of him, but his boys could hit a lot of our boys in that time. Unless you all disappear until I sound the all clear."

"Ain't nobody gonna wanna be runnin' out on you boss. What if you need back-up?"

"I have Kato."

"All two of youse, huh?"

"Well . . . and the F.B.I."

McSquintin said, "Oh, man, this just keeps gettin' worser an' worser…"

The Silver Mist was seated at his desk, watching two Alka-Seltzer tablets dissolve in a chaotic fizz of tiny bubbles in the bottom of his glass, when The Green Hornet stepped through the French doors that opened onto the terrace of his penthouse suite.

The Hornet gave the man credit. After an initial start of surprise, he did not pretend indignation or ignorance at the masked man's presence in his home. Instead, he merely sighed and set the glass down on the desk.

"I'll assume from the attire that you're The Green Hornet," he said.

The Hornet nodded. "I hear you've been looking for me."

"Not me, per se. It would be more accurate to say I've been encouraging my associates to seek you out."

"And kill me."

"Well," the Silver Mist said with a vague smile. "Yes."

"Nothing personal, though. Just business. Correct?"

"Always." The Silver Mist folded his hands across his stomach. He wore a blue cotton robe over gray silk pajamas and looked like someone's father sitting there in the early morning light. He nodded at the Hornet Gun clutched in the masked man's hand. "You, on the other hand, I see take it entirely personally. Anyone else would have sent an associate to kill me."

"You want me dead. That's reason enough to take it personally."

"If I may change the topic for just a moment," the Silver Mist said, gripping the edge of his desk to lean forward and retrieve his glass. "I wonder, seeing as I have been so careful to protect my identity in pursuit of this burdensome agenda, how you were able to unmask me, as it were."

"Business," said The Hornet. "Specifically, your *other* business, equally crooked but of the Wall Street variety."

Warren T. Reynolds III leaned back and took a swallow of Alka-Seltzer.

"Hostile takeovers all over Detroit, Mr. Reynolds, men whose integrity was once above reproach suddenly accused of fraud and malfeasance, forced from their own companies. And, always, the mysterious, privately held Peninsula Partners waiting in the wings to pick up the distressed companies at reduced prices. Any of this sound familiar?"

"Very much so. But impossible to prove."

The Green Hornet smiled. "You're not as clever as you think, Mr. Reynolds. Britt Reid's been working with the F.B.I. since the first moment he suspected someone was trying to frame him. They've already started unraveling Peninsula Partners by tracing the money back from Reid Communications. And, if I'm not mistaken, they should also be on their way over with a warrant for your arrest."

"Then you don't want to be here when they arrive any more than I do," said the old man, rising to his feet.

"Of course not. What I do want, however, is to leave behind the biggest mess imaginable for you to try and explain away."

"A masked intruder? That's not a mess, my dear Hornet. That's a legal defense."

Reynolds' hand came up, the barrel of a small caliber pistol pointed at

The Green Hornet. At the same moment, the door of the study burst open and six men, a couple of whom he recognized as having once been with various gangs, came spilling in with guns drawn.

"I also saw you press the signaling button under your desk," said The Green Hornet. A hornet-shaped dart flew through the terrace doors, buzzing over his shoulder and thudding into Warren Reynolds' gun hand. With a howl of pain, he dropped the weapon.

Kato stepped through the doors.

The Silver Mist's men opened fire.

The Green Hornet dove to one side. A burst from the Hornet Gun sent a choking cloud of green gas at the shooting thugs. Kato, fitting the boxy shape of a gasmask over his nose and mouth, dove through the swirling green plume, fists and feet flailing. The Mist's men had begun to spread across the room to surround the intruders, one pair moving right, two others going left, while the last two stepped into the room.

The Green Hornet fired off several more shots of gas, dropping the closest men into the start of several hours of unconsciousness.

"Kill them!" Warren T. Reynolds III thundered. He grasped his wounded hand to his chest as he backed away from the violence, seeking escape.

The Green Hornet vaulted over the desk.

Across the room, Kato watched his boss even as he fended off two burly opponents. The man in the green mask fought grimly and in silence, saddened by the day's task. When the telephone call came from the F.B.I. tying Reynolds, who served on the boards of almost all the corporations targeted by Peninsula Partners, with that mysterious company, Britt had not seemed surprised by the news. He had simply been crushed to find he had been betrayed by a man who he had called a friend since childhood.

"I saw it coming, Hayashi," Britt had told his friend at the time. "As soon as we talked to Dino Pavia, I knew it. I just didn't want to believe it. It was all those business terms he said the Silver Mist used, including his 'bothersome agenda.' That's one of Warren's little pet phrases."

Britt Reid was not a vengeful man.

But he could not abide betrayal.

From the pocket of his robe, Reynolds produced a .38. With a shaking hand, he pointed it at The Green Hornet.

"Stop or so help me God . . . !" the older man warned.

The Green Hornet barely paused and smiled, a ghastly, humorless smile.

"If you were going to shoot, you would have just done it," The Hornet said. "But you can't, can you, Mr. Reynolds? It's one thing to give orders."

The Green Hornet ripped the gun from Reynolds' hand and threw it across the room.

"It's something else entirely to look a man in the eye and pull the trigger yourself."

Warren Reynolds crumpled, like a masonry chimney collapsing onto itself, his face quivering and tears welling in his eyes.

Britt Reid did not want to see Reynolds cry, did not want to feel sorry for the old man. With a single blow, he knocked him unconscious, putting them both out of their miseries.

Behind his desk at the *Sentinel*, Britt Reid finished reading the afternoon edition's front page story detailing the activities of Warren Reynolds, a.k.a. the Silver Mist, including the revelation that Reid had been taking part in an F.B.I. sting to uncover the identity of the criminal and business mastermind.

Britt had returned to the office, prepared to write the story himself, only to find Mike Axford's investigative piece already on press.

"That's some mighty fine reporting, Mr. Axford," Britt said. "I needed the F.B.I. to dig up Warren's corporate connections. How did you manage it?"

"With a key to the back door of City Hall and about a dozen off-duty coppers helping me comb through municipal tax records all night long," Mike said. "By the way, the *Sentinel*'s gonna owe me for one helluva of an expense account for the drinks I'll be buying those boys tonight."

"The drinks are on me, Mike," Britt said. "And thanks, really. The Feds wouldn't let me tell you what I was into, but . . ."

Mike waved off the explanation.

"I knew you couldn't do nothing like they were accusing you of, kid. It just isn't in your nature."

Britt grinned. "The better angels of my nature, huh, Mike?"

"Yeah, something like that," Mike Axford nodded in agreement. "Never stop believing, kid."

NOW THAT WOULD BE TELLING

by Bradley H. Sinor

"They say that the heavens reflect the death of kings, but what about the death of a devil?"

Britt Reid let out a very long sigh before he looked up from the pages he had been reading. He had already read the story, twice, as a matter of fact. Dealing with it was not going to be easy, especially since Mike Axford, the reporter who had written the article, was on the other side of his desk. He had burst into the office of the publisher of the *Daily Sentinel*, dropping the pages on Britt's desk with a flourish.

"The Laymans?" asked Britt, though he knew the answer. The criminal organization headed by Vincent Layman, one of the biggest in Detroit, was Axford's latest obsession, even pushing his dream of seeing The Green Hornet in jail several notches down on his to-do list.

"You bet," said Axford. He grinned and ran his hand through the unruly red hair that looked like it had not seen a comb in years. "This is the kind of good old-fashioned journalism I've been trying to show those young idiots you've been staffing the news room with."

"So are you trying to be a poet, Mike?" asked Britt as he looked over at Axford. The other man had not sat down, but stood near a large world globe on the other side of the publisher's desk, slowly turning it with two fingers.

"Britt, what are you talking about?" Axford stared at his boss for a slow moment, not seeming to understand the question.

"Well, for one thing, this lead. It reads like something written in Mrs. Douglas' eighth grade poetry writing class, not a front page story in the *Sentinel*," said Britt, tapping the pages in front of him.

"Okay," Axford nodded. "Just maybe I was a wee bit melodramatic, but it fit when I heard that old man Layman had had a stroke. It was like

God himself had enough of that reprobate and decided to balance things out a bit."

"I don't know about the involvement of the Almighty in this story, but what I do know is that in the pages of the *Sentinel* we go with facts, not philosophical platitudes," he said.

Britt picked up a red pen from the corner of his desk and crossed out the first three paragraphs of the article; he then went on and marked several other parts. Out of the corner of his eye the publisher could see Axford's face grow as red as his hair, but he knew the reporter would only sit there and sputter, something he had seen him do many times over the years.

"If the old man dies, this could be the beginning of a major gang war. I'll even bet that damn Green Hornet will be going after a piece of the Layman pie," said Axford.

"You see The Hornet everywhere," chuckled Britt. "But I do agree with you; if Layman dies, then we have the potential for a lot of problems. The thing is, from what I understand, he's recovering."

"You've cut the guts out of this thing," Axford said and stared at the pages that Britt passed back to him.

Britt ignored his old friend and touched the button on his intercom. "Miss Case," he said, "would you take Mike's story down to the newsroom? Tell them to put it inside. If you hurry, we can still make the early edition."

After his secretary had departed, Britt Reid looked across his desk at Mike Axford. "With everything so chaotic, this might be the chance to get the goods on Layman, so get off your butt and get out there and find us proof to back up your story. Just no more bad poetry, please, I'm not sure I can take it."

"No, promises," laughed Axford as he headed toward the door. "But mark my words; I'm sure that damn Green Hornet is going to turn out to be hip deep in this. Hell, he might even be behind it."

Britt smiled. At least Mike had gotten one thing right; The Green Hornet was going to be involved, just not in the way Axford expected.

"It was very definitely attempted murder," said District Attorney Frank Scanlon. "The fact that old man Layman survived it just proves how lucky that cagey old wolf is."

Officially, Scanlon was not meeting the publisher of the *Daily Sentinel*, and certainly not giving him confidential police information. In fact, as far as anyone knew, Scanlon was at home, not sitting in Britt Reid's den.

Britt reached over to the carafe of coffee that Kato had just brought in.

He took a whiff of the dark brown liquid and realized that it was the brand that Scanlon liked. Given that the District Attorney had arrived at Reid's townhome less than two minutes before, it was a bit of surprise. He looked over at his friend, who was standing at the edge of the couch, but saw only a slight smile on the young Asian man's face.

There were times when even Britt forgot that Kato was standing close by. The ability to fade into the background had saved not only Kato's life, but also Reid's on more than one occasion, both as the publisher of the *Daily Sentinel* and as The Green Hornet.

"Is it possible that, whoever the assassin might have been, he actually didn't intend to kill Layman, but rather scare him?" asked Britt, turning back to his visitor.

Scanlon had one of the sharpest legal minds that Britt Reid had ever encountered. The District Attorney drew his glasses off and proceeded to carefully clean them, a move designed not only to clear his vision, but to give him time to formulate an answer.

"I don't know, Britt. It turns out this was a very rare poison, a mixture of a paralytic agent and some other things similar to nightshade. Thankfully the doctor who was having dinner with Layman recognized what has happening and knew how to treat it. He served in Southeast Asia and had seen it before. Our lab might have missed any traces of the stuff if he didn't tell them what to look for. In that case, you would have been running an obituary rather than Axford's rather vitriolic, but accurate, diatribe," said Scanlon.

"That's Mike for you," laughed Reid. "I take it the fact of the poisoning is being withheld by the police."

"Yes. Right now, not even Layman knows it. He thinks he actually had a mild stroke, and I prefer to keep it that way. The doctor who saved his life is willing to cooperate, at least for awhile. He's afraid of what the Laymans would do if they knew he was working with us."

"Their reputation for not tolerating whistle-blowers got a boost last month," said Reid.

A few weeks before, during the demolition of a warehouse building in the harbor area, a man's body had been discovered. He had been identified as Aristae Lima, an accountant who had disappeared two years ago, just when he had been about to turn state's evidence against the Layman gang.

"If you don't mind me asking, would there have been an odor of sour milk on Layman's breath?" said Kato.

Scanlon arched his head around; he had obviously also forgotten that Kato was standing there, and that realization seemed to bother him slightly.

"There was no mention of anything like that, though it's hardly the sort of detail that most doctors would put on their medical report," he said. "I take it you have a thought on what might have happened?"

"I know of several herbs," said Kato, "particularly one called Evening Flower, that if properly prepared could mimic the effects of a stroke. Most are fairly rare, and even if someone could get his hands on them, the assassin might find himself suffering the same fate as his victim, if he was not very careful."

"Since we didn't find any bodies lying around the restaurant, other than Layman's, I think we can assume the attacker knows what he's doing," said Britt. "Is there any place in town that someone could get any of these drugs?"

Kato thought for a moment, and then nodded. "I know of one on Garibaldi Street."

"Not the most fashionable area of the city," said Scanlon, looking at Britt. "If you go there, you should be very careful."

"Of course," he said. "But *I* won't be going there."

The slight hornet-like buzz of the engine always brought a smile to Britt Reid's face. There were times it seemed like only yesterday that he had first heard it, when he and Kato had taken the Black Beauty out onto the streets.

The sleek vehicle moved quickly through the city streets, carefully staying away from the main parts of the city. Not that many people, even the police, would recognize the car as belonging to The Green Hornet, because even the official reports varied on just what it looked like, which suited The Hornet.

To say that the neighborhood was run down was to put things lightly. There were mostly abandoned buildings, interspaced with some warehouses and a few businesses. The store they searched for was a combination grocery store and herb shop.

The Green Hornet reached up and readjusted his mask slightly. He heard a muted chuckle coming from the driver's compartment.

"No comments from the peanut gallery," said The Hornet.

"Of course not. I wouldn't dream of such a thing." There was the slightest tone in his voice that told The Green Hornet his associate had a smile on his face. "We're two blocks from the store. As I recall, there is a side door which should serve our purposes."

"No, I think that we will use the front door, this time," said The Green Hornet. "After all, we are just paying a friendly visit to a local merchant."

There was no sign of anyone on the street beyond a stray cat sitting on a bus stop bench nearby. The Hornet could see a single set of neon lights glowing inside the shop. After a quick check of his weaponry, Hornet Sting, and gas gun, The Green Hornet stepped out of the car and headed inside the store. Almost as an afterthought he flipped the cracked plastic *Open* sign that hung on the door over so the words *Closed Come Again* were visible. Kato also came inside but remained close to the door in case there were any unexpected visitors.

Standing behind the counter in the center of the store was an Asian man who looked to be anywhere from his late forties to his sixties, standing behind one of the counters, a sandwich and a soda can in front of him.

"Frankly, I would have expected tea," said The Hornet.

The man replied in Mandarin Chinese, then paused and took a bite from his sandwich.

"I think we're getting off to a bad start," said The Hornet. "I know perfectly well that you speak English, so can we go from there." The Hornet picked up a small brass Buddha that looked more like something that could be found at any tourist trap in Detroit's Chinatown.

"True, but some of the people who come to my shop expect to hear me speaking Chinese, so I endeavor to give them what they want. It helps business. As for the soda, well, I never did develop a taste for tea; as far as I'm concerned it's vile even with heavy doses of sugar added. Besides, as you well know, there are advantages to doing the unexpected," he said.

The Hornet nodded. "Very true, sir. So what should I call you?"

"That would be Samuel Langhorne Chan. My father was a huge Mark Twain fan. You can either call me Mark, or Sam; I've been known to answer to both," he said with a smile "I would be a fool if I didn't already know who you are. I hope you don't think that I am a fool, sir. So what can I do for you?"

The Hornet picked up an orange from a small box containing a half dozen of them. He carefully cut it into sections and passed several to Sam and to Kato.

"No, you are not a fool, Doctor. You are a man who risked everything for freedom and wound up having to struggle, since the authorities wouldn't recognize your medical degree. So you ended up here, selling traditional herbal cures and groceries, and trying to keep the wolf from the door."

"But The Hornet makes it in anyway," chuckled Sam.

"True, but I'm just here for information. I'm seeking the names of anyone who might have recently purchased supplies of an herb called Evening Flower," said The Hornet.

"Nasty stuff; use it wrong and it is an almost incurable poison. Use it in the right proportions and with the right other ingredients and it can do much to alleviate pain and speed the healing process," said the older man.

"There are many things in life such as that," said The Green Hornet. "I suppose that your words are an oblique way of admitting that you have had someone come in asking for Evening Flower."

"I suppose I could claim doctor-patient confidentiality," said Sam.

"You could, but I doubt that it would hold up in court, given the circumstances," he said.

"True, though it might be interesting to see you pressing the matter in the legal arena," said Sam. "Yes, someone did come in and purchase some of the herb. Unfortunately, I can't give you a name, she never gave me one. Would a description help?"

"Her? Yes, that would be most helpful," said The Green Hornet.

"I thought as much," he nodded. "She was in her mid-twenties, shortish blonde hair, stood around five foot three or so, and had a slight East Coast accent."

"You have a good ear. Did she say why she wanted the herb and wasn't going to a regular pharmacy or doctor?"

"I did not ask for details. All she said was that a friend of hers had been injured in a sports accident, something to do with gymnastics, and did not trust more conventional medicine. I will say that she was a most convincing liar, for she even supplied me with details of the accident." The older man picked up his sandwich and took a small bite out of it, as if to signal he had said all he had to say.

"You suspected she was lying and still you sold her something that could be used as a poison?"

"Anything can be deadly if used wrong: a car, a table knife, even a bottle of soda. As for lying, many of my customers lie about what they are seeking. Many times the lies are as much for themselves as for me."

"You mentioned that she had an East Coast accent?"

"A slight one. Some years ago my niece married a man named Winchester from Boston, so I got to know the accent quite well."

"You've been very helpful. You wouldn't happen to have had a security camera running at the time?" said The Green Hornet.

"I wish I could afford that sort of system, although I suspect it would make many of my customers extremely nervous, smacking too much of China and the secret police. Those are things they do not want to be reminded of," said the older man.

"Quite understandable."

"However," Sam said, with a half smile. "I might just be able to assist you in another way." The older man picked up a pencil and began to sketch on the back of an envelope. His hand remained steady as his pencil flew back and forth. A few minutes later he passed a sketch of a young woman's face across the counter to The Hornet.

"I must say, Doctor, you are a man of many skills."

Sam picked up his sandwich and held it up. "I even make a pretty good ham and cheese."

"On that point I have no doubt. Thank you, Doctor. I trust that you will not mention our discussion to anyone," he said.

Samuel Langhorne Chan took a swallow from his soda. "Discussion? Since I haven't had any customers this evening, how could I have had a discussion with anyone?"

The Hornet touched the brim of his hat in farewell as he and Kato turned and walked out the door.

"Did you believe him?" asked Kato as the Black Beauty pulled away from the curb.

"Yes. He had no reason to lie. Remind me to make some inquires regarding his current status; perhaps he might do better for his community if he had a medical license again," said The Hornet.

"Will do. So where to now?"

Before The Hornet could answer, the car phone behind his seat began to beep in a slow steady beat.

"Up late, are we, Frank?" he said picking up the phone.

"It's part of the job," said the District Attorney. From the background sounds, The Hornet could tell that Scanlon was calling from the radio phone in his official car, probably at crime scene. "We've got a situation. Jerik Taylor is dead, apparently by natural causes. The emergency room doctor says that it was a stroke, just like his boss. He was nearly sixty and reportedly had a heart condition."

Taylor was the number two man in the Layman organization; he had a reputation for using a straight razor and a Louisville Slugger baseball bat to enforce the gang's wishes.

"And his breath?"

"Smelled like sour milk," said Scanlon.

"Looks like whoever is behind this has got a hit list and Taylor's name has been crossed off," said The Hornet. "We may have a lead: a young woman, blonde hair, athletic, with an East Coast accent and some knowledge of herbal medicine."

There was a long pause before Scanlon spoke again; The Hornet could hear him talking to other officers at the crime scene. "Let me do some checking," he said finally. "We'll talk in the morning."

"Come to my place for breakfast." The Green Hornet held the phone in his hand for a moment. This was definitely not like Scanlon. If anything, he thought the man seemed a bit distracted.

"Do you think this is the girl who bought the poison?" asked Scanlon as he shoved a thin file across the top of Britt Reid's desk in the privacy of the newspaper publisher's townhouse. The television was on but turned down, leaving the hosts of a local Detroit morning show moving in pantomime, but neither man was paying attention to it.

The newspaper publisher picked up the brown folder and flipped it open. The file had only a few pages in it, mostly appearing to be a condensation of what was obviously a bigger one. It was the summary report of the death of Aristae Lima. The man had been about to turn state's evidence and testify about the Layman organization when he had vanished without a trace.

"I remember the case," said Britt. "Layman, Taylor and a third man named Joseph Keene were the last ones seen with Lima, and then the man just vanished off the face of the earth until a few weeks ago."

"True, but what I wanted you to see is on the last page, which gives the bio material we have on Lima."

Britt skimmed that page and stopped when he saw what the District Attorney was talking about.

"A daughter, Arianna, who would be twenty five now," said Scanlon, producing a picture from his inside jacket and laying it on the table. Britt twisted his lip a moment, then pulled out the sketch that Sam Chang had made, laying it next to the photo of Arianna Lima. The resemblance was close enough to satisfy both of them.

"She lived in Maine while going to the University of Maine at Orono; she was pre-med. According to our records, she was a champion gymnast who would have made the Olympic team, but for an auto accident," said Scanlon.

"So where is she?" asked Reid.

"That's a damn good question. After her father's body was discovered she dropped out of sight. I think we may have our assassin; she's decided to avenge her father by killing men who she believes murdered him," Scanlon said. "But why wait this long?"

"Maybe she kept hoping that he would come walking in the door one day," said Reid. "Then, when they found his body, her hopes were crushed."

"If she is the one behind this, we've got to find her, before she gets to Joseph Keene, who is, I suspect, her third and final target," said Scanlon.

"Okay, what's the rest of it?" asked Britt.

"Joseph Keene did not kill Arianna's father; he wasn't actually with Layman and Taylor when the killing happened. But they both swore that he was their alibi, which made him one of the main suspects."

"And we know this why?" asked Britt. There were several scenarios running through his mind just then, but one thing experience had taught him was to not jump to conclusions.

"Because Joseph Keene is an undercover policeman. He's spent years working his way into the Layman organization. We could have arrested Layman and Taylor on the Lima killing with Keene's evidence, but we've waited in order to be able to take down the whole organization. The problem is Arianna Lima thinks that Keene had a hand in killing her father, so he's next on her list."

Joseph Keene stared across the table at the two men who sat there smiling: Alexander Maclean and Finn Armstrong. They had arrived at the offices of Layman and Company a few minutes earlier, ostensibly to offer condolences on the death of Jerik Taylor and hopes for Layman's recovery.

Keene had been expecting them, or any of a half dozen others, to walk through the door since he had been awakened from a sound sleep with the news of Taylor's death. Maclean and Armstrong represented an Irish gang from the south side that had been nibbling at several areas in which the Laymans currently held sway. They were, for the moment, more an annoyance than anything else, but that could change and escalate to a threat without a lot of provocation.

"I thank you for your concern, Mr. Maclean, Mr. Armstrong. But Mr. Layman is expected to make a full recovery and it wouldn't surprise me to see him back here in the office within a week, at the outside," said Keene.

"I'm very glad to hear that. The reports we were getting were his recovery was still heavily in doubt," said Armstrong. He had a slight Irish accent that, at times, shifted over into sounding like someone doing a bad impression of an Irish accent. "That doesn't change the reason we're here."

"Really?" Keene said. "Why don't you tell me more?"

Maclean nodded, pulling out a small notebook from his inside coat pocket. "Let us say, we've been taking a look at business operations in the western part of the city and think what you have been doing there could stand some improving. In fact, there are areas where you haven't exploited the full money-making potential. It happens that the people we represent are quite adept at that."

"Let's cut to the chase. I know all about your drug operations. We're prepared to allow it in our territory, but only under *our* supervision. I would imagine a split of, say, eighty-twenty, in our favor, would satisfy both sides," said Keene.

"That's not the way it works. The numbers are good, but you have them reversed," said Armstrong as he carefully unbuttoned his suit jacket.

Keene knew what he was trying to imply, that it was now easier to reach the gun he supposedly had in his shoulder holster. However, he recognized the style suit the man was wearing. Keene had three of them himself, and it was not cut to hide any kind of weapon.

"It's exactly the way it works, and if you don't think I was expecting an 'offer' like that, then you're insulting my intelligence," said Keene.

"Please. It wasn't as if we were going to come in here, guns blazing, and take over your operation. That's too much like something out of an old movie," said Maclean. "After all, I'm a businessman and just came here to talk about what I'd consider mutually beneficial business ideas. I think you need to make some new business arrangements; otherwise, things might get very cutthroat, perhaps in more ways than one."

"Threats are not what I consider a good way of doing business," said Keene. "Besides, I've already made my own business arrangements and am quite happy with them."

"And they would be?" asked Maclean.

That was when the side door to the conference room opened and The Green Hornet stepped through, followed by his silent companion. Keene scratched his lip with his teeth but remained silent; this was not something that he had expected. He'd heard of The Green Hornet, had even seen photos, but a part of him had considered the master criminal to be simply an urban legend.

Maclean was out of his chair and had taken two steps toward the intruders when The Hornet's cohort turned and launched himself at Maclean, landing a solid closed fist blow to the man's chest, followed by a kick that sent the man back against the wall. Two throwing darts materialized in the bodyguard's hands and then struck the table, imbedding themselves in the wood between the fingers of Armstrong's right hand.

"There are new arrangements, gentlemen; they are with me," said The Hornet, his voice controlled and even but still carrying a tone of "you don't want to mess with me." "I suggest that you take your friend and get out of here. You can tell your associates that I'm taking over the Layman operations and anyone else interferes at their own risk."

Armstrong sat still for a few moments, and then nodded. "I've always been one to know better than to spit when the wind was blowing in my face." Very slowly Armstrong got up and walked over to Maclean, who was starting to stir. The big man came slowly to his feet, stared menacingly at The Hornet's bodyguard for a moment, then turned and walked away with his companion.

"Nice entrance," said Keene. "I suppose now you are going to make a few demands of your own."

"Actually, I'm not going to make any demands," said The Green Hornet, as he replaced the Hornet Sting in an inside pocket of his overcoat. "I'm going to leave things exactly as they are, Officer Clegg."

His real name was not something that Keene had not expected to hear the masked criminal say. Given The Hornet's companion's fighting abilities, he wondered how much of a chance he had to make it to the door, or even back to his desk to hit the panic button that would bring building security.

"Officer?"

"Don't try to play me for a fool. I've been aware for some time that you're an undercover policeman working on the gang task force, with the intention of taking down the Layman organization. It suits me to have exactly that happen," said The Hornet. "How much longer before your task force is ready to bring indictments?"

"Off hand, I would say three to four months." It surprised Keene that he was talking so openly to a master criminal. "But to be on the safe side, I would guess six months."

"Good. You can tell Layman that you hired me to intimidate your 'competition.' As I said, I want this whole house of cards come tumbling down. But to do that I need you alive, so I think it might be best if you absented yourself from the office for a few days. Those fellows who just left might decide to make their own business moves."

"Actually, that's not a bad idea. We have a penthouse apartment that very few people know about in the Columbian building. Maybe I'll go there for a few days; it can't hurt," said Keene.

The Hornet motioned for his companion to follow him and stepped toward the door. "I think that is an excellent idea."

"But what will you be doing in the meantime?" asked Keene.

The Hornet looked at him and smiled, it was a gesture that sent shivers down the undercover policeman's spine. "Now, that would be telling."

The bell at St. Paul's Episcopal Church three blocks away was tolling one a.m., and the wind had gotten up. But the air conditioning units on the roof of the exclusive Columbian Apartments provided not only a wind break, but enough places for The Green Hornet and Kato to remain out of sight.

"How can you be sure that she will come?" asked Kato.

"Because Keene will lead her here. She was watching him while we were there," said The Hornet. When they had entered Keene's office, he had caught sight of something moving in the window of a building across the street. Since that building was unoccupied, the idea that someone was there and watching seemed the logical conclusion.

"That's why you told him to wait an hour before heading over here," said Kato.

Before The Green Hornet could say anything he heard the door to the stairwell open and close. The masked man motioned for Kato to move toward one side of the roof while he moved toward the other, leaving Arianna Lima access to the air vent that led to the Layman penthouse.

The sounds of the city around the building faded to a low murmur as The Hornet made his way along the west end. When he heard the sound of fighting, he took to his heels and crossed the roof in only a matter of seconds.

A small black-clad figure, with climbing gear strapped around her, hung from the arm of a long television pole, whirling around it three times just above Kato. The Hornet's partner, who was in an attack crouch, launched himself up into the air at the same moment, timing his own leap perfectly, to pull the intruder down to the ground in a single fluid motion.

Kato's opponent did not stop moving, twisting and jerking first one way and then the other, but he held on. Finally she was able to grab onto a television antenna and twist hard enough to free herself. The two of them faced each other, unmoving, each taking the other's measure. She dodged several blows from Kato, and was about to retreat toward the stairwell when The Green Hornet tackled her, sending them both crashing onto the roof.

Even in his iron grip she had squirmed halfway to freedom when a burst of Hornet gas from his gun turned her into a limp mass.

The Green Hornet knelt next to the girl; even in the dim light he could see the same features that were in Chan's drawing and Scanlon's photograph. From the pouch attached to her belt he brought out a small baggie with a grayish white powder in it.

"Evening Flower," he said, passing the baggie over to Kato, who put it inside his own jacket. A quick search also found a small pistol, as well as a knife. "I would say she had a plan B and C."

"Do you think we should tie her up?" asked Kato. "She might be more willing to listen to reason that way."

"I think we can take a chance." The Hornet reached down and gently patted the girl's cheeks. "I only gave her a quarter shot of the gas. Arianna, Arianna. Can you hear me?"

A moment or two later the girl began to stir, her head moving from side to side as she struggled to sit up. She seemed a bit confused at first, which was a side effect of The Hornet's gas.

"Arianna Lima, listen to me. We're not going to hurt you," he said, as gently as possible.

"Yeah, like I believe that one. The next thing you're going to tell me is you can make me a great deal on the Brooklyn Bridge," she said.

"Sorry," chuckled The Green Hornet. "I sold that last week. Would you be interested in some swamp land in southern Arizona?"

"Great, I fall into the hands of a criminal comedian who really needs to hire better writers," she said. "I suppose now you're going to turn me over to Keene? Or is he working for you?"

"Neither," said The Green Hornet, reaching down to help the girl to her feet. "He actually works for the city of Detroit."

"What are you talking about? The Layman mob is powerful but they don't own the city, at least not yet. And frankly, I don't care; Keene was one of the ones that killed my father."

The Green Hornet reached into his overcoat and brought out three folded sheets of paper that he offered her. "This is from a file in the District Attorney's office."

She took the pages and skimmed over them, then looked at both The Hornet and Kato. "Is this true?"

"Yes, Keene is an undercover cop. He had nothing to do with your father's death. According to my information, he even tried to stop it and get him away safely. He was just too late."

The Hornet watched a variety of emotions wash across the girl's face, and then saw her shoulders stiffen.

"Say I believe this, what happens next? You turn me over to the cops for doing the other two?" she asked. "Why are you sticking your nose into this whole thing, anyway?"

"Keene and his people are within four to six months of taking down the whole Layman organization and putting them away for a very long time. I'm not asking you to believe me. I'm just suggesting that you wait, give the police time to do this, and it's in my interests to have exactly that happen. Let that be your revenge," he said.

Arianna Lima stood there for a very long time; in the distance were the sounds of cars, horns, sirens, and even the cooing and cawing of pigeons and crows.

"I believe you; so for now, I'm going to do what you suggest, wait and watch. You can tell Keene, along with that useless District Attorney Scanlon, that I'm still out there. I'll give them a year; if nothing has happened, well then you can bet that green fedora of yours I'll come back and go after Keene. If I do, don't get in my way."

"Agreed. But if you cross me and end up cutting into my business, into my profits, then I will make your life a living hell," said The Green Hornet.

"Not to worry on that regard," she said.

"So, what are you going to do now?" asked The Hornet.

"Naughty, naughty, sir, that would be telling," Arianna smiled.

The Green Hornet wasn't a hundred percent sure what she would do. She walked toward the edge of the building and looked down at the street. Before The Hornet could say anything, she clipped the hook of the climbing rope she wore around her waist to a metal support on the building's edge and leaped over. In a matter of seconds, she was two stories down and scrambling in a window just below the penthouse.

"Should we go after her?" asked Kato.

"Not this time, we've done what we came here for" said The Green Hornet. "Keene is safe and Aristae Lima's killers will be called to account for their actions in a court of law in the not too distant future."

Kato nodded and the two men headed for the stairwell.

"What's the matter, Mike? You look like you've lost your last friend in the world," said Lenore Case as she walked up to his desk in the far corner of the *Daily Sentinel* newsroom.

The sight of Britt Reid's personal secretary, dressed in a stylish but businesslike skirt and blouse, never failed to bring a smile to Mike Axford's face. Although it seemed to Lenore Case that this time it was a little bit more forced than usual.

"Casey, Casey, it's this whole thing with the Layman gang. It looks like the District Attorney is going to nail the lot of them," said Axford, pushing his copy of the early edition of the *Sentinel*. The headline proclaimed a crackdown on criminal gangs and had a large picture, above the fold, of members of the Layman organization being led away in handcuffs.

"Now, Mike, don't get me wrong if I ask this, but isn't that a good thing?" asked Casey. She already knew where Axford's mind was on the case; he had been ranting about it for months, since the elder Layman's stroke.

"Of course it's a good thing, but Scanlon isn't even mentioning The Gre—"

"—en Hornet," Casey finished with a smile. She would have been seriously worried if Axford were not trying to find a connection to The Green Hornet in this case. "Did it occur to you that maybe, this one time, The Hornet might not be involved in this whole thing? After all, he is only one man; he can't be behind everything."

"You're beginning to sound like our boss," Axford said. "Not that, in most cases, it isn't a good thing. I just wish he would agree with me more about The Hornet."

"Mike, he just wants that solid reporting that earned you all those awards and a reputation as one of the best journalists in Detroit," she said.

Axford got a huge grin on his face. "I have a strong suspicion that Britt told you to say that, but thank you for saying it, nonetheless. Now, Miss Lenore Case, will you let this crazy Irishman do wonders for Mike Axeford's reputation and be seen taking you to lunch?"

Casey smiled and slid her arm into Mike's, saying, "Mr. Axford, sir, it would do wonders for *my* reputation to be seen having lunch with you."

SUMMER OF DEATH

by Barry Reese

Hidden in the heart of San Francisco lay a place where men toiled and died for the amusement of the idle rich.

The combat arena was a circular area, bounded by a chain link fence that offered protection for those viewing the bloody spectacle while simultaneously preventing the participants from escaping. The smell of sweat and blood hung heavy in the air and the accumulated heat of so many people pressed into a poorly ventilated area gave the proceedings the feel of an ancient Gladiatorial event.

There were a series of ceiling fans that hung over the combat area, but they mostly seemed to stir up the hot air, offering little in the way of respite from the stifling scene.

Men and women in fancy dress sat behind the fence, wearing Mardi Gras style masks over their faces. The disguises did little to hide their identities, but it was part of the game, part of the glamour. Here in the arena people cast aside their public faces and became someone new, someone more primal in their desires. Here they came to indulge in that most ancient of human pleasures: the sadomasochist urges that even centuries of so-called civilization had failed to eliminate.

Hayashi Kato crouched with one hand raised behind him and the other held straight out before his well chiseled body. He moved in a semi-circle, sweat running down his lean torso. He wore only his mask and a pair of loose pants while his opponent was dressed in sandals, corduroy slacks, and a vest. The man had been wearing a bead necklace when the battle had begun but Kato had quickly turned the jewelry into a weapon, nearly strangling the man with it before it had snapped. The beads had tumbled to the floor, becoming a perpetual hazard ever since. Twice, even the nimble footed Kato had nearly slipped on the beads, which rolled about the floor at the slightest contact.

Kato sensed that his opponent was tensing to strike and a dozen ways of incapacitating him sprang to mind. In truth, Kato could have ended this battle long ago, but Britt had asked him to make it look good so that the audience might be properly entertained. Kato and Britt Reid were as close as brothers and their trust in one another was unshakable. If Britt asked him to play these games of violence and death, Kato would do so. In Britt's roles as owner of the *Daily Sentinel*, and as The Green Hornet, he accepted Kato as a trusted advisor and partner, though most of the world saw Kato as a servant and nothing more. In reality, nothing could be farther from the truth.

The attack finally came, accompanied by an animalistic roar. Kato heard the cheers of the crowd but he ignored them, throwing up a block that caught the man's right arm under the elbow. Kato continued the motion so that his attacker's momentum carried him off-course, causing him to stumble and fall to the ground. Momentarily disoriented, the man was unable to evade Kato's next attack: a sharp kick with his heel to the neck. If he had so wished, Kato could have snapped the man's neck like kindling. But Kato was no deliverer of death. He would leave his opponent alive, so that he might someday learn the error of his ways.

Kato relaxed, letting his arms fall by his sides. He slowly turned to acknowledge the crowd, who screamed their appreciation. Some of them demanded that the fallen man be finished, but Kato merely walked away from his opponent. He let his eyes travel from face to face, as if memorizing the details. In the Far East, he had learned several harsh lessons about the depths to which humanity might descend. He had seen the yakuza and the zaibatsu destroy their own people, all in pursuit of power and money. And at the side of The Green Hornet, he had faced evil incarnate. But these people, screaming for blood, were some of the most disturbing that he had ever encountered.

And the fact that all this violence was being carried out in the heart of the Haight-Ashbury district of San Francisco, the epicenter of the peace and love movement, was even worse. Kato knew that back in his usual stomping grounds of Detroit, the city was laboring under a series of brutal race riots, indicating a fraying of society's fragile bonds. The youths who had congregated here in Haight-Ashbury were seeking a way of rebuilding humanity's faith in each other and though Kato felt some of their goals were being lost in the haze of rampant drug abuse, he admired their ultimate aims.

Kato saw a gate opening up before him and several men in dark suits entered to retrieve the fallen competitor. These were the guards who stood just outside the fence during the combats. Each was armed with an electric cattle prod, in case the gladiators proved bothersome. One of the men gestured for Kato to exit the arena and the handsome young Asian did so, but not before spotting his partner in the rear of the crowd. The Green Hornet was dressed for work, in his midnight green coat and mask. They exchanged a silent greeting, each nodding their heads almost imperceptibly. The Hornet was safely in the shadows, where few of the crowds would notice him, but Kato's keen eyes had caught the familiar glimpse of green.

The duo had been in San Francisco for less than forty-eight hours.

Mr. Gaunt poured himself a stiff brandy and glanced over at The Green Hornet, who stood impassively near the door. "Please, have a seat," Gaunt said. "Can I get you to something to drink?"

The Green Hornet's eyes were narrowed to small slits. When he spoke, he sounded nothing like mild-mannered Britt Reid. There were no traces of Britt's easy-going nature. His words were terse and spoken in a husky undertone. "You saw what my man could do. He's the best fighter you'll ever get in this two bit arena."

Donald Gaunt crossed over to a plush chair and sat down, crossing his legs. He held his glass in one hand and affected a slightly feminine air. He was painfully thin, perfectly in keeping with his family name. He wore a pair of well-shined shoes, dark trousers, and a white shirt. Over all of this was cinched a smoking jacket of deep purple. His silver hair was slicked back with so much oil that it gleamed in the light. "He was very impressive. His knowledge of kung fu is breathtaking. What was the style he was using tonight?"

"It's called wing chun."

Gaunt nodded and took a sip. He gazed around his study, which was decorated in an overly masculine fashion. On the wall behind him was a pair of African spears crossed behind a canvas shield, while a bearskin rug, complete with claws and head, lay on the floor. An oil painting of a naked woman dominated the wall next to The Green Hornet. It was as if someone had set out to create a room that could only belong to a heterosexual male. It was done so forcefully that it actually created the exact opposite effect.

"Tell me again how you heard about my operation, if you don't mind," Gaunt said. "Your exploits in Detroit are well known even in California, but I doubt the same could be said in return for me. I would think I'm such a small fish that you'd barely take notice."

The Green Hornet knew he couldn't reveal the truth about why he was here, though his errand of mercy was always present in his mind. As owner of both DSTV and the *Daily Sentinel* in Detroit, Britt Reid was never far from the news. When one his top reporters, Ed Lowery, had revealed to him that the son of wealthy Detroit native Dan Carpenter had vanished in San Francisco, he'd at first thought it anything but newsworthy. So many people had descended upon the California city over the past few months that its streets were lined with young people who thought they were creating a new culture for themselves and for the world.

But Lowery's instincts had told him there was a lot more to the story and, as usual, he had been right. A number of dead bodies had been piling up in the Haight-Asbury district, most of them burned beyond recognition. Those that had been identified all began to fit a definite profile: young men in their late teens or early twenties in excellent physical condition and with some knowledge of fighting, be it boxing or martial arts. When Lowery had pointed out that Dan Carpenter's son, Cal, had been a local boxing champion before falling into the free love movement, the appropriate red flags were raised.

Britt had known Dan Carpenter for years and had associated with him at various charitable benefits. But it wasn't that association that had led The Green Hornet to San Francisco. He hadn't decided to fly to the West Coast until he'd called in a few favors with District Attorney Scanlon and gotten access to the autopsy reports of the dead youths from San Francisco. Several of them had a strange chemical cocktail in their bloodstreams, one that Britt and Kato suspected would render them unable to control their violent tendencies.

In other words, someone was taking young men off the streets and drugging them into being warriors. Though the bodies were too burned to be sure, Britt was positive that each of these young men would have shown numerous bruises and marks consistent with combat. After informing the staff of the *Daily Sentinel* that he'd be attending a publisher's conference out of town, Britt had headed West, eager to uncover the truth behind this disturbing mystery.

Instead of sharing these reasons with Mr. Gaunt, The Green Hornet chose instead to play the role that was so familiar to him that it was almost second nature. To the men and women of the underworld, The Green Hornet was not a nocturnal avenger, he was one of *them*.

"You're cleaning up out here. Every big spender from Seattle to Mexico City is coming here for a piece of the action. I want in. And you have to like what you just saw in the arena. My man's the star you've been waiting for."

Gaunt pursed his lips and sloshed around the liquid in his glass. The masked man disturbed him greatly, not just because of his manner and reputation, but also for what he meant in the greater scheme of things. The arena had been a fun and profitable pursuit for many months, but now that it was attracting the attention of the likes of The Green Hornet, Gaunt wasn't sure how enjoyable the future would be. Then again, The Hornet might be able to bring in even more money, especially with that fighter of his.

"All right, Hornet, I'll cut you in, but only on the profits from the fights your man is involved in."

"Not good enough." The Green Hornet stepped forward, coming to a halt just a few feet from Gaunt. He pointed a gloved finger at the criminal, lacing his every word with hidden threat. "I know what you're doing here, Gaunt. I know about the drugs you pump into those boys if they're not willing to fight, and I can think of lots of applications for that. I want samples."

Gaunt thought about arguing on this point but he elected to simply shrug and say, "Of course. Perhaps you'd be able to refine the formula. At present, repeated dosages cause brain damage, making it a very short-term solution. But we go through fighters so quickly that it's sometimes necessary to draft the reluctant into service. Sort of like the war." Gaunt chuckled and The Green Hornet offered a thin smile, as if sharing the joke.

The Hornet turned and headed towards the door. He stopped just shy of the exit and turned to face his host. "I'll be here in plenty of time for the first bout tomorrow night. I expect you to have a sample of the chemicals you're using waiting for me. Don't try to hide anything from me, Gaunt ... or I swear I'll dump you into the San Francisco Bay and take over this entire operation for myself."

Gaunt said nothing until The Hornet was gone, but then he threw his drink against the wall. The glass shattered and its contents trickled down onto the carpet. Gaunt stood, his anger rising. He had built this empire and while he was certainly willing to share in any increased profits The Hornet might bring, he would not be treated like a servant.

His thoughts drifted to mysterious fighter that The Hornet had brought with him. Right now, the man would be recovering in the fighters' barracks . . . A smile slowly formed on Gaunt's thin lips.

I'll have your sample ready for you tomorrow night, Green Hornet, don't worry about that. You'll get a firsthand view of how effective it truly is. . . .

The Green Hornet left the building with great haste. The offices above ground were nothing unusual, and the elevator that led to the levels below was not easy to find. There was little to suggest that this was a place where men fought and died.

The moon hung in the sky like a thick ball of cotton; its edges were obscured by a thin layer of cloud cover. The night was surprisingly chilly to someone whose view of California was etched forever by photographs of bikini-clad beauties and the music of the Beach Boys. Britt knew that many of the young people who fled to this area came poorly dressed for the often-chilly San Francisco weather, and most of them were camped out in overcrowded apartments or in the public parks. The Summer of Love was quickly losing its luster as drugs, poor hygiene, and rampant crime polluted the hippie dream of free love and peace.

The area in which Gaunt's lair was housed was a fashionable one, just south of the heart of the Haight-Asbury district. At this hour of night, the only people on the streets were stragglers leaving the arena. Their expensive cars pulled away, carrying giggling, half-drunk owners back to their posh homes. Their masks had been discarded, left behind in the arena, and they almost appeared human once more . . . but The Green Hornet had trouble viewing them that way. Once he'd seen a woman begging at the top of her lungs for blood, it was difficult to see her as anything other than a monster.

The Green Hornet stepped into an alleyway, ignoring the newspapers and trash that blew past his ankles. A 1966 Chrysler Crown Imperial was waiting there. Though at first glance it looked much like the famous Black Beauty, this was not the vehicle that had become known to police officers and underworld figures alike. It would have proven too difficult to drive the Black Beauty cross-country, since police throughout the nation were on the lookout for any car matching its description.

The duo had instead opted to fly to San Francisco with their equipment safely hidden in their luggage. When Kato had first shown him the rental car he'd arranged for their stay in the city, Britt had smiled in disbelief, wondering just how his friend had managed to find a vehicle that looked so much like their own.

The Hornet expertly navigated through the city streets, heading towards the temporary headquarters he'd established in the top floor of a midtown apartment building. He'd rented the loft-style apartment using one of the many false identities that he'd cultivated specifically for these sorts of missions. It was always good to avoid leaving behind any kind of paper trail that might lead back to Britt Reid. The added factor of paying in cash generally prevented anyone from asking too many questions.

The Hornet parked his vehicle and checked the time, knowing he'd waited long enough. He reached into his emerald coat and retrieved a heavy gold pocket watch. As with the Black Beauty, the pocket watch was far more than it appeared. Kato's brilliance had transformed it into a sophisticated electronic device. Though it was typically used as a means for The Hornet to signal the District Attorney, it was capable of far more.

After setting the watch to 3:45 and pressing the stud on top, The Hornet watched as a small antenna projected outward. He then held the device up close to his lips and began to speak, knowing that his words would be transmitted to Kato via a miniaturized unit located in his partner's left ear.

"Gaunt believes my story and I expect he'll give me a sample of the chemical compound tomorrow evening. I'd still like to have the chance to study it before we shut them down. We have no idea how many men he's got who are addicted to this stuff, and it would definitely help if we'd have something to combat the effects. Keep an eye out for Carpenter's son. Take care, my friend."

In a dimly lit barracks, Kato lay on his back, staring up at the underside of his bunkmate's mattress. He had known that The Hornet would be contacting him within minutes of the fight, so he'd tried to find a quiet place where nothing would interfere with the small transmitter buried deep in his ear. The clarity had been so impressive that it sounded like Britt had been at his side, whispering every word.

Kato reached up and massaged the bridge of his nose. To any onlooker it would have appeared that he was attempting to combat a headache or some injury gained in the arena. In truth, he was checking to make sure that his disguise was still in place. The small mask he wore would have done little to keep Gaunt's men from eventually identifying him, but The Green Hornet had helped alter his facial structure with carefully applied prosthetics and makeup.

It was a subtle change, but just enough to keep anyone from confusing him for Britt Reid's chauffeur, should that question ever arise.

Swinging his feet over the edge of his bed, Kato stared around at his new home. There were twenty other men here, most of them lying silently on their backs. A few walked around somewhat aimlessly, their eyes looking sunken and hollow. Four of the men were strapped to their beds and they growled deep in their throats, occasionally thrashing about as they strained against their bonds.

These were men who had been "Juiced," to use the parlance of their captors. These men had refused to fight under any circumstances, even when offered drugs, prostitutes, or money. The last temptation was a ruse and all eventually came to know it—the money would be given to the fighters upon their exit from the fighting arena. But no one ever left the arena, except under the cover of darkness, his body wrapped tightly in a black bag.

Kato stood up, his eyes scanning the faces of the other men. He didn't see the one he had bested in the arena. Presumably, he was being treated in a medical facility. Kato chose not to believe that they would kill him outright. After being inside this place for just under twenty-four hours, he had come to the conclusion that the burned bodies belonged to those who had died in battle, not to ones that had been killed for having lost their fights. There were many here who had lost multiple bouts, he had learned.

Britt had reminded him to look out for the younger Carpenter, but Kato had seen no one who matched the photograph he had been shown. Of course, if Cal Carpenter had joined with the hippie movement as his father believed, his appearance might have greatly changed. While Cal had once been a clean-shaven man with a short hair cut, it was commonplace for young men to adopt longer hair and grow beards once they arrived in San Francisco. It was very possible that even his own father might have difficulty recognizing him now.

"Who are you looking for?"

Kato turned to see that the man in the bunk above was watching him. He was in good shape, with shoulder length brown hair and bright green eyes. His face was unshaven and thin. Like Kato, he was dressed in loose fitting pants and an oversized button up shirt. Both men wore sandals, as did everyone in the barracks.

"A friend," Kato replied, staring into the other man's eyes. He was pleased to see the light of intelligence still shining there.

"This isn't a good place to find friends," the other man said with a wry grin. He held out a hand and Kato accepted it. "Name's Doug. I saw you tonight. You move like greased lightning."

"Thank you, Douglas." Kato quickly noted that the man's nose had been broken recently and that he winced as he lay back on the back. "Are you injured?"

"Just the usual, man. So what are you doing here? What's your price for playing?"

"As I said, I am looking for a friend. His name is Cal Carpenter."

Doug's manner changed abruptly and he lowered his voice. "Are you thinking of breaking him out of here?"

"I am. Would you like to come with us?"

Doug stared at him as if the very idea was something not worthy of consideration. "No thanks, man. I don't want to end up being anybody's human torch, if you know what I mean."

"I know that I would prefer to die with honor than to live as another man's slave."

The words that Kato spoke came out with calmness but great strength and they appeared to touch something inside Doug. "Wow. That's heavy." Doug sat up again, grimacing at the pain he felt. He took a deep breath and appeared to be considering his next words. "I know where Cal is. He's recovering. Broke his leg in a bad fall the other day. He's good, that's why they're tending to him and not putting him down."

Kato's eyes narrowed. So Gaunt and his men did sometimes sacrifice those who couldn't fight any more. "If you know that you could die here, why do you not resist?" he asked, unable to restrain his curiosity. Freedom of self was such an important part of Kato's being that he found it difficult to understand someone being willing to throw that away.

Doug shrugged and looked away. "I used to do a little karate when I was a kid. Always liked sparring. When I came out here, I couldn't keep a job and needed some dough. So when a guy came around, offering me money and some hashish if I'd do a little sparring for people to watch, it sounded good to me. First night I was here I saw a kid die. The guy he was fighting was high on the Juice and went crazy on him. Snapped his neck and still kept beating him. I told Mr. Gaunt that I wanted to leave but he told me I could either stay and get my three meals a day while fighting at night or he could Juice me and I'd end up crazy or dead. Or both."

"But there are nearly two dozen of you here. You could rise up and fight. Resist."

"Gaunt's men have those cattle prods, man. Our fists aren't going to do much good against those. Besides, some of these guys like it here. They get their weed and sometimes they bring in girls." Doug shook his head bitterly. "But if you're serious about getting out of here, I'll give it a go. I saw you in there tonight. It was righteous, man. You were like the hammer of God."

Kato smiled. He heard the single door to the barracks opening and watched as a man pushed in a cart filled with cellophane covered plates of food. Two armed guards followed but neither seemed to be expecting any trouble. Still whispering, Kato asked, "Where do they keep the injured fighters?"

"Down the hall. There's a doctor and a couple of nurses who watch over them."

Kato nodded and quietly accepted his tray of food. After Doug had received his and the attendant had moved on with the guards in tow, The Green Hornet's partner said, "Eat. Get your strength up. In a few days' time, we will make our move."

Britt Reid woke up at six in the morning and immediately indulged in his daily ritual. He had a cup of warm tea, followed by an hour-long session of yoga and Tai chi chuan, both of which Kato had introduced to him.

Suitably refreshed, The Green Hornet then spent the day studying photographs that he'd taken at Gaunt's lair. He'd used a miniaturized camera that was hidden in the right sleeve of his jacket, carefully arranging his hands so that he might get clear shots of the men and women in the arena and of the fortifications surrounding it.

A few of the crowd had been easily identifiable, even with their party masks in place. He had one particularly good shot of the Mayor's niece, her pink tongue flicking across her lips as she relished the violence before her. When Gaunt's criminal empire finally crumbled, The Hornet would make sure that these photographs found their way into the public's collective eye. Those who had funded the operation were just as guilty as the man behind it all.

By the end of the day he had been able to fashion a mock set of blueprints for the hidden areas of Gaunt's building, including exits and security posts.

Checking the time and realizing that he had just twenty minutes to get to the arena, he donned the rest of his gear and returned to his rental car.

Once he was behind the wheel, he checked his gun to make sure that it was in functioning order. It was a modified automatic with an elongated barrel and was capable of emitting a thick cloud of sleeping gas. He also verified that the Hornet Sting was ready for action, testing to make sure that the metal baton could telescope out to its full length without any problem. He didn't bother turning on the sonic cutting device but he checked its power level nonetheless.

It felt strange to be doing these things without Kato at his side. Though their public roles required Kato to play the role of manservant and driver, it was safe to say that the younger man was as important a player in their shared war on crime as The Hornet himself.

With grim determination, The Green Hornet set off for another evening amongst human devils.

The Green Hornet was surprised—and not very pleased—to find that Gaunt was waiting for him in the front row of the arena and not in his office. From what he'd learned of Gaunt, the man typically watched the bouts via closed circuit television, enjoying the spectacle but not to the extent where he'd risk getting blood or sweat on his person.

Led by a guard who brandished an electric cattle prod in one hand, The Hornet was taken through the crowd. There was an almost palpable sense of excitement in the air and it turned The Green Hornet's stomach. How could these people be here, clamoring for blood, while elsewhere in the same city people believed they were fighting for the elimination of war in its entirety?

The Hornet's dislike of his surroundings wasn't the only thing keeping him on edge. Normally, he and Kato took extreme lengths to avoid doing anything even remotely public. Yet here he was, striding through a crowded arena, in his full Hornet regalia. Given the fact that almost everyone was masked and that no one wanted to look each other in the face for fear of being recognized, he felt somewhat assured that he was doing the right thing.

Gaunt was seated next to the one entrance into the arena. He looked like the cat that ate the canary and The Hornet was immediately put on edge. He saw that a small vial of gray-colored fluid was perched on the armrest of Gaunt's chair and relaxed somewhat. Perhaps Gaunt meant to follow orders, after all.

"Ah, Hornet. I was beginning to worry you were going to miss the first match. I decided to start with your young friend."

The Green Hornet glanced towards the arena and saw that Kato was already inside, pacing about like a caged tiger. Now he knew why the crowd was in such frenzy. They were anxious to see the arena's newest star strut his stuff. Something in Kato's manner didn't appear quite right, however. The Green Hornet stared at his friend for a moment, detecting an unusual eagerness in Kato's body language. Realizing that Gaunt was watching him closely, he tried to avoid looking concerned.

"You have the sample?"

"I do." Gaunt lifted up the vial and stared at it. "But looking at it under a microscope is hardly a fitting test of its properties. You really must see its effects up close."

The Green Hornet said nothing, though his hand began to drift down to the Hornet Gun inside his jacket. Something was very, very wrong. He quickly scanned the people seated around Gaunt and his eyes widened as several of them now rose from their chairs, drawing the ever-present cattle prods and brandishing them in the direction of the emerald-clad avenger. "What's your game, Gaunt?"

"The arena. That's my game. You should know that." Gaunt chuckled and leaned back in his chair. "I'm going to be known as the man who took down The Hornet."

"You going to have your men beat me to death?"

"Of course not. You've seen my operation. Can't you guess what I'm planning? Your friend in there had his food last night laced with the Juice. Another dose was administered a few hours ago. He's in a rage and ready to kill anyone who comes close. You should have seen the fight he put up when we tried to move him from the barracks into the arena!" Gaunt crossed his legs, pursing his lips in a prissy fashion. "Of course, what am I saying? You're going to get to see what I mean. Up close and personal."

The Hornet looked back towards Kato, noting out of the corner of his eye that the guards were opening the gate and gesturing for him to enter the ring. The Green Hornet considered his options, knowing that he could try to pull forth the Hornet Gun, but there might be a gun or two amongst the men. If there was, he'd be cut down before the gas could take effect.

"You're signing your own death warrant," The Hornet warned.

"Assuming you survive the fight with your friend, the best you can hope for is to be added to my ranks of fighters." Gaunt gestured for his men to begin herding The Green Hornet into the arena. The masked man didn't put up a fight, having come to the conclusion that he needed to play along for now. If he could somehow restore Kato to his rightful state, they'd have a much better chance of escaping than he would alone.

The gate was closed and locked behind him, leaving The Green Hornet facing his dearest friend. Kato stood like a tensed coil ready to spring, his eyes blazing. There was seemingly no trace of his ally's true self remaining. Kato looked like a killing machine and nothing else.

The roaring of the crowd reached new heights as Kato charged forward, sprinting at tremendous speed. When he got within a few feet of The Green Hornet, he jumped into the air, the heel of his right foot aimed directly for The Hornet's head.

The Green Hornet brought up an arm and deflected the blow, though the impact still reverberated down his limb and left it feeling numb. Kato landed on his feet and spun around with a backhanded attack that once again had The Hornet scrambling to avoid.

Though both men trained together, there was no denying the differences in their fighting styles. Kato was a natural; he moved with astonishing speed and grace. He was also learned in almost every fighting style known to man. The Green Hornet was more of a boxer, punching and feinting like a prizefighter. He was familiar with the martial arts, but he was far from Kato's equal.

Kato continued pushing his advantage, driving The Green Hornet back until the fence prevented any further retreat. The audience was going wild, throwing debris into the ring and chanting for blood. The Green Hornet knew that he would tire before Kato, whose drug-fueled blood system would not allow him to quit.

The Green Hornet managed to grab hold of Kato's shoulders, holding him long enough to drive a head butt into the younger man's face. Blood spurted from Kato's nose but he didn't seem to react to the pain.

"Hayashi-san!" The Hornet hissed. "You have to fight that poison! I need you!"

Kato's eyes narrowed and for a second The Hornet thought he might have succeeded in reaching his friend, but then agony lanced through his shin as Kato drove his own foot into his partner's leg again and again.

Buckling under the pain, The Green Hornet dropped to one knee. He reached out in desperation and grabbed hold of Kato's leg, yanking hard. He managed to dislodge his friend and Kato tumbled hard to the ground, the breath momentarily knocked from his lungs.

The Green Hornet glanced around and saw that no guns were trained on him at present. If any of the guards carried firearms, they had yet to draw them. The Green Hornet almost grinned when he thought that Gaunt's arrogance was going to cost him. The villain had been in such a hurry to throw The Green Hornet into harm's way that he hadn't bothered to have his guards search the emerald-clad mystery man. The Green Hornet still had his full complement of weapons at his disposal.

The Hornet quickly retrieved two small masks from the interior of his jacket, strapping one over the lower half of Kato's face before the Asian could revive completely. He wasn't sure how the knock-out gas would react with the chemicals that were already in Kato's system. Rather than risk his friend's life, he would help Kato avoid the gas, even if it meant that their private battle might not be over yet.

When The Hornet's own mask was in place, he stood and drew out

The Hornet gun. Though the range on the weapon was only around thirty feet, this was an enclosed area and he had enough fluid for over a dozen shots before he'd need to reload. The roar of the crowd was now changing to expressions of disbelief: the regulars had never seen anyone bring out a weapon like this before and several of them were wondering if this was supposed to be happening.

The Green Hornet aimed the first burst at the guards surrounding the gate, his eyes drifting up to the spinning blades above the arena. The ceiling fans, though ineffective in cooling the building, were more than capable of aiding The Hornet's gambit. They picked up the gas clouds and spread them quickly through the arena, increasing its range tremendously. The gas settled over the men at the gate and began its work. It took some time for the guards to react and several of them began to fall unconscious before others finally drew the firearms that The Green Hornet had been dreading.

Under other circumstances, The Hornet would have found the shocked expression on Gaunt's face humorous. The man looked simply stunned. Gaunt yelled for his guards to hold their fire and The Hornet had only a second to wonder why. When searing pain raced through his back, he realized that the villain was merely hoping to see his plans come to fruition. Kato was back and ready for action, having slammed both feet into his back, right into his kidneys.

The Green Hornet staggered, knowing that if Gaunt feared things were getting out of control and told his men to open fire, both he and Kato were dead men. The Hornet allowed Kato to rush at him again. This time, he shoved his partner hard in the chest, sending Kato sprawling onto his back. It would only take a second for Kato to reach his feet again but that would more than enough time for what came next.

He used the Hornet Gun once more, this time directing the spray away from the guards, focusing on the spectators.

Immediately, a panic began to take hold of the crowd. The bloodthirsty mob was now a frightened one, with several people shouting that the knockout gas was poison. Men and women who only seconds before had been screaming for the blood of others were now terrified they might have to shed some of their own.

They rushed for the exits, knocking some down in their haste. The surging crowd trampled those on the ground and their screams contributed to the general cacophony. All of this had the simultaneous effect of making it nearly impossible for the gunmen to get a clear shot at the two men in the fighting circle. The crowd was buffeting them about and one of the guards was even knocked to the floor, his gun kicked away in the mad rush.

The Green Hornet took all this in even as he tossed away the Hornet Gun, knowing he'd need both hands free to handle Kato. He whirled around to see his best friend driving a karate chop straight towards his neck. The Hornet was unable to block the blow and was nearly felled by the attack, which left him gasping in pain. Reacting instinctively, he slammed a fist into Kato's stomach and followed with an uppercut that knocked Kato back a few feet.

Kato high-kicked, catching The Green Hornet under the chin. The Hornet's teeth slammed together, catching the tip of his tongue. His mouth filled with blood.

Kato drove The Hornet to his knees again by boxing the bigger man's ears and then slamming an elbow into the top of his friend's head. As The Green Hornet knelt, gasping in pain and spitting out blood, Kato readied himself for the killing blow . . .

Kato stared down at the man before him and a series of images suddenly began to cascade through his mind's eye: he saw Britt saving him from drowning on the day they met; he saw himself garbed as The Green Hornet's driver, fighting at his friend's side; he saw himself sitting behind the wheel of the Black Beauty, chasing after a lawless criminal.

And most of all, he saw his friend's face, contorted in pain . . .

The Green Hornet looked up at that moment, thin rivulets of blood running down his chin.

"Kato!" he shouted, his voice rising above the din. "Don't do this! Don't be their slave!"

He saw something stir within Kato and it proved far stronger than any man-made chemical.

The Juice drove him to violence, but above all, Kato was a man of peace. He had mastered the arts of fighting not to bring pain to others, but to stop those who would make war. The day he laid down his arms and became a gentle man of love and peace would be the happiest day of his life.

And Britt Reid shared his convictions, through and through. To kill Britt would be like killing himself.

The Green Hornet prepared himself for the battle to continue. There were stars before his eyes, but he wouldn't give up, that much was certain. If he had to go down fighting, that's what he would do.

To his surprise, Kato's open hand appeared before him. "Let me help you up, Boss."

The Green Hornet took the offered hand and was pulled to his feet. He couldn't stop the smile that spread across his face. "You beat it, Kato. You beat the drugs."

Kato nodded quickly and Britt got the impression that his friend was embarrassed over his recent actions. "We have an audience, Boss," Kato said, obviously seeking to change the subject.

The sound of Gaunt sarcastically clapping reached The Green Hornet's ears and he turned to see that most of the crowd was gone now, though the injured and dying lay in their wake, moaning from the floor.

Gaunt and several of his men remained and Kato quickly counted guns. There were only two, the rest of the men being armed with electric cattle prods.

"Bravo, Hornet. I wouldn't have thought it possible if I hadn't witnessed it with my own eyes. But now, it's over for you and your friend. You're trapped."

While Kato scrambled to retrieve The Hornet's discarded gas gun, The Green Hornet drew out the Hornet Sting. The metal baton telescoped out to its full length and The Hornet slid his hands around the grips, wielding it like a machine gun. He directed the sonic beam towards the lock on the gate, which shattered under its effects. The guards backed away, the two gunmen drawing careful aim at the masked men.

"Mr. Gaunt, I'd like to appeal to your nature as a gambler," said The Green Hornet.

Gaunt seemed amused by The Hornet's audacity. Truth be told, he was quite stimulated by this entire performance. He loved the physicality of the arena and the danger it posed, but he rarely indulged in it so closely. That was why he'd allowed things to spiral so out of control. Like those drug-addled youths he'd thrown to the wolves, Gaunt was feeling addicted to the high. He quite simply wanted to see what came next. What would The Green Hornet do now?

"Go on," he said huskily.

"Your men versus the two of us," The Green Hornet stated. "We'll throw down our weapons if your men toss aside their guns. They're free to keep the cattle prods."

A few more guards were now arriving, bringing the total number to nearly twenty.

"Bad idea," one of the gunmen whispered to Gaunt. "Let us plug them!"

Gaunt shifted his weight from foot to foot. He licked his lips before speaking. "Hornet, you have a deal. I'm going to enjoy seeing the two of you beaten to death."

Muttering, the two gunmen put away their pistols, drawing out their electric cattle prods instead.

"We are vastly outnumbered," Kato pointed out, whispering to The Green Hornet.

"Seems unfair, doesn't it?" The Green Hornet said, enjoying the repartee with his companion. "They really don't stand much of a chance."

Side-by-side, they exited the arena and began fighting as one.

A week later, Britt Reid was in his office at the *Daily Sentinel*, holding a golf club in his hands and carefully lining up his shot. He tapped the ball, perfectly depositing it in a cup on the other end of the room.

Mike Axford rushed in, without bothering to knock. Axford was a former policeman who'd drifted into the role of crime reporter. He was a good man with one serious blind spot: The Green Hornet.

Brandishing a copy of the day's paper, Axford waved it under Britt's nose. "Did you see this? The Hornet's expanding his criminal empire! He was out in San Francisco with all the hippies!"

Britt nodded and motioned for Axford to back up as he retrieved the golf ball and set it up for another shot. "I read the article. Considering it was on the front page, it was a little hard to miss."

"I'm just wondering when the authorities are going to take this more seriously. It's bad enough that The Hornet is public enemy number one around here without him stinking up the West Coast, too! Holy Crow, I just don't know why nobody else is up in arms over this!"

"Maybe The Hornet's packed his bags and moved out of Detroit," Britt offered, sinking another putt.

"Nah. The authorities have captured this Gaunt guy who was running the club and most of his men, plus a good number of the customers, but The Hornet got away. I bet he's back here in Detroit already."

"Well at least some good's come out of The Hornet's trip out west. Gaunt was brought to justice and from what I've heard, Cal Carpenter is back home with his folks." Britt smiled at Axford. "Seems to me maybe folks should be thanking The Hornet."

Axford looked like his head was about to explode. He whirled about and headed towards the door. "Sufferin' snakes, sometimes I just don't know about you, Mr. Reid! That Hornet's bad news and I'm going to prove it!"

After the door was closed, Kato stepped into view, having entered the office via a little-used second entrance.

"Poor Mr. Axford," Kato mused. "I wonder what he would say if he really did find out The Green Hornet's identity."

"Hopefully we'll never find out. The fewer people who know the truth about us, the better." Britt stepped over to Kato and placed a hand on his friend's shoulder. "Any lingering effects from those drugs?"

Kato's smile never wavered. "Occasionally I still feel the overwhelming urge to hit you . . . but otherwise, no."

Britt's laughter rang out so loud that his secretary looked up and stared at the door in wonder.

THE WET AND THE WICKED

by David Boop

Hayashi Kato found his employer Britt Reid brooding in his study, with only a single light pushing back the darkness.

Besides being Britt's manservant, engineer, bodyguard and driver, he was first and foremost his friend and confidante. He owed the man his life, and if something weighted heavily on his friend's mind, it was Kato's place to help shoulder that burden.

The *Daily Sentinel* owner didn't even look up as Kato made his presence known. Instead, Britt slid a copy of the *Daily Torch* towards his friend. Reading, he saw that it was folded to the editorial page. Kato had already read the op-piece that morning, as he did all the local and national papers. He knew it contained a scathing attack on The Green Hornet, District Attorney Scanlon, and the Detroit Police Department.

"Why is this article any different than the hundred before it, Britt?"

Britt turned in his seat to look at up at Kato, dressed in his stark white servant attire. Few knew this unassuming man was most deadly person in Detroit and the one Britt trusted the most with his life.

"Because it *is* the hundredth. When we took down that crooked bookie last night, Kato, he was exactly our hundredth criminal behind bars. And yet, here, today, is one more article pointing a finger at the evil that is The Green Hornet. The evil that's me."

Kato dropped the paper in the trash can next to the desk. "But, you are not evil. People just believe that because pretending to be a criminal was an easier way to bring justice to those who do not respect the law. You do not, even as The Hornet, break any laws."

"But we've bent them, Kato." Britt got up and started pacing the room. "Bent them into a pretzel. And have we really changed anything? Fear of The Green Hornet hasn't stopped crime. If anything, the fact the cops haven't brought 'him' in makes them look incompetent and gives hope to every two-bit thug that they'll be just as lucky."

"Crime may not have stopped, but that is not to say you have not made a difference. Many people feel safer out there, even if they do not know why."

Not to be deterred, Britt said, "Name one."

"Miss Lenore."

Britt shook his head, ebon hair staying perfectly styled. "She doesn't count. She knows who The Green Hornet is. She knows we're doing all of this to try and make the world a better place." He balled his fists in frustration, signaling to Kato there was more about all this than an article.

Kato was confused. "What did you think, Britt, when you started this? That crime would go away?"

"No, but I hoped by now we could slow down, maybe even ..." He clenched and unclenched the fists.

"What? Quit?"

There was sadness in his friend's eyes that made Kato almost look away.

"How could I? How could I ever hope to settle down, Kato? Give Casey the relationship she subtly hints she wants from me? I've already put her in peril so many times. How could I expect her to love a man that has not even two, but three identities?"

Kato put a hand on Britt's shoulder. "Why do you not let her decide?"

But before they could answer, the direct line from Scanlon rang. Welcoming the distraction, Britt grabbed up the receiver.

"Yes, Frank?"

District Attorney Frank Scanlon was always serious, but not in a cold way. He knew they had a job to do and asked a lot of Britt as The Green Hornet. Even then, Britt could imagine Scanlon, thick glasses covering his furrowed brow as they talked.

"Hello, Britt. I caught wind of something and thought it might be best if you checked it out."

"What's that?" Britt turned on the speaker and set down the receiver so that both he and Kato could listen.

"You know Tate Tripper, Jr., right?"

"Trip? As well as anyone outside his family knows him. My father and his were good friends before he got all paranoid after the Lindbergh kidnapping. Being an airplane mogul, that hit close to home for Tripper, Sr. He built a mansion and made it safer than Fort Knox. Never dragged his family into the limelight again."

"Yes, and that recluse nature was passed down to his son. He's rarely seen in public these days, and when he does come out, it's always with an armed squadron."

Britt nodded. "I seem to recall that. I don't think the *Sentinel* has even a photo on file, nor of his son, Tripper the Third."

"That's the point. He leaves his fortress for only one event every year: the Detroit Gold Cup."

Kato saw Britt's eyes light up for the first time all day. "The hydroplane race? The *Sentinel* sponsors that."

Scanlon chuckled. "Trip is a hydroplane racing nut. His team has won every major race from Seattle to Tampa, except for the Gold Cup. He's spent a fortune this year acquiring the best driver in the world, Javier Jaskot. He's obsessed with winning as much as Trip is."

"But how do we fit into this?"

The D.A.'s voice dropped an octave as he got down to brass tacks. "Someone is planning on kidnapping Trip at the race."

It took awhile to get through the many levels of Tripper's security, but Britt finally connected.

"Britt Reid?" came the commanding voice of Tate Tripper, Jr. "Well, I'll be hornswaggled. It's been a dog's age. How are you?"

"Pretty good, Trip. Yes, it's been too long. I hear the family is doing well?"

"Why, yes! My son, Trey, is finally following in his old man's footsteps after years trying to 'find himself.' Started designing his own planes."

Kato saw Britt twinge just a little. After their previous conversation, the tormented man must be wondering when he'd have his own children at this rate.

"That's great! Hey, I hear you're the favorite for the Cup this year?"

"Yes, yes. I'll have the cup on my shelf or I'll string up every member of my race team!" There was fire in his voice the likes of which Britt hadn't heard since his own father.

"Well, as sponsor, I'd like to offer you something special. We have a secure private box. I was wondering if you'd like to be my guest. Bring your family with you. My security team can coordinate with your own."

Kato could tell that Trip was mulling it over. "That would be great. But only under one condition."

"Name it!"

"Is there enough time for you to get a boat in the race?"

Britt looked at Kato who shrugged, then nodded.

"Yes, it's doable. But why?"

"I want to make you a wager. If you win or even place, I'll give you the exclusive of a lifetime."

It was too good a deal to pass up. "You're on! Send me your security team's requirements, and we'll coordinate them with our own."

They hung up and Britt practically glowed.

"What is this all about, Britt?"

He smiled at Kato and let him in on his plan. "I'm going to do it, Kato. I'm going to stop this kidnapping as Britt Reid, not The Green Hornet. If this works, then I'll bury The Green Hornet . . . for good!"

The day of the Detroit Gold Cup came quickly. Kato, always the one to test his skills, had poured over designs for the world's top hydroplane racers. He sent some modifications to the manufacturer of the *Sentinel*'s boat through Britt and the results had been the sleekest, fastest boat the newspaper owner had ever seen.

"Kato! It looks incredible. Our driver will win, for sure!"

At first glance, the boat could have been easily mistaken for a flying saucer. It had been delivered to a private boathouse Britt rented under a pseudonym, so Kato could make some last minute tweaks. While there were a lot of variations in hydroplanes, the genius inventor had chosen something akin to a horseshoe crab. It was painted in the paper's blue and silver colors, the same as their softball team. It would be easy to spot against the reds and blacks of the other boats.

Kato stared at the ground nervously. Britt picked up on it immediately.

"You want to drive, don't you? It won't mean as much if you don't win it yourself, right?" Kato nodded. "What if someone recognizes you as my manservant? They could eventually connect you as The Hornet's sidekick."

Kato perked up. "I have already figured that out." He reached behind a box and pulled out a helmet with full facemask. "See? Like Racer X!"

Britt couldn't help but laugh. He was lightheaded, so filled with possibilities. So what if someone added one and one. After today, Britt Reid would be protecting this city, not The Green Hornet.

"Fine. But go before the truck gets here. I'm heading over to the grandstands. My guests will be arriving soon."

Kato, obviously pleased, headed out.

The *Sentinel*'s private box had to be the most secure place in the city, save for the prison. Britt himself had to go through several checks. As his guests mingled and ate food, he felt more confident than he had in a long time. Lenore Case noticed the difference.

"Britt, you look very dashing tonight!"

Britt took her in. "No, if anything, you're the sight to see, not the race."

She looked incredible. She'd spent some money on her hair and auburn locks cascaded around her face, drawing his attention to her green eyes. Casey blushed at the compliment.

"You're, um," she cast a glance around, but no one was in earshot, "rather bold today."

He grinned like the Cheshire Cat. "Maybe I am. Maybe it's because, after today, I might have something important to ask you."

Two men arrived into the booth and immediately headed Britt and Casey's way.

"But that," he whispered, "will have to wait for later."

She nodded and turned to see where Britt's eyes had focused.

Tate Tripper, Jr. was tall and lean. People stopped conversation as he walked by, almost as if he absorbed sound. Trailing a step behind the airline tycoon was a shorter, stockier man with identical features, almost like a funhouse mirror version. Britt surmised this was Tate Tripper the Third.

Trip teased, "You know, you could visit Chez Tate once and awhile. It's been what, some thirty years?"

Britt took Trip's proffered hand. "Yes, but last time I was there, your dad's guards almost arrested me when our baseball bounced down the driveway and we went after it. I didn't want to be an eight-year-old with a record."

They laughed and after Britt introduced Lenore, Trip indicated his son, "This is Trey. Every bit the genius engineer I am, and maybe even three times that of his grandfather."

"Not that anyone would notice," said the young man.

Trip admonished the boy, "Now, don't start that up in public, son. You don't want the media mogul here to print something in his gossip column." Trip laughed it off, but underneath, Britt could tell there was more. They walked over to their seats and prepared for the race's start.

"So what *will* I be printing? What's this big exclusive?"

Trey opened his mouth, but Trip silenced him with a look. "Let's just say, we're about to make a major sale to the government."

Trey turned red as his old man talked. There was something he wanted to scream, Britt figured, but fear of his father kept it in check. The airplane tycoon noticed.

"Oh, all right. It's a new plane were selling to the government."

Britt raised an eyebrow. This was big news.

"Yes," shot out Trey before his father could stop him, "for peanuts. We could have gotten so much more money on the open market."

Fury raged in the senior Tripper's eyes. "I'll see the damn plane in hell before I let it go to another country! We Trippers stand for something: freedom! If one of those Commie bastards got a hold of it, your grandpa would rise from his grave and throttle the both of us. Now let that be the end of it!"

Trey cowered at the ferociousness of his father's assault. The box had gone silent and Trip suddenly noticed. "I'm sorry everyone. Please forgive my outburst."

Britt, ever the host, pretended as if nothing had happened. "I think the race is starting. Let's move forward."

The Cup began in good form with both the *Sentinel*'s and Tripper Airlines' racers taking an early lead. Binoculars out, the crowd whooped and hollered as the racers approached their first of five counterclockwise turns.

"Your driver is handling the turn like a seasoned pro. Who is he?" inquired Trip.

"Let's just say that this driver in one of the best race car drivers in the world and wanted to test his hand at something new."

Tripper was alarmed. "This is his first race? And he's neck and neck with my world pro? Preposterous! You just don't want me to know that you got one of Javier's protégés."

Britt shook his head. "The *Sentinel* doesn't have the money you do. No, we just found a gifted driver and let him have his way with it."

Trip couldn't believe what he was hearing, nor seeing. They'd already completed one lap and the two drivers kept jockeying for position.

"So . . . it's a plane," ribbed Britt.

Trip chortled. "Guess the cat's out of the bag. Yes, a spy plane. Undetectable by current radar."

Britt went fishing. "The boy's right in that it would fetch an incredible price on the open market, more so on the black."

Glancing at his son, then back to the race, Trip softened. "It's his design and he wants the whole world to see it. Hopes to step out from his father's shadow."

Britt nodded thoughtfully. "I understand shadows and how long they extend."

The third lap finished, and a pride-filled Britt watched as Kato held his own against the best of the best in the sport. This play continued until just before the last turn into the home stretch. The *Sentinel*'s boat slowed just enough for Tripper Airlines' to cut him off. With the time left, it would be next to impossible for Kato to catch Javier. At the finish line, Trip's boat won by half a length.

Trip exploded, jumping up and down like a little kid. Everyone patted him on the back. Everyone except Trey, who used the confusion to exit, apparently wanting to be as far away from his father's long sought victory as possible.

Britt and Trip's plan for the winner circle was simple: have as many security guards there that could fit. The only people allowed on the suspended dais would be the race official, Trip, Britt, the winning driver, and six armed men. Another group of men would be stationed below the stairs and more would be scattered around the crowds and exits. None of the race attendees could get close and spotters were on the watch for anything suspicious.

"I wanted Trey here with me," Trip explained as he scanned the crowd. "He's never been happy with my security arrangements. Kept him from making friends. He doesn't realize that I did it for him, just as my dad did for me. It's a dangerous world, Britt. You just can't be too careful."

"I run a newspaper and television station, Trip. I know how dangerous it can be, but locking him in a castle isn't protecting him, you know. It's overprotecting. He's a man, now. Let him spread his wings some."

Trip seemed to contemplate this. Britt noticed someone else wasn't coming, either.

"Javier?"

"Exhausted from the race. Your driver gave him quite a challenge. You have to tell me who he is!"

The media mogul deflected the question by pointing to the trophy being carried by the race official to the winner's circle. It was a monster cup, easily four feet high with fig leaf handles like elephant ears on either side.

The race official spoke into the microphone once everyone was in their places.

"This is a very special day. There have been several times during my tenure as the Detroit Gold Cup organizer that I thought I would be presenting this trophy to Trip. So many close calls, but despite all those missed chances, he never gave up. This is perseverance. This is what America is about!" He waited a moment for the cheers to die. "So I ask you join me as I congratulate Javier Couture and the entire Tripper Airlines' team, and especially to the man who made this win possible, Tate Tripper, Jr. Congratulations on winning the Detroit Gold Cup!"

It happened so fast, that even hours later when Britt tried to describe the scene to Scanlon, he wasn't sure how they'd pulled it off.

After being handed the trophy, Trip grabbed it by the handles and hoisted it over his head. When he did, the cup exploded, sending pieces and smoke all around the dais. Britt, reflexively reached for the airplane mogul, but he was gone.

Instead, there lay a trap door in the floor that Britt nearly fell into. Below, Trip floated on the water wrapped in a plastic cocoon. Everyone looked up at the sound of an approaching hydroplane, and Britt got his second shock of the day.

A green hydroplane with The Hornet's logo came barreling towards the grandstand. A net shot out from the side and snared the sealed Trip. Before guns could even be drawn, boat and hostage were down the river, Trip bouncing behind like a skier.

Trip had been kidnapped right under Britt's nose and there wasn't a damn thing he could do to stop it.

The stoolie was suspended three inches off the ground. The Green Hornet had fistfuls of the weasel's jacket as he held him against the wall. Word had gotten out on the street about the crime lord's rage and it took The Hornet longer than he had expected to track the stoolie down. It wasn't the first time some other outfit had piggy-backed on The Green Hornet's rep, but rumor had it that because this time it'd been done in such an obvious fashion, Detroit's most wanted man was infuriated.

"Talk!"

"I don't know nuthin'!" Spit flew from the small man's mouth like a sprinkler as he shook his head back and forth vehemently. "Everyone thought it was you!"

The man was yanked within breathing distance to The Green Hornet's masked face. He spoke through gritted teeth, "But it wasn't. Who's out to get me, this time? You know everyone and everything going on in the underworld. Who's out to frame me? The Giordanos?"

"Dis wasn't a mob job or I'd know! I swear!"

Behind The Hornet, a similarly masked Kato finished off the few foolhardy souls in the hideout that had stood up to them on their quest to find the stoolie. Thumps echoed in the shack as men hit the floor one or two at a time.

The Hornet asked again, "We know you tipped off Scanlon to the kidnapping. Now, where did you get your information? *Talk!*"

"I-I just overheard somethin' down at the docks. It was just loose talk at a bar. 'Bout a boat. Dey needed it for a kidnappin'.''

"Who?" The Hornet shook him again.

"I never saw dem. All I know is dat da guy in charge said to make sure Tripper wasn't hurt. Dat's all! I swear to yas, dat's all!"

Back in the Black Beauty, Britt removed his hat and mask and wiped his brow. He'd never sweated so much before. He'd never been this mad at himself, either.

"You know that we might never be able to use that man for information again . . . . It is one thing to use the reputation of The Green Hornet to get intelligence, but you may be skirting the edge."

Britt averted his eyes from his driver's as they took him in via the rear view mirror. "Yes, I know, Kato."

Kato nodded. "You are not the only one who feels shame right now. I let someone slip a sugar-filled balloon into one of my gas tanks. I would normally do a more thorough check, but I let the excitement of the coming race cloud my normal judgment. I, too, have much to be angry about . . ."

Britt cut him off, "Sure, but you just lost a race. I lost a person due to my arrogance."

Kato slammed on the brakes and turned in the seat to face his friend. "Please, let me finish. I, too, have much to be angry about, but then I remembered a mantra I used in my youth.

"'Rid yourself of your arrogance and your lustfulness, your ingratiating manners and your excessive ambition. These are all detrimental to your person.'

"I needed this failure today to remind myself that I am nothing. And when I am nothing, I am everything."

Britt thought about this. He often wondered how Kato could keep so calm in the worst situations; ones that he, himself, let blind him with emotion.

"Lao Tzu?"

"Hai."

Donning the mask and fedora, The Green Hornet smiled at his friend, "Let's roll, Kato. Down to the docks."

"Hai!"

Together they drove up and down the port in stealth mode, looking for some sort of clue, when Kato spotted a man creeping near a dry dock. The wheelman pointed him out to Britt.

"Is that not that Mister Axford?"

The reporter passed under an alley light and his red hair confirmed his identity. They watched as he picked the lock on the building's door and slipped in. After a quick check of their equipment, they followed.

The Green Hornet and Kato weren't five feet inside the door before they heard the sounds of a fight. Rushing in, they found Mike being worked over by three thugs. Kato leapt the distance, landing a flying kick to the shoulder of the biggest guy. The Hornet entered the fray, spinning the hooligan holding Axford around and planting a right cross to his chin.

Kato's opponent was twice the Asian's size in height and muscles, but those were the odds Kato loved. Dropping down to a crouch, he swung his right leg around to strike just behind the large man's kneecap. This threw the larger man's jab off target and Kato was able to dodge it with ease.

The Hornet blocked a one-two punch from his thug with ease. Wanting to finish the fight quickly, he jack-hammered the man's solar plexus, knocking the wind from him. A chop to the back of the neck, as Kato had shown him, rendered the man unconscious. He looked up just to see Kato's sparring partner go down as the dexterous bodyguard jumped up and connected a spinning kick. This left one man who dove into the water instead of facing the combined might of The Green Hornet and his bodyguard.

Mike moaned as he got to his feet. Grabbing a life preserver from the wall, Kato slipped it down and over the reporter, trapping him. Axford snarled at them.

"I knew my tip would pay off! And here you are, the criminal mastermind himself! Where's Tate Tripper, Jr.?"

The Green Hornet turned away from Mike. He tried never to look the reporter in the face for too long, lest Mike recognize his boss's eyes.

"I have no idea. I was set-up. You've followed me. You know I don't do theatrics like that."

"Yeah, maybe you were framed this time," spat Axford, "but that doesn't mean you won't find a way to get your cut from the ransom."

Kato saw the man beneath the cowl flinch. If only they could let Mike in on the secret, but each time they added a person to the illusion, its effect was diluted. Instead, The Green Hornet made to leave.

"What? No gas? No knocking me out? That's not like you."

The fake mobster was about to say something when he spotted a piece of torn paper on the workbench. On it was one of his Green Hornet stickers.

"Why are you here, Axford?"

"I got a tip that the owner of this boat shop wasn't above doing some below radar work."

Reaching for another paper to write on, The Hornet scribbled a note. He talked to Mike over his shoulder. "In an hour, when you wake up, take this message to Scanlon."

"When I . . . ? Oh, damn!"

The Green Hornet turned and sprayed Mike in the face with the Hornet Gun. As Axford went down, he stuffed the note into the reporter's pocket.

"Where to?" asked Kato.

"Tripper Field."

On the way, Kato deviated from the route.

"Where are we going?"

"I have a surprise."

They pulled up to Britt's secret boat house. When they stepped inside, Britt's jaw dropped.

"So, this is what you were doing last night while I was tracking leads?"

"Yes." Kato grinned ear to ear.

The hydroplane had been almost completely remodeled. Painted the same midnight black as their car, it sported the similar green lights as the Black Beauty, as well.

"I call it the Black Barracuda."

Britt walked around it, feeling its smooth exterior. "You couldn't have done all this in one night?"

"No, this was my plan all along. I designed the boat to add special features after the race."

"What can it do?"

Kato reached in to the driver's compartment and pressed a button. Holes opened up on either side and missile heads poked out. "Everything the Beauty can do and more." He pressed another button and a harpoon point extended from the back. Kato stepped into the driver's seat and flipped one last switch. A glass dome slid down over him. "Emergency escape pod with bullet-proof glass."

"You outdid yourself this time, my genius friend!"

Kato tried his best not to let pride take over again, but even he had to admit it was a thing of beauty.

The Tripper Airlines Airfield was built on the Detroit River, not from the docks. Back in the early days, lumber for building airplanes was floated down from the north woods to the facility.

The Green Hornet stood on the outside of the racer, holding on to the foil, and considered their options. As Kato motored the Barracuda slowly towards the open dry dock, they could see dozens of limos with diplomatic plates parked by the warehouse doors.

Kato called up, "How did you figure out it was Trey?"

"That note in the shop? It had all the details of the race on in. The corner was torn, but there was just enough of the Tripper Airlines' logo left for me to recognize it from the plans Trip sent over to me. It didn't take long to figure out that Trey just wanted his father out of the way so he could put his spy plane up for bid on the black market. That's why the mystery man didn't want Trip hurt."

The dry dock angled up into a large manufacturing plant. Cranes could lift shipments out of the water and carry them to different stations for cutting, welding or painting. The frames of several aircraft hung in various stages, looking like skeletal remains of ancient birds recently dug up and reassembled.

It was quite an effect as the Black Barracuda arrived, The Green Hornet standing upright on its hood. He casually stepped off it and walked up to the gathering. Easily two dozen men stood near another seated dozen. Everyone was armed and many of the guns were trained on him. In front of the assembly, Tate Tripper the Third stood at a podium. Behind him, a plane, if it could still be called that, glistened in the factory's overhead lights. It was small and flat with wings that curved up like a manta ray. If he had to describe the color, the best he could come up with was "mirror."

"Sorry I'm late."

A general stood. He puffed out his medal-covered chest to mark his importance. His accent was decidedly Russian. The Hornet wondered how this man was walking around loose in America without a thousand C.I.A. agents swarming all over him.

"Who is this *durak*?"

Not perturbed, The Hornet walked up to stand next to Trey. "I'm no one's fool, General. I'm the one who made this auction a reality." He looked directly into the Tripper heir's eyes, begging him to disagree, "Isn't that right, Trey?"

Trey swallowed hard. "W-why, yes. The Green Hornet is the city's most notorious criminal mastermind, and if not for his involvement, we all wouldn't be here today."

The general sat down, but didn't look relaxed. Trey motioned for The Green Hornet to take a seat. Once he had, the auction started in earnest.

As the biding commenced, Kato finally had time to look at the other boat in the dock area. It was the fake Green Hornet hydroplane. Javier, the airline's driver, sat half out of his seat. He acknowledged Kato, one criminal driver to another, with the tilt of his head. Tied to the hood was a gunny sack. A muffled noise came from inside as it wiggled and thrust about trying to get loose. Kato deduced that the bag must contain Tate Tripper, Jr.

It didn't take long for most of the bidders to drop out with only two left in the ring: the Russian and The Green Hornet.

"$30 million," said the growingly-upset general.

"$40 million," countered The Hornet.

The military man challenged, "Who do you represent? No mere crook has that type of money."

The Hornet shot back, "I'm no mere crook. Crime pays well here, General."

"Hmmff!" He raised his hand, "$50 million!"

"$100 million."

The Russian stood up again, pounded his chest and yelled, "$200 million!"

Calmly, the bluffing Hornet eclipsed him, "$500 million."

There were gasps. The General called the bluff, "I demand to see this money! I am not afraid to show mine." He motioned back to where several guards held briefcases. "Are you?"

The Green Hornet got up. "It's in my boat." He walked towards the Barracuda, carefully checking his watch. As he stepped on board, he nodded to Kato. Kato pushed a button and missiles shot out from the hydroplane. The bodyguard had targeted a spot just above the big hanger doors in the front. The resulting explosion was the signal Scanlon, the Detroit police and the United States National Guard were waiting for. Sirens wailed outside as they moved in unison to surround the hanger.

Gunfire broke out as representatives from many countries, all believing they betrayed each other, went to war. Javier backed his hydroplane out of the dock. The Green Hornet jumped into the melee while Kato turned to pursue the boat.

Javier was already speeding up by the time Kato cleared the dock. Not caring about the package tied to his hood, the hydroplane was soon up to maximum speed. Kato, his driving at top form, cut the distance between them. Javier took the corners rough, fear guiding his hand, while the Barracuda's turns were precise and controlled. Within minutes, Kato was pulling alongside his opponent.

The Green Hornet dodged behind a file cabinet, a bullet embedding in the wood surface. One of the Russian General's men rushed up, and The Hornet had to break cover to face off against him. Too much was happening and he didn't like being out in the open while all of Detroit's law enforcement was sitting outside. The soldier swung and missed, but gave The Hornet enough room to pull out the Hornet Gun and spray him in the face. Two more advanced, and they, too, went down. As they dropped, The Green Hornet caught sight of Trey as the heir climbed up the ladder into the spy plane.

Needing to get closer, The Hornet launched himself at the closest foreigner, this one in Arabian robes. The Arab pulled a knife and tried to impale the masked man, but The Hornet's moves were quicker. He disarmed the sheik, wrapped him in a bear hug, and lifted him off the ground. Carrying him fireman style, he ran across the factory floor, doing his best to dodge both enemy and friendly fire. Once he made the underside of the plane, The Green Hornet dropped his unwilling shield and discovered a wide-eyed Arab, muttering and checking his robes for bullet holes.

"Thanks!" said The Hornet and tipped the rim of his hat. He climbed the ladder into the belly of the plane and closed the hatch just as it taxied out of the back of the hanger.

Kato stayed tight with Javier as they made their way down the river. For every twist and slice the world famous racer made, Kato matched him move for move. Unable to shake him, Javier pulled out a gun and fired at his opponent, causing Kato to lower the bulletproof glass shield.

The distraction was all Kato needed to pull ahead. Using the targeting scope, he lined himself up with the hydroplane and fired the harpoon. Timing it just right, the harpoon skewered the bow just below the hostage. Javier was forced to cut the engine or risk crashing the boat, an almost certain death for all concerned. Instead, he let the Black Barracuda drag him back to the factory.

Despite the gunfire, Trey's spy plane cleared the hanger without too much damage. So focused was he on preparing for take-off, Trey didn't hear The Green Hornet's approach until too late.

"It's over, Trey!"

He had the Hornet Gun out, but Trey cranked the controls, throwing The Hornet off balance. Trey shouldered him in the chest, causing the faux criminal to trip against the co-pilot seat. The gun dropped from his hand and fell to the floorboards.

Swinging the controls the other way caused The Hornet to fall forward and Trey elbowed him in the face. The Hornet stumbled backwards into the compartment and landed on the floor. The Tripper heir locked the controls before following the masked man into the back of the plane. Trey drew a gun, but The Hornet was faster. He swung a leg up and knocked the piece from Trey's hand. The kidnapper propelled himself at The Green Hornet, hands reaching for his throat, but The Hornet stopped the claws inches from their goal. Twisting, he knocked the younger man off balance and was able to get out from under him. They both got up and squared off.

"You don't get it, do you? Everything I've gone through? Living in the shadows, trapped by his fears, his identity! This was my chance to break the curse handed down to me; a chance to be my own man!" To Britt, Trey seemed to be talking not to the masked criminal, but to the man underneath. "Ruined, all because of you."

But it was The Green Hornet who answered, "Kid, you have no idea how good you've got it. Instead, you whine about woulda, coulda, shoulda. You didn't have the courage to play the cards you were dealt, and you didn't have the brains to pull off this stunt. Face it, you're going down."

"Not if I can help it!"

Trey turned back toward the controls. The Hornet realized he'd have to cross over the belly hatch to get there. Thinking quickly, he drew and extended the Hornet Sting. He blew the hatch just as Trey stepped on it. There was a yell as Trey fell through, followed by a short scream. The Hornet went to the controls and eased them off, before carefully dropping through the opening.

Trey lay on the ground, dead, crushed by one of the plane's wheels. Britt hated this turn of events, but in the end, it might have been best.

The National Guard military and police were approaching quickly. Kato called out from down by the river, having deposited a bound Javier and a freed Trip off by the docks. Seeing this as a cue to leave, The Green Hornet slid into the night.

Britt shook Tate Tripper, Jr.'s offered hand and gave him a sympathetic pat on the shoulder as they moved toward the door of his study.

"The government still wants to pay me for the plane, but it seems like such a paltry amount compared to losing . . ."

It wasn't the first time Trip had to pull himself together that afternoon. Good as his word, he gave the *Sentinel* an exclusive interview. He'd turned the trophy over to Britt once it was discovered that all the hydroplanes had been sabotaged by Trey's henchmen.

"Hold fast to the idea that it didn't fall into the wrong hands. There's a war out there, Trip, even if it's a cold one. You've done the right thing."

Trip nodded. He looked to Britt with sad broken eyes, "Next year? Detroit Cup? All on the up and up?"

Britt gleamed. "You're on!" But they both knew Trip would never race a boat again.

As he left, Kato showed Lenore Case in. He bowed and escorted Trip to the front door.

"It's so sad," she began. "He just wanted to protect his son and the one person he couldn't protect him from was himself."

"Yeah, but it's a long race. What separates the winners from losers is how we run it. Trey wanted it all, but you can't always get everything you want."

Seeing his contemplative expression, Casey said, "But sometimes you *can* get what you need. Which reminds me . . . weren't you going to ask me something back at the Gold Cup? What was it?"

She was catty and Britt liked her even more when she was like that, but the reality of what he'd just gone through put him firmly back in his place, a man with three identities—media mogul, faux villain, and the city's unacknowledged hero. None were complete without the others.

"It'll have to wait until a later time, Miss Case. For now, we've got a paper to put to bed."

Britt handed Lenore the tapes of the Tripper interview. Disappointed, she gave him a slight tilt of her head as she exited the room. Kato was there as she left.

"You could tell her."

He stopped puttering. "About? Wanting to leave The Green Hornet behind?"

"That . . ." Kato smiled. "And other things."

Britt leaned back in his chair and took in his bodyguard, best friend, and confidante. "I already have a lot to juggle, as it is. How could I fit husband or father into that right now? No, the city needs The Green Hornet."

"For now," Kato said slyly.

Britt had to chuckle. "Yes, for now. But I will say this, old friend. When the time does come, I will put the mask away for good and be just that, a family man. I won't live in paranoia the rest of my life, nor hide my family behind fortress walls to protect them."

A chime rang out, signaling D.A. Scanlon's approach through the secret entryway. Britt moved to pull the fake books which activated the hidden fireplace entrance.

The deadliest man Britt knew bowed slightly. "You will not have to. You will always have me."

Returning Kato's nod, Britt prepared himself for whatever Scanlon was bringing. He basked in their brotherly fellowship as he turned with him together to greet their guest.

"So true. So very true."

THE CARLOSSI CAPER

by Art Lyon

In a filthy alley on Detroit's beleaguered northwest side, a man in a disheveled brown-gray suit accepted a sheaf of papers from a shadowy figure. It was what some people quaintly call the "wee hours" of the morning—people who never deigned to visit the seedier pockets of the city. Across the street a camera shutter dilated open, paused, and closed again, the noise of it all discretely timed to coincide with the pulsating buzz and click of the tawdry neon sign above the "gentleman's lounge" next door. The photographer smiled to herself and watched as the two mysterious-looking figures went their separate ways into the night. She skittered off, barely able to contain the heady mixture of pride, excitement, and anticipation. This was going to be a good one.

Morning light pierced the blinds of the executive office of the *Daily Sentinel*. It warmed the grain of the wainscot paneling, accented the room's trim, modern lines, and cut a tall, stark silhouette of Britt Reid, owner and publisher of the *Sentinel*. He stood close enough to the blinds to get a good view of the city through the slats. He was dressed like the kind of man who cared less about who designed his suit than simply buying it someplace reputable—and reputable looked good on him.

His personal secretary, Lenore Case, stood beside him as she always did this time of day, with a steno pad folded over to a blank page and a freshly-sharpened pencil. They'd been there for some time now, but the paper was blank and the pencil still sharp as a tack. She held them in one hand now, at her side. He gazed out at the city, and she at him.

Outside, the city had come to life again. It wasn't always the life everyone wanted, and downtown wasn't what it used to be. But this was where he was needed, and he couldn't do what he did without people like Miss Case. Casey. The way the lines of her dress interrupted the bands of light streaking through the blinds was easy on the eyes, but he was too obsessed with weighty matters to appreciate it—and she knew it. Britt broke the long silence.

"If my sources are right, he's out there somewhere right now. . ."

"That 'Carlossi' character you mentioned? What's this all about, Britt?"

"Vincenzo Carlossi is a high-society, international smuggling specialist for organized crime outfits. He's here for a reason, but what's he moving and how's he getting it in or out of the country? That's the key. The Green Hornet will be busy for a while, I think—I can't expect the explanation to just fall into my lap."

The door to Britt's office being thrown open was only briefly preceded by a muffled argument about whether it should be opened or not, and the tones and timber of the argument were only too familiar.

"Hello, Lowery!" Britt got it out with a dubious but amused smile before the man could even stop his barreling gait up to Britt's desk.

"I'm sorry, Mr. Reid, but this is important!" As usual, Lowery looked like he hadn't changed out of yesterday's clothes. It was hard to say, though, because Lowery's usual look was flushed and frenzied, red-brown hair shoved into a tufted shock, all packed into an unbuttoned, lifeless brown-gray suit.

"Clicker" Binny, camera slung over her shoulder, dismissed him with a casual roll of her eyes and wave of her hand. "Oh, it's always important with you. The least you could've done is knocked on the man's door!" Clicker was plainly tired, but as chipper and put-together as ever,

Lowery continued. "Well, no one was in the outer office, so I. . ."

"So you just figured you might as well barge in?" Britt finished, trying to hide his amusement.

Miss Case knew a good cue when she heard it. "This is what I get for abandoning my post." She left the room and made a point of closing the door with respectful emphasis.

"What about me?" Britt called after her in mock desperation.

Clicker's eagerness almost drowned out her nicely-affected southern lilt. "Begging your pardon, Mr. Reid, but don't mind him. He means well and all, I guess. It's just this story. . ." She blew and then brushed aside a loose bright-blonde curl from a trendy updo. "It's a doozy!"

Britt leaned back in his chair. "Well, 'doozy' me up."

Lowery rolled right into it. "It started with an anonymous tip, see, from someone in one of the projects. Guy's got a chemistry degree or something, and he's been testing things where he lives and other places, old and new, even some under construction right now—"

"—all of them tenements and apartment blocks, in the worst neighborhoods in town. . ." Clicker added.

"—places like that, and he's found all sorts of toxins leaking from foundations and walls and who knows where. Now all the places were built by Etna, who—"

"—like every other construction set-up in town is—"

Lowery glared at Clicker with a mixture of irritation, surprise, confusion . . . and admiration. "You read all this?" he asked her, flapping around the manila folder he'd been clutching in his sweaty hand the whole time.

"Yeah, and I can walk and chew bubblegum at the same time, too!" she shot back.

Britt raised an eyebrow and gestured at Casey's outer office door. "I'm sorry. Would you two like me to leave as well?"

Lowery and Clicker stopped their banter and tried to look respectful. Britt almost regretted having to break the silence. "Etna, like every other construction company in town, is in the hands of organized crime. I'm familiar with the union situation, you two."

"Oh, for cryin' out loud, Lowery—show him the stuff!" Lowery, somewhat abashedly, handed the mangled and stained bundle to Britt.

"Good thing you don't work in the mail room, Lowery. . ." Britt commented. He snapped off the rubber band holding it all together and started methodically laying papers out on his desk.

"Controlling the unions isn't enough for them, I guess," Lowery continued. "Now they're making even more money—off of government contracts, mind you—by buying this junk—"

"—with our tax dollars." Clicker inserted.

". . . with our tax dollars! Smuggling in cheap materials, and pocketing the difference!"

"And risking lives in the process, in the poorest areas of town—the lives of people no one listens to," Britt added grimly. His eyes narrowed, moving from one set of papers to another. Then he looked up at the two again with a strange light in his shrewd eyes. "Some of these buildings your informant tested are under construction right now, you say?"

"The sites are all listed out with the toxins and their sources, and we've got a reliable breakdown of the whos, whats, whens, and wheres." Lowery replied, indicating a stapled set of papers. Clicker was anxious, one hand on her camera. "And I've got loads of pictures, Mr. Reid—good ones, too! A real play-by-play! Copies of contracts, location shots of the sites and materials, candid stuff from union reps and city hall folks we've been trying to get answers from. . ."

Britt stood up, all action now. "Keep it up, you two! Get this piece written. Clicker, you might get that pictorial you've been talking about. But be careful. This is the big leagues, the kind of crime The Green Hornet would like to horn in on."

Lowery agreed. "And if we know about it, you can bet that crook's working on a way to get a piece of the action."

Later, once he had the office to himself again and Miss Case had cleared his schedule, Britt Reid picked up the phone, flipped a hidden switch on the base, and made a special secure call. When the other end picked up, there was an alarming roaring in the background Britt couldn't identify.

"Hayashi? What is that noise?"

"Nothing to worry about, Britt! Just trying something out in the garage here."

"Well, I've got more for you to try out, I'm afraid. I need you to set up the chemistry gear, to confirm some evidence I'm sending in," he said as he pulled the sheaf of papers together. "And get the Black Beauty ready. Tonight we have a few stops to make—as The Green Hornet and Kato!"

Later, as the veil of encroaching night drew over the city, Britt Reid abandoned his role of newspaper publisher and donned the guise of the mysterious figure in midnight green feared throughout the city: The Green Hornet!

He strode into the private garage and workshop level of Britt Reid's townhouse. There he found Kato, known, in the black outfit and mask he now wore, only as The Hornet's swift and silent right hand.

"Ah, Boss, you're here! Good—everything's ready." Kato gestured at one of the work tables, where a small chemical laboratory had been set up. Kato's gloves were off and he was cleaning the black soot off a pair of identical burn marks off the garage wall—the wall directly behind The Green Hornet's sleek rolling arsenal, the Black Beauty. The Green Hornet eyed the evidence a little dubiously, looking back and forth between the Black Beauty and the matching blast marks.

"Is this what you were doing when I called? Trying out some new kind of fuel, Kato?"

"Yes, Boss—and then some!" Kato replied with a devilish grin.

The Green Hornet trusted Kato implicitly, but it was hard not to be curious. "All right—your tinkering's never let me down before. Let me know when you have it worked out." He moved on, turning to the work table. "What can you tell me?"

Kato set aside his cleaning. "I got the package you sent, and this informant's work was very thorough—everything checks out." Kato's degree in chemistry was just one of the myriad talents he brought to their war on crime. "In fact . . . we went to school together."

"You're kidding."

"No, sir. I made some calls, and he's been getting the chemicals and equipment for his tests from some of the same places I do. The handwriting seemed familiar at first, and then there are some technical references, specialty stuff, and . . . if this informant's at home in the projects. . ." A rare discomfort seemed to possess Kato for a moment. "Well, there weren't many non-whites in that degree program. Like myself, he was someone determined to stay and help this city any way he could."

Behind his mask, The Green Hornet's eyes narrowed in concern. "I understand, Kato. Keep his identity to yourself, though. It's best if as few people as possible know his name until there's a legal case and protection available."

"I guess that's the safest thing." Kato was pensive for a moment, and then turned back to the papers and reports. "I made several calls, and was able to trace the countries of origin of some the stuff, based on chemical content, U.S. Commerce and Trade regulations, and the like." He pointed out several annotations to The Green Hornet as he flipped back and forth through the documents.

"Wait a minute. . ." The Hornet interrupted, checking and rechecking several sources. Then he stood up straight, pushing back his shadow-green fedora as he scratched his head in surprise. "What do you know—it did fall into my lap!"

"Boss?"

"Some of these sources match the movements and transactions of a smuggler I've been keeping tabs on."

"Two birds with one stone?" Kato offered. "Of course, I can't confirm any of my—of this informant's findings without actual physical samples of the suspect materials."

"I was thinking the same thing, old friend. But we need to make one stop first." The Green Hornet smiled grimly—it was time for action.

"Let's roll, Kato!"

DiSano's was a fancy steakhouse and show bar, with high-stakes poker and a lot more hush-hush going on upstairs. It was a favorite among the city's criminal elite, and a favorite place for them to bring anyone they wanted to impress—or wanted in their pocket.

The Green Hornet and Kato left the armored Black Beauty backed into a little-used, dead-end alley behind the establishment. They entered through the kitchen entrance, almost casually, so that it was several seconds before anyone recognized the notorious duo passing in their midst. Kato made his usual quick survey of the room and its contents.

Someone rushed for the door out into the dining area. A steak knife pinned his sleeve to the door frame. Kato had a veritable armory at his disposal in such a well-equipped kitchen—the knife had just been the closest thing at hand. He made a pointed "Shh!" gesture at the would-be squealer, who did what he could to get out of the way as the ominous figure of The Green Hornet came near.

A beetle-browed man-mountain stuffed into a cook's smock slunk toward a corner shelf and a conspicuous black bag. Kato nodded to The Green Hornet to make sure he'd noticed this. They knew they could rely on a distraction very soon.

The two masked figures slipped into the shadows of the dining area. The right crook would give up the information in a pinch, but The Green Hornet knew something of Carlossi's habits, and a lot about those of the local malfeasants. Carlossi thought he was too good for this town, and wasn't one to linger regardless. His first night in town, Carlossi would be here.

The dining area was intimate for such a large space, with alcoves, booths, and antechambers, all of it thick with smells and smoke and talk. The occasional client climbed the shadowy stairs at the back up to the second-floor rooms.

Kato looked to the top of the stairs. "Gambling?"

The Green Hornet cracked a wry smile. "Or something. . ." He'd have to make this place a priority. There were probably a dozen crimes being committed under this roof right now.

The great thing about a building full of guilty consciences is that somebody's bound to get antsy and make a mistake. The Green Hornet and Kato were listening closely for what they knew was coming. From the now too-quiet kitchen came the sound of a gun bolt being cocked. The Cro-Magnon-looking fellow lumbered out of the kitchen trying to look nonchalant with an M3 "grease gun" at his side.

A few guests noticed with expressions ranging from horror to irritation. At the same moment, the searching eyes of the thug and a nearby patron met those behind the two midnight-green masks.

"The Green Hornet!" someone yelled.

The two masked men exchanged a glance, and that was all that was needed. Years facing all manner of sticky situations together laid out the next few moments clearly before them.

Kato vanished into the shadows. The Green Hornet barreled into the man-mountain shoulder first before the thug knew what was coming at him, slamming him back through the kitchen door and into a cacophony of pots and pans and water. Then everything was plunged into darkness. Patrons started crowding to the main entrance and the faint glow of street lights. Kato grinned slyly and raced into the kitchen. A moment later a blinding flash lit the place like a lightning bolt, accompanied by a split-second roar and rush of air. The place erupted into a full panic.

The Green Hornet and Kato emerged from the kitchen brushing traces of baking flour from their dark suits. The Hornet gave his partner a grim, satisfied smile. Kato was about to say something about fine carbohydrate dust and industrial stove-top burners, but stopped in his tracks as they both saw a man in a white suit rushing up the stairs.

"Carlossi!" The Hornet said, almost to himself. He eyed the two armed goons letting Carlossi through at the top of the stairs, and exchanged a knowing look with Kato.

The Green Hornet bolted for the stairs. Kato ran and leapt up on to the bar, covered the length of it, vaulted the handrail, and appeared amidst the two surprised gunmen. While Kato provided the hoodlums with quick trips to the bar top below—one over the banister, and one through it—The Green Hornet disappeared up the remaining stairs and into the chambers above, tossing a black hand-held device to Kato as he went. "Bags and doors! Fire her up!"

He powered after Carlossi into a small, paneled game room and a packed poker game sent pell-mell by the din below. The Green Hornet doubled over a thug with a blow to the diaphragm and wrenched another goon by the lapels. Kato leapt into the room, rolled to the floor, swept the legs out from under a third opponent, and was back on his feet across the room, pressing buttons on the Black Beauty's remote control pad. Faster than seemed possible, the device was inside Kato's jacket as he side-stepped a blow, snatched the fist in its path with his own hands, and twisted the goon into a joint-wincing knot.

Men were coming up the stairs. Men with guns. Kato looked expectantly to his partner. Against the outer wall, flushed with fear and indignation, Vincenzo Carlossi furtively looked for a way out. It was hopeless. This intrusion was going to make his dealings very difficult, if not impossible.

"Who are you people? What gives you the right . . .?"

The Green Hornet glared at Carlossi, whose complexion chilled. "New in town? I know who *you* are—and I know why you're here. . ." he said ominously and for all to hear. With his gaze still fixed on the recoiling man, The Green Hornet charged straight at him . . . and past him, up onto the large octagonal poker table and out the window with a crash of shattering glass. Kato was gone with him, like a shadow.

Men poured into the room waving guns around like flashlights. The Green Hornet and Kato landed on a multi-chambered air bag atop the Black Beauty that deflated almost completely the instant they made contact with it. It automatically jettisoned as they rolled off the roof of the car and into the waiting open doors. By the time anyone made it to the window, all they heard was the receding, unmistakable buzz of the infamous Black Beauty.

It wasn't much later when The Green Hornet and Kato, watching from the sleek, shadowy car in a darkened alley across the way, noted Carlossi's hurried exit from DiSano's amid the throng of confused, fleeing patrons.

"Looks like we made an impression, huh Boss?"

"The game is definitely afoot, old friend," The Green Hornet agreed from the back seat, "but you and I aren't what Carlossi's afraid of most right now. No, we let the mob bosses know that we're onto him, and suddenly this whole building materials racket is looking pretty dicey—all because of him. He doesn't have many choices right now but to get out of town as quickly as possible."

The Green Hornet eyed the situation outside Di Sano's. "Get the tracker ready, Kato. . ."

Kato opened the targeting panel on the dashboard and made some adjustments. A thin tube shifted into view below the Black Beauty's front grill. The quick sound of a high-pressure air gun was followed by a small distant metallic slap, and the tube retracted back into the car's body.

The Green Hornet switched on the viewer mounted behind the forward seats, and confirmed a readout.

"We've got him, Kato! Nice shooting. With that miniaturized tracer magnetically fastened to Carlossi's car, we can track him anywhere in town. It'll take time for him to arrange his escape, and with any luck he'll lead us right to anything he's smuggled into the country."

"Time for a couple of construction site visits?" Kato asked.

"And then a battery of tests in that lab of yours. We might get to kill two birds with one stone on this caper yet!"

Back at The Hornet's lair, the two unloaded construction material samples from the Black Beauty. The Green Hornet arched a curious eyebrow. On both sides of the trunk's floor ran two new compartments. He feigned ignorance.

"Is it just me or is the trunk smaller than it used to be?"

"Is it? I hadn't noticed. . ." Kato replied nonchalantly.

"We need to find you a new hobby. . ."

They removed their coats, hats, and masks and worked into the night, duplicating and double-checking the tests detailed in the informant's research. Britt kept track of Carlossi's car via a monitor nearby.

It was the pre-dawn hours before they were satisfied they had been thorough enough.

"It's all true, then?" The Green Hornet asked.

"It looks like it, Boss."

"So. . ." The Green Hornet leaned against a work table and sifted through the likely scenarios. "It looks like Carlossi is smuggling material *in* to the country, but he just got here . . . he wouldn't tell anyone where it was until he closed the deal, but with his clients scaring him out of town. . ." He stood up straight. "He's got too much invested to cut his losses. He'll want to sell that stuff somewhere—anywhere—and the only way to move that kind of bulk out of the country discretely and fast is across the river by boat, under the cover of night."

Stripping off his safety gloves, Kato had stepped over to the electronics area of the workroom.

"Boss!"

The Green Hornet snapped out of his analysis and shot a look over at the display screen with the tracker's status.

"Great Guns—Carlossi's car is at the docks right now! There's no time to lose, Kato. Fire up the Black Beauty!"

As they neared their fateful destination on the river, The Green Hornet restlessly anguished over the time they had lost. He gauged their speed and the time the crooks had had to do their dirty work. Kato eyed his partner in the rearview mirror and had no qualms about pushing that sleek wonder to its limits. The Black Beauty streaked through the night in silent mode, a blur in the fog that had formed along the waterway.

Suddenly, the dimmed lights of a small container carrier ship were discernable through the mist—and they were just now pulling away from the vacant dock.

"It's no use, Kato—we're too late."

Kato tightened his grip on the wheel. "I've got it Boss. . ."

The ship was one-hundred meters from stem to stern, with large cargo containers lined up on either side of its long, flat deck. The wide aisle in the middle was lined up directly with the end of the dock, which jutted out into the river. Kato saw the only opportunity they had. He slammed the pedal to the metal, and the center of the steering wheel popped open to reveal a red switch and small radar screen The Green Hornet had never seen before. From behind him in the car came a strange click-clack. Outside, two rudder-like aileron panels sprung open on both ends of the Black Beauty's reinforced rear fender, exposing hidden exhaust ports. There was the sudden hiss and whine of escaping pressurized gases. The ship was still pulling straight away from the dock, several meters out and getting further by the second.

"Uh, Kato—about that test of yours in the garage . . . how did that go?" There was too much trust between them for doubt, but this was a surprise in a tight situation.

"We're about to find out. Hold on, Boss!"

What felt like a barely-contained explosion at the back of the car heaved The Green Hornet and Kato into the backs of their seats, as the twin blasts of ignited rocket fuel—a green-hot flame thanks to Kato's propellant mixture tinkering—shot from the new openings. Kato white-knuckled the steering wheel to keep the Black Beauty pointed at the receding ship's lights. The car bolted forward like a bullet from a gun, left the edge of the dock behind, and disappeared into the fog that blanketed the river.

In that airborne span of tense, breathless seconds, Kato's eyes were locked on the radar screen showing the Black Beauty and the ship as he corrected thrust and flight to guide the hurtling car safely to its target.

Out of the fog, the half-dozen henchmen huddled before the wheelhouse on the ship's deck saw two fierce, green eyes cut through the night with a roar like a dragon. The Black Beauty rocketed over the water in the wink of an eye and landed with a scraping lurch right down the aisle on the ship's deck.

Sparks flew as the careening car skidded along a cargo container on one side, but Kato kept her barreling toward the horrified criminals. He finally brought it to a screeching, sideways stop at the last possible instant practically on top of them. The Green Hornet and Kato sprung their doors bodily into the closest goons.

A stunned henchman dropped his shotgun to the deck. Two more leveled pistols. Kato replied with two lightning-fast throwing darts. They whizzed a terrifying hair's-breadth from the goons, striking the wall of the wheelhouse directly behind them.

It was all the distraction The Green Hornet needed; he caught their weapons from underneath and using his momentum shoved the guns up and the goons into the wall, twisting the pistols out of their hands.

Kato scooped up the dropped shotgun and in a whirl of blows quickly thrashed its previous owner and the one remaining hoodlum into bruised and plaintive submission.

The Green Hornet looked up to see Vincenzo Carlossi bolting up the stairs to the enclosed wheel-deck.

"Get back here, you!" he yelled.

The Green Hornet bounded after him and caught a handful of the back of Carlossi's white suit jacket. He yanked him down the narrow stairs, spun him around by the lapels and pulled him close.

"It's over, Carlossi. Tell your man at the helm to turn this packet around and surrender."

Carlossi spat in what he knew was vain defiance.

The Green Hornet glared at Carlossi and tilted his head toward his partner. "Kato. . ."

As quick as thinking, Kato let fly a final dart. The helmsman jolted back. A sudden, small spray of cracks appeared when it imbedded itself in the wheelhouse window, with the needle-sharp tempered steel point and stylized insect wings . . . of a green hornet.

An "anonymous" radioed tip about the arrival of smuggled goods, with just enough detail to get the right level of attention, had the dock well-stocked with police. They peered into the fog at the muffled sound of a ship's engine approaching, ready to make arrests and earn some points. Suddenly, just as the container ship touched the dock in the mist, with an infamous buzz backed by the roar of rocket propulsion the Black Beauty vaulted out of the haze, onto the dock, and disappeared past them into the night.

Inside that sleek wonder, the two crimefighters left the police far behind.

"So, Kato," The Green Hornet mused. "How do you think the story will run? 'Green Hornet Strikes Again! Masked Criminal Plots to Take Over Mob Union Stranglehold?'"

They both cracked a smile at that. "This city is something else. . ." The Green Hornet added. Kato saw that his crime-fighting partner was feeling some of the weight of the multiple roles they played, of the life they led.

Kato decided to cheer up the moment. "I wasn't sure we had enough propellant for a second jump. . ."

The Green Hornet laughed, sat back, and decided not to ponder an alternate ending to their night's work. The Black Beauty streaked along through the breaking dawn.

"Let's bring her in, Kato," he said with a small satisfied smile.

Lowery and Clicker got the story they wanted, though Clicker made some noise about it not featuring enough pictures. She had to agree in the end that it wasn't a picture kind of story. Her heart was in the right place and she had all the determination a publisher could hope for, and Britt Reid made a note of it.

Lowery, of course, had to point out that The Green Hornet got away again.

There wasn't a bar in town where the two of them would blend in together, but this one was close. Hayashi Kato found who he was looking for and approached with a genuine smile. He didn't get out like this much at all. He shook the black gentleman's hand.

This was the man whose handwriting he had recognized, whose notations, references, and phrasings they had both picked up from their chemistry professor years before. This was the man Clicker had surreptitiously photographed in the alley. This was the informant. Tonight, though, he was just an old friend.

"Hello, George." Kato said. "Been keeping busy?"

SOLDANUS, THE SULTAN OF CRIME

by Gary Phillips

"That was a great run by Farr against the Bears Sunday, wasn't it?" Colson Admundson said. He sampled his JB and soda, while also puffing on his unfiltered cigarette.

"I hope Landry's shoulder is okay," Britt Reid responded. "He got pretty banged up in the fourth quarter," he added. "Of course by then I was more interested in the leggy blonde I'd brought with me to the owner's box. Who knew watching big, sweaty guys smash into each other would make her so . . . giddy."

"You old dog," Admundson leered, clinking his glass against Reid's, who was drinking ginger ale.

Seemingly aloof to his surroundings, Reid, newspaper publisher and local television station owner, was keenly aware of the movements and rhythms of the crowd in the large hall. He was attuned for any disturbance in those vibrations. He smiled politely at a waitress in platform shoes and hot pants strolling by, perfectly balancing a tray of wine in long-stemmed glasses on an upturned hand.

"I've got two hundred bucks on the Lions over the Vikings," Admundson said. "I hope everyone's healthy." He added, joking, "That won't spur an investigation by the *Sentinel*, will it, Britt?" Admunson was the Vice President of community relations at a large construction firm. What that really meant was he was a fixture in the offices of local politicians at the City-County building, which was Detroit's City Hall, making sure his projects went through.

"We'll keep it our secret, Colson." Both men laughed lightly and each drifted off to mingle with others in the crowd. Reid said hello to Keith and Mary Finlay, who together owned and operated several supermarkets in Detroit proper and out into Dearborn and Royal Oak. He talked golf and about President Nixon's recent landslide reelection with Mitch Xanthes, an auto parts distributor for American Motors. Xanthes was trying out a new look, complete with sideburns, mustache, and Haggar polyester flares. Reid schmoozed some more, and soon found the crimson nailed hand of Sandra Deavers on his upper arm.

"You should be proud, Sandra. You've done good," Reid commented to the pretty dark-haired philanthropist. She'd helped pull together the Maxton fundraiser.

"Like you, I just want to see our city come back, Britt." She smiled up at him.

He smiled back.

"Working out at the gym, huh?" She squeezed his muscle and kissed him on the cheek, her dangling earrings tinkling. "Or is running from one pretty woman's boudoir to another keeping you trim?" Her smile had enough wattage to light Cobo Arena.

"My nights are lonely and unfulfilled, Sandra." Absently, he fingered the fob on a chain to his pocket watch. The fob was the Japanese kanji symbol for enlightenment.

Her mascaraed eyes watched him over the martini glass she'd put to her lips. "I could change that."

Before he could answer, mayoral candidate Rudy Maxton blew into the mic at the podium. "Hello, hello, I guess this is on." He adjusted the mic's flexible extension and said, "I want to thank each and every one of you for coming out tonight despite the weather. But this is Detroit and we're used to hardship and dealing with that, aren't we?"

Applause and whoops went up.

Maxton had been a community activist, a firebrand to some, a change-maker to others. But he was the first black mayoral candidate in Detroit's history to garner a sizable white following. He was a contender. McNulty, the old line white incumbent, had resorted to subtle and no-so-subtle race baiting in some of his radio ads. This had ratcheted up tensions in the city.

Maxton sported a neat Fu Manchu mustache and close cropped hair, wearing a three-piece bell bottom suit and open collar shirt. He continued, "Our city has been called Motown and the Motor City, we've been up and we've been down, our people divided at times, but we've always come together when it counts. I intend to throw out deadwood and run a clean administration. We've had enough of corruption. This is what my campaign is all about, uniting us, not dividing us, no matter what one's color or creed is."

There was applause again. On the other side of the ballroom, a side entrance banged open. In came four men in work clothes, gloves, and ski masks, brandishing serious weaponry. There were three security guards about who reacted.

"Hold it," one of the guards said, drawing the revolver in his holster.

One of the masked men, holding a Thompson machine gun, strode toward the guard, who fired directly into the intruder's chest. This had no effect. The masked man butted the guard in the head with the stock end of the Thompson; the guard dropped to the floor. One of the remaining guards, a retiree from the General Motors assembly line, had also gotten his gun out, a .45. But its bullets were also ineffective, even though he took a head shot at one of the masks.

"Forget it pops," the man he shot at sneered. He slapped the guard with a pistol, disarmed him, and herded him over with the others.

Four more invaders came through the main entrance, similarly attired and wielding Sten guns and M-16 assault rifles. One of them wrapped and padlocked a chain on the latches of the twin entrance doors. Murmurs went through the crowd. Unnoticed, Britt Reid had his pocket watch out, and after using his thumb to move the hands to a specific time, pressed the stem. A small antenna protruded from the watch, and then retracted.

"This is exactly what it looks like ladies and gentlemen," the leader of the robbers announced. He held his SMG sub-machine gun aloft toward the ceiling as he walked among the frightened and wary. Another gunman escorted Maxton, the mayoral candidate, from the raised podium to join the rest. "Don't be shy and don't be penurious. Give till it hurts." Five of the crew now surrounded the bunched together four hundred or so. The other three proceeded to remove diamonds and gold from the women and paper money from the men, and dump the haul into burlap sacks, like cruel imitations of Santa Claus.

"Let's have it, slick," one of the intruders said to Reid. The newspaperman willingly handed over his wallet. Now was not the time to challenge these men. Too many innocents could get wounded or killed.

Their collecting finished, the octet moved backwards, guns on the crowd, toward the side entrance. The door was propped open with a cylindrical cigarette receptacle. As the robbers exited, the leader paused in the doorway and said, "It's been fun, folks." He sprayed bullets toward the ceiling, causing three of the large chandeliers to crash to the floor, glass exploding outward. People screamed and ducked, the lights flickering as well. The side entrance clicked shut, locked.

"Britt, Britt," Sandra Deavers yelled in the confusion as the crowd surged about.

Reid was at the padlocked front entrance. Fortunately for him, this area was darkened and his actions unseen. As bodies bumped and collided at his back, he sprung the lock deftly with a burglar tool. He opened the door. "All right, now, we can get out," he said loudly. "Just be calm and orderly, let's keep cool."

"Like Britt said," Rudy Maxton echoed, "everybody's okay so there's no reason to panic."

The gathered slowed. A Pistons basketball players with a bubble of an afro stepped in front of Reid and used his size to help direct people.

"Thanks, Curtis," the newspaperman said.

"No problem, Britt," the tall man answered.

Reid was to the side in the doorway and departed quickly through the main area as he spotted Sandra Deavers heading toward him. She came out of the ballroom, looking around, hands on her well-toned hips.

He turned a corner, out of her sight, and heard her declare, "That man."

The newspaper publisher jogged along a hallway to the bathrooms and on through a service area lined with tray carts. In no time he was outside, on the side of the building along a narrow alleyway. A light snow was falling again. The sleek Black Beauty drove up and idled, the back door automatically opened by the black-masked driver. Given the icy roads, special studded winter tires had been put on earlier that day. Reid got in as the car took off.

"They're on Lafayette," the taciturn driver announced at the wheel as Reid changed his clothes.

"Excellent, Hayashi," The Green Hornet said.

Only the sound of crunching snow was heard as the Black Beauty exited the alley and came onto the street. The specially baffled motor was on stealth mode. Traffic wasn't heavy given the time of night and condition of the roadways. It wasn't hard locating the robbers. They assumed they weren't being pursued. Kato had previously eyeballed the cars they'd escaped in when he'd circled around to pick up Reid.

Via a snitch nicknamed Squirrel, The Green Hornet had encountered on another matter a few days ago, the rumor was there might be a hit on the Maxton event—a fundraiser the community-minded Britt Reid had already RSVP'd to as coincidence would have it. That's why Kato and the Black Beauty were camped near the Tucker Hotel on Cadillac, where the fundraiser was held.

Some of the gang were in a 1970 cobalt blue Pontiac GTO, racing slicks on the rear, and the others in a '68 Javelin with bondo slathered on one fender, a super-charger sticking out of the hood. The tricked out cars cruised side-by-side toward the expressway. The robbers had removed their masks to avoid undue attention. The Black Beauty's headlights were on infra-green, aiding in making the car hard to see at night. Inside the machine, the two crimefighters could see clearly given the treated windshield. The neon and electric signs of passing storefronts were reflected in undulating streams on the car's polished ebony hull like it was a motorized shark honing in on its prey. Suddenly the GTO revved, the men inside having spotted The Hornet's darkened vehicle when it passed under the lights of the brightly lit Stegman used car lot.

"So much for the element of surprise," The Green Hornet said evenly.

Kato glared straight ahead, depressing the accelerator. He smiled thinly. Now this was getting good.

One of the thieves in the back seat of the Javelin stuck his body partway out and let loose with a machine gun burst. The bullets bounced impotently off the Black Beauty's armored shell. Kato handled the big car expertly and sped to the passenger side of the Javelin. The side window came down and a muzzle flashed at them again as Kato used the heavier and squatter Black Beauty to bump the attacking car. Momentarily, he sent the Javelin into its companion GTO. The Pontiac crossed the double yellow and a station wagon, its horn blaring, swerved to avoid a collision.

"I know," Kato intoned flatly, "we have to be careful of the civilians. They don't."

The Javelin screeched on its brakes, pulling back, giving the ones in the GTO a clear shot. The muzzle of a bazooka protruded from the GTO.

"Got it," Kato said. He sped up, knowing that's what the bazooka's shooter was anticipating and would be aiming slightly ahead. The bazooka was triggered while simultaneously Kato stoked the brakes and wrenched the steering wheel, causing the Black Beauty to fishtail. The shell rocketed past the driver's side, not an inch between it and the car. The projectile exploded a mail box, blowing it up while its concussive force blew the windows out of a television repair shop and a Laundromat.

Burning envelopes rained down like little meteorites as the GTO screeched around a corner leaning on two wheels, the Black Beauty right behind it. What cars were on the street either got out of the way or the combatants zoomed around them. The Javelin took off in another direction.

Patrons entering or exiting the Bent Moose Saloon gaped at the high speed chase as it roared by. One of those witnesses was Mike Axford, crime beat reporter for the *Daily Sentinel*.

"Holy Crow," he muttered. He watched as an emerald colored gas cloud erupted in the street. Small balls of the stuff were fired from the front grill of the Black Beauty and broke open on contact. "What the hell is that green devil up to now?" Axford wondered aloud.

Kato brought the black car through the pall which dissipated more slowly due to the cold. The GTO was right behind but given the heavy plume, its occupants couldn't see clearly enough to fire the bazooka again—at least for a few seconds. The masked adventurer leaned out an open window and aimed his Hornet Sting sonic baton back at the GTO's front wheel. A brief distinct buzzing sounded as the sonic device shattered the front brake caliper of the Pontiac. One of the robbers fired his machine gun, but The Hornet ducked back inside his car.

The GTO's driver pumped the brakes, but the destroyed caliper bled brake fluid. Under normal conditions, the car would have come to a rest, but at the speed they were traveling and with an iced street, there was no stopping. The car slid sideways, shuddering, and rolled over. The vehicle skidded on its top and smashed into the concrete and iron pylon of the overhead expressway. The Green Hornet and Kato were out of their stopped car and to the crashed vehicle in several bounds. Pasted on the expressway arch just above the destroyed GTO was a flyer for a rally in support of Mayor Winston "Win" McNulty, the incumbent.

One of the three in the car crawled out of the wreck, reaching for an M-16 that had fallen nearby. Kato threw a dart into the back of his hand and he yelped. The martial artist was on him and a quick hand chop to the side of the robber's neck stilled him. The Green Hornet used a brief burst of his Sting to loosen one of the car doors. Out tumbled two canvas bags of loot.

Sirens fast approaching, The Green Hornet shined the beam of a small flashlight on the car's other two occupants, dazed inside the wrecked car. Kato took the thieves' pictures with a small camera. One was Caucasian, like the one Kato had knocked out, and the other Asian—Chinese he surmised. The white one who was still inside the GTO, with the bazooka he'd shot jammed against him, had smashed his head into the windshield. Pieces of glass were embedded in his bloody face and head. The Asian man groaned.

Kato announced, "We better go."

"Right," The Green Hornet said, distracted. Each carried a canvass bag to the Black Beauty, and they took off as the police cruisers skidded onto the scene.

"Shouldn't we go after him?" the rookie officer driving said to the training officer beside him, Sergeant Burke.

"Forget it, kid." Burke leaned over and turned the engine off. "I've chased the Black Beauty before and wound up wrapping my squad car around a light pole and filling out enough paperwork to make you cry in your beer for a week. And that was in good weather."

Axford jogged over, saying hello to Burke, whom he knew. He'd seen the two mystery men carry the bags away. He bent and looked close at the robber who'd been cut up by the smashed windshield. The reporter smiled a lopsided grin.

In the rear seat of the Black Beauty, The Green Hornet wasn't smiling.

"What's worrying you?' Kato asked as he drove dark on the back streets, heading for the secret garage.

"The one who aimed the bazooka at us."

"Yes?"

"I recognized him, Hayashi. More importantly, I saw Axford coming across the street when we left. He knows who that man is too."

"Bad news?"

"Bad news, *doshi*," The Hornet said, using the samurai term for fellow swordsman.

The exclusive in the morning edition of the *Daily Sentinel* was a front page, above-the-fold story by Mike Axford, recounting how The Green Hornet had robbed other robbers. Three men were in the hospital jail ward. One of them, who apparently shot a bazooka at the elusive Hornet and his often silent partner in crime, was a member of the Detroit Police Department who'd been suspended for bribery and excessive force charges.

"Our beleaguered police chief, mindful this has played into the notion in the black community that the mayor would do anything to keep his job, has a press conference scheduled at Frank Murphy Hall of Justice later this morning," Axford said. "Of course I'll be covering it."

"Good, Mike," Britt Reid said to Axford in the city room. The customary din of electric typewriters churning away and phones jangling could be heard around them. A few old timers still clung to using their manual typewriters. Small clouds of cigarette smoke hung over a few desks as well.

"But we need to get to the bottom of this," Reid added. He didn't have to remind Axford of the race riot that had destroyed property and race relations in the city in '67. Both men were keenly aware of how hard it had been to rebuild lines of communication since then—tenuous as they were even now.

"That Hornet is mixed up in this somehow, Britt, and I'll dig it out," Axford said. "I wouldn't put it past him to want to see all the city go up in flames to feed his twisted ego. Not only do we have that crooked cop Elmore Estleman in the GTO, there was an out-of-town muscle, and this Asian fella too. No ID on him, but when the police questioned him, his heavily accented English had them figuring he was fresh off the boat. Otherwise a guy his relatively young age would be from around here. I'm heading out now to meet with an immigration source of mine."

"Okay, Mike, keep on it," Reid encouraged. How curious it was, he'd often noted, that the interests of being a newspaperman were at cross purposes to his being The Green Hornet. Though in the end, weren't both sides of him about the pursuit of justice?

"You figure The Hornet's importing some Oriental dancing girls, Mike?" Ed Lowery, another reporter, walked by, perusing a sheaf of papers. "Gonna open up a club or have a harem?"

Axford, already heading out, quipped, "Jerry Lewis ain't got nothing on you, Lowery." He guffawed as he left.

As Reid turned away, city editor Gunnigan gestured at him to swing by Lowery's desk. Reid headed that way and listened in on their conversation.

"So, is this mad scientist legit?" Gunnigan asked the reporter.

Lowery looked up from his papers. "Kirk Exton was a mechanical engineer at Ford, then left for someplace called El Segundo near Los Angeles, to work in aerospace and defense contracting, top secret stuff it seems. He retired early with money he'd invested wisely. His wife had passed, so he came back home to Detroit about six years ago."

"What's this Exton got for us?" Reid asked.

"Not exactly sure yet, Boss," Lowery replied, "but it might be a breakthrough in something he calls clean energy."

Gunnigan raised an eyebrow. "Well, you better go feel him out, see if he's on to something or just howling at the moon. Could be he inhaled too much rocket fuel or who knows what out there in La-La Land."

"Yeah," Lowery chuckled. Like a lot of rust belters, they shared a one-dimensional view of the West Coast.

Reid nodded at the men and headed to his office.

"You were right, take a look at this," Lenore Case said as she entered his inner office with him. Using a remote control, Reid's personal secretary turned up the volume on the television set built into the wood paneling of one of the walls.

". . . We're very concerned that this might go deeper than one rogue police officer," a tall, clean-headed black reverend was saying to a television reporter in front of a storefront. "I pray this isn't about the establishment seeking to silence a good, honest candidate."

Casey turned the volume down again. "I've already gotten a couple of calls from the blue hairs in Birmingham, worried their black maids are sending secret messages to the militants." She wasn't joking.

"I know Reverend Markham," Britt said, indicating the television screen. "We've worked together on urban renewal projects. He'll voice his opinion, but he's no bomb thrower."

She stood close to him, each breathing in the other. "Then let's hope The Green Hornet gets a handle on this soon."

He looked at her for a beat or two. "Good thing he's not alone in this."

"Indeed."

The masked individual who called himself Soldanus, the Sultan of Crime, had his hands behind his back. He gazed out the cathedral window of an abandoned brewery, looking onto the Detroit River below. He was a middleweight-built man of above average height, boxy shoulders in a two-piece gray pin-striped suit, and dark blue gloves. A dark blue mask covered his entire head. There were eyeholes, but his eyes were obscured by some reflective material behind the slits. A fedora rested flipped over on its crown on his desk. His factotum, Rasmussen, entered the tastefully decorated office.

"I can't get any information from our contact in the police department," he said to Soldanus. "The three are under guard by the chief's hand-picked men."

Soldanus turned to look at him. "No matter. Even if one of them talks, they know nothing of the larger picture. We go forward."

"What about The Green Hornet?"

"He wants to muscle in on our action so much, let's give him a real taste."

Rasmussen showed even teeth.

In loose chinos, black T-shirt, and a light windbreaker, Hayashi Kato moved along the cramped rear corridor of the Bow Wah Bakery on Peterboro. The business was located in Chinatown. A sweet smell crinkled his nostrils in the confined space. Through the morning and early afternoon, Kato had shown the picture of the presumed Chinese man the police held to specific people—some supposed solid citizens and others among the underworld. A word here, some cash there, had led him here. He arrived at the door he'd been instructed to knock on and did so. There was a peace symbol sticker on it. Kato was not surprised when one man appeared at the near end of the corridor and two others from the way he'd come. Going into himself, he got ready.

"You're one nosy dude, you know that?" one of the men said in Chinese.

"So I've been told," Kato also responded in Chinese. The closest one attacked with a flying kick. Kato ducked and threw him into the other two who were rushing forward. The hallway was so narrow, there was no way they could come at him side-by-side. Kate went on the attack.

The crimefighter blocked his opponent's fist and executed a palm strike. The two went at it fast, their feet and hands blurs. Kato did a double elbow hit to the man's cheek. He followed with a punch to the groin, then a knife-hand strike to the man's collar bone. *Crack*. Then another blow and another broken bone. Kato finished him off with a half-round kick to the head. The first one went down. The second one attacked.

In just a few seconds of combat, Kato realized this one had more skill. His hooking punch clipped Kato hard. Flow and feeling, flow and feeling, Kato reminded himself. Open palm down, he deflected the man's kick. The attacker followed with a step-down move. Kato countered. Back and forth they battled in the close quarters. Then an opening came and Kato delivered an upward strike. Using an unorthodox style put the second one off-balance. Switching up again, Kato employed American-style boxing techniques learned after long hours of sparring at the prizefighter's Mecca, the Kronk Gym.

He delivered a one, two, combination upstairs on his opponent's head, then downstairs to his stomach. Hunching forward, tucking in his head, Kato surged forward like he was going for the championship belt. The other man's blows cascaded on Kato's upper shoulders and neck. He responded by swiveling his hips and put one, two more dead center in the man's gut. He added a left uppercut that connected solidly and made the other man stumble backwards. Economy of motion, Kato reflected. Switching back again to wing chun, Kato delivered a straight on kick, combined with a back hand strike. Three times he repeated this maneuver, in a blink. The back of the second opponent's head broke the plaster of the wall as he reeled back. A punch hand slice to the throat keeled him over, giving him trouble breathing.

The last one was on Kato. They tumbled and grappled. Their hurtling bodies broke in the door with the peace symbol and they fell in. The remaining attacker back flipped out of the way, producing a knife as he came out of his crouch. Kato removed his nunchaku from inside his windbreaker. A knife sweep had him backtracking. He barely blocked a follow up thrust with the end of the nunchaku. He spun and leaped up, used an overhand strike with the nunchaku to the man's temple. Back on his feet, Kato moved inside of another knife thrust. He grabbed the man's knife arm and used ju-jitsu to flip him. Getting him down on his back, Kato didn't let the man's arm go. Turning his body, he snapped the third attacker's elbow. Twin strikes of his foot to the other man's face knocked him out.

Sweating, blood on his lip, Kato walked over to the one he'd struck in the throat. Tapping the end of the nunchaku against the man's forehead, he awoke groggily.

"About this gentleman," Kato began, showing him the captured man's picture.

As Hayashi Kato obtained information and communicated such to Britt Reid, Mayor Win McNulty was leaving the assignation apartment he kept under an assistant's name in the industrial suburb of Warren on a quiet, tucked away street. With him was a pert twenty-four-year-old campaign intern and former manicurist, who'd proven oh-so-supportive of hizzoner. There was a chill wind and she shivered slightly on the stoop. The mink bomber jacket she wore was just a little shorter than her mini-skirt.

"Oh, big daddy," she said drowsily, "I think I need some more warming up." She giggled and played kissy face with the much older and married man.

"Sadly, my sweet, duty awaits." Arm-in-arm, the two descended the steps to his Lincoln Continental parked around the corner.

"Die, pig," the first shooter said, popping up from behind a set of trash cans. He fired a round into the mayor's chest.

The second shooter put a bullet in the man's head before he'd fallen to the ground. As the assassins ran off, the pretty woman screamed and cried. The two shooters wore ski masks and gloves. This she accurately reported to the police. Yet in less than an hour after the shooting, word on the street was that black militants had killed the mayor in retaliation for the Maxton incident.

Elsewhere, Ed Lowery had waited for an hour in a coffee shop. Kirk Exton hadn't kept their appointment. He'd called the man's house again, but got no response.

"I appeal for calm and reason at this time, my fellow citizens," Britt Reid said directly into the camera, his fingers clasped before him on the spare desktop. He was broadcasting a live appeal at his local television station, DSTV. "I realize the attack on the Rudy Maxton event and now this terrible tragedy this afternoon involving our mayor has us on edge. But there are those who would not allow or want the light of justice to shine on the guilty, and have us succumb to vicious rumors and innuendos. I would ask you to please let the authorities do their jobs and catch these criminals. Let's give Deputy Mayor Ryan our full support as he takes over in this stressful situation. Know too that along with the police and legal system, I will, as someone who values the public trust you've shown for this television station and the *Daily Sentinel*, bring my resources to bear in this time of crisis."

Reid continued a while longer, then concluded, asking for calm again. The screen faded to black and after a canned announcement, the station went back to its afternoon movie, a Bob Steele oater. On a popular black radio station in town, Reverend Markham had made a similar call for reason.

"Good job, Britt," Sandra Deavers said to Reid as he stepped out of the broadcast booth.

"What brings you down here?"

"You know I sponsor a young ladies association in one of the public schools. I wanted to show them the station and, well, I was hoping you might spare a few minutes to talk to them about careers in news and broadcasting." Behind Deavers were several teenaged girls who looked about awkwardly.

"Of course."

After his brief talk, Deavers kissed Reid on the cheek. "You're a doll."

"Talk to you."

"It's a date." A couple of the teenagers giggled as Reid walked away.

"Britt, there's a call for you on line two," one of the news producers said.

"Thanks, Scott." Reid walked to a post and clicked on the blinking red tab of the push button phone attached to it.

"Can you talk freely?" District Attorney Frank Scanlon said on the other end.

"Not exactly," Reid answered.

Scanlon chuckled. "Then you'd better keep a poker face. I have a possible lead to this Soldanus you asked me about earlier, the one Kato learned about." He went on and Reid listened, saying little, betraying nothing in his features.

Before sundown in a Grosse Point Woods dining room, where cut crystal glasses were the norm and an original Gauguin hung on a wall, a husband, wife and their two young children enjoyed a meal of rare roast beef with sides of mashed potatoes and steamed green beans. They didn't hear the low hiss of sleeping gas that issued from the timed gas canister in the air vent. The husband's face plopped right into his mashed potatoes.

At that moment in a number of well-to-do homes in the Woods and greater Grosse Pointe area, variations of this scene played out as residents keeled over from the contents of hidden sleep gas canisters.

Docile inhabitants and pets made robbing those homes so much easier.

Miles from Grosse Point, Rudy Maxton was shaking hands and greeting the last wave of patrons at the custom car show at Olympia Stadium.

"Oh, no, I don't for a minute believe in any sort of conspiracy out to get me," Maxton assured a middle-aged white homemaker. "I'm as concerned as the rest of us at finding out who assassinated the mayor."

"You've got my vote, Rudy," she said, clasping his hand.

Maxton, accompanied by two campaign aides and two recently-added bodyguards, walked by a display of a prototype hydrogen cell motor.

The motor exploded violently.

At sundown, after forays into a secret casino in Greektown and a drive out on Eight Mile Road, The Green Hornet and his chauffer, who said little as well, let their actions do the talking.

Five hoods lay in various stages of hurt around the office of a mobbed-up waste hauling business in Clawson. One was hanging partway out of a broken window, letting the cold in. The Hornet finished the sixth one off with a short jab to the face, busting out two teeth. The hood sagged to his knees. He was prevented from keeling over due to the masked man in the midnight green topcoat holding him by his longish hair. The Hornet bent down to lean in close to the bruised gangster.

"Now, about this amateur Soldanus trying to angle in on my territory," he said sibilantly.

After their talk, riding in the back of the Black Beauty, The Green Hornet got a call from Lenore Case on the Beauty's radio phone. Only a select few had this number. "What's up, Casey?"

"It's all over the wires," she said. "Rudy Maxton is in bad shape at the hospital after an attempt on his life. A riot has already begun near Olympia Stadium, and is spreading. Police are swarming the area. Naturally Axford is going out there. It's bad, Britt."

The Hornet squeezed the receiver tightly. "Okay, Casey, see if you can reach Reverend Markham. No doubt he and other black leaders will be heading there too. I have his private number." He recited it to her and added, "Hayashi and I are en route to what I hope will solve this situation before it gets too out of hand."

"I damn sure hope so." She severed the call.

Soon the Black Beauty was driving slowly along a Gross Pointe residential street. It pulled in at a specific mansion. There were lights on in the house. Close to the porch there was a sign among the hearty rhododendrons announcing a private patrol. The rear of the house overlooked a private dock on the Detroit River. There were several such private docks up and down this part of the coastline. Out front, The Green Hornet and Kato alighted and proceeded forward. A sniper with a suppressor on the barrel of his rifle with an infra-red scope had The Green Hornet in his crosshairs. He was on the roof of the mansion where they'd parked.

On the other side of the large house, Soldanus, Rasmussen, and seven others were already away in a twin engine fishing boat that had been anchored at the dock. A faint buzzing as if by a large insect came and went in the night air, but the departing criminals didn't pay any attention to the sound. One of the hoods, a former sailor, piloted the craft, which also towed a portable tool shed on pontoons. In the shed were crammed millions of dollars in original art, jewels, and gold looted from the old money homes in this suburb. Much of it had been obtained from hidden family safes whose doors were blown off with plastique. The boat headed for one of the many uninhabited islands not far away in the channel. The water hadn't frozen over yet, though there were a few ice floes. Their destination was called Celeron, a wildlife preserve.

Reaching the island, the gangsters disembarked. By prior arrangement, each hired thug would get a small knapsack containing a combination of bearer bonds, cash, jewels and gold. A number of the houses they had robbed had bullion illegally tucked away—Soldanus had known this beforehand. On the beach were several small boats, some with motors, previously brought to the island. The hired gunners would depart from here to parts unknown. There were reptiles, badgers, and birds among saw grass that reached more than seven feet high.

The swag was divvied up. Rasmussen spoke in Russian on a walkie-talkie.

"It's been a pleasure doing business with you, sultan," one of the men said, shaking the ganglord's smallish hand. The hoodlum turned and a dart entered the side of his neck, shutting down a nerve to his brain. As he sank to the ground, The Green Hornet's sleeping gas swept over the beach. There was enough wind to drive it away quickly, but not before two more gunsels were overcome. The Hornet used his Sting to destroy the outboard motors of the fishing boat.

"Get him," Soldanus yelled. "The Hornet wants your money."

The four remaining hoods produced hand guns and spread out into the saw grass. Soldanus and Rasmussen ran to the fishing boat and removed a trussed up and gagged man. They hurried to the first boat they reached. This one only had oars. "Get our contact in Ontario to meet us out in Lake St. Clair," the masked gangster bellowed.

Rasmussen nodded as he began rowing, badly, the walkie-talkie at his feet. "This is hard, he complained.

"Faster," Soldanus yelled.

Back on Celeron, it wasn't long before The Green Hornet and Kato, threading their way through the tall grasses, took out the thieves using their fists, feet and weaponry. They had the advantage of night filters in their masks' eyelets. Though this didn't give them vision as clear as day, the lenses did allow them to distinguish forms better. This had allowed The Hornet to spot the sniper on the roof when Kato had driven the Black Beauty to the burgled mansion. Wary and walking toward the home, he'd brought up his Hornet Sting, aiming it at the sniper. The rifle had exploded. Disoriented and injured, the would-be killer had fallen off the roof, breaking an arm and both legs.

On their way out to Grosse Pointe, The Hornet and Kato had discussed how the mobster at the waste hauler had been insistent about a particular neighborhood block that was Soldanus' target. That was too specific and, presuming a trap, they had been prepared. Thereafter, he and Kato had borrowed a rowboat and taken off in the dark after the fishing boat, following the sound of the motors. Reid had been a champion rower in college.

Now, as Soldanus and Rasmussen tried to get away, The Green Hornet and Kato were soon closing the gap in the borrowed rowboat.

Soldanus fired a handgun. His aim wasn't bad but The Hornet's was better. The Sting sounded its sonic song again and he blew a hole in their rowboat. Rasmussen stopped rowing to get his gun out, but Kato's dart, thrown into his upper chest, released a puff of sleep gas, sending him to dreamland. Soldanus dove into the icy water and began swimming. The Green Hornet took off his coat and went in after him. Two quick punches to Soldanus' masked face subdued the mastermind, and The Hornet began tugging him back toward his own rowboat.

Meanwhile, as the crooks' boat sank, Kato rescued the sleeping henchman and the bound figure.

The dazed Soldanus, the unconscious Rasmussen, and the drugged captive were crowded in the rowboat. The Hornet turned the tied up man over.

"You know him?" asked Kato.

"Yes, it's the missing scientist," he breathed. "Kirk Exton."

On the Ontario side of the lake, a man stood in a small motor boat. He looked through his infrared binoculars, witnessing the capture of Soldanus. He did have a Makarov handgun, but he weighed his options. Grumbling to himself in Russian, he made his decision and motored back to the Canadian shore.

"Now, let's see who's been getting funny with me." The Green Hornet pulled Soldanus' mask off, revealing a wet and bruised Sandra Deavers.

The surprised Green Hornet maintained his poker face. Squeezing her arm, he noted the padding in the suit to bulk up her frame. Probably had lifts in her shoes too.

"You got guts and brains, lady. But you're through, sultan. Nobody squeezes me out."

She shivered.

The following morning at his home, Britt Reid handed a cup of coffee on a matching china saucer to Lenore Case. She sat on a stool at the bar-like kitchen counter. The morning headline in the *Daily Sentinel* reported the riots in text and pictures. But the local television news last night had footage of Sandra Deavers, wrapped and padlocked in anchor chain, on the doorstep of the police department. The Green Hornet had strategically conversed with a few street types, and word had spread that it was Soldanus behind the mayor's killing and attack on Maxton, who was expected to recover.

Soldanus had done this to enflame racial tensions and cause a major distraction for the police, so she could pull off her robberies. As the truth became known, an uneasy quiet had settled on Detroit.

Casey crossed her legs, showing a lot of thigh in her short robe. "So all this bedevilment was really about kidnapping Kirk Exton, the mechanical engineer."

"Mostly," Reid said, sipping his coffee. "Don't know what made Sandra go over to the other side. Though I do know, from an article in our archives from the society pages, she'd made two trips to Russia last year, supposedly on behalf of goodwill purposes."

He went on. "Hayashi found out one of her henchmen, who we initially perceived was from China, was really from Eastern Russia. Sandra, as one of the sponsors of the Maxton fundraiser, was able to switch out the bullets for blanks in the guards' guns."

"She meant to deliver Exton to her Soviet masters so they could force him to develop his hydrogen cells for engines aiding their military expansion," Casey said.

"So she proudly admitted to The Hornet," Reid acknowledged. "She also contemptuously made a point about stealing from the bourgeoisie, the very people who'd invited her into their homes for dinner parties, charity meetings, and what have you. That's how she was able to plant her remote controlled gas canisters. She'd met Exton at a reception at one of those parties. Being as charming as she could be, she of course got the widower talking about his invention." He sipped his coffee thoughtfully.

"The sad truth is, though, she was able to inflame racial tension quite easily," Casey said. "We have a long way to go in this city, Britt, in this country."

He smiled at her. "The philosophers have only interpreted the world in various ways; the point is to change it."

"Thomas Jefferson?" she frowned.

"Karl Marx, Miss Case."

She dipped her head slightly in appreciation. They finished their coffee.

THE DANGEROUS GAME

by Eric Fein

A pall hung over the city of Detroit like a black widow spider closing in on its prey. Tensions still ran high from the July riots that spilt the already divided city further apart. And now, as 1967 was staggering to a close like a boxer past his prime, more blood was being spilled.

Less than a week ago, a sniper started picking off citizens as they went about their business. The victims didn't have anything in common other than they all seemed to be targeted at random. In each case, a single shot to the head or chest by a bullet loaded into a .458 Winchester Magnum rifle cartridge killed them. Of course, the papers had a field day when it became clear that there was a sniper on the loose. One of the gaudier tabloids, the *Daily Torch*, called the sniper the Motor City Shooter.

Despite the city's spasms of violence, Bill Cooper was having a good day. He was an ad man for the Gilbert Ad Agency. He was on his way home from work after a very successful presentation to one of the firm's biggest clients.

Now, Cooper walked along Woodward Avenue in midtown Detroit to pick up flowers and wine to celebrate with his wife. She had been against him traveling with the sniper on the loose. However, he refused to live his life in fear. Besides, he told her, there was something like 1.5 million people in Detroit. It was unlikely that the sniper would pick him.

Other people must have felt the same as him because the streets were crowded. Still, anxiety and fear were palpable on the streets of Detroit.

Cooper passed a street musician who played *Flight of the Bumblebee* on his trumpet. Now there was a brave soul, Cooper thought. Hearing the melody made Cooper smile. He couldn't remember where he heard it before but it didn't matter at the moment—

The world went black for Bill Cooper at 5:13 p.m. in the middle of the street. He crumpled to the ground like a broken G.I. Joe action figure.

A woman walking two feet to his right saw what had happened and screamed hysterically. Everyone stopped to see what the commotion was about. There, lying in the street, was Bill Cooper in his crisply pressed charcoal gray suit, a bullet hole dead center in his forehead. The back of his skull and most of his brains were splattered across the sidewalk looking like a Jackson Pollock painting.

One moment, everyone was frozen in place. The next, there was an explosion of activity as people ran for cover. They ducked into the nearest open doors they could find, leaving Bill Cooper's corpse on the now quiet street.

In the twenty-four hours after Bill Cooper's murder, two more citizens of Detroit were also killed by sniper-fire. Sam Halifax, a twenty-year old college student, was shot as he ran laps in the park. He was on an athletic scholarship and his coaches thought he showed great promise for qualifying for the next Olympics.

Inga Meyerson, thirty, was a nurse at the county hospital. She was on her coffee break smoking a cigarette in the hospital's ambulance bay when her pretty freckled face was shattered by the sniper's bullet.

That brought the total number of deaths from the sniper up to seven. News of these deaths sent the city into a fresh wave of panic. The police had no answers and too many questions.

Of all the Detroit papers covering the attacks, the *Daily Sentinel* presented the facts in the most straightforward and honest manner possible. Its owner, publisher, and editor, Britt Reid was an energetic young man dedicated to publishing the truth no matter where it took him, and doing right by the citizens of Detroit.

When it became clear that there was a sniper at large, Reid had turned his office into a command post for his staff. Reporters young and old ran in and out for briefings and instructions. Reid paced behind his desk as his secretary, Lenore Case, who answered to the nickname Casey, took notes. This scene had taken place every day since the shootings had begun.

At the moment, Reid was in a closed-door meeting with Casey and Mike Axford. Axford was one of the *Sentinel*'s best reporters. He was a former policeman who had a hard charging style and never took no for an answer. He had cracked many important cases.

Reid and Axford were used to having heated exchanges about the stories that Mike covered. This time was no different.

"I'm telling you Britt," Axford said. "The Green Hornet is behind this. I feel it in my gut."

"Come on, Mike," Reid said. "Maybe, what you're feeling is the chili you had for lunch. The Hornet may be a criminal but he has never gone after the general public in any way."

"That we know of," Axford said. "This could be a dramatic shift in his operations. Maybe he's got something big planned."

Reid shook his head sadly. He respected Axford, but the reporter could be exasperating at times. None more so than when he was grinding his ax about The Green Hornet. That could be stopped if Reid let him in on his secret that he, Britt Reid, was in fact The Green Hornet.

Reid had pledged long ago to rid Detroit of its crime and corruption. He was motivated by the memory of his father, Henry Reid. Henry had been the publisher of the *Sentinel* before Britt. He had been a crusading journalist who passed on his passion for truth and justice to his son.

Henry had the misfortune of angering members of Detroit's crime syndicate to the point that they had him framed for murder. He was sent to jail and before he could be cleared, died there. This led Britt to dedicate his life to his father's principles of journalistic integrity and to create the alter ego, The Green Hornet, which allowed him to deal with criminals on terms they understood.

Only three people knew of Britt's secret life: Lenore Case, District Attorney Frank P. Scanlon, and Reid's valet and chauffeur, Kato.

The ringing of the phone interrupted Reid and Axford's argument. Casey answered it, "Mr. Reid's office." She listened then said, "Send it up now."

She hung up the phone.

"What was all that about?" Reid said.

"The front desk," Casey said. "There was a package left for you marked urgent."

Through the large glass panels of Reid's office, they could see the messenger step off the elevator. Casey went out to meet him and took the package. She walked back into the office and handed it to Reid.

It was in a large manila envelope. He sat at his desk and put it on the desktop. Casey and Axford flanked Reid on either side and watched.

Reid looked over the envelope. Other than his name printed in block letters on the front, there were no markings. There was something bulky inside the envelope. It was about the size and thickness of a pack of cigarettes.

Reid used a letter opener to slit one end of the envelope. He carefully looked inside, then took out the contents. There was a letter and a small gift box. He glanced at the letter, grimaced at what it said, and handed it over to Axford. Reid opened the box to find a single large caliber bullet lying on a cushion of cotton. The bullet had a silver tip and on its casing the symbol of The Green Hornet had been perfectly etched.

"What is all this?" Casey said.

"It's a red herring," Axford said. "I bet The Hornet delivered it himself."

"I doubt that," Reid said.

"Would someone please tell me what is going on?" Casey said.

Axford handed her the letter. It read:

TO: BRITT REID, PUBLISHER, THE *DAILY SENTINEL*.

YOU MUST PRINT THE FOLLOWING MESSAGE ON THE FRONT PAGE OF YOUR EVENING EDITION OR MY NEXT VICTIM WILL BE A CHILD. TO PROVE I AM THE REAL DEAL, THE ENCLOSED BULLET IS THE SAME AS THE ONES I USED ON MY VICTIMS, .458. WE BOTH KNOW THAT THE CALIBER OF THE BULLETS HAS NOT BEEN RELEASED TO THE PUBLIC.

TO THE GREEN HORNET:

I'VE SENT THIS PAPER A BULLET WITH YOUR SYMBOL ON IT. IT'S MY CHALLENGE TO YOU. THE THROWING DOWN OF THE GAUNTLET, IF YOU WILL. I CHALLENGE YOU TO FIND ME BEFORE I FIND YOU.

LIFE IS A DANGEROUS GAME. CARE TO PLAY?

THE MASTER SHOT

"My goodness," Casey said. Her face had gone pale and tight. She handed the letter to Reid. "What are you going to do?"

"What can I do?" Reid said. "I have to print the letter. I have no doubt that he will carry out his threat if I don't do as he says. After all, he's killed seven people already."

"Come on, Britt," Axford said, face red with frustration. "You know that this is just a way for The Hornet to make himself look innocent. If he's one of the sniper's victims, then he can't be the sniper. But I know that's malarkey."

"Okay, Mike," Reid said. "You feel so strongly that The Hornet is in on this, then I'm making that aspect of the story your assignment. See what you can dig up."

Reid turned to Casey. "In the meantime Casey, get Clicker Binny down here. I want photos of the letter and the bullet. Then, I want you to bring these things over to D.A. Scanlon. I'll arrange that now."

"Yes, sir," Casey said and left the office.

Axford followed her out. When they were gone, Reid took out his pocket watch. He set the hands to 1:50 and pressed the stud on top of the watch. A small antenna shot out of it and emitted a signal that would be picked up by Frank Scanlon.

Detroit's District Attorney was deep into the day's paperwork when the tiny receiver in the earpiece of his eyeglasses picked up The Hornet's signal. He closed the file he was reading, put it back in his "In" box, and dialed Britt Reid's direct line at the *Sentinel*. "Yes, Britt," he said.

Reid's voice came over the phone line. He quickly explained about the letter and bullet. Scanlon was floored.

"I'll come over right now to get it," Scanlon said.

"Not necessary," Reid said. "I'm sending Casey. She'll be there soon. Oh, Frank, I'm going to want that bullet back tonight. Can you arrange that?"

"I think so," Scanlon said. "You will give it back to me, right? It won't look good if evidence goes missing on this case."

"I'll get it back to you tomorrow," Reid said.

"Okay," Scanlon said. "I'll stop by tonight."

Britt Reid lived in a townhouse on a quiet street. There was a secret entrance that D.A. Scanlon used to gain access to the building. An ingenious hidden elevator built deep within the building brought him up to Reid's living quarters. The wall with the fireplace and mantle rose to reveal Scanlon in the elevator cage. He stepped off it and into Britt Reid's living room.

Reid was standing at the bookcase opposite the hidden elevator. He pushed back the books that he had only a moment before tilted down and out of position on the shelves. These specific books were rigged to the apparatus that controlled the secret elevator. With the books back in their normal position, the wall and fireplace slid back into place.

Reid and Scanlon shook hands. Kato entered bearing two cups of coffee, cream, and sugar on a tray. He was dressed in black slacks and white jacket. The clothes camouflaged his lean, lethal body honed by years of martial arts training. Kato set the tray down on Reid's desk.

"Hello, Kato," Scanlon said.

Kato nodded and handed him a cup and saucer and then poured the coffee from a silver coffee pot. Scanlon took it, said "Thanks, Kato," and sat down in the chair facing the desk, setting his cup down on the coffee tray. The evening edition of the *Sentinel* sat on Reid's desk. The shooter's letter was printed on the front page. Scanlon nodded at the paper and said, "Are you sure running the letter is the right thing to do?"

Reid leaned back in his chair, "I think that whether we run the letter or not the shooter is going to strike again. This way, there is a chance that the gratification he gets from seeing his letter in print might keep him from hunting for fresh victims, at least for a little while."

"God help us all if he strikes again," Scanlon said. The stress of the last week showed in his face. "I don't know how much more bloodshed the city can tolerate before cracking up."

"The citizens of Detroit are tough," Reid said. "They've survived other horrors and they'll survive this one. You have the bullet?"

Scanlon took a small envelope that held the silver-tipped bullet out of his breast pocket and handed it to Reid.

"What did the lab boys have to say?" Reid said.

"Not much," Scanlon said. "It's the same make and caliber as the bullets taken from the victims—except for the silver tip and the hornet engraving. There were no fingerprints other than yours, Miss Case's, and the photographer's. What good is it to you?"

"I'm going to trace it back to its maker," Reid said. "That will give me a line on our sniper."

"And if it doesn't?" Scanlon said.

Reid smiled at his friend, "It will, Frank. Trust me on this. There are only a handful of people with enough money, skill, and ego to commission a bullet such as this or build it. We know from the letter the shooter wants me to hunt him down. In the bullet he has delivered to me the key to finding him."

"It's a trap, Britt," Scanlon said.

"Of course it is," Reid said. "I would expect nothing else. But I plan on making the shooter regret the day he stepped foot in my city."

"I'd settle for him in a jail cell. Well, I should be going," Scanlon said. "Let me know if you need anything else."

"I will, Frank. Thanks," Reid said.

The two men stood and shook hands.

Reid pulled down the appropriate books on the bookcase to reveal the elevator once more. Scanlon got on it and it ascended to the exit.

"Let's go," Reid said. "It's time for The Green Hornet and Kato to take action."

"Right," Kato said.

In minutes, Reid and his valet were battle ready. Reid wore a short brimmed fedora and long coat, both midnight green in color. A molded black-green facemask, with a stylized hornet symbol in the center of it, hid his true identity.

Kato wore a black mask similar to The Hornet's, minus the symbol, as well as a black chauffeur's uniform and cap. They entered the garage where Reid's everyday car, a Chrysler 300, sat. They went over to the wall, flipped a few switches. Special grips attached to the wheels of the car.

Suddenly, the car and the floor flipped over to reveal a sleek black customized 1966 Chrysler Crown Imperial called the Black Beauty. The car, modified by Kato, held many lethal secrets including a gas cannon, Hornet mortar, oil slick, and rockets.

The car was armored plated. To compensate for the added weight, the Black Beauty had a cutting edge suspension and a super powerful engine that overpowered any other vehicle on the road.

Kato got into the driver's seat and The Hornet in the passenger compartment in the back. The Hornet went through the weapons checklist: Hornet Sting, Hornet gun, and Hornet scanner. Satisfied that everything was in order, The Green Hornet said, "Let's roll, Kato."

"Right, boss," he said.

He turned the key in the ignition and the car roared to life. The door to the garage lifted and the Black Beauty slid out, down the hidden alley. The wall-sized billboard that masked the alley opened to allow the car access to the street. It was deserted.

"Where to?" Kato said.

"Downtown. Ivan's Pawnshop," The Hornet said.

Kato kept to the side streets to avoid the public. He had the car on silent running so that it moved through the streets like a steel ghost.

Ivan's Pawnshop was on a street with a record store, a barbershop, and a check-cashing store. Across the street were a twenty-four hour diner and a cab company. Kato avoided the storefronts and came up through a side alley. He stopped the car near the pawnshop's backdoor and cut the engine. The Green Hornet and Kato exited the Black Beauty and entered the shop.

Inside, the smell of sweat, cigarettes, and stale beer hung in the air. The Green Hornet and Kato stood silent just within the doorway and looked around. They were in the storeroom. It was packed with musical instruments of all shapes and sizes, as well as TV sets, fur coats, antique vases, and other household items. A stack of western and mystery pulps from the 1930s and 1940s sat moldering in a corner. There was a doorway with a grimy translucent plastic curtain that led into the front.

The sound of a TV, tuned to a western, could be heard. Kato took point as the two masked men walked to the front of the store. They paused, standing in the shadows, in the hallway that opened up behind the shop's front counter.

They saw a short fat bald man who resembled Humpty Dumpty sitting behind the counter watching a 13-inch black and white TV set that sat next to the cash register. The fat man wore gray slacks, a white shirt with a dirty collar, and a moth-eaten V-neck sweater. His face was pockmarked from decades of bad acne and bad eating. He smoked a thick, black cigar that was clenched tight in the corner of his mouth.

The Green Hornet pulled out his Hornet gun, stepped over to the fat man and put the gun to the back of the man's head. The man gasped. His cigar dropped to the floor. The Hornet ground it into shreds under his heel. "Nasty habit, Ivan," The Green Hornet said.

"Whatever you want, take it," Ivan said. "I'm no hero."

"Neither am I," The Hornet said and removed the gun from Ivan's head.

Ivan turned slowly to see who was behind him. His face paled at the sight of The Green Hornet and Kato.

"Whatever you're looking for, I don't have it," he said. "I don't fence stolen goods anymore. Honest."

"I don't care what you fence," The Hornet said. "I'm here for information."

"I don't do that business either," Ivan said.

"Everyone on the crooked side of the street in this city knows that you have contacts in every dirty racket going," The Hornet said.

The Hornet put a hand on Ivan's shoulder. Ivan flinched, looked into The Green Hornet's eyes. They were as cold and hard as a pair of brass knuckles. Ivan gulped. "I don't want any trouble, Hornet. My heart can't take it."

"Answer my questions and you won't get caught in my sting," The Hornet said.

The Green Hornet held up the silver-tipped bullet in front of Ivan's face. Ivan's eyes went wide. He was no longer panic-stricken. The gears in his head were turning over, calculating the bullet's monetary value.

"Who made the bullet?" The Hornet said.

Ivan went to take the bullet, thought better of it, and said, "May I?"

The Hornet handed him the bullet and Ivan pulled a jeweler's loupe from the pocket of his pants. He stuck the eyepiece into his left eye and held the bullet up to the light. "Top quality silver," Ivan said. "Engraving is exacting yet graceful. Bullet itself is well crafted."

He handed the bullet back to The Hornet and put his loupe back in his pocket. "Only two guys I know could have made it. One's doing a dime in the can for weapons possessions and other assorted indiscretions that the Feds frown on."

"And the other?" The Hornet said.

"Roger Lyle," Ivan said. "He's real high-class. At least that's what he wants the public to think. He's a jeweler by trade. He's got a gallery on the other side of town. He makes jewelry for the high society set. But he's been known to do special commissions—gold plated .45s, platinum coated daggers— for special clients . . . of the broken nose variety. You know, the kind you don't want to meet in a dark alley."

"Good," The Hornet said. "Do yourself a favor and don't give Lyle a friendly heads-up about us or we'll be back."

"Hand to God, Hornet," Ivan said. "My lips are sealed. It gets out that I helped you, I'm a dead man."

The Green Hornet held his gun up and stuck it under Ivan's chin. "Just keep reminding yourself about that because if you double-cross me, I'll know about it and I'll be back and I won't be happy.

Ivan was sweating. "I'm on your side. Honest."

The Hornet said nothing, turned and left. Kato gave Ivan a hard stare and followed his boss out the back.

Roger Lyle's gallery took up the first floor of a four-story brownstone. Kato parked the Black Beauty on a side street and the two men stuck to the shadows as they approached the building. The lights were off in the gallery but on in the top floor apartment. They stood at the gallery's front door.

"You want me to pick the lock?" Kato said.

"No," The Green Hornet said. "Let's make a statement."

The Green Hornet pulled out his Hornet Sting. It resembled a foot-long metal baton. He pulled on one end of it and the Sting telescoped out so that it was now three feet long. The Hornet aimed the Sting at the door lock and pulled the trigger. A high-frequency sonic burst zapped the lock, blowing it up. The door swung open. The Hornet and Kato entered. Kato shut the door behind them.

The gallery was elegantly furnished. There were several display cases filled with Lyle's jeweled creations. A painted portrait of Lyle hung over the main counter.

Motioning to it, The Hornet said, "He's not *too* taken with himself is he?"

Kato smiled. "There has to be at least three million dollars in gold and diamonds here."

They heard heavy footsteps coming down the stairs from behind a closed door.

"And here comes the security system," The Hornet said.

As if on cue, the door burst open. Two muscle-bound men in dark suits and carrying automatic pistols rushed out. The Green Hornet and Kato leaped into action. Kato was a blur of hands and feet. He disarmed the first attacker with two well-placed kicks: the first to the hand to get rid of the gun and the second to the sternum. He followed this up with a slashing blow to the throat. The gunman grunted as he was propelled back and crashed into a small display case. It shattered under his weight and he landed on the floor with a loud thud.

Before he had even hit the ground, The Green Hornet was making short work of the second man. The Hornet grabbed a large solid silver plate from a display stand and threw it at the second attacker like a discus. The plate slammed into the man's head before he could even take aim at The Hornet. He was out cold before he hit the ground. The Hornet stepped over to him and kicked his gun across the room.

The Hornet turned to Kato who stood over the other unconscious man, smiling.

"Nothing like some after dinner exercise to make you feel alive," The Hornet said.

Motioning to the men on the floor Kato said, "I don't think they would agree with you."

The Green Hornet and Kato went up the stairs to the top floor. The door to the apartment was open. Inside, they found Lyle's living quarters furnished with sleek modern furniture made of plastic, chrome, and leather. The dining room table had been set for two. The plates held the remains of dinner.

A closed door stood at the far end of the living room. They went over to it. Kato tried the door. It was locked. He kicked it open, shattering the doorjamb. They were now peering into a bedroom. The ceiling was mirrored. The centerpiece of the room was a giant circular bed with a scared blonde cowering under the covers. The Hornet stepped into the room. The blonde pulled the blanket over her head and sobbed.

"Take it easy, miss," The Green Hornet said. "We won't hurt you. We have business with Roger Lyle."

The blonde showed her face. It was a pretty face, even with tears and mascara running down it.

"He's not here," she said.

The Green Hornet allowed a brief smile and said, "Come now, Miss—?"

"Melanie Miles," she said.

"Miss Miles, are you suggesting that Roger Lyle left someone as enchanting as you all alone in this big house?"

Melanie looked away.

The Hornet took a step closer to her. "You wouldn't want to lie to me, Miss Miles."

Her eyes widened and she took a deep breath and whispered, "He's in the closet behind you."

"Thank you," The Hornet said. "I suggest you gather your things and go home."

Melanie slipped out of bed. She was wearing a black silk negligee that showed off her long legs. She grabbed her clothes from where they hung over a chair and hurried out of the room.

The Hornet and Kato turned their attention to the closet door.

"Come out, Mr. Lyle," The Hornet said. "Or, we're coming in."

There was no response.

"Okay, shoot it up," The Hornet said.

Kato smiled.

The closet door popped open. Lyle, in a blue silk robe, ran out. "Don't shoot!"

Kato grabbed the man by the arm and spun him around so that he flew onto the bed. Lyle scrambled up and turned to face his attackers. The Hornet was now standing at the side of the bed closest to Lyle. Kato stood on the other side of the bed. He was silent with arms crossed over his chest.

"The money's in the safe," Lyle said.

"We're not here for money," The Hornet said. "I want information about this."

He pulled out the silver tipped bullet and held it up in front of Lyle. Lyle kept his composure, save for a fleeting look of recognition that The Hornet caught.

"I never saw that thing in my life," Lyle said.

The Hornet shook his head sadly. "I have it on good authority that this is your handiwork. You have two options: tell me who you made this for or my friend here will adjust your fingers so the only thing you're ever able to craft again are finger paintings—and very bad ones at that."

Lyle breathed hard.

"I can't," he said. "My clients demand confidentiality."

"Okay," The Hornet said, nodded to Kato.

Kato smiled, cracked his knuckles, and took a step toward Lyle. Lyle scurried away like the rat he was.

"Wait," he said. "You're right. It's my work. But it was a one-time thing. It was a gag."

"You don't read the papers," The Hornet said.

"What?" Lyle said.

"This bullet was sent to the *Daily Sentinel* by the Motor City Shooter," The Hornet said. "That makes you either the sniper or his accomplice. Doesn't matter to me which one you are. What does matter is that this sniper business is causing the cops to turn up the heat on the streets. It's interfering with my operations. The sooner the sniper is caught, the sooner things go back to normal. Understand?"

"Yes," Lyle said. "Hey, how'd you get the bullet?"

"That's none of your concern," The Hornet said. "You have bigger problems at the moment. One being that my temper is growing short. Last chance, who hired you to make the bullet?"

Lyle looked at Kato and then back to The Hornet. He sighed, ran his fingers through his hair. "Pike. I made it for Jonas Pike."

"The head of Pike Industries?" The Hornet said.

"Yeah, that's the one," Lyle said. "He's also an expert big game hunter. I made it for him two years ago before he left on one of his African safaris. We met at a show at my gallery. He admired my work and we got to talking about the city and crime and you came up. He said the city had become an urban jungle and you were the biggest game to hunt.

"I made a joke about using special bullets, like to kill a werewolf. He liked that idea. He sent over a bullet for me to use and $10,000 in cash for my services. You've got to believe me. I thought he was kidding. I didn't think he was crazy. If I did, I never would have made it for him."

"We all know that's a lie," The Hornet said. "You've done business with just about every mob in the city. You'd rip out your own mother's gold fillings and melt them down into bullets if you were paid enough."

Rage passed across Lyle's face. He wanted to strike out at The Hornet, but he knew better. He sat silent as they left. He hoped the sniper would get them.

"Where to now?" Kato said. He was once again behind the wheel of the Black Beauty and The Hornet was in the back seat.

"Home," The Hornet said.

He glanced at his watch. It was going on 10 p.m. Reid picked up the handset to the car's radio phone and dialed a number. The phone rang three times before it was picked up on the other end.

"Hello?" a man's deep voice said.

"Jonas Pike?" The Hornet said.

"Speaking," Pike said.

"Mr. Pike," The Hornet said. "This is Britt Reid of the *Daily Sentinel*. It's just come to my attention that you have returned to the city after being away for quite a while and I would like to interview you personally for a feature article in the *Sentinel*'s Sunday edition magazine."

"I'm flattered," Pike said. "I'll expect you tomorrow morning at seven. My butler does an excellent Eggs Benedict."

"Seven?" The Hornet said.

"Don't be so shocked," Pike said. There was a touch of sadistic amusement in his voice. "The early bird gets the worm and all that. That's one of the first things you learn as a hunter, Mr. Reid."

"I'll see you tomorrow morning, good night," The Hornet said.

Reid and Pike ate breakfast on the terrace of Pike's duplex apartment. Pike owned the 20th and 21st floors of his apartment building and had linked them with an interior staircase and private elevator. From the terrace, the city looked almost clean and dreamlike. Pike had been right about his butler. The Eggs Benedict were excellent.

Pike was a tall, tanned man without an ounce of fat to his fifty-year-old body. His steel gray eyes were sharp and intense. The two men made small talk for most of the meal until the dishes were cleared and they were left alone to enjoy their coffee.

"Mr. Reid," Pike said. "As much as I enjoy the attention from the media, I know you didn't come here to welcome me back home and find out what my plans were."

"No?" Reid said. "Then why did I come here?"

"It's obvious," Pike said. His face cracked by a broad smile that showed white teeth the size of Chiclets chewing gum. "You want me to tell you what I think about the sniper running riot through the city. Correct?"

Reid smiled. "Well that was one of the things I wanted to ask you about."

"Let me tell you that in theory thinning the herd is part of nature's plan. We think nothing of it to kill an animal in the wild for sport or for food. But let a person die and people beat their chests and wail. It's a lot of baloney."

"You're not seriously advocating that what the sniper is doing is a good thing," Reid said.

"No, my dear boy," Pike said. "You misunderstand me. I'm saying that life is one big dangerous game. We all know that at some point we'll lose at it. We make up rules and laws that we abide by in the hopes that death will do the same. Only it doesn't. When it's your time to go does it really matter if it's from a heart attack, a car accident, or a bullet? You're dead just the same."

"Pardon me for saying this, but you sound like you've watched *The Most Dangerous Game* one too many times," Reid said.

Pike looked at Reid with shock that soon gave way to laughter. "My dear Britt, how did you know that was one of my favorite films?"

"Lucky guess," Reid said.

"Sometimes, luck is all you need to stay alive," Pike said.

"You're not concerned for your safety, with some mad shooter running loose in the city?" Reid said.

"On the contrary," Pike said. "I relish it. I have stared down charging rhinos and lions protecting their prides. One man with a gun doesn't scare me."

Reid glanced at his watch. "Well, Mr. Pike—"

"Call me Jonas," he said.

"Jonas," Reid said. "I really must get going. I have a busy day ahead of me. Again, thank you for your time and the breakfast. I enjoyed our conversation."

"So did I," Pike said. "By the way, the Captains of Industry Association is throwing me a dinner tonight. Why don't you come? I'll have your name put on the guest list."

"Thank you," Reid said. "As the publisher of the *Daily Sentinel*, I'm already on the list. I wouldn't miss it for the world. That reminds me, I was talking to a friend who heard that you have a most unusual hunting trinket that I would love to see."

"Really?" Pike said. "Which one? I have so many."

"It's a sliver tipped bullet with The Green Hornet's symbol carved into it."

Pike's face grew dark and pinched. "Who told you about that?"

Reid waved his hand, "It was at a party. I don't remember when or who. It was just an interesting tidbit. That's why I remembered it."

Pike stood and walked into the other room. Reid could hear him rummage around his desk. Pike came back into the room, annoyed. "It's missing. I could have sworn I locked it in my desk drawer before I left for my safari. My mistake. I must have put it in my safety deposit box."

Either he is innocent and hasn't even seen the Sentinel*'s front page with his bullet on it or he is not only the sniper, but the world's greatest actor*, Reid thought.

Pike smiled but it was forced. Reid nodded, "Another time perhaps."

"Certainly," Pike said.

As he got up to leave, a man in his late twenties entered. He was dressed in a blue suit and drank orange juice.

"Good morning, father," the man said. "I see you're back to your usual business rituals."

"Ah, Britt," Pike said. "I want you to meet my son, Karl. Not only has he a head for numbers but he is an excellent hunter."

"I wonder where he got that from?" Reid said and they all laughed.

Reid shook hands with Karl. The man had a firm grip and looked Reid in the eye with a face that was warm and friendly.

"Well, this has been wonderful," Reid said. "I'll send you a draft of the article tomorrow for you to proofread."

Jonas Pike rose and shook hands with Reid. "I look forward to it. My butler will show you out. See you tonight."

The dinner honoring Jonas Pike was as Reid thought it would be: drawn out and boring. It was held at the Sheraton-Cadillac Hotel, one of the city's finest. The cream of the city's high society was present. They were all eager to court Pike's good graces should they need his help down the road. Karl Pike sat at a table with some of the other young executives of Pike Industries. He seemed to thrive on the attention given to him and his father.

Reid was still wondering if Jonas Pike was the sniper at the end of the evening. He hadn't seen enough of the man to determine the issue one way or the other. He just knew that Pike marched to his own drummer. He was part Henry Ford and part Frank Buck.

Outside, there was a heavy police presence to protect the patrons leaving the dinner. He was approaching his car when a woman shouted hello to him. His response to the greeting saved his life because he changed his direction and moved his head just a few degrees. The first gunshot rang out. He could feel it race by him before shattering his windshield.

Reid hit the ground and crawled between two cars. The parking lot was a madhouse. Men and women screamed and ran in all directions seeking cover. Police officers shouted orders but no one listened.

As quickly as it had begun, it was over. This time the sniper had killed two people, a banker and his wife. They had been lifelong residents of the city and spent all their extra money on helping the agencies that aided Detroit's underprivileged. Their bloodied bodies lay twisted in the parking lot.

Reid, rage boiling within, got up, brushed himself off, got into his car, and drove off into the night.

The Black Beauty prowled the streets of the city. Inside, The Green Hornet sat in the back seat and spoke to D.A. Scanlon on the car's radio telephone.

"You had quite a night," Scanlon said.

"One I'd like to make sure is never repeated," The Hornet said. "Did the lab boys come up with anything from the evidence they collected from tonight's attack?"

"Yes," Scanlon said. "The sniper used the building across the street from the hotel. He left his brass lined up in a neat row on the ledge with a note addressed to you.

Scanlon read him the note:

HORNET, I WAS HERE. WHERE WERE YOU?

"Obviously, he's taunting you," Scanlon said. "He seems intent on goading you into finding him. Why?"

"I don't know for certain," The Hornet said, "But I should have an answer by the end of the night. I'll talk to you later Frank."

The Hornet hung up the phone and said, "The Pike residence, Kato."

Kato parked the Black Beauty in a dark alley behind the building. They used the basement entrance to gain access to the high-rise and took the service elevator up to the 19th floor. A key was needed to access the elevator entrance to the 20th floor. So they forced open the fire stairs after they neutralized the fire alarm wired to the door. This gave them access to the hallway on the 20th floor and the entrance to Pike's apartment. They found the door to it unlocked.

Inside, Pike's duplex was dark and still. The Hornet switched on the lights. The apartment was in disarray. Furniture was turned over and broken. There were smashed glasses and paintings hung askew on the walls.

The Green Hornet and Kato searched the first floor room by room. They found Pike's butler dead in the kitchen, a bullet hole in the back of his head. There were bloodstained footprints that led out of the kitchen and to the spiral staircase that offered access to the second floor of the apartment.

Hornet gun in hand, The Green Hornet climbed the stairs with Kato close behind. The staircase brought them into a large trophy room stocked with mounted animal heads, weapons of all kinds, trophies, and framed pictures of Jonas Pike with celebrities and three U.S. Presidents.

Jonas Pike had been shoved into a desk-sized trophy case. The glass had shattered underneath him. Blood pulsed from two bullet holes in his stomach and dripped into a puddle on the floor.

The Green Hornet and Kato leaned over Pike.

"Kato, call for an ambulance," The Hornet said.

"No. It's too late," Pike said.

"Where is your son?" The Hornet said.

"R-roof," Pike said, and died.

They raced up to the roof. At the access door they stopped and listened. They heard nothing.

"I think this calls for a gas dart," The Hornet said. "We can use the smoke from it as cover to get through the door." The men donned small gas masks to protect themselves from the knockout gas in the dart.

From his coat sleeve Kato produced one of the darts. It was six inches long with a sharp steel point at one end and stylized wings on the other that acted as stabilizing fins. He threw the dart so that it landed in the center of the roof.

As the smoke seeped from it, the shooting began. The Hornet and Kato went in opposite directions. Bullets kicked up pieces of roof as The Hornet ran. The bullets came at them from the edge of the roof of the neighboring building. This building was one story higher than Pike's building and there was a space of four feet between them.

Karl, still unseen, turned his attention to Kato and had him pinned down behind some boxes. At the same time, The Hornet jumped the gap between the two buildings. He grabbed onto the other building's fire escape, pulled himself up onto it and began to climb it as quietly as possible. He could just make out Karl's shadowed figure peering over the roof. A bullet whizzed by The Hornet's head. He froze and pressed himself against the ladder to lessen the target he offered Karl Pike.

"Karl, it doesn't have to end this way," The Hornet said. "Drop the rifle. We can talk."

"I don't need your help," Karl said.

"Trust me," The Hornet said. "You do."

"What do you care about me," Karl said. "You're just a criminal."

"True," The Hornet said. "But, I'm also a businessman. With your father dead, you stand to inherit everything. Right? We could work out some kind of deal that would benefit both of us."

"You're right," Karl said. "I do inherit everything. It was a perfect plan. Set dear old daddy up to be a victim of the sniper and have the sniper turn out to be The Green Hornet. Then have The Hornet killed by me, the grief-stricken son.

"My father dies in a blaze of glory, The Hornet takes the fall and I am praised for being heroic and a great shot. I take over the family business and finally get to live life the way I want to live it.

"But dear old dad had to ruin it. He got suspicious. He confronted me when we got home tonight. I guess I shouldn't have stolen his Hornet bullet. It tipped my hand before I was ready. He actually threatened to disown me and turn me into the police.

"You believe that? That son of a bitch kept me sitting in the sweltering African bush for a year so he could shoot whatever tickled his fancy and I'm the crazy one."

As Karl ranted, The Green Hornet climbed up a few more steps. Meanwhile, Kato also moved closer, crouching behind a large electrical unit, so that he had a better view of Karl.

"I can help you show the world that you were better than your father," The Hornet said.

That caught Karl's attention. He noticed The Hornet was closer to him and smiled. "You're toying with me, Hornet. I'm done being toyed with."

He leaned over the edge of the roof and had The Hornet dead center in his sights when Kato threw a Hornet dart. It hit Karl's hand as he was about to pull the trigger. He screamed, lost his grip on the gun, and without thinking, lunged for it. He lost his footing and fell. The Hornet jumped off the ladder, caught Karl in mid-air, and landed on the rooftop.

Karl leaped for The Hornet, but Kato stepped up and rendered him unconscious with a well placed strike to the neck.

"Thanks, Kato," The Hornet said. "That should keep him out of trouble until the police arrive."

Below, the sounds of police sirens grew louder.

"That's our cue to get out of here," The Hornet said. He made sure to collect the spent darts as they left the roof. The Green Hornet and Kato were in the Black Beauty and far away from the Pike duplex by time the police arrived.

The next morning, Britt Reid was back to work at his office in the *Daily Sentinel* building. He was meeting with Casey and Mike Axford. Reid wore an amused expression as he listened to Axford talk.

"I'm telling you, Britt," Axford said. "I don't care what the police say. I know The Green Hornet was behind this sniper thing. The police report said that Karl Pike's hand had a puncture wound from some kind of dart. Now, who but The Green Hornet uses weapons like that?"

"I don't know, Mike," Reid said. "Maybe some kids were having a dart contest nearby and things got out of hand."

Axford's face got redder than normal and his chest puffed out. Reid kept his face impassive and Casey hid behind her note pad.

"Fine," Axford said. "Make jokes. One day you'll see that you've been wrong and I've been right—that The Green Hornet is the worst criminal there is."

Axford stormed out of the office. Casey, her face lit up by the prettiest smile there ever was, shut the door and turned back to Reid. "Sometimes you push Mike too far, Britt."

"I know," Reid said. "He just makes it so easy. Now where was I?"

"You were dictating your editorial about Jonas Pike and his son," she said.

Reid got serious again. "Right," he said and began speaking again. As he did, he thought about the events of the last few days and what Jonas had said to him at breakfast. Though Britt disagreed with most of what he had said, there was one thing that resonated with him. Sometimes, life really was a dangerous game.

BEAUTY IS AS BEAUTY DIES

by James Mullaney

"Excuse me, you can't come in here, sir. *Sir?*"

Even on a good day Britt Reid was only vaguely aware of the voices outside his office, and this was stacking up to be a very bad day. Accounting had finally followed through on a weeks-old threat to send up some insurance actuarial tables in which Britt had zero interest, and for the past hour he'd felt the slow kick of a chorus line warming up in the wings behind his temples. He needed aspirin, and fast.

Britt reached for the intercom to buzz his secretary and it was only when he tore his eyes away from the mind-numbing paperwork that he heard the stressed voice of Lenore Case amid the drone of voices beyond his closed door.

"Sir," Casey insisted, a sharp edge in her tone. "I said you can't—"

And then another voice, not Casey's. Britt wasn't sure whose voice it was. It could have been male or female, for it was little more than a terrified gasp.

"He's got a gun!"

The exclamation was followed at once by panicked shouting. A great frightened clamor rose from the *Daily Sentinel*'s city room. And then Britt heard it. A gunshot.

The sharp slap to his eardrums brought Britt to his feet in a flash. As he bounded across the room he heard a second shot. Even as he flung open the door to find the city room in chaos, a third pistol crack was screaming over the panic.

Men clambered over desks in a desperate race for exits. Papers scattered as if in the wake of a mini-cyclone. A sturdy Smith-Corona had crashed from an upended desk and the ribbon had snagged a fleeing foot, unspooling from typewriter to hallway.

"Britt, get back!"

Gunnigan, city editor of the *Sentinel*, had taken command. He was puffing mightily as he charged the unseen intruder. Another shot and Gunnigan was falling with a grunt to the scuffed floor, an unmoving heap of rolled-up shirtsleeves and suspenders.

Britt saw the flash from the muzzle before he saw the gunman. A fat hand sticking from the sleeve of a grimy trench coat; hand and gun jutting from behind a pillar. A great looming shape behind, spilling in either direction; now moving, lumbering into view. The gunman was a hulking figure, with black hair cut short to a bullet skull. Maybe a fighter in younger days because he still had that grace that was hard to lose, but middle age had turned muscle to fat. Dead, pig-like eyes blinked incessantly as the big man marched past Gunnigan's body.

Many had fled but a few of the men had gathered their wits. Two reporters and a copyboy charged the gunman.

The brave fools weren't going to make it. The shooter was too quick and he'd caught their movement from the corner of his eyes. He was already turning, already a fat finger squeezing down on the trigger. At least one of them would take another bullet.

"Hey! Did the society page miss your sweet sixteen?"

Britt was shouting even before he realized he was running headlong at the gunman. The distraction worked. For an instant the gunman's attention was divided between the crowd before him and the voice behind. He opted for the voice.

The big man was surprisingly quick on his feet. The gun flashed around, unblinking steel eye nearly level on Britt's chest. But in that moment just before he fired, the trio of charging men tackled the gunman from behind.

The mass of bodies struck with the full force of men propelled to heroics by fear and adrenaline. The gunman lurched sideways into a column. The copyboy must have played some ball in high school. He was a little guy, but scrappy. He screamed a warrior's whooping cry as he took the gunman around the legs. One knee buckled.

The gun wavered, tried to find a target. By now Britt had eaten up the distance to the shooter. He grabbed the big man's wrist in both hands and slammed it against the column. Another discharge. Britt felt the bullet whistle a few inches from his forehead. Somewhere, a window shattered.

Britt hauled back and slammed harder. This time there was a crack of bone and the fat hand sprang open. The gun hit the floor with a thick thud and skittered into the corner near the water cooler.

The second knee buckled and the shooter became a massive lump of black overcoat on the city room floor. The three men who had tackled him wrestled him flat.

Two more men charged out of nowhere to help pin him down. It was all over.

Britt didn't take time to catch his breath. "Hold him down. Ed, make sure someone's called for the police and an ambulance." One of the men disengaged from the pile and raced to a phone while Britt hustled over to Gunnigan.

The *Sentinel*'s city editor was unconscious but breathing. Blood soaked the front of his starched white shirt. Gunnigan had fallen on a clean sheet of typewriter paper. Britt very carefully slipped it out. It was crisp and new. No blood. That meant the bullet was still inside. That could be good news or bad. Belly shots were tricky that way.

"Cops are on their way up, Mr. Reid," Ed Lowery called as he trotted over to Britt's side. "Ambulance will be here any minute."

Britt's brow was furrowed. "What the hell made this guy snap?" he muttered as Ed crouched down beside him.

"Since when do nutjobs need a reason?" Ed asked, still panting.

Britt took a deep breath and exhaled. Gunnigan would probably pull through. He was a tough buzzard. One casualty. No matter how you sliced it, it could have played out a lot worse.

"Oh, boy," a voice said. "He's part of the Scorpion gang."

Britt felt his head clear, *sharply* clear. Like a wet cloth wiping clean a dirty chalkboard. It took a massive effort to keep the shock in check. When he turned, his face was bland even though every muscle in his body screamed. The copyboy was sitting on the gunman's chest and was pinning the gorilla's arm to the floor with one foot. Sticking out of his trench coat sleeve was a wrist as fat around as a country ham. And on the inside of the wrist was stamped a bright green scorpion outlined in red.

"What's he doing here, Mr. Reid?" the kid asked.

Britt's voice was perfectly level, completely controlled. "Beats me, son." He was grateful for the distraction of the police who chose that moment to come charging off the elevator and through the city room's main doors.

Britt tore his eyes from the tattoo and took a step forward. Only then did he finally see the other body.

They had all missed it tucked away behind a desk near a row of battered filing cabinets. A thin girl in a smart yellow blouse and conservative orange skirt.

Lenore Case's auburn hair was splashed across her face. She did not move.

"My God," Britt whispered.

"She must have hit that desk awfully hard. X-rays show a swelling on her brain. I'm reluctant to order surgery. I'm still hoping we won't have to operate. We'll know more in the morning, Mr. Reid."

The somber faced doctor clutched a clipboard to his chest. The two men stood side by side next to Lenore Case's bed. A small window looked over the parking lot where a lone police unit sat amongst a handful of cars. Moths and other night insects buzzed silently around the parking lot lights.

The crisp white sheet rose and fell with Casey's rhythmic breathing. An IV tube snaked from a suspended saline bottle to one thin arm.

"Simply terrible. Tsk. The brain is such a tricky thing. And they say she tried to disarm the gunman all by herself?"

This was one thing about which all eyewitnesses agreed. Casey had first tried to coax the nuisance intruder from the city room but when he drew his gun she had been the first to react to the danger. Not by running, which would have been the sane thing to do, but by jumping on the behemoth's back. He had shrugged her off like a shawl and she'd apparently struck the back of her head on the way to the floor. No one was sure about the last part, for by then gunfire had ignited the stampede that had cleared the room.

"They still don't know why he went on a rampage?"

"No," Britt said.

The doctor was shaking his head at the madness of the modern world as he ducked around the curtain that separated Casey's cubicle from the rest of the intensive care unit. He did not acknowledge or, indeed, even seem aware of the presence of the thin young Asian man in the plain black suit who stood just outside the curtain. Britt's young valet had his back to his employer and was watching the activity near a room at the distant end of the hall, where two uniformed police officers stood silent vigil.

The curtain to Casey's cubicle rustled shut and Britt was alone with his secretary.

"I guess I don't have a right to chew you out," Britt whispered. "Fools rush in, right? But hold the weight limit down next time. How about you only go after maniacs who outweigh you by a factor of three?"

Casey's lips were parted but no words passed them; just the steady slip of breath from a battered body fighting to heal itself.

There was a stainless steel water dispenser on a small table next to the bed. Britt wet his handkerchief and touched the damp cloth to Casey's dry lips. If he expected a reaction, any kind of acknowledgment that the bright young girl was still awake inside somewhere struggling to get out, he got none.

He was brushing a lock of Casey's hair from over one eye when the curtain lifted. Britt straightened up quickly but it was only Kato. His valet nodded down the hall.

"They are getting ready to leave."

At the far end of the hallway the policemen had been joined by two doctors and an orderly. The orderly was struggling with a wheelchair in which was crammed the hulking gunman from the *Daily Sentinel*. His right arm was wrapped from elbow to hand in a fresh plaster cast. His left wrist was handcuffed to the wheelchair.

Britt's lips thinned. "Time to go to work, Kato."

Patrolman Frank Barton of the Detroit Police Department had better things to do.

"They need a chaperone, call a damn sergeant. They get paid to drink coffee all day, they can babysit this goon. What am I, the delivery boy?"

The ambulance driver still wasn't talking. Barton didn't know what the guy's problem was. Ever since they'd loaded the Sentinel Shooter (that's what the radio was calling the nut) into the back of the ambulance for the ride to headquarters, Barton had tried to engage the driver in conversation, but it was like he couldn't hear or something. The driver was always adjusting the mirror or fiddling with the radio. Barton still hadn't gotten a look at the guy through the small window that separated the cab from the rear. Even the rearview mirror was angled in such a way that Barton couldn't get a glimpse.

"How 'bout you?" Barton asked, turning away from the silent driver as they left the hospital parking lot. "You ready to sing, Kong?" The cops had come up with their own name for the as-yet-unidentified gunman.

Kong's good arm was handcuffed to the gurney on which he sprawled. The gurney was angled and afforded the criminal a view of traffic behind the ambulance. Barton's partner was following in a squad car.

"I'm an innocent victim," Kong grunted. His gaze was directed not at Barton, but at the trailing patrol car.

"That tattoo says otherwise. You may as well tell me who Scorpion is.

They'll get it outta you anyways downtown. What? Did I say something funny? What's with the smirk?"

Kong was still looking out the rear window of the ambulance. For the first time since his violent appearance at the *Daily Sentinel* two hours before, there was a sparkle of knowing humor in the dark depths of his ink-black eyes.

Barton followed Kong's gaze . . . and gasped.

There was a second car in the street, this one behind the trailing squad car.

The black Crown Imperial had appeared out of nowhere. It must have been in a side alley, lying in wait like some jungle predator. With a silent surge of speed, the sleek black car flew up beside the squad car. Barton could see the look of shock on his partner's face. He hadn't expected it, hadn't seen it until it was on top of him. The young cop instinctively stomped on the gas and the patrol car zoomed forward, chewing up the distance between the cruiser's front grille and the ambulance's rear bumper.

"Back off!" Barton screamed.

No good. Bumpers met with a hard thud that rattled tin boxes of medical equipment off shelves and tossed Barton roughly to the floor.

Kong lunged for Barton's gun but the cop was faster. Weapon drawn, he aimed the barrel at Kong's forehead. "So that's it!" he snarled. "You're working for *him*."

A squeal of tires. Barton twisted around in time to see The Green Hornet's car leapfrog ahead of the cruiser so that it was directly behind the ambulance. Immediately the road behind the black car became a patch of dark liquid and the squad car was suddenly spinning wildly out of control. It slammed a telephone pole in a crunch of twisted metal and a hiss of smoke. Barton's partner was climbing from the wreckage as the ambulance raced around a corner, the Black Beauty glued to its tailpipe.

"Get us to the station!" Barton screamed, scrabbling to his feet. And for the first time he finally got a good look at the driver.

The blood drained from Barton's face.

The driver was wearing a felt hat and green mask. Barton hopped over the medical junk for a better look. The seat's headrest had blocked the driver's green coat. Barton aimed his gun at the back of The Green Hornet's head.

"You're mine," Barton announced.

The Green Hornet smiled. "I don't think you want to do that." He didn't turn, didn't slow down. The ambulance flew on, the Black Beauty following as if on a leash. They were heading for the waterfront.

"Pull over," Barton commanded.

The Hornet not only failed to comply, his foot pressed harder on the accelerator. Barton lurched back, grabbing the gurney desperately. The gurney, locked in place for the ride, rocked hard then was still.

"I said stop this car!"

They were picking up speed. The cop squeezed off a wild warning round that punctured a hole in the roof.

"Shoot him and we'll crash!" Kong screamed.

But Barton was suddenly no longer interested in firing his weapon. He had dropped his gun and was clutching his throat with both hands. Kong made a move for the gun, but all at once his own large mitts grabbed instinctively for his own throat. Then came a kind of euphoric lightheadedness, and when he finally noticed the green mist that was hissing in from the driver's compartment, Kong was already drifting into a deep slumber and the driver—who was now wearing an oxygen mask— was saying something that sounded like, "Good night. Be seeing one of you soon." But Kong could no longer be sure of anything because the darkness of a dreamless sleep had clamored up from the silent shadows to claim him.

"Wake up, sleepyhead."

A dark shape rippled in the musty air. A ghost with a sepulchral voice that reverberated deep in the gunman's slowly waking brain.

Through the foggy twilight haze, Kong was vaguely aware of the man standing before him. Then all at once the image seemed to coalesce, to find sharp focus.

They were in a warehouse. It was empty, save a few broken boxes. The concrete floor stunk of ancient oil. Kong was sitting on the floor, the abandoned warehouse office to his back, his hands bound behind him to a rusted column. His broken wrist ached.

The Green Hornet did not give the shooter much time to absorb his surroundings. When he saw Kong was awake, The Hornet leaned in close, so close Kong could see clearly the famous hornet insignia on his green mask.

"I assume the Scorpion staged that show at the newspaper to draw me out. Sorry to disappoint, but I do things on my terms. Where is he?"

"Go pound sand," Kong growled.

"That's not how this is going to work." The Hornet reached down with both gloved hands and grabbed fistfuls of the gunman's shirt. He dragged the big man up until they were nose-to-nose. Kong winced at the fresh pain in his wrist. "You think I don't know what's been going on? That jewelry store heist last week? The two bank jobs the week before? He's been trying to get on my radar for weeks. Ordinarily I don't bother with penny ante thugs, but he's finally got my attention. What does he want?"

Kong's broad face split into an evil grin. "Dollars to doughnuts he's already got it."

The truck was dark red. The big trailer was light gray, but dirty. It had been many years since it had last seen a sponge and soapy water.

Detroit's waterfront was always a buzz of activity, so it was not unusual for trucks to come and go at all hours. If anyone even saw the red truck at this late hour, no one paid it any mind as it chugged through shadows and alongside ruptured chain link fences and dilapidated buildings. On the dashboard in front of the driver was a silent walkie-talkie which he did not touch. He was listening carefully.

"They seen him, so it's gotta be close," said his nervous partner in the passenger seat. "Harry would've radioed if it took off north, and there's no other way out."

"Quiet," the driver whispered.

The walkie-talkie suddenly squawked to life. "Found it," a staticky voice laced with anxiety hissed. "South alley, the old Wallingford Meatpacking warehouse."

The driver quickly dropped the truck in gear and brought the big rig around to the abandoned meatpacking plant. He found Harry waving his arms and motioning to cut the truck's engine. Behind Harry was the dark shape of a car.

The Black Beauty was camouflaged by the shadows of the alley. When the truck was within a few yards, the driver cut the engine. The instant the motor was silenced, the trailer door rose and a dozen men in gas masks scampered out.

The interior of the trailer was lined with thick panels, soft to the touch. A new high-tech addition that stood in stark contrast to the weathered exterior.

A ramp was lowered to the ancient asphalt and a four-wheeled jack rolled down to the parking lot. As the jack was positioned beneath The Green Hornet's car, two more men hustled down the metal ramp hauling a thick length of chain.

The hydraulic jack whirred and the black car began to rise. The men jumped back when the car came suddenly to life.

The engine buzzed like an angry insect. As if possessed of a mind of its own, the car's rear tires spit gravel and nearly caught the asphalt, but the high-pitched whine and stink of burning rubber stopped once the tires lifted completely off the ground. The instant there was nothing but air between tires and pavement, a spray of green mist from unseen nozzles flooded the damp night air. The men in their gas masks hustled unharmed through the fog and hooked the chain to the underside of the car. A whir came from the depths of the trailer and the Black Beauty rolled up the ramp and disappeared inside.

It was over in less than a minute. The small army of men disappeared in back with the car, the rear door was pulled shut, and the truck's engine purred to life.

A single voice squawked over the walkie-talkie. "We got it," the driver called. "He still in the warehouse?"

The response was a whisper. "I'm watching him right now."

"Looks like we're in the clear. Just in case, give us cover."

The truck and its precious cargo hugged the shore on its way through labyrinthine alleys and parking lots, chugging off into the chilly Detroit night.

The Green Hornet knew that he was a sitting duck when the small pane of dirty glass shattered near the second story catwalk.

The first bullet chewed a pulpy divot five feet up on the column to which he'd tied the Sentinel Shooter. A second bullet was screaming for his back when he felt the full force of a lunging body slamming him out of the projectile's path.

Kato had been lurking in the dark, eyes peeled for danger. He came out of nowhere, threw The Hornet out of harm's way. The two men crashed through the flimsy plywood wall of the old office in a hail of falling panes of filthy glass and shattering wood. From outside the wreckage of the office there came a sudden, inhuman grunt from Kong and all at once the column to which he'd been tied was torn loose with a wrench.

"The boss'll send you a thank you note!" Kong yelled.

With the column gone, a huge chunk of ceiling tore free. Chunks of dirty panels and cob-webbed insulation came down, and as The Hornet and Kato were buried under the collapsing debris and cloud of dust, he caught a glimpse of a laughing Kong as the gunman, arms still bound behind him, stumbled out the warehouse door.

The uniformed guards rolled back the high chain link gates the instant the truck rumbled into view. The old tractor trailer with its top secret cargo sped onto the grounds accompanied by three dark sedans.

The sprawling complex occupied four city blocks. Three words adorned signs on guard shacks, gates, and factory walls: *Lanyard Motors Corporation.*

Old Herbert Lanyard often bragged that he owned one of Detroit's biggest auto companies, but all he owned was hype. LMC's buildings had not seen fresh paint in a decade, there were potholes in the parking lots, and at this late hour there were few vehicles in the employee lots. Three shifts had run round the clock at LMC for decades, but the second and third shifts had ended fifteen years ago. There was now barely one shift, supplying cars for one Central American government, and rumor had it even that contract was going to Ford.

The red truck passed unmolested deep into the Lanyard complex. Near a test track, a hanger door opened revealing a bright interior. The truck steered through the opening and was swallowed up by the big building.

Inside the hanger, the Black Beauty was brought down from the trailer. This time when the green mist came, one man who had not secured his gas mask properly had to be carried from the massive hanger. As the unconscious worker was carted past him by two engineers in white coats, Herbert Quentin Lanyard released a grunt of disgust.

"Who is that fool, Bosch?" Lanyard demanded. He did not acknowledge the hulking Kong, who took up a snarling bodyguard position behind him.

"Elmer Wright, Mr. Lanyard," replied Dr. Emil Bosch, Lanyard's handpicked Director of Special Acquisitions.

"Well, don't leave him in here. Dump him in the hall."

"Yes, sir." Bosch directed the men to haul Wright from the room.

"Incompetence," Lanyard grunted. "I won't brook incompetence."

"Yes, Mr. Lanyard."

Herbert Lanyard was an octogenarian with a fringe of steel gray hair swept up and pasted onto an otherwise bald pate. He was six feet two when he'd dropped out of sixth grade to take a job in a bicycle shop and he never, ever hunched. His spine was rigid, his eyes were sharp and his thin lips were pinched in a perpetual grimace.

"I also won't brook lollygagging. Back to work."

"Yes, Mr. Lanyard."

The small observation room in which Lanyard and a handful of his employees stood was separated from the hanger by a thick sheet of glass.

The Black Beauty and the men in clean white coats who were hustling around her were dwarfed by the hanger's great size. The huge room was empty save a few equipment lockers. Soft white panels identical to those that lined the trailer covered walls and ceiling.

Inside the observation room, a half-dozen seated men worked feverishly while against one wall highly evolved computers whirred and clicked loudly. Lanyard eyed the bulky computers with mistrust. To him they were nothing more than oversize cigarette vending machines with turntables glued to their faces.

"A scam, these computers," Lanyard said to no one in particular. Kong was trying to scratch under his cast with one fat finger; the others continued to work. "You don't build a car with computers. You build it with this and this and these." He touched heart and head and displayed a pair of gnarled, arthritic hands, respectively.

One of the seated engineers wore a pair of bulky beige headphones. He pressed the left earpiece and as he turned a dial on the console before him he nodded excitedly. "I'm picking up some kind of radio signal, Dr. Bosch. I think it's calling for help."

"What's that mean *exactly*?" Lanyard demanded.

"It means that the car is likely radio controlled, as I suspected," Bosch said. "At minimum it means it can send a signal to let him know where it is at any given time."

"What about now?" Lanyard's voice was perfectly level and those who did not know him might mistake the evenness of tone for calm. Those who had worked for him for even a short amount of time understood instinctively that a visibly angry Herbert Lanyard was far less dangerous than this deceptively unruffled specimen. The seated engineer became very quiet and shook his head with certainty. Bosch, still standing, shook his head as well.

"No," Bosch agreed. "The panels we designed muffle the signal. It's not strong enough to penetrate. It's more or less contained, bouncing off the walls."

"I don't like equivocation, Bosch, especially where The Green Hornet is concerned. Nail down that 'more or less.'"

"He'd have to be on top of us to pick it up. The road is too far away. We're so deep inside the complex there's simply no way. It's safe."

Lanyard exhaled a cloud of acid-fueled halitosis. The show of irritation broke the tension in the observation room. "It'd better be." He stabbed a long finger to a red button on the nearest console and his booming voice echoed out over the big hanger. "I want that car stripped down to the ball bearings," he snapped at Bosch's team. "I want its secrets and I want them yesterday." He released the button. "I'll be in my office, Bosch." He started to leave. "And Bosch," he added, pausing at the door. The terrifying calm returned to the CEO of Lanyard Motors Corporation. "If I go down, mine won't be the only body bobbing in the river. Clear?"

"Perfectly, Mr. Lanyard, sir."

Lanyard was so quiet as he left the room—his grinning bodyguard Kong in his wake—that the only sound Dr. Emil Bosch heard was the audible gulp in his own throat.

Britt Reid sat in his office at the *Daily Sentinel*, three stacks of files on the desk before him. He had called down to the paper's morgue for all information on the top crime kingpins in Detroit, ostensibly for a story on organized crime. In truth, he hoped to find this so-called Scorpion, the elusive criminal who had set a perfect trap to snare the Black Beauty.

It was dispiriting to see the corruption and violence that plagued the city he loved stuffed into so many bulging manila files. The thickest file had a clean white piece of tape on the tab on which were the neatly typed words: "Green Hornet."

"At least *you're* out of the running." He took the Hornet file and tossed it to the far corner of his desk.

As he dragged open yet another file, Britt winced and massaged his shoulder. A falling beam had clipped him in the warehouse office collapse. Still, it could have been worse. Thanks to Kato he had escaped with only a few minor cuts and bruises.

When the phone rang, he glanced out at his secretary's empty desk before reaching for the receiver. "Britt Reid."

"Mr. Reid, Doctor Harrigan. You left instructions to call."

Britt sat up straighter in his chair. "Any changes?"

"The good news is that Mr. Gunnigan has turned the corner. Surgery couldn't have gone better. No post-op complications. He's already awake."

Britt steeled himself. "What about Miss Case?"

"Unchanged, I'm afraid. She's still unconscious. I've ordered a new set of X-rays. We'll know by morning if we'll have to operate. I'm sorry, Mr. Reid. I wish I had all good news for you. If it helps, I've seen people in far worse shape recover fully."

They spoke for only a few minutes longer, Britt pressing for details about Gunnigan's and Casey's treatment. When he was satisfied they were receiving the best care available he thanked the doctor and hung up the phone.

Britt studied the files for two more hours but failed to make any headway. He had the nagging feeling that what he was looking for wouldn't be in the regular files. "What am I missing?" he asked the empty room.

He gathered his coat and left the office, taking note of a copy of the latest edition of the *Sentinel* on a desk in the half-lit city room. A blaring headline read:

Green Hornet Helps
Daily Sentinel Shooter Escape

When he arrived at home, Britt found Kato working under the hood of Britt's convertible. There was a pile of old automobile magazines stacked on the workbench and a wastebasket stuffed full with old newspapers and rags. With nothing else to do, Kato had spent the afternoon tinkering and cleaning around the garage.

"I talked to Scanlon but he hasn't heard a peep," Britt announced when Kato glanced up, a look of silent concern on his face. "If the Scorpion doesn't tip his hand soon, I'm afraid the Beauty might be gone for good. Or worse."

The thought of the Black Beauty's awesome weaponry in the hands of a criminal mastermind—a real one, one more shadowy and elusive than Britt's alter ego—was too terrible to imagine.

Britt noticed the pile of car magazines. A yellow hotrod with silver mag wheels and painted flames was posed like a *Playboy* centerfold on the topmost cover. When he saw the hotrod, an old memory stirred at the back of Britt's brain.

"Hold on. Scorpion. Kato, why didn't I think of it before? *Scorpion.*"

In another instant he was tearing through the stack of magazines. He found one from several years before. The date was about right. He flipped hastily through the pages until he found a full page ad. He glanced up, a look of triumph on his face.

"I can't believe I've been so stupid. The Scorpion. Kato, it's not a who, it's a 'what.'" He held out the magazine so Kato could read the advertisement.

There was an image of a vehicle that looked like a compact sports car that had been extruded from the tailpipe of a Brink's truck. It was blockish in the wrong places, unwieldy in those parts that weren't blockish, and about as sleek as a cinderblock. The aggressive text that accompanied the picture screamed:

Introducing the Lanyard Scorpion!

Herbert Lanyard was a man out of his time.

The other founders of Detroit's great automobile enterprises had fallen away to death and retirement as the decades passed, but Lanyard stubbornly refused to leave his corner office. It was true that fresh blood brought with it new ideas. Without it, Lanyard Motors stagnated.

Lanyard resisted change and innovation, insisting America would always buy the quality products of LMC. But as time wore on, the bottom fell out and red leached into the black. The Sixties came and no one wanted to buy his cars any longer.

When, after years of resistance, Lanyard finally saw that change was inevitable, he set about in a panic to try to right decades of lousy management with one grand gesture.

Sporty cars were all the rage, and so Lanyard himself designed one. The Lanyard Scorpion, the costliest blunder in automotive history. He had nearly been laughed out of the business.

His company was failing. Age had overtaken him. For Lanyard there was only time for one last Hail Mary pass. But despite the seeming success of his carefully laid plan, failure was still clinging to Herbert Lanyard like a stench.

"What do you mean you can't open it?"

"It seems to have run out of knockout gas," Dr. Bosch said, broad face glistening with sweat. "But when one of my people tried the door handle he was electrocuted. He's in the infirmary now. We can wait for the battery to run down, but it's not losing juice. There might be more than one."

Lanyard looked at the sleek skin of the Black Beauty. That car possessed secrets that would restore his fortunes, if only his fool employees could unlock it.

"You said you tapped into the radio signal."

"I might have. I'm not sure."

"Bosch, I want you to open this car, and I want you to do it right now."

Bosch took a bulky remote control, as big as five decks of playing cards, from the pocket of his lab coat. He drew out a silver antenna which he aimed at the Black Beauty. Inhaling deeply, he turned a fat black button.

There was a whine that made the hair in Lanyard's ears itch. Something unseen whirred and clicked on the black car. Lanyard and Bosch had no idea what had made the sound until a moment later when a pair of rockets screamed from the front of the vehicle and blasted a hole in the distant wall of the hanger.

In the ensuing chaos following the blast, many things seemed to happen all at once. Lanyard tripped and fell to the floor. Far off, sheets of white panel, stained black and burning, collapsed with the wall to the floor. Engineers ran in panic away from the blasted section of wall.

Bosch was screaming to his frightened team. "The radio signal! We've got to get that wall sealed up!"

Too late.

It was impossible. Lanyard would not have believed it had he not seen it with his own eyes. A truck appeared, headlights flashing bright, speeding toward the opening.

It was *his* truck. The specially outfitted rig Lanyard's men had used to steal the Black Beauty. It came up fast, a square peg aimed like a massive spear for the round hole created by the black car's rockets. The truck didn't slow, it crashed the wall, tearing a larger hole and raining down chunks of roof as it bounced into the hanger. All eighteen wheels screamed and tore tracks of fat black rubber as the big rig jackknifed and slid a long and painful groan across the wide floor until it came to a stop precisely where its driver intended, within six yards of the Black Beauty. The doors popped open.

Lanyard's jaw dropped in shock.

"Thanks for opening the door," The Green Hornet announced, dropping lightly to the hanger floor.

Bosch grabbed a wrench and ran for the masked man. The Green Hornet sent a single gloved fist square into the engineer's jaw. The white coated man whirled a little pirouette and disappeared behind the Black Beauty.

"Aaaaarrggghh!" The terrible, guttural roar came from the observation room. Through the door charged Kong, cast raised above his head like a club.

A swift movement from the driver's side of the eighteen wheeler.

Lanyard barely saw The Green Hornet's young henchman move. A fist flew out and caught the giant in the throat, stopping Kong dead in his tracks. A knee to the belly doubled Kong over and the sharp chop of a hand connected to the thick meat at the back of the big man's neck. Lanyard's unstoppable bodyguard collapsed, a mountain of quivering polyester.

"I hate to cancel your plans, Lanyard," The Green Hornet said. "So which highest foreign bidder were you shipping it to, the Russians or Chinese?"

Panting, Lanyard struggled to his feet. The old man's comb-over had come unglued from his scalp and strings of wild hair hung in crazed knots.

"I don't care about rockets and machine guns. Hang those gizmos. I want the *car*. Imagine an entire fleet of them in showrooms from Maine to California. Kids these days only want dazzle. Picture your car in bright green, red. They'll be drag racing it, going to drive-ins. They'll love the hippie green headlights, that outer space buzzing noise it makes, the fact that it's the fastest thing on four wheels. It'll be the biggest sensation since hula hoops. I can make you legit."

"It's not for sale. You knew that or you wouldn't have stolen it."

"*Everything's* got a price."

"You can't meet it. Face it, you're a failure. No one wants your cars, Lanyard. If they did, you wouldn't have to resort to robbing jewelry stores to get my attention. Your problem was that tattoo. Your genius there—" He nodded to the unconscious Kong, over whom Kato stood guard. "—and his cohorts got those tattoos of your Scorpion on their arms. It led me right to you."

"I hadn't thought of the tattoos when this started," Lanyard said. "He and the others worked on the Scorpion production line. When the press created the Scorpion gang it worked perfectly into my plan to draw you out. The Hornet *had* to meet the Scorpion."

"It just proves how little you mean to this town these days, Lanyard. In the Motor City no one even remembered your failure of a car. In another ten years they won't even remember your name."

"In ten years no one will even recognize this town," Lanyard insisted with growing fury. He skin became ashen and his lips seemed to have taken on a bluish hue. "I've seen the future. We're getting killed on domestic production. Eventually it'll be imports as far as the eye can see. The Japanese are going to swoop in like kamikazes and kill the U.S. auto industry. You'll see." Spittle launched violently from between Lanyard's bluing lips. "That'll happen over my dead . . . *it'll happen over my dead. . .*"

With a ragged gasp and bloodshot eyes growing wide, the auto manufacturer clutched one bony, veined hand to his chest.

The funeral for Herbert Quentin Lanyard was one of the largest ever in the Motor City. A parade of cars from the earliest ever produced to the most recent top-of-the-line models streamed from the Lanyard Motors lots to the grounds of the Lanyard estate where the old man was rolled inside the family mausoleum on his last set of wheels. Absent, but noticeably so to only a few, was the most famous automobile in Detroit.

The funeral details were front page news in the latest edition of the

Daily Sentinel, folded neatly on the nightstand of Lenore Case's private hospital room. A side story mentioned that the Sentinel Shooter had been found tied up in an eighteen wheeler outside Lanyard Motors along with several accomplices in the Scorpion crime wave.

Casey rustled the sheets and exhaled, slowly opening her eyes.

The lights were low. It had been day when she last awoke. It was night now. A guest stood vigil in a dark shadow in the corner of her room, just out of sight of the parking lot light shining through the louvered window.

"Are you still here?" she asked groggily.

"Went home to change."

"Oh. Business as usual."

Casey heard Gunnigan's unmistakable growl from a distant room. The *Sentinel*'s city editor was shouting about a typo that had in his brief absence somehow made it onto page one, and was using language far too colorful for a public hospital ward.

"I'm under the weather one day and the whole place goes to hell. Until I'm back, I want everything run past me. What? Courier it over, I don't care, and you can start ten minutes ago!" The sound of a phone slamming down echoed through the ward, followed by the soft voice of a harried night nurse.

Gunnigan was snarling, "What do you mean? I *was* whispering," as Casey heard another sound, this one coming from the parking lot. It was a high-pitched whine. It approached like a soft raging specter and stopped beneath her window. No one else heard. Gunnigan's tirade was the perfect cover. In the corner, the figure stirred.

"No rest for the wicked, huh?" Casey said.

"Not if I can help it."

From the shadows near the window stepped The Green Hornet. "You take it easy, Miss Case. And if that boss of yours gives you a hard time for taking a few extra days off, you send him to me."

When the figure in green pulled open the door, Gunnigan was again on the phone and the ward was once more in turmoil. Someone was suggesting his phone be unplugged. Her visitor looked back, smiled, and just like that, The Green Hornet was gone.

A few moments later, Casey heard the sound of tires squealing and the buzz of the Black Beauty's engine fade into the distance. And when she closed her eyes she knew that she and all of Detroit slept safe and secure once more.

AULD ACQUAINTANCE

by Matthew Baugh

Kato struck hard and fast. His fist slipped between flailing limbs and connected with the unyielding torso. The dummy twisted and Kato parried low, then high, as wooden limbs lashed at him. A third limb thrust at his face and he bobbed away, then bobbed back to hit the torso and limbs with a flurry of punches and elbows.

"That's no way to treat a lady," Britt Reid said from the doorway of the exercise room.

Kato stepped back from his opponent, a heavy wooden post with several projecting limbs. The dummy fighter continued to twist from side to side, slashing the air until the young Asian man touched a switch on the wall.

"That's the strangest dancing partner I've ever seen," Britt said, grinning. He was immaculately clad in a tuxedo, his dark hair perfectly in place.

"It's a 'wooden man' for gung fu practice," Kato said. "Usually they don't move, but I rigged a motor on this one." In contrast to Reid, he wore baggy black pants and a sleeveless t-shirt which revealed lean but powerful muscles. He picked up a towel and wiped sweat from his face and neck.

"Why not just use the old-fashioned kind?" Britt asked.

"That's fine for traditional forms, but not for fighting. It teaches you to be too rigid and predictable. It's better to be ready for your opponent to do the unexpected."

"Just the same, this isn't the way I imagined you'd be spending Valentine's Day."

Kato smiled with one corner of his mouth. "Not really my holiday."

"Well, it's mine, this year at least. I'm heading downtown for a charity gala."

"Who are you going with?"

"Stella Robinson," Britt said with a rueful smile.

Kato knew the young woman, the daughter of a Detroit society family.

291

She was blonde, pretty, spoiled, and about as interesting a conversationalist as his training dummy.

"Shame you can't take Casey," he said.

"She'll understand." Britt glanced at his platinum wristwatch. "I'd better get going; Stella doesn't like to be kept waiting."

He left and Kato moved to a heavy punching bag to work on combinations. As he moved into a broken rhythm of hands, elbows, knees and feet, his mind wandered. He felt bad for Lenore Case, Reid's secretary. She was not only as pretty as any of the city's Stella Robinsons, but she had a good heart and a sharp mind. He understood how Britt's pose as a wealthy playboy helped in their fight against crime, but Lenore deserved better.

I hate *Valentine's Day*.

Kato's attacks picked up speed and fury as he thought about being alone. Usually it was something he dismissed, but tonight he couldn't help remembering. He thought of shy little Reiko who had given him his first kiss when she was fifteen and he thirteen. There had been Xiuying, Sifu Guo's tomboyish daughter who had swapped mischievous smiles with him as they sparred. Where would that have gone if she hadn't been promised to someone else while still a teen? Then there was Joanna, whom he had rescued and sent away. They had never even kissed but he thought of her often. Finally there had been the gentle Annie Chiu, taken from him by a stray bullet.

Kato finished with a barrage of punches and a leaping sidekick that bent the heavy bag in half. His arms and legs were trembling with the energy of his exertions. He shook his head, surprised at his emotions. He'd known that working with The Green Hornet would be a lonely, secretive life. Posing as a criminal by night and a meek domestic servant by day left him little opportunity to be himself and no time to share his life with another. He thought he had already come to terms with that.

Kato showered and changed into a bathrobe. He sat on his bed and gazed at the landscape on the wall, a monochrome work by the Japanese painter, Sesshu. With a few strokes and spatters of ink the master had created a gnarled tree in the foreground and massive rocks fading into the mist behind it. Kato tried to relax his body and empty his mind, focusing only on the painting, drawing from its serenity.

The phone rang.

With an expression of annoyance he rose and went to answer. The expression vanished when he saw that the scrambler circuit had been engaged. That meant it was one of a small handful of people, Miss Case, District Attorney Scanlon, or. . .

". . . Tim Nektosha," the voice said. "I need to talk to The Green Hornet right away."

"He's not here," Kato replied.

"Damn! This is urgent."

"Talk to me."

"Look," Tim said, "no offense but I really—"

"Hold it," Kato said, his voice cutting through the other's like a whip. "Your options right now are talk to me or hang up and wait for The Hornet to contact you. What's it going to be?"

"Fine," the man said after a moment. "We got hit at the casino tonight."

"How much was taken?"

"Nothing, they came in on motorcycles and tore the place apart, sent a few people to the hospital and started a fire. We only just got it put out."

"Motorcycles?"

"Yeah, they must be part of a club. They were all wearing black vests with a skull in a Viking helmet stitched on the back."

"That sounds like the Berserkers," Kato said. "They're a Detroit based club; but I don't know what a biker gang would hope to accomplish."

"You got me," Tim replied. "I did manage to catch one of them, though. If you and The Hornet hurry down you can ask him yourself."

The Black Beauty sped silently down I-94 at over one-hundred mph. The big sedan was as silent as a ghost. Kato sat at the wheel, clad in black chauffeur's livery and a mask. Thanks to 'infra-green' headlights and a specially treated windshield, he could see the road and the traffic easily while running dark.

He turned off at the Chelsea exit and whispered through the sleepy little town and onto the Reservation Road.

Tim worked at the Three Fires Casino on the Ojibwa-Potawatomi Reservation. The place had been operated by the mob until The Hornet had run them out months ago. He had done so with the help of a young Potawatomi Army veteran named Tim Nektosha. He was a good man who had gotten caught up in organized crime until The Hornet stepped in. Now he ran the casino, making sure the proceeds went to the people of the reservation. Nobody messed with him as it was known he was The Green Hornet's made man.

Not until tonight.

Kato passed the side road that led to the casino and continued on. The fires seemed to be out, but he could see the lights of Tribal police cars and fire trucks from Chelsea. He slowed as the road narrowed to slightly less than two reasonable lanes of crumbling asphalt. He turned onto an unpaved side-road which tested even the Black Beauty's suspension, and followed it as it wound its way to a little farmhouse and an old barn, both sporting new coats of paint. A new tractor and a pickup truck sat in the yard. Other than that, things looked the same as they had before Tim had started working for The Hornet. The Potawatomi, he had heard, didn't flaunt their good fortune but found ways to share it with their neighbors. He liked the tradition, and that Tim was holding to it.

He stopped the car and moved to the house. The door opened before he reached it and an athletic young man ushered him in. Tim Nektosha had changed in the months since Kato had seen him. He wore a silk shirt and bola tie now along with expensive-looking cowboy boots, and his black hair, once military-short, had grown out enough to underscore his Potawatomi blood. He didn't wear any jewelry except for a chain around his neck. It looked like it probably held a charm of some kind, hidden by his shirt.

The prisoner was a lean blonde man in his early twenties. His hair hung in a single braid that reached to the middle of his back and he sported a scraggly beard. He wore worn jeans and a back leather vest, open to reveal the tattoo of an eagle on his chest. A golden hoop hung from one ear. He sat on an old sofa with his hands cuffed behind him.

The man forced a laugh and swore when he saw Kato.

"Man, you are one twisted cat," he said. "It ain't time for that kind of get up until Halloween."

Moving so quickly that his actions barely registered on the eye, Kato plucked a Hornet-shaped dart from his sleeve and hurled it at the biker. The missile passed neatly through the loop of the earring, pinning the man's head to the back of the couch. He struggled for a moment to dislodge it, but the dart was too firmly rooted. He subsided with a defiant glare.

"You talk when I tell you to," Kato said, letting his voice take on an arrogant edge.

The man forced an ugly laugh. "I ain't telling you nothing," he said. "Berserkers don't squeal."

"Then I don't have much use for you, do I?" Kato asked, producing another dart.

"When Snake and the boys get hold of you, they're gonna do a lot worse than play darts."

"He had this on him," Tim said passing Kato a note, a neatly folded scrap of yellow paper. Kato felt a jolt of fear in his chest as he looked at it.

Hornet, the note said,

You know what I want: an alliance between the two of us. Until you agree, I'm going to hurt you by hurting the people you care about, starting with your oldest friends.

"Who gave you this?" Kato asked.

The man sneered and Kato felt a touch of admiration for his nerve. Getting him to talk could take a long time—longer than they had.

"It was a woman, wasn't it?" he said. "Blonde hair, green eyes, nice-looking."

The biker looked startled, then resumed his tough-guy expression, but Kato had his answer. He pulled out a different dart and threw it at the biker, striking him in the center of the chest.

"Hey!" Tim shouted, but the dart, rather than skewering the man, released a small cloud of green gas on impact. Startled, the biker inhaled some of the gas. His eyes rolled up and he went limp.

"What are you doing?"

"I know what I need," Kato said, recovering the darts he had thrown. "I didn't want him to hear any more of our conversation."

"Okay," Tim said. "So, what's this all about?"

"Get in the car. I'll tell you on the way."

I hate *Valentine's Day.*

Britt Reid returned his date's smile, with effort, and wished he were somewhere else. It wasn't that Stella Robinson was unattractive. The pretty blonde had chosen a strapless gown that showed off her curvaceous figure well, in a blue fabric that accented her eyes. When it came to beauty, charm, and social pedigree, Stella could hold her own with any woman in the room. Unfortunately, Britt found her painfully boring.

Stella Robinson's world seemed to start and end at Stella Robinson. She cared about clothes, galas, and gossip but had a distressing lack of curiosity for anything outside her social circle. She didn't seem interested in the space race, or the dangerous tension between Russia and China, or for that matter, the growing social unrest in Detroit. Britt had broached those topics on different occasions only to be answered with an incredulous stare that said, 'But what does that have to do with *me*?'

That wasn't a problem he'd ever had with Laura. His former fiancée was a brilliant woman and it was her penetrating mind as well as her beauty that had intoxicated him. He shuddered, remembering how close he'd come to marrying a woman capable of murdering her own father. Still ... he had to admit he'd have preferred her company to this.

The woman he would *really* have enjoyed bringing, he realized, was Lenore Case. She had not only a sharp mind but she also cared. Laura's curiosity came from a restless drive to control people; Casey's grew out of a deep sense of compassion.

The problem was that unspoken rule he and his secretary had somehow settled on without either of them actually saying it. She knew that he was The Green Hornet and that meant there was not going to be any romance between them. She would never do anything to make the world suspect his secret.

That really doesn't make sense, Britt thought. *How would us being involved interfere with The Hornet?* It was something that seemed logical when he talked to her, but at moments like this, it sounded idiotic.

His thoughts were interrupted by a soft buzzing from his pocket watch, a signal that someone was trying to reach The Green Hornet. He glanced at Stella, who had stopped talking and was pouting at him.

"Am I *boring* you, Britt?"

He grinned as carelessly as he could. "Not at all Stel, but I just remembered a phone call I need to make. Will you excuse me for a moment?"

It was clear that Stella had no intention of excusing him, but Britt ignored that and went to a bank of phone booths in the foyer of the opulent ballroom. He dialed the number for the Black Beauty's radio phone and was rewarded a moment later when Kato answered.

"Bad news, Boss."

"What is it?" Britt asked.

"A biker gang hit the casino," Kato said. "The Berserkers. Tim broke it up, but it sounds like Laura Cavendish is back."

"Are you sure?"

"She left one of her yellow paper notes. It sounds like she's after Tim's family."

"What?" Britt raised his voice in surprise. "How could she know?"

"She has a way of finding things out," Kato replied grimly.

Britt was quiet for a moment as he tried to figure all the possibilities of his enemy's new plan. "Where's Tim's father?" he finally asked.

There was a pause as Kato relayed the question, then: "He's at the Detroit Institute for Cancer Research, room 318."

"You and Tim do what you need to and wrap things up there; I'm going to check on him."

"Right, Boss."

"Are you going to tell me what this is about?" Tim asked. "Who is Laura Cavendish?"

"She's a crazy woman," Kato said, choosing his words deliberately. "She has a history with The Green Hornet and likes playing mind games."

"Why would she be after me, or Dad?"

"The boss's family and the Potawatomi go way back," Kato said. His hand darted out to catch the thong around Tim's neck and pulled the charm, a silver bullet, out of his shirt.

"Do people know you wear this?"

"I guess," Tim said. "Dad gave that to me a couple of months ago and I've been wearing it ever since. Why? What does it mean?"

"There used to be a masked gunfighter who carried these," Kato said. "Ever hear of him?"

"Sure, but I thought that was just folklore, you know?"

"He was real, and he's The Hornet's ancestor."

A look of astonishment crossed Tim's face. "Your boss's mask makes more sense all of a sudden," he said. "So . . . does this bullet mean the masked gunfighter helped my family?"

"More than that. There was an Indian who rode with him; a Potawatomi."

"Yeah?"

"Do you know your family history?"

"No, there was a lot of chaos when Dad was a kid and we lost touch with any relatives." He paused and his eyes widened. "You can't be saying what I think you're saying."

"As nearly as the Boss has been able to figure, you're that man's closest living relative. As far as he's concerned, that makes you as important as a long-lost brother."

"But how would this woman know about that?"

"She knows all about the masked man and his partner. The way the boss tells it, her great-grandfather practically stole the state of Texas before they stopped him."

Tim's eyes widened again. "If she's after me then Hanomah could be in danger."

"Who?"

"Hanomah Return, I've kind of been seeing her. She's an intern at the Reservation Clinic, and she's on duty tonight."

"Britt, are you sure you won't come up for some coffee?" Stella batted her too-thick-to-be-natural lashes at him and he noticed the perfectly applied ebony slashes on her upper lids. He had to admit, she made a lovely picture.

"Sorry, Stel," he said. "I really do have to get to the *Sentinel*."

She caught his arm in both her hands. "I'm sure I could find *some* way to help."

"That's sweet of you to offer," Britt replied, gently freeing his arm. "But I'm going to have to pass. I'll make it up to you, I promise."

He gave Stella a quick peck on the lips then hopped back into the white convertible and sped away, leaving her fuming on the sidewalk in front of her building.

A few moments later Britt pulled to a stop on a side street near the Cancer Center. He hated using the convertible but with the Black Beauty out of town he had little choice. He pressed a button under the dash which caused the license plate to rotate out of sight and a false plate to move into its place. Another button raised the soft top—not the usual one, but a flashy green cover. Kato had installed a second soft top which helped to camouflage the car and gave him a little concealment. The top up, he opened a hidden panel in the driver's door and withdrew a dark green trenchcoat with matching fedora and mask. A gas gun completed his transformation into The Green Hornet.

He slipped out of the car and circled to the rear of the building. The Center was smaller than a regular hospital and, at this time of night, much quieter. A frown crossed The Green Hornet's face as he noticed a cluster of motorcycles in the lot.

Laura's men had beaten him to their target, but they were still in the building. The frown changed to a grim smile as a plan formed in The Hornet's mind.

They left the unconscious biker by the side of Reservation Road and Kato used the car phone to tip the police, then sped toward the clinic, Tim riding shotgun. He pulled a .45 automatic pistol from his waistband and checked the clip.

"We don't use guns," Kato said.

"You have got to be kidding," Tim replied.

"We don't kill. You know that."

"Yeah, but this is different."

Kato shot the young man an intense sideways glance.

"Fine, no guns," Tim said, anger in his voice as he placed the weapon on the seat. "So what do I do if I can't shoot them? You want to go back to my place so I can pick up a tomahawk? Maybe a bow and arrows?"

Kato pressed a button on the dash and a panel in the passenger door slid open to reveal a slender pistol with a dark wooden grip and a barrel of green tinted steel. Tim lifted the strange weapon and looked it over.

"The boss' spare," Kato said. "It fires a stream of liquid that turns to gas as soon as it hits the air. Anyone who breathes it is out for several hours. It works best indoors; any wind at all messes with the range."

"Thanks," Tim said. "Look, I'm sorry, but I don't see the sense in this. I mean, it's noble not to take a life and all, but we're giving these goons a big advantage."

"It's a waste of time to complain about resources you can't use," Kato said. "Try thinking about the best way to use what you've got."

Tim slipped into silence. Kato felt for him, especially going into a situation where people he cared about might be in danger.

"You love her?" he asked after a few moments.

"Hanomah? It's . . . complicated."

"Either you love her or you don't."

"I *shouldn't* have any feelings for her."

"In my experience, feelings don't have much to do with 'should' and 'shouldn't'," Kato said.

"Look, no disrespect to you or The Hornet, but she deserves better than someone who's involved in this kind of stuff. Besides, her father's a cop, Reservation Police on the Tsichah land."

Kato grunted. The two were silent until the clinic came into view around a clump of evergreens. The building was a wide one-story structure with a single entrance that opened directly onto a gravel parking lot. A few people, staff and patients by the looks of them, huddled near the building as a score of bikers circled and roared through the lot. The men wore the same black and silver leathers as those who had attacked the casino.

"I feel a little out-gunned," Tim said.

"Don't worry," Kato replied. His black-gloved hand reached out to flick a switch on the dash.

"You're not going to use the rocket launchers, are you? The clinic —"

"Relax," Kato said. "The Black Beauty has more tricks than that." He gunned the big car forward, scattering the motorcycles and clipping two in the process. As the Black Beauty passed, it emitted a thick plume of green gas. Most of the bikers managed to get clear, but at least half a dozen went down. The next moment a volley of pistols and several shotguns sounded as the remaining men opened up. Kato smiled as he heard the slugs ricochet harmlessly off the heavily armored body and bullet-proof windows. Unless one of the gunmen had an anti-tank rifle they were in no real danger.

Kato spun the Beauty in an arc that seemed impossibly tight for such a big car, narrowly missing the front door of the clinic. Now that the building was behind him he raised the front grille revealing a battery of rocket launchers, each powerful enough to demolish a car.

"How many left?" he asked.

"Was it my turn to count?" Tim asked. After a moment's hesitation he added, "I've got eight down, eleven up."

Kato pressed a switch and a rocket shot from the car to strike the ground in front of a cluster of cycles. None of them went down, but the blast panicked and scattered them.

"For someone who doesn't want to kill, you play pretty damn rough," Tim said.

"I apply force where I need to," Kato replied. He fired another rocket, this time blasting an abandoned bike to flaming rubble. "Beating the enemy with brute force is one thing, but winning without fighting is the goal."

The Black Beauty surged forward again, but as it did, Tim gave an oath, opened his door and flung himself out. Kato's gaze shot to the rearview mirror where he saw five more gang members in black and silver leathers leaving the entrance, dragging a small, dark-haired woman in a lab-coat.

The distraction lasted only for an instant, but it was long enough for one of the bikers to blind-side him. The man rode close enough to fling a large vodka bottle with a flaming rag in the top. The makeshift missile shattered against the Black Beauty's armored hood, spreading burning gasoline across the front end.

Kato allowed himself a frustrated snort. He was off his game to let something like this happen. He threw a switch, closing the grille, before the fire could reach the rockets. As the blazing car lunged through the knot of bikers, the flames on the windshield made visibility almost impossible. Kato hoped the bikers had the reflexes and the common sense to get out of the way. He felt a glancing impact as a motorcycle careened off his left fender.

Then he was through and spun the Beauty to a stop. He flicked the wipers on, hoping to sluice away some of the burning gas. Through the fire he could see the remaining bikers (nine by his count) trying to rally. He saw Tim at the entrance, fighting a group of men, and he hit the accelerator.

Tim had recognized Hanomah Return as the men pulled her from the building, and the shock had overridden all the discipline he'd learned serving in Vietnam. He barreled out of the car toward the men. A heavy-set Berserker with a long, scraggly beard tried to run him down but Tim sidestepped the bike and his gun discharged a thick stream of green gas into the man's face. Another biker, this one on foot, pulled a revolver, but the gas gun made short work of him too.

He was starting to develop some respect for his weapon when a thrown tire-iron caught him in the wrist. He felt a burst of pain and dropped the gun. Three men, fists swinging, moved in on him before he could pick it up, and for a moment it was all he could do to cover up.

One of the men reached behind his back for a weapon and Tim kicked him in the side of the leg. The man stumbled to one knee and Tim caught him with his own knee in the side of the head, laying him out on the gravel. The second man had some karate training and threw a roundhouse kick at his head. Tim caught the kick and swept the man's standing leg.

The final man had drawn a Bowie knife. Tim leaped back as the biker lunged, but the tip of the weapon caught him, tearing his shirt and cutting a bloody furrow down his ribs. The Berserker grinned and moved in, confident of his kill. Tim took a step back, feigning weakness.

When the knifeman lunged again, Tim spun to the side, the blade missing him by barely an inch. He caught the biker's wrist and, with a practiced movement, twisted the arm behind him. The man gave a cry of pain and dropped the knife, but Tim kept twisting until he felt the bones in the man's elbow come apart.

The karate fighter was back on his feet. This time he'd pulled out a snub-nosed revolver, which he aimed at the center of Tim's chest.

Suddenly a flaming black juggernaut skidded between the two men. The biker fired three shots, but they ricocheted from the Black Beauty's metal skin. The driver's door opened and Kato sprang out. His right foot arced up in a lightning fast crescent kick that slapped the gun from the berserker's hand as he aimed it. Kato used his momentum to spin his body, adding this force to an unexpected side kick that doubled the biker over. Moving like a dancer going through choreographed steps, he stepped in and struck the back of the man's neck with a chopping blow of his hand. The Berserker went down.

Tim watched in awe. The driver had disposed of the man more quickly than he would have believed possible.

"Get in the car!" Kato yelled.

Tim glanced around. In the chaos of the fight he'd lost track of

Hanomah. After a second he saw her; she had been loaded into a sidecar on one of the motorcycles that was speeding out of the parking lot. He scooped up the fallen gas gun and clambered into the car, pulling the door shut after him.

"They've got Hanomah!" he gasped.

"Not for long," Kato said. "Hold on."

In a spray of gravel the Black Beauty shot after the fleeing motorcycles. In moments they were careening down the decaying asphalt of Reservation Road. The hood still blazed but the flames had dwindled to merely decorative. Kato winced as they hit a pothole and he struggled to keep the vehicle on the road. On a good stretch of highway the Black Beauty could have overhauled even the powerful motorcycles, but on a road like this that was impossible.

"So what now?" Tim asked. "We can't use rockets or gas. If anything makes him lose control at this speed, Hanomah's dead."

"We wait," Kato replied. "They'll make a mistake."

A shotgun blast rattled off the back windshield and Kato caught sight of the rest of the bikers in pursuit.

"You've got rocket-launchers in the back?" Tim asked.

"That's overkill," Kato said. "This is better." He threw a switch that caused a set of sprayers in the undercarriage to spread a film of oil on the road behind them. The Berserkers hit it doing more than seventy and began to topple. Kato shifted his attention to the bikes in front, trying to make up ground.

He estimated they were fifty yards behind and closing as they approached the outskirts of Chelsea, then a railroad crossing light ahead began to flash and the gate came down. Kato glanced left and saw a westbound freight train coming fast on the crossing.

"They're not going to make it," Tim said. His voice was calm, but Kato sensed the tension rolling off the man like waves. He remained silent and coaxed more speed out of the big car.

The Berserkers reached the track at almost the same moment as the train and shot across in front of it. Kato heard Tim hold his breath as the bikes seemed almost to brush the front of the locomotive.

One didn't make it. With a sickening crunch of metal on metal, the motorcycle and its rider were hurled clear of the track. Kato turned the Black Beauty into a sideways skid and came within inches of becoming another victim of the train. As they came to a stop, he heard Tim start to breathe again.

"They made it. The bike with Hanomah made it. She's alive."

"I think so," Kato agreed.

"But they're getting away," Tim said, staring bleakly at the endless procession of boxcars.

"No. There's one more trick I can try."

Jason Nektosha started to rise from his hospital bed.

"Sir, the doctor said you were to lie still."

He looked at the nurse, a stocky woman about his own age, with the outthrust jaw of a Marine drill instructor.

"I was just going to change the channel," he said nodding to the television on the bureau as a howling band of Apaches raced across the screen.

"You don't like this?"

Jason shrugged. He didn't mind westerns so much. Something about white actors in makeup pretending to be Indians and speaking pidgin-English was so absurd that he found it funny, but he had to be in the right frame of mind.

The nurse frowned and twisted the dial until the image of a sleek spaceship moving across a starry background appeared on the screen.

"Leave it there," he said.

The nurse glared at him, as if questioning his choice.

"Leave it there," he repeated. "I like Mr. Spock."

She left him and Jason tried to settle into the rhythms of the program, but his mind wouldn't quiet down. He was grateful to his son for bringing him here where his cancer could be treated, but he hated the hospital. He was too polite to say so, but he hated the businesslike manner of the doctors. The nurses were a little better, but no one talked to him like the people did at home. How was a man supposed to heal without his friends and family around?

He closed his eyes for a moment. When he opened them he realized that he must have dozed. The lights and television were off and the only sound was someone moving in the hallway. Jason Nektosha felt as if he was the only person in the whole building, alone in this colorless, antiseptic place. The clock said midnight but he didn't feel sleepy. For most of his life, Jason had awakened with the dawn and spent the day working his little farm. This place had thrown off his body's rhythms, and distanced him from the nurturing routines of earth and sky.

Jason grunted, scolding himself for his bout of self pity. His mother had told him that regret for things that couldn't be changed was a waste of time. Better to take what life offered in the moment. He switched on the bedside light and picked up the novel Tim had left for him, a slender paperback titled *Dandelion Wine*.

He glanced up as the door opened, admitting three tough-looking men dressed in white, like orderlies.

One of them, with a ponytail and the build of a weightlifter, snatched the book from him and started to toss it away. A second man, leaner and taller, with a pleasant face and a neatly trimmed beard, caught his wrist.

"Geez, Animal," he said. "Show a little respect. The guy who wrote this is a genius."

"Sorry, Dean," the bulky man replied, looking a little frightened.

"What is this?" Jason demanded.

"Don't get upset," Dean said. "We're just taking you on a little ride. When we're done with our business, you can come right back."

"Yeah, Chief," the third man said. "No need to go on the warpath." He was a thin, rodent of a man who apparently liked to laugh at his own jokes. He stopped when Dean shot him a venomous look.

"Bones, you keep watch," Dean said. "Animal, get the wheelchair."

Jason watched as the men moved to obey. He'd been living close to his own death for too long to feel much fear, but the situation seemed so unreal.

"You want to kidnap me?"

"It's not the best time to discuss it," Dean said, pleasantly. He caught Jason's arm in a powerful grip and dragged him to his feet. The older man struggled against him for a moment before he was seized by a racking series of coughs that drove him to his knees.

"Geez, don't lose a lung," Dean said. "Bones, I need some help."

"Bones can't hear you," said a voice from the door.

Jason managed to look up and saw a tall silhouette in a fedora and trenchcoat. His reading light shed just enough illumination to reveal that the man wore a mask.

"The Green Hornet," Animal whispered.

Before the big man could move, The Hornet raised his gun and fired a stream of gas at him. Animal gasped once, loudly, then collapsed across the wheelchair.

Jason heard a sharp intake of air and realized that Dean was holding his breath. The false orderly released his arm and charged through a plume of green gas to tackle The Hornet. The two went down in a heap with Dean on top. He rose and began raining down lefts and rights as The Green Hornet brought up his arms to fend off the blows.

Jason struggled to his feet, fighting off another fit of coughing. He looked around for something that he could use as a weapon. When he glanced back at the fight, the situation had changed. Dean leaned back too far winding up for a punch and The Hornet arched his back, toppling the man to the side.

In a moment they had both scrambled to their feet. Dean jabbed at the man's masked face but The Hornet slipped his head to the side and countered with a right cross to the jaw. While Dean was stunned, The Hornet pressed his advantage by landing a left hook to the ribs and finishing with a powerful right uppercut.

"Are you all right?" The Hornet asked.

Jason sat on the bed and struggled to master his breathing. "I'm fine," he said. "Thank you."

"I didn't do it for you. These punks are trying to move in on my territory. I don't tolerate that."

"Maybe," Jason said. "All I know is, since you ran the mob out of our casino and took over, the tribe's getting a lot more money. There are people on the Rez who see you as a hero."

"You think I'm some law-abiding citizen?"

"No, but the white man's laws don't usually do us much good. You're kind of like—" Jason broke off as a mild coughing fit seized him.

"Like Robin Hood?" the masked man asked, irony thick in his voice.

"I was going to say like our hero, Nanabush, but Robin Hood works too."

"Don't fool yourself." The Hornet bent and scooped up Dean in a fireman's carry. "Nobody seems to have heard that scuffle," he said. "If you think you owe me anything, give me a few minutes to get to the stairs before you call for help."

The Hornet slipped out the door.

Jason watched after him for a moment, then grinned.

The phone in the armrest of the Black Beauty rang. Tim glanced up as Kato answered. He had been watching a closed-circuit monitor that depicted the fleeing bikers. It had amazed him when Kato first launched the scanner, a disc-shaped miniature helicopter carrying a remote camera. Tracking Hanomah and her abductors had consumed all of his attention, but there was only one man who could be on the other end of the phone.

"Yeah, Boss?" Kato said, then waited for a moment, listening. "Your father's okay," he said to Tim, then continued to listen.

Tim turned his attention back to the monitor, still listening to Kato's end of the conversation.

"We're following some Berserkers," the black-clad driver said. "They've got Tim's friend . . . No, we had some bad luck with a train . . . They're just outside the city now . . ."

"It looks like they're pulling into a biker bar in Wayne," Tim said. "It's near the intersection of Wayne Road and Michigan Avenue."

"We can be there in an hour," Kato said. "You should—" He stopped, obviously having been cut off. A moment later he spoke again. "Right, Boss."

"What's the plan?" Tim asked.

"He's not waiting for us." The driver's voice was grim.

"What's he doing? If he rushes in there they could kill Hanomah."

"Don't worry," Kato said, his voice grim. "He's going to do whatever it takes to get her out of there."

The Snake Pit Bar & Grill was a windowless one-story roadhouse on the edge of a seedy residential area. Peeling paint and unkempt yards were common, and the occasional junked car on blocks completed the depressed feel of the neighborhood. The Green Hornet scanned the area, noting the number of bikes in the lot. His stomach tightened as he counted seventeen. At least there was an empty lot separating the roadhouse from the nearest homes. He didn't want the inevitable violence to affect civilians. He opened the secret panel and pulled out a cylindrical device—something Kato had been working on.

Dean stirred in the back seat and tried to sit up. The fact that his hands were wired together behind his back made this simple task difficult. The Hornet caught him by the collar, hauling him up and spilling him to the pavement.

Dean swore. "What is your problem, man?"

"Recognize where you are?"

The biker glanced around, stopping as his gaze rested on the bar. "Man, are you suicidal, or what?"

"Who's in there?" The Hornet asked. "Who's running this sad little operation?"

"You think I'd tell you?"

"Doesn't matter. You and I are going to walk inside in a minute and you're going to make the introductions. You're also going to make sure your little friends don't try to shoot me."

"Yeah?" Dean said, forcing a chuckle.

The Hornet held the cylinder up for the man to see. "Were you in the military, Dean? Do you know what this is?"

"It's a Mark-3 hand grenade," the biker answered, the forced levity gone from his voice.

"Good," The Hornet said. "If you know that, you probably know that this holds eight ounces of TNT and is designed specifically for killing everyone in a closed space, like a bunker . . . or a biker bar."

"You're freaking nuts!"

"You know what they say," The Hornet replied. "Suicidal loves company." He pulled the pin but kept a firm grip on the grenade, preventing the lever from coming loose. "If anyone shoots me, I let go of this and . . . well, you know what happens next, don't you?"

Dean nodded and The Hornet pulled him to his feet.

"So, who will I be talking to?"

"Snake," Dean said. "Our chapter-head is Snake Dumont. He owns the bar."

"Any civilians in there? Waitresses? A barman?"

"No, just wall to wall Berserkers, waiting to kick your—"

The Hornet interrupted the boast with a stiff shove.

Moments later Dean waved off a couple of bikers posted as sentries and the two men entered the bar. Usually a room like this would have been raucous, but the patrons—all men wearing black leather—were deadly serious as they watched him enter.

He saw Laura Cavendish at a back table dressed in her Yellowjacket outfit, a distaff parody of his own trenchcoat, mask, and hat in yellow. A lean man slouched next to her with the arrogant assurance of a king. He was shirtless under his black vest and The Hornet saw a cobra tattoo on his left bicep and a rattlesnake coiled on his right forearm. Near the pair a small woman with black hair in braids sat in a chair, her hands tied in front of her. Her slender face was streaked with tears, but she watched the room alertly. He knew this must be Hanomah Return and felt a tug of admiration for the courage he sensed under her fear.

A giant with a shaved head wearing a single gold earring stood behind Hanomah. He was more than six and a half feet tall and powerfully muscled, but what caught The Hornet's attention was the snub-nosed revolver he held to the woman's head.

"You must be Snake Dumont," The Green Hornet said to the tattooed man. "You've put your money on the wrong horse this time. I've faced this 'lady' before, and always beaten her."

"Really?" Snake said with a slow grin. "From where I sit she looks like the winner. You make one wrong move and Mr. Clean will blow the squaw's pretty little head right off her shoulders."

Normally, The Hornet would have pretended not to care. Unfortunately

Laura's presence made that impossible. She knew him too well. The tightness in his stomach increased and his nerves seemed to sing with electricity. He had to play this just right.

The Hornet gave Dean a shove, sending him to the floor, and raised the grenade. Several bikers swore as they recognized the device. Snake Dumont only chuckled.

"You really *that* crazy, man?"

"I was crazy enough to walk in here alone. Here's the deal: I don't like kidnappings so you let the girl go and we can settle this, one way or another. Refuse and I drop the grenade; hurt her and I drop the grenade; shoot me and I drop the grenade."

The room fell dead quiet. The Hornet could hear Hanomah's ragged breathing and the nervous shifting of some of the Berserkers. Then Laura laughed, a harsh, self-assured sound that he had grown to hate.

"He's bluffing," she said.

The Black Beauty slid to a stop two blocks from the roadhouse. The scanner had shown The Hornet enter twenty minutes earlier and, so far, there hadn't been any kind of commotion to indicate a fight.

"You think he's okay?" Tim asked.

"The boss would have gone in prepared for anything," Kato replied. "I don't think they could have taken him out without a big fight."

"But we can't be sure."

"No. Not without eyes inside. We'll need to figure a quiet way to get past the guards."

"I have an idea," Tim said. "There was a package liquor store a block over, wasn't there?"

Lil' Moses Brannon flipped his butterfly knife open and closed unconsciously. It was a habit he'd picked up in the Navy and one that he still fell into when irritated. It bothered him to no end that he had pulled guard duty while Snake was inside, face to face with no less than The Green Hornet. It didn't help that his partner, Badger Hanson, was in his stoic mode. The older biker was leaning against the wall by the door, arms crossed over his barrel chest, expression hidden behind shades and a neatly trimmed beard shot with gray.

Brannon considered saying something smart to Badger. It was hard to restrain himself, even with the man wearing his little white button that read "COME NEAR ME AND I'LL KILL YOU."

Just then he saw the Indian, a young guy with his shirt half out staggering in their direction, clutching a brown paper bag just big enough to hold a bottle of Thunderbird.

Brannon muttered an oath. This was not a good time to have to deal with a drunk.

"Hey, man . . . you open?" the Indian asked, his voice slurred.

"Been hittin' the fire-water pretty hard, huh, Chief?" Brannon said.

The Indian's grin widened and he lurched closer. Lil' Moses started to step toward him when Badger caught his arm.

"Nice clothes for a drunken Indian," he said, his tone suspicious. Brannon looked the man over again; his rumpled suit did look expensive. Something was wrong with the picture.

The Indian brought the bag up and he could see that what he'd thought was the neck of a bottle was actually the muzzle of a gun. The weapon fired a stream of gas and the world turned green.

Kato counted down on his fingers: 3-2-1, then he and Tim burst into the room, small gas filters covering their mouths and noses. He took in the situation as Tim spread a stream of gas around them. At a glance he saw The Green Hornet holding the grenade, the Yellowjacket and her thugs holding Hanomah at gunpoint, the breaker box on the far wall, and the horde of armed bikers, many of whom were turning to train their weapons on him.

Acting almost faster than could be believed, Kato plucked a dart from his sleeve and sent it across the room to lodge in Mr. Clean's hand. The bald giant roared in pain and fury as he dropped his gun. Before the weapon hit the floor, Kato launched a second dart at the breakers. At the same moment The Hornet flung the grenade into the midst of the Berserkers, sending them scrambling in blind panic.

Several things happened at once. The dart pierced the thin metal lid of the breaker box to the circuits beneath. There was a bright flash as it shorted out and the lights in the room went dark. The grenade hit the floor but, instead of exploding, it began to issue a cloud of green gas.

Kato smiled as the disguised weapon caught the men off guard, plunging them into unconsciousness. The Chinese strategist Sun Tsu had once written that all warfare is deception. Kato and The Hornet had worked hard to master that lesson; the gas bomb disguised as an explosive was their latest twist.

He stepped into the mob, hands and feet moving in swift arcs, stunning and breaking bone where they landed. He could sense The Green Hornet and Tim Nektosha doing the same close at hand.

Despite the gang's overwhelming numbers, this was fairly easy. The Berserkers were surprised, disoriented, and the gas was taking its toll. Only a few in the back of the room—the Yellowjacket and her little group—had managed to avoid it. As they moved out the back door, dragging Hanomah with them, The Green Hornet and Tim pushed after them. Kato decided to play rear guard, making sure none of the gang still in the building had a chance to follow.

Snake Dumont burst out of the back of the roadhouse, followed by the yellow-clad woman he had fallen for. Gorgeous, ruthless, and smart, she was what he'd always imagined his ideal woman would be. Not that she was his woman yet, but Snake was confident that would come.

At the moment, though, things weren't going well for either of them. Mr. Clean came out next, still dragging the Indian woman with him.

"Dump the squaw, Clean!" Snake shouted. "Just kill anyone who comes out that door."

The giant nodded, sending Hanomah sprawling to the dirt lot with a shove and drawing a huge Bowie knife. He was Snake's best man. They'd been together for six years and Mr. Clean followed his orders with child-like trust.

"Idiot!" the Yellowjacket, snapped. "I thought your gang was tough enough to handle two men."

"It was three," Snake replied coldly. He hadn't risen to his position in the club by being a hothead and it irritated him that his ally was losing her cool. There would be plenty of time for recriminations after they got away. Besides, she could have given him better intelligence on The Hornet. Still, a little fit of pique was nothing that couldn't be fixed.

"Start the car," he said. "Clean and I will keep them off your back till we can all get away." Drawing a .357 revolver he turned just as The Green Hornet came out the door.

Mr. Clean slashed at him but The Hornet ducked past the blade and kept running. Snake lined up a shot, but the giant was right behind The Green Hornet. He hesitated, not wanting to risk his flunky. That hesitation was enough for The Hornet to pull out a metal truncheon and throw it. It caught Snake's wrist, causing him to lose his grip on the gun.

He was dimly aware of the Indian emerging from the back of the roadhouse and tackling Mr. Clean to the ground. He heard tires throwing up dirt and gravel and turned to see the Yellowjacket peeling out of the lot in her lemon-colored Mustang convertible.

This day is just going all to hell, he thought.

The Green Hornet stalked closer and Snake grinned at him.

"You have got some real style, man," he said. "Is it too late to talk about switching allegiances?"

"Why don't you look me up when you get out?" The Hornet replied. He raised his gun.

"Can't take me without cheap gadgets, huh?" Snake said. "Maybe The Green Hornet isn't so tough after all."

"Why not?" The Hornet said with a crooked smile. "I don't have a problem teaching a punk like you a lesson in respect." He pocketed the gun and moved forward, bringing his fists up.

"Bad move, baby!" Snake said. "I fought Golden Gloves."

He launched a blindingly fast combination at The Green Hornet, only to see the masked man neatly parry his flurry. He pressed the attack and was rewarded with a stiff left jab that staggered him back.

Snake backed away as he realized that the masked man could box. His hand went to the waistband of his jeans and came back with a switchblade which opened to reveal a six-inch blade. The Hornet hesitated when the weapon came out and Snake grinned.

"Shoulda kept your advantage, man," he said, and moved in with an underhand stab. The blow would have pierced The Hornet's heart but the masked man managed to twist aside at the last instant and caught Snake's wrist. His free hand pounded a short right hook into the biker's kidney, then another, then another. Reeling in pain, Snake sank to his knees, the knife falling from limp fingers.

"Remember this the next time you or one of your associates thinks about crossing me," The Hornet said, then a green-gloved fist sent Snake Dumont to oblivion.

Tim struggled against the massive Mr. Clean. He'd managed to take the big man off his feet but overpowering him was proving a lot harder. He was a good wrestler, all-state in high school, but Clean was stronger than any opponent he'd ever faced; plus he had a knife, something his coach had never told him how to deal with.

The giant had managed to get on top and was forcing the blade closer and closer to Tim's face with one hand while he choked him with the other. Tim had both hands on Clean's wrist, trying to keep the knife back but that left him helpless to escape as he ran out of air.

Come on Hornet! he thought. *Come on masked driver guy! I'm not too proud to admit when I need a little help.*

The blade pressed a little farther, until the tip drew blood from his cheekbone. He shoved and twisted with all his strength, but he only pushed it back for a second, then darkness began to close in from the periphery of his sight and his struggles didn't matter any more.

Kato stepped out the back door, satisfied that the Berserkers has all either fled or been overcome by the green gas. The first thing that he saw was the giant Berserker bending over Tim Nektosha with a knife. The woman—Hanomah—rushed at him with a brick in her bound hands and brought it down on his bald head.

The big man grunted in pain and sent the woman sprawling with a backhanded blow. He rose to his feet and stepped toward her, knife still in his hand. Tim lay still but Kato couldn't see any serious wounds.

"Hey!" Kato shouted and hurled the last of his darts. It caught the giant in the arm but didn't make him drop his weapon. He turned, plucked out the dart, then threw his Bowie knife.

Kato turned just enough to let the blade fly harmlessly past and smirked.

"Not so smart to throw away your only weapon."

"I don't need a weapon," the bald man said, striding forward. Kato side stepped away from the building, making the giant come to him. His arrogant pose was useful in angering an opponent, but inside he was calm as he analyzed the big man. Mr. Clean was obviously very powerful and his reactions to the brick and the dart showed a ridiculous tolerance for pain. His size could mean he was relatively slow, but it also gave him a dangerous advantage in reach.

The giant lunged forward, closing the distance with a right hook. Rather than fade back, Kato did the unexpected, ducking forward under the swing and slamming a one-two combination to the big man's unguarded armpit and ribs.

Clean grunted, and spun, swinging a wild haymaker at Kato's head. This time the masked man did lean back, just enough that he could feel the wind from the swing on his face. His foot shot out, catching the giant on the side of the knee and almost sending him down. Clean was back up in an instant and Kato circled away, moving with the smoothness of a ballroom dancer. Clean followed, but more cautiously.

He's like a bull, Kato thought, *aggressive and durable; but a bull can be baited.* He lowered his guard and offered the big man a mocking smile. "Not doing so well, are you."

Mr. Clean snarled and swung a massive fist, but Kato danced back, arms at his sides, staying just out of reach. Clean swung again, with the same result, then spread his arms and charged. This was what Kato had been waiting for. He caught the big man's wrist in one hand and vest with the other, spinning to the side and shooting out his leg at the last moment in an improvised version of the judo throw, tai otoshi. Mr. Clean went over Kato's leg and struck the ground with bone-jarring force.

In an instant, Kato was on the man's back and had locked his arms around Clean's bull-like neck in a choke. The giant struggled, but the hold cut off the flow of blood to his brain and not even his great strength could help him. In seconds, his struggles weakened and finally stopped as he succumbed to unconsciousness.

Kato rose to his feet, dusting off his black uniform.

"You picked a tough one," The Green Hornet said, as he walked up.

"Not tough enough. How about yours?"

"I got the gang leader." The Hornet frowned. "Unfortunately, Laura got away again. Still, it's a victory, and no casualties on our side."

Kato turned to see to see a recovered Tim, talking quietly to Hanomah as he untied her wrists.

"Any way we can use the Scanner to follow her?" The Green Hornet asked.

"I'm afraid not," Kato said. "Its power's just about gone."

"Then she's escaped again. Kind of ironic."

"What's that?"

"All three of us coming together like this: me, Laura, Tim. Kind of like our ancestors."

"I suppose so."

"He's a good man," The Hornet said. "Maybe we should consider making him a bigger part of our little organization."

"Maybe not," Kato replied. "I'd hate to see him give up what he's got just to help us."

He turned to watch the two. Tim had finished untying Hanomah but still held her hands in his. He continued to speak quietly and, even in the moonlight, Kato could see the worry on his face. He knew that feeling well. He thought about the women he had known and wondered if this was one of the rare ones who could understand and accept. Then Hanomah's arms went around Tim's neck and she stretched on tiptoe to kiss him.

The Green Hornet nudged Kato's shoulder.

"I love Valentine's Day, don't you?"

MEMORIES OF MY GRANDFATHER, RAYMOND J. MEURER

Afterword by Lisa Meurer Long

My name is Lisa Long Meurer, and Raymond J. Meurer was my grandfather. For many of you, his name is not familiar, but to us grandkids, he was so much more. On paper, he was partner to George W. Trendle, the man behind WXYZ, home to *The Lone Ranger*, *The Green Hornet*, *Sgt. Preston*, and so many other classic radio shows. Yet outside of "work," he was active in his community, and an accomplished musician, often playing with popular dance bands of the 1940s.

You just seem to know when you meet someone really cool. The people around you act differently and you overhear interesting remarks. I had that unique experience as a small girl with my grandfather, Raymond J. Meurer. He was a very busy man and I did not see him often, but when I did the atmosphere changed. He had a twinkle in his eye and a gentle smile . . . and he was mysterious. I remember hushed conversations about the Lone Ranger and radio stations. I saw books and toys that I was not supposed to play with. I heard stories about Canada and someone named Sgt. Preston of the Yukon. I remember the day my father dressed in a real astronaut suit; the housekeeper told me that my grandfather had written a book called *The Space Eagle* and my father was on his way to a "studio" to make a picture for the cover. Then there were "buzzing" sounds and laughter and all sorts of excitement over some fellow named Kato. Next there was this really cool television show that we were told that we all had to watch. I remember the handsome man in the green mask and I remember hearing the name, Bruce Lee.

I can recall someone saying that "The Green Hornet had landed in Michigan" . . . and one day my grandfather was in his upstairs office (a place the three of us kids were not supposed to go into) . . . and I heard my grandfather call my name. He invited me in and I sat at his feet and he started talking. He shared with me that his grandchildren were very special to him and how many things he had done in his lifetime were meant to be a blessing for us. He used words like "providence" and "legacy"—words an eight-year-old was not familiar with but . . . it sounded amazing. The television show ran only one season but the characters, stories, and legacy have continued.

We are pleased that The Green Hornet and Kato are back in the public eye. We trust that a new generation will become familiar with The Green Hornet and that the "buzz" will continue for generations to come.

My grandfather would be proud.

Proudly,
Lisa Meurer Long

RAYMOND J. MEURER: MAN WITH MANY HATS

Afterword by Tim Lasiuta

Raymond J. Meurer was a man whose impact on America during the 1930s, '40s, '50s and '60s was substantial, yet seemingly invisible. He, in addition to being a jazz musician, church organist, theatre and exhibition representative, is perhaps best known for his work with WXYZ, the Lone Ranger, and Green Hornet Inc.

He was born October 16, 1904 in Detroit to Mr. and Mrs. Alois Meurer. Part of a large family that included two sisters and four brothers (Alous E., Erhard F., Carl J., and Henry D.), he spent most of his life in and around Detroit. His father, Alois, was a prominent Detroit musician who passed on his love of music to his family. Raymond proved particularly adept musically, making his debut at age eighteen on station WWJ, broadcast live from the Blue Room at the Cadillac Hotel. In the 1930s, he sang with the Russ Morgan orchestra, gaining the attention of George W. Trendle.

He was strong academically, studying law at the University of Detroit, and upon graduating, was employed by Mr. Trendle for his fledgling WXYZ station as chief legal counsel. His education in entertainment law served him well, as he was responsible for negotiations with Republic and Universal for the *Lone Ranger* and *Green Hornet* serials, and the landmark *Lone Ranger*, *Sgt. Preston*, and *Green Hornet* television series. He supervised the complex licensing contracts for all of Trendle-Campbell-Meurer properties, as well as setting the moral tone, along with Fran Striker, for the Lone Ranger television series.

Not only was Mr. Meurer active with WXYZ, he served on many national theatre and exhibition boards (such as the American Federation of Musicians), and acted as legal counsel for the Teamsters and Firefighters. After the sale of the Lone Ranger to Jack C. Wrather in 1954, and subsequent sale of Sgt. Preston in 1957, Mr. Meurer moved to Boca Raton for two years, then returned to serve on the board of Michigan Consolidated until 1968. He remained active, trying to sell a musical, and return the Ranger to television. As late as 1967, Mr. Meurer was very active in Detroit, serving on the board of the University of Detroit, and the University of Detroit Law School. After the 1967 Detroit riots, he again served the city, this time being part of reconstructive efforts.

In addition to his legal skills, he wrote a book, *Space Eagle*, in 1967, as well as a children's novel (never published), and he wrote a song for the 1968 Richard Nixon political campaign, "Richard Nixon, I am the One." He was a lifelong member of St. Josephs in Detroit, serving as Chief Organist for most of his life.

His marriage to Beatrice Daudlin produced one son, Raymond J. Meurer Jr., who worked with his father at WXYZ in a variety of roles. Raymond J. Meurer passed away on October 15, 1974, one day short of his 70th birthday.

DAILY SENTINEL MORGUE
Author Biographical Notes

MATTHEW BAUGH has been writing fiction for seven years, including stories for Moonstone's Green Hornet, Avenger, Phantom, and Zorro anthologies. He lives and works in the Chicago area where (contrary to persistent rumor) he does not have a heavily armed black car concealed under the floor of his garage that he uses to fight crime. He does not know anyone named Kato but does have a black cat who works hard to keep him in line.

Denver-based **DAVID BOOP** is a single parent, full-time employee, returning college student and author. His pulp novel, *She Murdered Me with Science*, came out in 2008. In addition, he has over a dozen of short stories and two short films to his credit. He's had over forty jobs since age thirteen, including a stint as professional Beetlejuice impersonator. His hobbies include the Blues, Mayan history, and film. You can find out more at www.davidboop.com.

DEBORAH CHESTER is the internationally published author of 38 novels. Her credits include *The Alien Chronicles* for Lucasfilm Publishing (named to VOYA's Best Books for Young Adults list in 1998), and an *Earth 2* tie-in novel, along with Ace fantasy titles, *The Sword, The Ring, The Chalice, The Pearls*, and *The Crown*. Her short story, "The Street That Forgot Time," was published in *Twilight Zone's* 50th anniversary anthology. Under the pseudonym C. Aubrey Hall, her latest book is *Crystal Bones*, a YA fantasy from Marshall Cavendish. For more information, visit www.deborahchester.com, www.faelinchronicles.com, and www.debchester.wordpress.com.

VITO DELSANTE is a comic book writer. He's written for DC Comics, Marvel Comics, Image Comics, and Simon & Schuster, among others, and his stories have been reprinted in other countries. He lives in New York City with his wife, Michelle, and two dogs, Kasey and Kirby, and wears glasses. www.incogvito.com.

F.J DESANTO is a producer, writer, and creator who has co-produced films such *The Spirit*, an animated version of *Turok: Son of Stone*, and is co-producing the upcoming feature film adaptations of *Doc Savage* and *The Shadow*. He executive produced *Talking with Gods*, the documentary about the life of Grant Morrison, and has written for DC Comics and contributed to Tokyopop's *Star Trek: The Next Generation Manga*. His first original creator-owned series will be published by DC Comics in 2012, and he is currently at work on new *Star Wars* comic project for Lucasfilm and an original graphic novel for Archaia.

WIN SCOTT ECKERT holds a B.A. in Anthropology and a Juris Doctorate. He is co-author (with Philip José Farmer) of the Wold Newton novel *The Evil in Pemberley House*, about Patricia Wildman, the daughter of a certain bronze-skinned pulp hero (Subterranean Press, 2009). He also edited and contributed to *Myths for the Modern Age: Philip José Farmer's Wold Newton Universe* (MonkeyBrain Books), a 2007 Locus Awards Finalist for Best Non-Fiction book. Win has written tales featuring many adventurous characters, including Zorro, The Avenger, The Phantom, The Scarlet Pimpernel, Hareton Ironcastle, Captain Midnight, and Doc Ardan. He has co-edited and written tales for two volumes of Moonstone's Green Hornet anthologies, and has stories forthcoming in Moonstone's *Sherlock Holmes: The Crossovers Casebook* and *Honey West*. Win also wrote the Foreword to the new edition of Farmer's *Tarzan Alive: A Definitive Biography of Lord Greystoke* (Bison Books, 2006) and the Afterword to the reissue of Farmer's Sherlockian crossover novel *The Peerless Peer* (Titan Books, 2011). Win's latest release is the encyclopedic two-volume *Crossovers: A Secret Chronology of the World* (Black Coat Press, 2010). He lives in the Denver area with his wife Lisa, three cats (Belle, Buster, and Spike), and two dogs (Mischief and Trouble, who more than live up to their names). Find Win on the web at www.winscotteckert.com and www.pjfarmer.com/woldnewton/Pulp.htm.

JOHN EVERSON is the Bram Stoker Award-winning author of the novels *Covenant, Sacrifice, The 13th, Siren*, and *The Pumpkin Man*, all from Leisure Books. He's also penned several short fiction collections including *Needles & Sins, Vigilantes of Love* and *Creeptych*. His short stories have appeared in more than 75 magazines and anthologies and have been translated into Polish and French. John shares a deep purple den in Naperville, IL with a cockatoo and cockatiel, a human skull, and a mounted Chinese fowling spider named Stoker. For information on his fiction, art and music, visit www.johneverson.com.

ERIC FEIN is a freelance writer and editor. He has written dozens of comic book stories featuring characters such as The Punisher, Spider-Man, Iron Man, and The Green Ghost. He has also written more than forty books and graphic novels for educational publishers and has written stories for Moonstone's *Sex, Lies, and Private Eyes* and *The Avenger: The Justice Inc. Files* anthologies. As an editor, he has worked on staff for both Marvel and DC Comics. At Marvel, he edited *Spider-Man, The Spectacular Spider-Man*, and *The Web of Spider-Man*, as well as limited series and one-shots including *Spider-Man and Batman: Disordered Minds*. At DC Comics, he edited storybooks, coloring and activity books, and how-to-draw books.

JOE GENTILE keeps pretty busy running a publishing company, but in his spare moments has managed to write graphic novels and short fiction about: Buckaroo Banzai, Kolchak the Night Stalker, Zorro, Sherlock Holmes, Werewolf the Apocalypse, The Phantom, The Spider, The Avenger, and many more! One of his latest projects was the critically acclaimed graphic novel *Sherlock Holmes/Kolchak: Cry for Thunder,* which will soon be expanded to a full-fledged novel. When he's not writing, editing, or publishing, Joe plays the bass guitar and enjoys a good life with his wife Kathy, and their pack of personality-ridden dogs Apollo, Artemis, and Callie.

HOWARD HOPKINS (www.howardhopkins.com) is the author of 34 westerns under the penname Lance Howard, six horror novels, three children's horror novels and numerous short stories under his own name. His most recent western, *The Killing Kind*, was a

December 2010 release and his most recent horror series novel, *The Chloe Files #2: Silver of Darkness*, is available now. He's written widescreen and panel comic books and graphic novels for Moonstone, along with co-editing and writing for *The Avenger Chronicles*, and will soon bring The Golden Amazon back for a new generation of readers. He's also created a new pulp heroine called The Veil, is the editor of the upcoming *Sherlock Holmes: The Crossovers Casebook* and *Honey West* anthologies, and has had stories in *The Spider Chronicles*, *The Green Hornet Chronicles*, and *The Captain Midnight Chronicles*.

ART LYON is an illustrator, designer, colorist, and writer who believes that telling stories is one of the most important things people do. He has contributed to Eisner Award-winning comics and graphic novels for major comic book publishers, and has designed and illustrated book and album covers, cartography, comics, websites, and role-playing games. "The Carlossi Caper" is his first published fiction. Art lives with his lovely and talented wife and two delightful, rascally children in Bloomington, Indiana. Visit ArtLyonArt.com to view Art's portfolios and look at his past, current, and upcoming projects. Contact him at artlyonart@gmail.com.

PAUL KUPPERBERG is the author of the mystery novel *The Same Old Story* and the short story anthologies *Two Tales of Atlantis* and *In My Shorts* (available from buffaloavenuebooks.blogspot.com). He scripts the bestselling *Life With Archie: The Married Life Magazine*, and has written numerous short stories, essays, articles, and more than two dozen books of fiction and non-fiction, as well as over 800 comics for DC, Marvel, Archie, Bongo, and others, including Superman, Green Lantern, Captain America, Spider-Man, the Archie gang, Scooby Doo, Bart Simpson, and his own creations, *Checkmate!, Arion Lord of Atlantis*, and *Takion*. Follow Paul at kupperberg. blogspot.com.

JOE MCKINNEY is a sergeant in the San Antonio Police Department who has been writing professionally since 2006. He is the Bram Stoker-nominated author of *Dead City*, *Quarantined*, *Apocalypse of the Dead*, *Dodging Bullets*, *Flesh Eaters*, and *Dead Set*. His upcoming books include *The Zombie King*, *St. Rage*, *Lost Girl of the Lake*, and *The Red Empire*. As a police officer, he's received training in disaster mitigation, forensics, and homicide investigation techniques, some of which finds its way into his stories. He lives in the Texas Hill Country north of San Antonio. Visit him at joemckinney.wordpress.com for news and updates.

JAMES MULLANEY is the ghostwriter, author or co-author of 26 novels, including four books in the "New Destroyer" series. He's written for Marvel Comics and co-authored The Destroyer series guide *The Assassin's Handbook 2*. He is currently working on a new action-adventure series. His website is www.jamesmullaney.com and he can be reached there, on Facebook, or by email at housinan@aol.com.

From his secret lair in the wilds of Bethlehem, Georgia, **BOBBY NASH** writes. A multitasker, Bobby's certain that he doesn't suffer from ADD, but instead he . . . ooh, shiny. When he finally manages to put fingers to the keyboard, Bobby writes novels, comic books, short prose, novellas, graphic novels, screenplays, and even a little pulp fiction just for good measure. Despite what his brother says, Bobby is not addicted to buying books and DVD box sets and can quit anytime he wants to. Really. You can check out Bobby's work at www.bobbynash.com, www.facebook.com/bobbyenash, www.twitter. com/bobbynash, www.lance-star.com, www.BloodyOldeEnglund.com, and more.

GARY PHILLIPS draws on his experiences ranging from political action committee hack to delivering dog cages in writing tales of chicanery and malfeasance. His most recent mystery novel was *The Underbelly*, about a sometimes homeless Vietnam vet's search for a disabled friend disappeared from Skid Row. He was editor of the bestselling *Orange County Noir* anthology, and has short stories in *Damn Near Dead 2*, *Too Much Boogie*, and *Shaken*, a Kindle-only collection done for Japan quake relief. For Moonstone he writes various characters including Operator 5 and That Man Flint. Please visit his website at: www.gdphillips.com.

BARRY REESE is a member of the New Pulp movement. His credits include: *The Rook Chronicles*, *Rabbit Heart*, *The Damned Thing*, *The All-New Official Handbook of the Marvel Universe*, and *Lazarus Gray*. Barry is married to artist Cari Reese.

BRADLEY H. SINOR has seen his work appear in numerous science fiction, fantasy, and horror anthologies such as *The Improbable Adventures of Sherlock Holmes*, *Tales of the Shadowmen*, *The Grantville Gazette*, and *Ring of Fire 2* and *3*. Three collections of his short fiction have been released by Yard Dog Press: *Dark and Stormy Nights*, *In the Shadows*, and *Playing with Secrets* (along with stories by his wife Sue Sinor). His newest collections are *Echoes from the Darkness* (Arctic Wolf Press) and *Where the Shadows Began* (Merry Blacksmith Press).

Like The Green Hornet, **PAUL D. STORRIE** debuted in Detroit. He's been writing comics professionally since 1998, working for numerous publishers, including Moonstone Books, Marvel and DC Comics. His prose debut was a short story in Moonstone's 2007 *Werewolves: Dead Moon Rising* horror anthology. You can find out more about him at his website Storrieville.com or by following him at twitter.com/storrieville.

MICHAEL USLAN is the originator of the Batman movie franchise and Executive Producer of all the films from *Batman* to *The Dark Knight Rises*. His autobiography, *The Boy Who Loved Batman*, will be published by Chronicle Books in Summer 2011.

DAN WICKLINE is a published writer and photographer. Born in Norwalk, California, he currently resides in Los Angeles with his wife Debbie and three cats: Tiger, Panther, and Crash, and dog Artemis. Dan has written for Image Comics, IDW Publishing, Humanoids Publishing, Zenescope Entertainment, Avatar Press, Cellar Door Publishing, and Moonstone Books. Recently Dan has written the re-launch of *ShadowHawk* for Image Comics and the on-going *Sinbad* series for Zenescope. If you would like more information about Dan Wickline, his work, or wish to contact him, please visit www.danwickline.com.